Black Shawl

Victor Sage was born in 1942 and lives in Norwich where he is a Reader in English Literature at the University of East Anglia. His first novel, *A Mirror for Larks*, was published in 1993.

Victor Sage
Black Shawl

SECKER & WARBURG
S&W
London

First published in Great Britain in 1995 by
Martin Secker & Warburg Limited,
an imprint of Reed Consumer Books Limited,
Michelin House, 81 Fulham Road, London SW3 6RB
and Auckland, Melbourne, Singapore and Toronto

A CIP catalogue record for this book
is available from the British Library

ISBN 0 436 43967 0

Typeset in 12/14 Perpetua
by Deltatype Ltd, Ellesmere Port, Cheshire
Printed in Great Britain by
Mackays of Chatham plc, Chatham, Kent

To Karin, Alex, and Nina
χωρίς τη φιλοξενία και την
υποστύρηξη των οποίων
αντό το βιβλίο θεν θα είχε
γραΦτεί

Contents

Acknowledgements

I wish to express my warmest thanks to the following people who talked with me about this book before, during, and after it was written and who gave unstintingly of their time and ideas: Elsa Amanatidou, Ruth Parkin-Gounelas and Dimitri Gounelas, Roulis and Elizabeth Heliotis, George Kalogeras, Alex Lagopoulos and Karin Boklund-Lagopoulou, Jina Politi and Elsa Soultana-Yioka. My special thanks are due to Barbara Hatzidou (and to her brother and parents) who kindly consented to interrupt her holiday and give a two-hour interview to a total stranger; and to Dimitrios and Athena Zouros whose hospitality to me was truly extraordinary, that is to say, truly Thracian. Thanks also to staff of DEE who patiently answered my questions; and for their courtesy and efficiency many thanks to the staff of the Newspaper Collection of the Thessaloniki Public Library. Any mistakes are, of course, not their responsibility, but my own. Finally, thanks to Jeanetta for typing in THE VICTORIAN TRAVEL JOURNAL.

For some of the mythological information in the book, I have drawn heavily upon the following: R. Guénon, *Symboles Fondamentaux de la Science Sacrée*, Paris, 1962, and M. Eliade, *Histoire des croyances et des idées religieuses*, vol. 1, Paris, 1968. The texts and translations of *rebétika* songs are taken from: *Rebetika: Songs of the Old Greek Underworld*, eds. Katharine Butterworth and Sara Schneider, New York, Komboloi Press, 1975.

I

Zenophilia

SPRING TO AUTUMN, 1987

Spring

They all thought of Eel-Pie as a pocket of resistance, a place where you could get good smokes and good talks – too much of it sometimes, as with all good things – but which none of the inhabitants, unlike the visitors, even dreamt of as 'hippie'. Kelly had an eye for this kind of culture. She'd been round it, one place or another, all her life. In her book people who made work were serious, period. Especially serious when they sold their stuff. Sure, there were some wide-boys and some idlers, but on the whole it was – thanks to Henry, who owned the boat-yard and rented them their workshops – a world whose productive rhythms had not collapsed into 'efficiency' – that pimply, pseudo-American-business-school, *military* bullshit everyone on the island could smell a square mile off.

It was a rough little spot, not like Santa Cruz where Kelly had been doing her jewellery in the seventies. The Rolling Stones had long gone, their hotel turned into a block of flats. In winter, the island's labyrinth of workshops and half-built boats, the aisles between heaps of spare parts and old pumps whose origin, and even function, was known only to the few, its slipways and alleyways down to the river, all became a mudbath. There was only one way on and Kelly had to haul everything over there herself by hand, unless the lads had the motorised trolley they used at the boat-yards, which just fitted the one-person wide, hump-back bridge and equally narrow lanes.

3

Kelly had long been used to living in a world of 'lads', as they called them in Britain, and she thrived on it. She had a good eye. She could shoot a rifle and she played darts like a demon up in the White Swan, knocking them all dead – literally, at Killer – with those long, accurate strokes from the shoulder, turned sideways on like a man. The lads never gave Kelly any trouble. They called her 'Red'. Because of her hair, but almost everybody knew she had Indian blood. Not hard to spot, anyway, with those epicanthic folds. If they did try it on, she took them to bed, once only, and promptly (like a red-haired witch, one of them remarked with fraternal bitterness) turned them into her brothers.

Kelly treated them all like her brothers, brothers she never had, goggling at her with that hopeful, wistful look on their faces as she stood there in one of the crêpe, wrap-around tops that emphasised her big, freckled, swimmer's shoulders and directed them where to put the packets of raw materials for her jewellery, or the logs for her stove.

'Hey, Red, where d'ya want this, mate?'

Mate? Loved it.

That was what was so strange about Roger.

She nudged her friend Sal. Mmmm, over there, yum-mee.

The party was a Saturday-nighter on the Sections.

The Sections was what everyone called a certain row of houseboats on the river at Richmond, and some people that Kelly knew on Eel-Pie –boat-building types – had taken her and Sal along with them for a laugh, together with some of the others – the painters, the cello-maker, the violin-makers, the cartoonists, the guitar-makers, and Drago the sculptor who made Dogon masks.

'Christ, what you want him for, Red?' moaned Sal, looking down her nose at Roger; 'he's so straight.'

It had been a long time since Kelly had really had any activity in the romantic department, but she surprised herself at the way she made up to him. He was real neat, old-fashioned-looking, like some old Hollywood star from the 1940s, Joseph Cotton-type – incredibly handsome, Kelly thought, from the left-hand side, where she deliberately stayed for most of the party – and he had this clipped, no-nonsese way of talking and looking at things. It refreshed her, she decided, and she started glancing at herself sidelong, amused at her own reactions to everything when in his company, occupying a new space in which she seemed to be given a lot more room than she was used to getting for herself. Maybe it was because he was older and she felt the challenge of an older man. Maybe it was because he was travelling, and she wanted to travel again. Maybe it was black-and-white movies. Who knew? Who cared? With that lantern-jaw, he was definitely Marlboro country anyway.

After the party, they sauntered back along the towpath from Richmond bridge in a thick dawn mist, dodging the wet sprays of blossom – Kelly kind of liked the way he held them back for her – deep in discussion of his trip to Greece. Roger was a civil engineer who was working in Athens as a consultant to a firm there. He had come back to visit someone, he said, who had just had an operation.

Kelly bit her lip. She found herself already wanting to know who the 'someone' was. *So soon do we make a possession of what pleases us.* She'd read it somewhere and it was her joke against herself if her collector's passion got out of hand. But she was too intent on what he was saying about his experiences in Greece to intervene – she didn't want to miss anything – and so she let it go.

Kelly's Greece was the islands in the 1970s. She'd sold her jewellery all around – on Kos, Rhodes, Mykonos, Corfu and, of course, on Crete, and she had picked up some tourist Greek. But Roger was really into the North, Macedonia, going through the gritty struggles of everyday life, the difficulty, and the comedy, of trying to get things done for nationalised industries in a Byzantine bureaucracy which went to bed or went fishing between 2.0 and

6.0 p.m. everyday. He talked and talked, not about the islands, but about mainland Greece, the differences between North and South, moving with an easy fluency through the contrasts and the anecdotes in his warm, ex-Midlands voice.

They paused, standing on the centre of the steeply curving bridge looking down into a bowl of mist that hid the water completely and gave Kelly the drunken urge to straddle the rail, whip up her skirts, and parachute right into it – Docs first, wheeeee! – while he was telling her the story of the peddlar who sold a talking parrot to a man just as the boat was leaving Piréas harbour.

The peddlar shouts up to him, just as the boat moves away from the shore, '*É*, the parrot can't talk after all . . .' 'That's OK,' shouts the man to the peddlar, 'the money I gave you is all dodgy. But at least I can sell this dumb cluck to some other sucker, whereas you, *re maláka* . . . !'

Kelly was still laughing at this story, and the way Roger drew it out, when she unlocked the padlock, slid back the big galvanised door and led the way into the boat-yard, past the slipways, up to her attic studio, through the trap-door with its two pulleys and hanging counterweight, which Roger paused to take in his hand and weigh, thoughtfully, before coming up any further.

There was a bed under the sloping roof and this they sat on, their knees drawn up like children, drinking the mint tea she fixed him, while she told him about one of the boys who had been killed recently on the slipway downstairs. Her mood had suddenly changed as the pictures and then the words came haltingly back to her.

Three of them had been working stripping the keel under a big boat when she had begun to roll. Two had ducked down underneath where there had been a space beside one of the trolleys, but the young man, through lack of experience, had tried to climb out of the slipway up on to the side, and the boat had rolled on him. Kelly had run down with the rest to see what she could do, but there was nothing. The boat had pinned his chest over the sharp brick parapet at the side of the slipway. The lads were all around him, one of them holding his hand, uselessly. He couldn't talk, but he could just about understand the surprise of dying. By the time they got the ropes on the boat and eased him out, it was too late. They took him out by water; the people along the river knew – word was already out – and a surprising number came to the water's edge to give their salute as he passed.

Roger picked the chunky mug out of her hand and took the two of them together – flowered, cheerful, a pair, handmade by Sal – over to the other side of the studio where her workbench stood. He put them down and lingered there, examining her tools and the pieces she had been working on.

Roger was really taken with some of her stuff on the table, he said. She didn't know whether he was just trying to be tactful and distract her. She ended up by going over and showing him. There was a medallion, one in particular, he kept staring at and turning over.

'Masonic?'

On the one side there was a circle with a cross in it and on the reverse three concentric squares linked by four right-angled lines.

'Older, Druid,' said Kelly. Then she laughed. 'At least, I got them out of this book on Celtic and Druid art. The wheel, that's the earthly paradise . . .'

'How come?' he asked.

'D'you know anything about Indian philosophy?' asked Kelly, glancing up at him, her shoulder brushing his as they stood side by side at the bench.

'Sorry, didn't have time for that where I come from,' said Roger.

'God,' she breathed, 'I thought everybody knew about Indian philosophy. So where in hell's name *do* you come from?'

'Nuneaton. Anyway, I thought they were Druid . . .'

'These shapes all go back to the lotus flower, this circle with a

7

cross in it. See, the lotus blossom spreads outwards from the point in the centre which is the centre of the world . . .'

He was staring at her.

You're really into all this, aren't you?'

'Guess you could say,' Kelly breathed. She was beginning to lose her melancholy amid her favourite things, as she took the medallion and, frowning, rubbed it against her skirt.

'And what's that on the other side?' said Roger, bending to turn it over in her hand.

'The squares? One within another?'

'Yes'.

'Oh, *that*, that's the celestial Jerusalem . . .' She held the medallion up to Roger's collar against his neck and squinted at it in the light from the velox window in the roof. 'Hey, let's have a look at it on . . .' And she undid his collar with deft hands and slipped it over his greying curls which felt so springy under her fingers.

He smiled down at her, unable to stop touching it.

'Hey. Now *you're* the celestial Jerusalem! Yeah. Kind of gets you, doesn't it . . .' She watched as his finger moved in circles over the lines in the silver, the nail following their curves to the central square, where it rested. 'It's the triple enclosure. It has this kind of magical feeling. This one was found on a Druid stone in France. There's a lot of this triple-concentred stuff in Celtic art too. You feel you're really moving into the centre of something, uh? It's Greek too, y'know?'

She looked at him, deciding his nose was kind of Greek, kind of Hollywood Greek, while she told him about the similar emblems they found on the Acropolis, and the spindle of the world.

'Hey, you know Plato's description of Atlantis?'

He didn't.

'It's kind of neat,' said Kelly. 'It's another triple. Only circular this time . . . Y'know, like the old Hindu *Meru*, the triple enclosure round the centre of the world . . .?'

8

'You really do know a lot . . .' said Roger admiringly. 'I had no idea . . .'

'No idea what?' said Kelly. 'No idea people who made jewellery had anything upstairs?'

She tensed, and stared openly, frankly enquiring.

'No idea . . .' he began, smiling under her stare, 'there was so much to it . . .'

For a moment, she suspected him of patronising her, as he raked along the bench, diplomatic, evasive now, picking up another piece, tilting it to the light and murmuring.

But her eagerness was too great. She plunged past him: 'See, this is the two of them together . . .' She ignored the one in his hand and insisted on another, without a chain, which she had just been working on and had not quite finished.

He turned it over.

'It's the same on the other side,' he said, slight disappointment in his voice.

'Yeah, but look at what it is . . .' she said.

They stared at it together.

'Double Dutch to me . . .' He was resigned, apologetic for his earlier tone perhaps, she thought, though she couldn't read him at all. 'What is it?'

'OK, it's a triple square, *see*?' She was playing with him now and they both knew it, using the voice of a kindergarten teacher. 'But with the second square tilted into a diamond here, *see* . . .'

'See, dumbhead?' he paraphrased, laughing.

'See, oh unaccustomed, uninitiated one,' she smiled back.

'And there are four right-angled lines coming from the corners of the diamond . . .' he said, rising to the bait.

'So. How many triangles?'

*Tri*angles?' He frowned like a dreamy boy, and Kelly started to laugh. 'Oh, I see . . . er, twelve . . .'

'Correct. You can cut stones like this. Beautiful. Rubies, big diamonds. They have to be big. And you know what this figure means?'

He caught her tone.

'Oh holy one, oh High Priestess, I know nothing of it.'

'That's the quadrature of the circle. Look, this is interesting, you're an engineer,' she was explaining now, breaking off the game. 'The old priests used to inscribe the signs of the zodiac in this figure . . .'

'The Byzantine Basilica. That's the only squared circle I know,' he said. He asked for a sheet of paper, and she gave him her Rotring architect's pen. With swift, confident strokes, he drew the picture of a circle inside a square. 'That's the dome,' he said, 'looked at from above . . .'

Kelly smiled up at him.

'I know,' she said, 'the old guys did it deliberately. It's the rotational cycle. Between heaven and earth.'

'Bullshit. It's a question of stresses,' he said. 'Sorry!'

'It's the wheel and the square together . . .' said Kelly. 'Hey, c'mon, Mr Architect, Mr Engineer, Mr Scientist, Mr *Man*!' She nudged him again with her elbow as she spoke.

He was looking along the bench by the wall where she had set out some brooches and buckles. He picked up a disc-like bracelet with a double chain of tiny links, which was engraved with a dripping lance on one side and on the other a wheel with six radii.

'The wheel, that's the cup,' she said, 'the receptacle, the rose of the world . . . It's Rosicrucian . . .'

'And this?' He turned it over.

'Don't tell me you don't know what *this* is?' said Kelly, with soft scorn. 'Think what it looks like!'

'No idea,' said Roger, who meant it.

'Well, I take it you've got one . . .'

He looked politely puzzled still.

Kelly sighed. 'OK, think of it as the sacred lance that was put into Jesus's side on the cross . . . remember that?'

10

'God, from infant school,' said Roger. 'My sadistic Methodist teachers were quite fond of the story . . .'

'Well, this fellow Joseph of Arimathea collected all the blood in a cup, the Holy Grail, and brought it to Somerset?'

'Oh all that Round Table stuff,' said Roger.

'Round Table? Wheel?' said Kelly.

'Oh come on! That's going a bit too far!'

'No,' she said. 'There's no such thing as going too far. Oriental religion had it all, it's the same – Prakriti, see, the universal substance, the lotus flower, which is the receptacle for all the rays emanating from Purusha . . .'

'Pretty sexy stuff,' said Roger.

He seemed to have got the idea now and was obviously trying to lead her away from the workbench and back to the mattress in the corner.

'Hey,' Kelly warned him with a giggle, 'that's right. But that's the *lowest* level of manifestation . . . You can only go up from there . . .' She was holding on to his shoulder, starting to laugh as she walked in a wobble on the mattress, like a trampoline acrobat.

'Suits me,' said Roger. 'I'll be the dripping lance, if you'll . . .'

'Provide the lotus, uh? Jest don' drip too soon, my man! Hell, this conversation's getting worse by the minute!'

Kelly sat down, took out her tin and rolled the joint. She didn't give a monkeys, by then, if he *was* a cop.

She crossed her legs and lit a couple of joss sticks and, as she narrowed her eyes and blew out the match, her mood had changed again.

'Why does it keep getting harder to survive?' she asked, in her special American, little girl's voice.

'Maybe it's time to get up and go,' said Roger. He was resting his back against the wall at the other end of the mattress and staring at her, at what she hoped was her hair, her best feature, in what she prayed was fascination.

11

Kelly put down the unlighted spliff by the side of the mattress and thought about it.

She had sold her boat to get this workshop studio so that she had enough to cushion her and buy materials. For three years she'd been reasonably happy here, so the idea of upping and blowing whatever capital she had left was hardly appealing. On the other hand, she had tied herself into a tight little circle, so she couldn't travel any more without giving up her workshop and her contacts, who would find someone else to get their jewellery from. Soon find someone else, that was it, that was what they all said. So you had to dig in, hunker down, and endure. If you *had* something, no matter what, you had to hang on to it.

'Nah!' she said in her fake south London, reaching down and lighting it. 'Not unless somebody paid me . . .'

It was not a hint, she swore it was not. Would Kelly do that? Anyway, he ignored it, whatever it was.

But immediately, from that moment on, Kelly started planning the trip in her mind. Scheming about how she could do it and keep her options open. Almost absent-mindedly, she patted the mattress beside her.

And he turned out to be cool. All right for smoking with and quite funny, quite goofy, when he relaxed. Nice, curly hair and in quite good shape, considering he was fifty, good teeth, good strong body.

Of course, Kelly had to sort out his breathing. It was the same with all these Brits, they held their breath. Generally got all choked up and red in the face.

Kelly was simply the best yoga teacher in town and she spent half of Sunday working on Roger, making him relax.

'I don't go for all this Hare Krishna stuff,' said Roger.

'You're confusing things. I bet you don't even know what the Krishna means?'

He didn't.

'Krishna is black, right? Arguna is white? OK, now black is the principle of non-manifestation, it's the state of non-being, and white is manifestation, mortal being in the world. Get it?'

'Yin and Yang?'

'That's right, Paramatma and Jivatma . . .' She was sitting behind him now, stroking his forehead. 'Now, think of "It" as black, and "Me" as white . . .'

He was looking doubtful, trying to crane over his shoulder.

'It's *you* who mentioned the Krishna, not me!' said Kelly. 'C'mon, let's give it a whirl. You've obviously got it on your mind . . .'

After she had taught him a few chants, Kelly went to the bathroom to get her oils. She was just about the best masseuse she had ever met, too. She took the condom out of the cabinet and slipped it into her mouth, popping her tongue into the bubble, because, even with a guy like Roger, you could never be too careful these days.

They spent the rest of Sunday rambling round their biographies.

Kelly was the daughter of an Irishman and a Sioux Indian woman. The principal thing that had happened to Kelly was that she had seen her mother Ruth Windcloud shot down by McClusky. She had been inside the mobile home but she watched it through the window. Ten years old. They used to travel around, state to state, not really stopping anywhere, and there was booze and there were alterations, usually in the evening when the driving had stopped. On this occasion, Kelly had been locked in because she had showed her old man some lip. McClusky was starting to get drunk. She could see the two of them near the fire embers, arguing either about money or about the young guy at the gas station that Kelly's mother had been getting fresh with, according to her father. All of a sudden he picked up the shotgun and she started running away from him towards the mobile home.

Kelly was looking through the window. She saw it all. He levelled the gun and she saw it kick up as he squeezed off a barrel into her mother's back. They were staring at each other, Kelly and Ruth Windcloud, with the glass between them and her mother kept on running towards her. The thing Kelly couldn't get out of her mind was her mother's frown as she bit down hard on the air, bucked like a piece of big game on TV and rolled over once too often, ending up just short of the steps.

After that it was a series of homes. But luckily Kelly was a person with a powerful sense of her own destiny and she had come through it all, independent, ready to travel just as soon as she could. She just had to get away from all those guns. Now she liked it in England, but she wouldn't mind going back to maybe Spain or Greece, because she'd heard through the grapevine things were happening there.

Roger had dropped out of a steady job with a government department to form his own engineering company which designed civil engineering projects. He was from the Midland Counties of England. He had had a happy lower-middle-class childhood in Hinkley, which he tended to call Nuneaton, and had done his training at Birmingham University.

Kelly didn't understand him at first when he said he was a 'right-wing Labour man' and he had to explain. He didn't approve of Tony Benn or Arthur Scargill or Ken Livingstone, all of whom Kelly thought were pretty well OK (at least they *did* things . . .). Roger's great ideal, he said, was Hugh Gaitskell. Kelly had never heard of him. Roger was quite proud of himself for not going off with the Gang of Four, though Kelly wouldn't have minded if he had, because she thought they were pretty well OK too (at least they were trying to *do* something . . .).

Roger married his local girl, Thelma, in 1960 and they had two children and lasted together eleven years. Roger lost two stone over the divorce and started riding a bicycle. Then he met Barbara and lived with her and her kids. Nowadays, things were not so good between them. For the last five years they had been geographically separated, while Roger worked some lucrative contracts in the Middle East, places like Saudi Arabia, commuting here and there, and things appeared to have just worn out. It was a pity, said Roger, because he liked Barbara. She was intelligent, good company, had three nice kids. But . . .

'No sex?' said Kelly.

'That's right.'

'You think *I'm* intelligent?'

'Of *course*,' said Roger.

Kelly sang: 'Born. In the USA.' She nudged him. 'Hey, din' go to no college, Mister. Better watch out who you're messin' with . . .'

Kelly and Roger made a pact. She would come out to Greece and join him, in a few months' time, just as soon as she could get the money together and make some extra pieces of jewellery ready to sell, and they would travel. She wanted to see all that Macedonian gold he'd told her about.

The medallion she gave him to keep.

Autumn

The machine-gun burst of Greek over the intercom sounded like the Captain welcoming everyone on board. The young woman in the black leather jacket sitting on the aisle side of Barbara, her eyes as black as coals under a great buoyed-up bush of curly black hair, stopped chewing her gum for a second and then burst out laughing.

Barbara waited for the English translation: 'Captain Cháros and the crew would like to welcome you on board . . .'

'I don't get it,' said Barbara aloud.

The young woman along the seat, who had piled up her Harrods and John Lewis bags in between them, was chewing again.

She turned to Barbara: 'Of course,' she said cheerfully, 'Captain Death and his crew . . .'

'Oh, Charon,' said Barbara, 'the ferryman?'

She stared out of the window at a small clump of west London weeds which began to move back under the wing as Captain Death opened the throttle.

This was a funny way to start. It was a Sunday too. Was it all going to end in tears?

Barbara had been in two minds about coming, but her children had finally persuaded her. She had agonised for months. It hadn't been at all easy, because no one gives up a job, even at some corny little college like St Dunstan's in Leytonstone. And it was entirely against her principles to give up her independence, but they had all got together and persuaded her to come. She needed the space, they said. And why shouldn't she have some space for herself? They didn't need her, they argued, rather too decisively, she thought, and was ready to be hurt. Was it so easy to dismiss your mother from your young lives? But she knew what they meant . . . And they were right, she thought. Here was an opportunity, so why not?

'You do mean the Styx, don't you?'

The girl pulled down the bright green scarf that was thrown across her throat and loosened her jacket, digging in the breast pocket with two fingers and bringing out her cigarettes and a *briquet*, as she explained that it was an old Olympic Airways joke. Captain Death frequently did OA262, the shuttle run between Heathrow and Thessaloniki.

'I'm flying on to Athens,' said Barbara, not quite knowing why she said it so hastily.

The girl smiled. 'You'll probably still be with him.'

The seatbelt sign came on. They braced themselves involuntarily as the drumming of the wheels, cut at shorter and shorter intervals by a seam in the concrete, began to intensify into an alarming set of vibrations until, when Barbara looked out of the window, the tarmac under the shaking wing had turned into a blur.

She turned to look along the seat again at the young woman who was already looking at her and whose confident, steadily masticating jaws faltered for a moment as she shrugged: 'Actually, he's not far off retirement.'

There was a moment of solemn silence while they looked at each other and then they laughed, and they were still laughing when the drumming of the wheels suddenly ceased, the backs of the seats rising in front of them until the aisle had become a forty-five-degree ramp.

Antigone reminded Barbara of her eldest daughter, Kate. But

she was much more serious and focused, Barbara learnt, than Kate. She was a young lawyer, Barbara judged about thirty-one, quite a bit older than she looked, whereas her Kate was twenty-eight and still didn't know what she wanted to do. Antigone had popped over – her English was extremely good – to see her friend Sarah in Slough for the weekend. She was living in Athens, but now, on the way back, she was going up to her village in Macedonia for a day or so to see her family. Her brother, Yannis, would meet her at Thessaloniki.

Antigone explained, waving her cigarette as she talked, that she was working on her first case – defending some terrorists against the police.

Barbara stared at her, amazed at her confidence. She had too much make-up on for Barbara's tastes and her teeth at the front were sadly irregular, so Barbara couldn't think of her as beautiful, but she was very striking. Quick, warm, and sympathetic, switching rapidly between English and Greek to accommodate the various lags in Barbara's understanding, Antigone was somehow more forthright than an English girl of her generation. More solemnly committed to everything, to confront it, to explain it. Or was this Barbara's own response to a loss of nuance in the unfamiliar?

Another burst of Greek music on the intercom left Antigone humming and tapping her business-like black shoe against the seat in front.

'I don't know what this is. I know the song but not this version. It's insular,' she said in English.

Barbara laughed.

Antigone frowned. 'Why are you laughing?'

'In English that would be an insult. It would mean provincial . . .' said Barbara smiling.

'I don't know which island,' Antigone started to say, and then a beautiful bold smile spread into her cheeks. 'Oh, I see . . . no, it is literally . . .'

It was Barbara's turn to smile. 'Insular,' she said, completing the turn. 'No, it's me who misunderstood . . .'

'Have you been to Cyprus?' said Antigone after a little while.

'My accent, all those boos and baas . . .' Barbara laughed. 'You spotted it . . .'

She explained that years ago she had been an army wife on Cyprus and had learnt some Greek then. And she had augmented her meagre store over the years by taking various courses here and there. When the air-hostess brought their food, Barbara had the temerity to wish Antigone 'Kalén órexe!' and the air-hostess smiled and raised her eyes at Barbara and they were all laughing at the undemotic ending she had unconsciously used, which led the talk on to politics and language. Fuelled by retsina, they were chattering away like magpies, easy and natural, swapping volumes of information without caution.

Barbara felt lucky on this flight. She felt unburdened. She was able to tell Antigone in a low voice about her operation, the hysterectomy which she had dreaded and which she had spent the last months recovering from and which, oddly, had given her a sense of freedom she couldn't put a name to.

It was a paradox. As she talked about her tired self to this young woman, Barbara felt enlivened. As she detailed her convalescence – those empty weeks in which she'd had ample opportunity to observe the struggle to survive of people in south London, amidst the stress, the debt, the depressing boom, the sheer bragging self-deception of public rhetoric, while every-where, progressing with a combination of open flotation and viral stealth, spread the dismantling of public institutions – Barbara repelled these burdensome phenomena that still scarred her memory, one by one, with every word, as if mounting on her own descriptions, like the aircraft itself ascending through the turbulence, into lighter, calmer air.

Antigone explained to Barbara her feelings about PASOK, Andreas Papandreou's Pan-Hellenic Socialist Movement Party, which was coming to the end of its second term in power in Greece. She explained she was virtually a child of PASOK, or, at least, she still identified closely with the aims of the first PASOK government of 1981. She described what it felt like for the whole country to be united at that point after the fall of the Junta. The exile and torment of the generations before hers had ended. PASOK, she felt, had, without exaggeration, taken Greece into the twentieth century and instituted essential steps to modernise the whole social system.

'I thought it was that other man – sorry, I can't remember his name – who had taken Greece into the twentieth century,' said Barbara, remembering all those books Roger had taken out of the library and which she had surreptitiously read.

'Venizélos? Ah, but PASOK broke the dam,' said Antigone.

'What do you mean?' asked Barbara.

Antigone described the cycle of anti-communist fear and military pressure which had paralysed the Left and which previous liberal administrations could not get out of. Karamanlís, an honourable but hardly socialist politician, had legalised the Communist Party and stabilised the language, but PASOK had taken these reforms much further, giving them a soil in which to flourish. PASOK created the impossible for Greece, she said, a centre-left political space.

'And this political space is a *public* space,' Antigone insisted. 'Up to that point, the history of Greece could be written in little envelopes, in *fakelakia*.' She gave her broad smile and crisped thumb and forefinger.

Barbara proposed an arc of intersection: as Margaret Thatcher's star had risen, like the truly perverse historical event it was, in the West, blackmailing the people of Britain – middle and working classes alike – into following her evangelical retreat into a face-grinding, belt-tightening fantasy of 'Victorian Values', Papandreou's star had risen in the East . . .

'The South-East . . .' said Antigone, holding up her hand. 'We must have this right!'

20

'. . . the South-East – then – of Europe, and created a Greece of the future, whose social fabric was woven from a new broad alliance between middle and working class. At the very moment Mrs Thatcher declared she didn't believe there was such a thing as "Society", so Andreas Papandreou did the opposite: he won the support of the people on the streets for a social concept, a public life free from corruption. How's that!'

They laughed at Barbara's sudden rush of political astrology, the product of an unexpected, champagne-like, moment of confidence and euphoria, whose bubbles were already beginning to go a little flat: 'Well, almost,' she said.

And then, after a silence, she asked, 'And has he delivered it?'

'What?'

'The future?'

'PASOK has made significant advances. I feel it as a woman. I'm grateful to all those women who worked in the party organisation of PASOK who struggled for the final abolition of the Greek Family Law, and the women who worked on the Prime Minister's Council for Sex Equality until it was upgraded to a General Secretariat . . . now they've decentralised the whole machinery, those women, and in every prefecture of the country there's a network of Equality Bureaux . . . they even rewrote all the school-books to express the principles of equality . . .'

Barbara felt a mixture of emotions as she watched the activity of the young woman's face, the expressiveness of her features and the casual, hopeful way in which she believed the history of the present to be her own history: weariness, or was it a streak of maturity, made her feel this was all too neat. Hadn't they been through all this in England? And how far had the tides of the Women's Movement ebbed, since the 1970s? Barbara had been very active in the National Abortion Campaign, and when the Corrie Amendment debates came round she was active again in marches and campaigning. But this was a limited issue about which she felt strongly. She knew well that the Equal

Opportunities Commission felt that it was extremely difficult to police the practices of employers and she guessed, as she listened to Antigone's rather wistfully earnest textbook speeches, that this must be all the more true of Greece.

Antigone was laughing. 'I just thought of that poster that was circulating in Greece, the one with Margaret Thatcher as Scarlet O'Hara in the arms of Ronald Reagan, and behind them the world exploding in a nuclear firestorm.'

'And the caption: "Gone with the Wind." God, it really did seem as if one of them was going to press the button. Yes, the SWP did it in England,' said Barbara. 'Funny, it's already somewhat pathetic to think of that now . . .'

'Pathetic?'

Barbara suddenly realised Antigone didn't understand, because it was another Greek word:

'I . . . I mean . . . I don't mean . . . *pathitikos* . . . er, I mean it in the English sense . . . er, you know . . .' she waved her arm, 'pitiable.'

But it didn't matter. Antigone was nodding. 'For us it is important still,' she said. 'We want Greece to be a nuclear-free zone. Andreas has promised . . .'

Here Barbara did sit back a little and feel a superior irony creeping into her responses, while Antigone's voice, as rich and innocent as a baroque flute, went on to detail Papandreou's election promises to get rid of the American bases.

'Good luck to you,' said Barbara. 'We in the Labour Party never managed it. Ronald Reagan doesn't even have to ask our permission to bomb his enemies from British soil . . .'

Whether it was personal or not she couldn't tell, but Antigone, it seemed, had a special aptitude for hopefulness, an absence of world-weariness, a shiny patina of unjaded energy which Barbara both envied and felt sharply as a rebuke to herself. But at the same time, she mused, as they became aware of the Pindos mountains through the cabin window and the good Captain announced they

22

were beginning their descent into Thessaloniki, these young people had something slightly righteous, slightly evangelical, about them compared with old Sixties-types like herself.

She realised, as she unpopped her ears and they exchanged addresses, how absorbed she had been; she hadn't thought of Roger once during the whole flight, except to explain at one point in a polite exchange that he was her partner – well, he was actually her *husband*, she confessed – and she was going out to join him.

They kissed in the aisle, she and Antigone, and promised to contact each other in Athens, a promise Barbara really meant to keep.

For a moment she slipped her fingertips under the raven-black bunch of curls at the back of Antigone's neck and bounced them lightly, as if weighing them. 'I've been meaning to tell you,' she whispered, glowing from all their talk, 'how lovely your hair is!'

Antigone shook it, as if to prove her point, and Barbara could still feel the brief pressure of the young woman's hand on her arm after she had disappeared through the exit door, leaving her to plod on towards Transit Passengers.

Roger was standing at the back of the hall near some glass windows, talking to a silver-haired man. He broke off and waved, on tiptoe and waggling the fingers of his raised hand.

'So you got here,' said Roger. 'Barbara, this is Panos Panagópoulos . . .'

Roger's companion's eyes were huge and dead – fishbelly-blue orbs that hung and swivelled over her in a fashion so remote that she felt as if she were shaking hands with an iguana. His dripping silver locks ran in greasy rails from a sharp widow's peak to the back of his head, where they finished in a series of nasty curls at the nape of his neck. His head, however, was tiny in comparison to his enormous pear-shaped body with its great hands and

23

feet, the latter size tens at least, standing splayed at each side like a clown's feet. The yellow, pocked face thrust forward, curving upwards into a snub-snout, accentuated by a tobacco-stained brush on the upper lip that ballooned from under the nostrils and blocked them completely. Barbara watched the perpetual roll of the muscles in each cheek as his gums and teeth ground together. The mouth, which seemed an integral part of the snouted, upward-thrusting, bristling mass, was a lateral undulating sulk through which his voice, whose every microsyllable grated on her ears like a handful of pebbles thrown into a barrel, pushed its way past a single, leaning, yellow tooth.

There was no point in being angry. She knew what Roger was like, but *why* did he have to bring a stranger, when they hadn't seen each other for eight months?

They bent heads together and searched for a place to place their dry lips, humming 'Mmmmm . . .' Panos smiled on, checked his watch while they bumped faces, and then took Barbara's hand in his, covering it with his other one.

'So young, so charming,' he breathed. 'I had no idea . . .'

'Taverna . . .' said Roger, picking up her bags.

Panos was from DEE, the electricity company, it seemed. They urgently had to talk over some business.

They climbed into Roger's Toyota. Panos sat in the back, leaning forward immediately and hanging on the two front seats. Every time she turned Barbara felt his eyes running over her like water, prying by their own weight into her blouse, flickering down through her belt on to the place where her thigh was raised, and spilling down her tights into her sensible shoes, even swirling round her ankles, looking for a lower level like dirty water emptying out of a bath.

'Picked a pretty bad time to come, actually, Barbara,' said Roger, his eyes on a cyclist negotiating a puddle of oil.

'Thanks very much,' Barbara said. 'What a charming welcome!'

Roger turned, puzzled. 'Country's falling apart,' he said indignantly.

She tried conquering her irritation at his self-importance. 'What's going on then?'

'Serious bloody anarchy, that's what's going on . . .' He switched into his English-accented Greek: 'Isn't that so, Pano?'

'We have some problems at the moment,' said Panos. His shy smile glittered at her over the seat-back while his eyes tried to get into the gap between her blouse collar and her neck.

She turned and he flicked his eyes up to hold hers.

'What kind of problems?' she asked in her Cypriot Greek.

'Bloody Prime Minister's running around with an air-hostess,' said Roger. 'Did you see that picture in *Eikónes*, my God!'

'No, I didn't!' said Barbara pointedly.

'Bloody outrageous,' said Roger to the removals truck which was approaching on the wrong side of the road. He flashed his lights. 'Out-bloody-rageous . . .' he said as the truck pulled in at the last minute, horn blaring.

'*A re maláka*! Wanker,' shouted Roger, lifting his two hands off the wheel and throwing them up into the air like a juggler.

She stared at him. He was wearing a medallion.

'What was *in* the picture?'

'She looks as fat as a cupboard and she is reaching out to hold his hand,' said Panos.

'Doesn't sound too bad to me . . .'

'In a *stateroom*?'

'With this horrible sick smile . . . That was the caption, wasn't it? "A certain smile" . . .' said Panos.

'Well, it still doesn't . . .' Barbara began.

'Have you seen the nude ones?' said Panos to Roger.

'Cripes, no,' said Roger, 'I didn't know . . .'

'Nude photos of the Prime Minister,' she said, perversely.

'No, of Dimitra,' said Panos. 'You know, there was a journalist who got hold of them and was showing them round . . .'

25

Roger laughed into the windscreen. 'Absolute tart,' he said, whinnying. 'No wonder the place is going to the dogs.'

'Is that Demeter,' said Barbara, 'the goddess of fertility?'

'You know something,' said Panos to Roger, 'she used to be in love with a chemist at the bottom of Methymnis Street. I know the guy . . .'

'So do I,' said Roger. 'Tall guy, dark, balding, putting on a lot of weight . . . wears a blue denim shirt from the Sixties . . . What, *him*?'

'That's him,' said Panos. 'Sometimes when he wasn't there Dimitra used to serve in the shop . . .'

Roger turned to Barbara. 'The shop is near the flat,' he said.

'Poor woman,' said Barbara.

'*Our* flat,' said Roger, 'in Kipselis . . .'

'But I thought PASOK was doing well,' said Barbara.

'PASOK's had it,' said Roger. 'Kaput.'

Panos sighed at her, a wall of garlic. 'I'm afraid he's right . . .'

Roger drove the car almost up against the bumper of the car in front and pressed the heel of his hand on the horn button.

'Come *on*, move over, *re maláka!*' he shouted.

Panos laughed. She looked over as she felt his hand on her arm, placed there with the flamboyant confidentiality of an actor about to draw the attention of another actor. She followed his gaze down to a crushed packet, the aperture of which he was holding towards her between thumb and forefinger.

'No, he's blown it,' said Roger. 'It's only a matter of time before this Cretan bank thing blows. They can't keep the lid on the thing much longer.'

Barbara gave a little smile and threw up her chin an inch, in the Greek fashion, to indicate the negative.

'What's that all about?' she asked from the centre of a cloud of blue smoke.

To her astonishment, Panos passed a lighted cigarette over Roger's shoulder and fastened it into the corner of his mouth, where it hung and bounced while Roger explained to her that

26

PASOK had been using the Bank of Crete as their honey-pot, but that the Bank of Crete was run by a total crook called Koskotás, a Greek-American, who had milked the economy of millions of dollars and was probably an agent of the CIA.

Roger, who had never smoked in his life. Medallion man.

Finally, after they had stood on the corner of the street outside the fish taverna in the rain for what seemed like an eternity, while Roger took his leave of Panos, several times over, they climbed into the Toyota and drove back. Roger was full of energy. Barbara looked sidelong at his familiar lean-jawed face, illuminated by the passing cars, and smiled to herself.

'What are you talking to Panos about?' she asked.

'Oh! business,' he said airily.

'Roger,' said Barbara gently, 'relax. It's me.'

He looked sideways and frowned. His hair had flopped sweatily over his brow and he looked completely demoniacal for a second, like a psychopath in an American movie. He said, 'Security, actually.'

'For Christ's sake, Roger, *don't* be so pompous!'

'I'm serious. Greece is being visibly undermined by certain groups. It is in the interests of certain people for the experiment in Greek democracy not to work.'

'What people?'

'Communists largely, plus the extreme right. All sorts of people. The CIA seems to be fiddling about here, as usual.'

'So, what do *you* know about security?'

Roger whistled through his teeth at an approaching cab which had poked out from a side street. He was driving far too fast, Barbara saw. He waved his arm magisterially at the cab driver who could not possibly have reacted.

'Now, you stay exactly where you are!' he shouted.

They went by on the pavement.

27

'There's no need for this. Slow down,' said Barbara.

'What's the matter, Barbara?' said Roger.

'Stop showing off.'

He slowed down and they rolled, still too fast, over some cobbles, Barbara's bottom lip banging against her teeth.

'Want to get back,' said Roger.

'I shall get out if you don't slow down. What if a policeman . . . ?'

'Don't be ridiculous,' said Roger. 'This is Greece.'

Barbara looked out of the window at the warehouses, and the unlit alleys that snaked away between them.

'I don't think you'd like to get down here,' said Roger, who had followed her gaze.

'You're avoiding the question,' said Barbara.

At last, he began to explain. There was a serious point, it seemed. The country was in domestic chaos, particularly in the public sector. DEE and OTE, the nationalised electricity and telephone companies, were going to put up prices by twelve to fifteen per cent. The teachers and pupils in schools and universities were on the streets, herding to the Ministry of Antonis Tritsis in vast numbers, protesting against his imposition of a new Educational Law, which, among other things, took away their right to have a minimum number of textbooks paid for by the State. The new Health Service instituted by PASOK was running into trouble and staff – including doctors – were selectively on strike at major hospitals. Athens, stifling under a silvery cloud of pollution, was full of rotting refuse sacks. And the banks, particularly the National Bank of Greece, were on strike.

'So?'

'Well, everybody's coming out. There's bound to be trouble in DEE, Panos's electricity company. The signs are all there.'

'Sorry,' said Barbara. 'I'm being a bit slow. I thought you said it was a public corporation. How can it belong to one man?'

'It is. DEE is a state organisation run by a management . . .'

'Then how can . . .'

28

'Panos is a director.'

'But you said Panos's company!'

'For God's sake, Barbara. Just a manner of speaking. Anyway, the point is the union structure includes a communist faction and an extreme right-wing faction . . .'

'So the chances are there will be industrial action if the prices go up. Sounds perfectly normal to me . . . ?'

'Yes. But it's deeper than that. If there's a strike in DEE, it's almost bound to be political, because the management are seeking to modernise working practices . . .'

Barbara sniffed. 'Sounds like a very *managerial* sort of a phrase . . .'

Roger grinned.

'I *have* been talking to Panos,' he said.

'I can see that. What are these practices?'

'Productivity agreements, some changes in the pension scheme . . .'

She knew what it was now that made him seem different. 'By the way, what's wrong with your tooth?'

'Chipped it. The one next to it got knocked out by an American.'

Barbara stiffened. For an instant the whole vision came to her. The sleazy bar, Roger, smoking a cigarette, receiving a blow that knocked the cigarette flying out of his mouth and made the blood gush down his chin . . .

He licked his lips. 'Gave as good as I got,' he said, drumming his two hands on the bottom of the steering wheel.

Barbara shook her head. 'Sorry. Good try . . .' she said.

They burst out laughing together. They hooted into the windscreen.

'I suppose you were fighting over the girl . . .' said Barbara.

'What girl?'

'You know, Roger, the one who gave you that medallion . . .' she murmured, with a sudden stare at him.

29

'Oh, this. I bought this. D'you like it? No, actually, it's much more banal. I fell down because I wasn't looking where I was going. You see, there aren't really any pavements in Greek cities because everyone builds his own building and he's responsible in law for the bit in front of it. So they put all sorts of fancy arrangements all at completely different levels. It's one of the basic culture shocks.'

'What, falling down?' She was scornful. Why didn't he admit it?

'Yes, actually . . .' Roger passed a hand lingeringly over his lips. 'No, I meant the absence of street planning, any planning, come to think of it . . .'

'Do you want to carry on with the lecture you were giving me?'

'Ah yes,' said Roger, without a flicker. 'Where were we? The management is trying to introduce changes in the tenure of jobs, and at least in a limited way tie pay and conditions to productivity. At the moment, if you join DEE you get a job for life . . .'

'Wouldn't be "accountability" by any chance, would it?' said Barbara ironically.

'They don't use the word here.'

'I don't care about that. We all know it's a Thatcherite concept . . .' Barbara was beginning to feel an obscure burn of anger.

'No, no,' Roger said, the pomposity returning in a parody of a lecturing manner. 'It goes back *long* before that . . .'

'Skip the history. I know it,' said Barbara, trying to rein in the desire to reach across and fiercely tweak his ear. 'The point is that you are talking the language of the management.'

'Panos is . . .' said Roger.

'Sounds like the existence of the deity, "Panos is". Panos is . . . a lecher,' said Barbara suddenly.

'I was about to say before you so rudely interrupted me that Panos is . . . a director . . .'

30

Barbara stared across the space between them on the front seats as if it were a huge natural distance like a ravine. Up in the roof of the car, beyond the ravine, the thunder clouds were massing.

'You said that before. So what can you do to help him?'

'Well, he's actually helped *me* in a number of ways,' said Roger.

Barbara put her hand inside her top to adjust a strap that had crossed and ran her fingers under it, tracing it up to her shoulder where it cleared finally. She felt his eyes on her while she performed this operation – flicking, checking, roaming where they had been edging to go but had been previously restrained, she assumed, by the severity and watchfulness of her glance.

The lift had a mirror in it, a full-length plate-glass mirror. Roger opened the door, his hand extended. As Barbara passed in she felt his fingers brush her hip. They moved as she moved, sliding down to her buttock, where they performed a friendly little pat. Barbara stared at their knuckles and veined backs in the mirror and, while his head was turned to press the switch for the third floor, she peeped over his shoulder and winced at her wincing image.

'Don't,' she saw herself say.

'Don't what?' said Roger, bending towards her as if he were deaf and sliding his arm awkwardly round her shoulder, while they both stared at the floors peeling away in front of them.

'Well,' said Roger, taking her coat from her shoulders, 'what do you think?'

Barbara had indeed been thinking, but only minimally about the flat. She was registering the degrees of drift between them, trying to deal with the fact that she didn't like his attitudes, his voice, even the way he was standing now and asking her what she thought. He's turned into someone else, she heard herself think, the phrase passing as if on an illuminated electronic noticeboard.

Immediately she began to anticipate the next thought as it slid across the black screen of her mind, so that she had the curious sensation of not quite catching it.

Is this . . . She struggled with the unarticulated thought, inclining her head, but the tail-end had flashed off into the darkness.

'Mmm . . .' she said aloud, aware that he was looking at her sharply.

'Very enigmatic,' said Roger, hanging the coats up.

As he moved away, the thought which had already passed on the screen passed again, this time quite clearly: *Is this what you've given up your independence for?*

'Big, isn't it. How did you find it?' she said.

Guilt pressed lightly in. She'd only just arrived, for God's sake. She took his arm, in a gesture of appeasement he could only have misunderstood, and they moved towards the yellow and black three-piece suite which stood round a small coffee table in the regulation square of the Greek salon.

Barbara took off her shoes while Roger mixed the drinks. She wanted a soda water. He had a large Cutty Sark.

'Greeks love Scotch,' he explained.

She lay back on the sofa with a sigh. She was feeling very confused and she sat up again, almost immediately, and doubled her legs under her.

He came over and she hoped he would sit in the armchair, but he sat heavily on her tucked-up feet instead, not seeming to notice, while he explained how he had found the flat and the role of the estate agent.

It was the first time he had ever bribed someone, he said. All his friends had warned him that he would almost certainly need to do this if he wanted the flat quickly and Panos had come with him to help. They had taken the estate agent, who was called Chrissoula, to a taverna. Panos had found out that Chrissoula was New Democracy, the conservative party, from a family in Piréas

32

he knew, and before long it seemed to have been arranged that Chrissoula's brother would come to Panos and would be given a position in DEE. Roger hadn't been able to follow the Greek at certain crucial points in the discussion, which seemed to dive into a series of 'ticks' and 'tacks' and 'tsaka-tsakas' with appropriate hand movements. When they re-entered standard Greek, Panos had laid his hand on Roger's shoulder and said, *'Ol'endáxei . . .'*

Afterwards he explained that Roger would need to give her twenty-five thousand drachmas, which he would take to the shop in an envelope when he went to sign the contract the next morning. She was expecting this.

The queue at the bank had been impossible because of the strike. There were only certain days of the week on which you could get any money at all. Roger had arrived late at the shop and had actually blushed, he confessed, when he took out the envelope and folded it into the contract he had signed.

'What's this? Oh . . .' said the girl, 'thank you . . .'

He refilled his glass from the cupboard. Barbara was glad of the respite provided by his narrative. The flat was not untidy, because Yiannoula came twice a week, but it had a batchelor, unlived-in air. *She* certainly didn't live here, the medallion girl. The pictures on the walls were vintage Roger – crude maps and prints which resembled the sort of thing you got in a bank or a railway carriage. The marble floor was clean, but the few rugs it had on it were scant and all the same blue colour. The shelves were made of terracotta, free-standing units piled one on top of the other in faded greens and oranges. The dining table was a small round affair with a plastic top. It all smelt a bit musty.

Barbara eased her feet from under Roger's thigh as he talked. She rubbed the pins and needles away, wondering what she was going to do with this slightly distasteful, boyish, middle-aged stranger who appeared so proud of the bed he had found in the flea-market and who had learnt how to bribe estate agents.

'It's really sound,' he said.

She had no idea what this remark meant. Did it refer to the bed, or the investment?

'You still haven't answered my questions,' said Barbara, who had begun to shiver slightly. She got up off the sofa and smoothed down the awful plum-coloured skirt which she had bought specifically for travelling.

'Where are you going?'

'Don't tell me you've got stocks and shares too . . .' she called from the bedroom. 'Just getting my . . .'

She felt his hands on her shoulders on either side and his hot breath in the hair on the back of her neck.

'Please don't,' she said.

She was thinking this was uncomfortably close to Celia Johnson in *Brief Encounter*, when he spun her round so suddenly that she fell sideways slightly and staggered, putting out her hands on to his shirtfront and pushing against the chicken's egg of his breast-bone.

'Just pleased to see you,' he breathed, cocking his chin forward and charging it into her neck, between her shoulder and cheek. She winced at the sandpaper scrape and, finding her spine curving towards him under the pressure of his hand on the middle of her back, pushed hard against his shirtfront. But as she threw her head back to get rid of his guzzling mouth from her neck, his other hand joined the one on her spine, already planted there in the mode of an over-zealous ballroom dancer, and the two hands slid downwards, squeezing their way with great huge painful pinches of the flesh of her buttocks.

Barbara pushed sharply.

'Ah,' she cried, pulling her head back further. But this only had the effect of pushing out her pelvis against him which he took advantage of by crooking himself over her.

Barbara felt as if she were wrestling with a giant crab, whose great plated belly and wriggling underneath bits were pressing into her while the two massive claws locked around her from behind, opening and shutting and pinching painfully the flesh in the small of her back and the top of her thighs. Something rigid began to butt into her at the front, repeatedly, with small sharp movements, while she could feel him saying something into her neck, his dead voice vibrating inaudibly against the skin of her jugular vein.

'Stop. It.' She cried through gritted teeth as her wrists began to collapse their resistance while his nostrils soughed, hot and horse-like, against her cheek and ear.

She was just as suddenly released and he was standing two feet in front of her, much taller because her shoes were off, panting slightly, and smiling at her.

'So pleased to *see* you,' he whimpered through his teeth, sucking back a drop of saliva that rolled out on to his bottom lip as he spoke.

'I'm tired,' she said, moving round the bed; 'it's been a long day.'

'Of course,' said Roger. 'But you don't know how much I've missed you . . .' He made a movement.

Barbara looked at her watch.

'Good God, is that the time!' she said, exasperated at the ruse.

They had a brief conversation about the two hours' difference but she could see he wasn't listening.

'Look, I'll just go and get ready for bed. I haven't even unpacked yet . . .' She flicked some hair back from her eyes.

'You don't need to do that,' he said, and repeated it with an odd, upward-moving intonation.

'Of course I need to do it,' said Barbara sharply and pushed past him.

He spread his hands and stepped aside. 'I'm sorry,' he said, 'I just . . .'

In the bathroom Barbara's trembling hands moved amongst her things, putting the shampoos and conditioners and all the other bottles she had bought for her trip on the shelf under the

35

mirror. She didn't want to look at herself, nor to admit at any level what had just happened. She had no name for it. It made no sense to her. But, as she laid out her Body Shop scents and her new dispenser of Revlon conditioner, she became aware that her skirt had slewed right round so that the zip, which was normally at the side, was now at the back.

She stared full into the mirror and wrenched her skirt round into its proper position. The strange woman with the tremulous lips and hands and the one red eye looked back at her, the hair fallen like a heap of straw over her forehead.

'Pull yourself together,' she said aloud and plumped her hair from the back.

'Barbara?' said his voice through the bathroom door.

The woman in the mirror took a deep breath.

'Yes?'

'I'm just going out to . . . get some cigarettes.'

'OK,' said Barbara, taking a tissue and starting to work on the damage.

'Won't be long. You go to bed.'

Barbara snapped awake in the dark at the sound of voices. She lay trying to distinguish them. At first her mind simply registered the different sounds in a blur, but then she disentangled the treble whimper of a child in the flat above from the deeper voices that seemed to be coming from along the corridor. She rolled over slightly and opened her eyes. Roger was not there. Above, the child started to yell: '*Babá*! *Babá*!' Barbara felt, in a perfect equilibrium of discomfort, the insistence of the cry and her own helplessness. Her tongue moved around its rank dry cavity. Her nose was blocked and she had been breathing through her mouth. Down below, the dull reminder of her bladder began as soon as she moved.

Barbara had no idea where the light was. Nor could she

remember where the furniture was situated in the bedroom. There was a chair somewhere near the door. She sat up in bed and lifted the sheet and coverlet, gently, swinging her pyjama-clad legs over into a gulf whose darkness seemed all the thicker for having no palpable features beyond the edge of the bed. She sat for a moment while she listened to two deep laughs one after the other and a cigarette smoker's cough.

As her lowered feet touched the parquet, steps pounded across the ceiling, their urgency evidently competing with the scream the child's cry had almost reached. It stopped immediately.

Barbara put out her hands like a sleepwalker, and launched off with a few lame, sliding steps. She felt there might be anything in front of her in the thick darkness and, stiff with anticipation, she braced herself for a collision.

The voices drew her towards the door and eventually, after feeling the wall and making out the corner of the room, her absurdly patting hands came across a light switch and then the jamb of the door. She moved down to the handle and turned it, revealing the hall as if on a screen, the door seeming to fold back rather than swing forward in the darkness. A faint light came from the sitting-room and Barbara began to find her sense of direction returning. She knew where the bathroom was and steadily she pushed off on to the marble, aware of the pyjamas flapping at her ankles. She walked towards the light.

Barbara passed the door to the sitting-room. She could see a corner of something that looked like a map and a glass of beer.

Roger was saying in English, 'What about Ptolemaida?'

'There's only one exit at this point . . .' came Panos's growl.

Smoke poured thinly through the crack in the door, a few twirls catching the light.

Barbara walked up to the door and pushed it with her fingertips.

'Look, what you need on this parapet is railings. No one can get up on it then. Here, and here, and here,' said Roger in Greek, suddenly looking up, his fingers still stabbing into a corner of blue river that ran between the raised folds of the map.

Panos turned his head and they stared silently at her as she stood in the doorway. She was suddenly aware of her pyjamas clinging between her thighs. She felt one of her breasts slide under the loose material of her pyjama top and, almost involuntarily, she made a gesture with her right arm to contain it, while her left hand completed the movement it was already committed to , rising high up behind her head to grasp a handful of hair.

For a full second she stood blinking in the doorway at the tableau in front of her.

'Barbara,' said Roger.

'What time is it?' said Barbara, faking a yawn and moving a leg to free the trapped material. Panos's iguana eyes rolled down the front of her pyjamas, looking for a gap. She went into the theatre of waking, even crossing one bare foot over the other as she spoke, in an appeal for pathos that tracked intimately a night of childhood when she had got up and stood in the doorway of her parents' bedroom while they had been making love. She had stood then, too, in the glare of the two sets of eyes from within the room, while she yawned a yawn to harmonise the interval.

Roger stood up.

'It's about two, Greek time. Shall I . . . ?'

Shall I what?

'No, no,' said Barbara beginning her turn. 'I'll be fine.'

She drilled her smile down at Panos, whose eyes automatically flicked up, hanging there, ready again to leap like fish in formation at her profile, to catch a flop in the material and wriggle in between the buttons at the front.

'You two carry on,' said Barbara, spinning on her bare heel and marching off with lowered head. She swished her way across the hall to the bathroom door, her feet slapping on the marble, while they stood in silence, looking out of the lighted space.

38

*

As soon as they had climbed into his orange, electricity company pick-up, Yannis started going on at her about the chaos at the recent union conference.

He was not so much teasing, as taunting her, she knew, with accounts of PASOK voting tactics. But she was too tired for this old game, and steered him on to the family.

Antigone looked down, fingering the three red roses wrapped in silver foil which lay in her lap. She sneaked a look sideways at Yannis as he drove. The sly, always understated smile that nestled under his hook nose recalled their bouts of slack-jawed laughter in between constant arguments about politics. Yannis, who had been a communist since the age of sixteen, was never really PASOK and kept calling PASOK voters papists and vegetables. Privately Antigone considered him properly passionate but publicly, for her, he was far too romantic and utopian about his politics. On his shelf in the bedroom, even now he and Elleni were married, Antigone was willing to bet, he kept his copy, not just dog-eared but worn and battered with reading, of the Russian encyclopaedia, though he had long ago left the official Moscow party and joined KKE-ES, the Communist Party of the Interior.

They passed several cars hooting loudly in convoy as they came into the outskirts of Thessaloniki. Young basketball fans hung out of the windows waving drinks and yellow banners.

'Ares?'

'Yes. They must have won.'

'Bravo Thessaloniki!'

'They've got Galis basically . . .'

'And Yannakis, come on . . .' said Antigone, 'and Soubotitz.'

'Ah, but it's Galis who's the real playmaker . . .'

'Get away with you!' said Antigone, laughing, 'it's a *team*. Never mind all this political crap, Yanne. Tell me your news.'

'Eleni and Tassos are fine.'

39

'Does he sleep at night?'

Yannis laughed. 'Like a faggot . . .'

'And Eleni. Tell me about her . . .'

He looked ahead at the road, fingering his chin.

'She's happy, I think. There's some trouble with her father and some land that's bothering her at the moment because her mother keeps ringing up. She doesn't like me working so late, but we're fine. A bit hard up – we're saving up for some new furniture now . . .'

'I'm looking forward to seeing them,' said Antigone happily. 'And now, how's my little mother and father . . . ?'

'Socrates is the same as ever. The *kafenéio* is . . . the *kafenéio*. But . . .' He sighed.

'What is it?'

'Oh, I don't know, she keeps worrying about the money . . .'

'What, the field?'

Antigone and Yannis came from a village up in the Pierian mountains. Their father, Socrates, kept the café in the square, a casual all-purpose institution which could turn into a taverna or a roastery when required. They had all had to serve in this café during their childhood. Remote, surrounded by high mountains, the village was relatively rich. It owned seven thousand goats and on the side of the old road from Veria, where the land was flatter and more fertile, there were tobacco fields which formed the main income for the villagers. Recently, Socrates had sold one of these fields to a merchant businessman and, according to Yannis, the guy had not come through with the money.

'Eleni and I go up every other Sunday. And whenever we go, she's always on at me . . .'

Antigone exclaimed as she looked out of the window. 'The Toumba!'

They were passing through Ano Toumba, a maze of streets grouped around a neolithic burial mound, and one of the fastest growing areas of the city. Antigone had lived here with their aunt, Theia Soula, while she had been a student.

'Look up there. PAOK's football ground . . .' said Yannis.

But Antigone had already turned away and was staring down through the concrete balustrade of the bridge into the *réma*, the ravine that meandered down from the heights and crossed under the road at this point. There were shacks in the *réma*, and Antigone put her hand on Yannis's arm, straining to catch sight of the roof of Kyra Barba's little home-made house tucked in between its steep walls.

'Oh, shall we call in?' she said suddenly.

Yannis looked at his watch. 'Too late. She's in bed by now.'

As they made their way down Konitsis Street, a large, orange number fourteen bus made its way towards them.

'They're still running,' said Yannis.

'The buses?'

'And the trains. But not for long. I think we are going to have a long hard winter this year.'

They came to Egnatia Street and Yannis drew up at the lights where National Defence Street crossed.

'*Amán!*' he said. 'Look at this!'

Antigone had been looking with curiosity at the university building, where she herself had studied for four years and now her sisters, Fotini and Katerina, were both there.

He was staring at the lake in front of them, a huge overflow of swirling black water, almost a metre deep in places, which covered the whole of the crossing between the streets.

'The drainage system in this town hasn't improved,' said Antigone.

'What do you expect in Greece?' said Yannis, as they rolled off through the flood with the rest of the queue.

They took the Veria road, getting deeper into the discussion of family politics. Antigone was the eldest. From an early age she had become famous for consulting her own interests and making out a case for them. It was assumed that she would end up as some kind of lawyer because she was one of those children who behaved like one. Had she reminded him, she and Yannis could have laughed about the time she challenged Socrates's right to punish her, after he had denied her a request for an ice-cream. Father and daughter had gone at it like hammer and tongs. Antigone had been patient and persistent in her own defence. It had been Socrates who had lost his temper at what he called her habit of twisting the facts.

It was Antigone they had looked to to sort out situations when they arose, and she had accepted the role, she reflected, with alacrity. She now saw that the discussion of family politics which she had initiated in order to postpone a ritual argument about politics in general with her brother was shifting into an account of her responsibilities. Yannis wanted her to talk to their mother and get her off his back. This was the implication, she thought, of his particular selection in the catalogue of facts.

'I'm working at weekends to help them as it is,' said Yannis as they moved out through the harbour area of the city towards the road to Katerini and Veria. 'She doesn't seem to recognise that I've got a family to look after now . . .'

Antigone was wondering whether it was Eleni. She sensed that Eleni and her mother didn't get on. The two families were known to each other. Antigone and Yannis's people were Romano-Vlach in origin, on their mother's side. They came from Macedonian nomadic shepherd stock, a closed community, which had lived for centuries by transhumance, the seasonal herding of stock over hundreds of miles of mountain pastures from villages in the Verian plain and the remote pastures of the Pindos mountains.

The Vlachs had spoken their own language, which was more closely related to Romanian than Greek, and had their own traditions. Whole villages used to be left empty, to be returned to when the animals were brought back for their seasonal pasturing in that area. Their mother, Matoula, could remember these trips across the mountains from her childhood, though later her

42

parents began to settle all the year round in Veria. When she was small the Vlachs were fiercely independent and self-sufficient. A race apart, literally stateless for centuries, they were out of the reach of the Turk in the high mountain villages of the Pindos and they often still had their own businesses in animal products – in sheep's and goat's milk and yoghurt.

Sometime after the Second World War Vlachs had been asked to choose whether they would become Romanian or Greek. A whole branch of the family, including Matoula's sister, Pascalena, had gone to Romania, a choice which had caused much bitterness and estrangement amongst those who had stayed behind and become Greek, like Matoula, in order that she could marry Socrates. But now the others were suffering so dreadfully under Ceaucescu, there was, ironically perhaps, some chance of reconciliation.

Eleni's family were farmers from the plain of Veria, who had recently become relatively well-off due to the damming of the river Aliakmon and the draining of the littoral plain. This had created a modern system of irrigation and allowed the farmers to institute an intensive system of fruit and vegetable cultivation in the rich, dark soil of the reclaimed land. Eleni's family were New Democracy people, though Eleni herself had revolted from them before she married Yannis. Antigone knew that her mother was sceptical of Eleni, however, even though she never spoke against her. The flat they had moved into in Veria had been Eleni's *proíka*, her dowry, from her mother and father.

Yannis was asking her in code to intervene with their mother and take the heat off the newly married couple.

Antigone sighed and looked across at her brother. She didn't want to get into all that.

'And how's the old goat?' said Yannis.

Antigone had long ago confided in Yannis about the old goat. This was her name for Loukas Karchakis, the Athenian company lawyer she had met in her last year at university at a law conference. He had taken an immediate fancy to her, in fact she suspected that his only reason for being there was to cast an expert eye over the young female graduates. Loukas had bombarded her with gifts and then seduced her in a hotel room in downtown Thessaloniki, right in the middle of her last exams. He had taken her out with a rather *louche* provincial set to all the usual out-of-the-way tavernas in the city and she had spent a fortnight, bored stiff, on his yacht in Chalkidiké at Porto Carras, where he had laid siege to her without success. That was about as much as Antigone could take of the old goat.

In the mean time, however, he had offered her a place as a young trainee in his law firm in Athens, which she was careful to accept only after she had broken off her relationship with him. But he was constantly trying to win her back by a series of elaborate favours, phoning her at night, just when she was about to go to bed, with some new scheme or offer. He was tireless, the old goat.

'É, same as ever,' said Antigone. 'But he got me this job, which is my first big break. I can't complain . . .'

'Yes, I saw your picture in the paper,' said Yannis. 'We all looked at that and said, "Now Antigone's a big shot . . ." Mama and Babás are so proud of you . . .'

She wished the guy hadn't taken that photo of her outside the preliminary hearing, advising her client, Christos. She was leaning right across, whispering in his ear, her lips extended almost to the point where they touched the lobe of his ear and her fingertips lightly holding the back of his neck above the collar. Everybody teased her about this full-page colour photo of her kissing the young terrorist, when all she had been doing was making sure that he understood his rights in a crowded and noisy room. The picture had somehow made them all put a mental caption on it.

The lights of Veria twinkled against the dark mass of mountains.

'So what's going on in this case?'

'Looks like a police set-up. They *already knew* what was going to happen – the records show that they had filed the case against Lekas at dawn on the day he was shot. Before it happened. Now you and I know that no policeman is going to start making out charge sheets at dawn or 6.30 a.m. in *Greece*, I ask you, without something funny going on . . .'

'Who are they in with?'

'They're a group of middle-class boys playing at being the Red Brigade. Some of them are a bit paranoid. Most of them are good right-wing nationalists from respectable backgrounds . . .'

'That's what I thought,' said Yannis. 'So the police are having a field day?'

'Yes. Looking for weapons all over Athens. So far they've come up with two caches and they're trying to nail about thirty people they've identified as having contacts with the Lekas group.'

Including Manos, she thought. Her client, the spoilt, slightly paranoid Christos, conformed perfectly to the description she had just offered Yannis, even though she believed in fact he had been unjustly arrested and beaten up by the police. The insubstantiality of their charges showed that they had very little to actually go on.

But Manos was different. Manos was a poet, slightly raffish, streetwise, who hung out on the fringe of this group. He lived and wrote in a one-room apartment and seemed to spend a lot of time on his own. He came from a large family in Plaka. All his brothers had been in the navy, and Manos would soon be going too, if he were not arrested. Manos's hair was perfectly cropped all over his beautifully ovular head, his hand movements were extremely delicate, and his voice – like the voice of all his brothers – was high and womanly. He spoke in a soft chattering. Antigone thought that all the boys must be replicas of the mother whom she had never met. The whole family seemed to be crazy about cats.

Antigone was preparing herself for the news, one day soon, that Manos, too, had been arrested.

'Then they'll try and fabricate a connection to the Seventeenth of November,' she said aloud, suddenly thinking how the remark applied to Manos too. She thought of his innocent face in newspaper pictures juxtaposed with police portraits of dead members of Greece's most feared terrorist group.

She looked out of the window at the twinkling lights at the foot of the dark mass of mountains. It was another world down in Athens and she had to admit she was amused by the intensity of some of these wild tearaway young men who were so crazily romantic about everything. She was in two minds whether she wanted to be in Athens and it was Manos and some of his friends, at the moment, that kept her there. She passionately believed that their rights should be defended. But she had also detected a vein of something else in her feelings about Manos. He never called, he just turned up at her flat. At first, she had not noticed how strange it was of her never to be annoyed, especially when she had lots of work to do and her papers were strewn all over the living-room table. But then on one particular occasion, quite recently, when she opened the door, in walked Manos with a bag full of something which he took straight into the kitchen and started to boil without asking her. After a few minutes the whole apartment had been filled with the scent of lemons. When she had asked him why he had done this, was he going to cook them for something, he had simply laid his head on one side and smiled.

'Because they smell so good,' he said.

Out of the hessian bag he was carrying he had also taken a little squeeze-box, engraved with pastoral scenes of an eighteenth-century type, and sung to her, the aroma of the lemons stealing into the sunny room, the old song by Charhákos about the Civil War soldier who doesn't want to be asked by his wife what is in the old photograph on the wall. 'Don't ask me about that, Maria,' he keeps saying, and the key to the song – here Manos held up his hand and called her attention to it, emphasising for her the very part of the verse – lies in the way the old soldier reveals that it is a photograph of his old comrade-in-arms, his sergeant, who turned out after the war to be a communist. On the other side.

Antigone had sat at the table, her pen poised over the paper, as if politely waiting for him to finish. In reality she wanted him to go on, so that she could carry on looking at the arch of his very soft eyebrows, smell the aroma of the lemons and study the way that he inclined his head with such a winning pathos that a real sadness arose inside her at the repeated words, gathering significance each time he uttered them: *'Me me pikráineis állo piá'* – don't embitter me, Maria, once again.

This was a moment she had not shared with anyone, not even with herself. Only now, as she sat in the car listening to Yannis talking about the effectiveness of the Seventeenth of November Terrorist Group, did she realise she was thinking about it again: the bitterness of the song was the pain of another generation, not hers, and certainly not Manos's, and yet this rather strange boy had the gift of bringing it home to her.

'And all this stuff about the keys to the Simca . . .' Yannis was saying.

Antigone agreed the keys were just a red herring put up by the police.

'I wish we didn't have to go up the top tonight,' she said suddenly. 'Can't we just stay at the balcony and go up to the village in the morning?'

Their new apartment in Veria was on the street referred to locally as 'the balcony' because it looked out directly over the fertile plain of Veria from the bluff in the foothills on which the town was built.

'No way,' said Yannis, laughing. 'It's more than my life is worth. They're all waiting for you, and I promised Mamá that I would bring you straight from the plane. She's made food, and everyone's at home waiting . . .'

'And then I'll come down to you and Eleni tomorrow? Please?'
'You'll come down to us tomorrow.'
They took the road off to Vergina.

She sat on the end of Katerina's bed and unpacked her things from their tissue paper. They were both the same size, though Katerina was not as tall as Antigone. They looked at her new shoes and her new, very well cut two-piece in dark blue, of which she was so fond because it carried such a chaste, severe, professional air with it. When Katerina held it up, the skirt was too long for her.

'Look, I can wear it with lots of different things, don't you think?' said Antigone.

'Mmm . . .' said Katerina. 'Not really my colours . . .'

As a student, Katerina wore her regulation uniform. She had a big dark coat for winter, a few different blouses, three pairs of good sailcloth Lee jeans, some heavy knitwear, a short striped skirt in pale blue and mauvy-pink stripes and three pairs of shorts, for summer. She kept these clothes ironed and pressed to perfection so that there was always a knife-edge crease down the jeans and on the arms of the blouses.

Two of the blouses had originated with Antigone. She looked at Katerina as she sat on the bed with legs crossed in her pyjamas.

'Hey, Ninaki,' she whispered, 'this is for you.'

Antigone had brought her a slinky woollen dress in dark red.

Katerina glowed as she leapt off the bed and held it in front of her. She dashed for the mirror. She turned full on, she turned sideways, she ran her fingers through her hair while she held the dress clipped tightly at the top against her, so that it hung down over her knees.

'Length all right?' said Antigone, anxiously getting up off the bed and standing behind her.

'It's beautiful,' said Katerina, pirouetting. She threw the dress

48

down on the bed and shyly turned her back while she took off her pyjama top.

'I have to see this on,' she said. 'Is it really from London?'

Antigone was delighted. She had spent hours in Oxford Street trying to get all her purchases right and this was the one she had taken the biggest risk with. There wasn't much you could do with such a garment except give it to someone else if it didn't fit.

She looked at her sister standing over her with the dress down over her pyjama legs. She was taking a cigarette out of the packet. She held it up and Antigone nodded. Katerina put two cigarettes in her mouth and slinked comically over to the dresser to get the ashtray and lighter.

'*Pouláki mou*,' said Antigone, 'you look terrific. You're going to be a wow at those Institut Français parties . . .'

'Yeeeeh . . .' said Katerina, through pursed lips, as she lit the two cigarettes together with one flash of the lighter.

Katerina. She was growing up fast. Antigone and she had never been close until the last few years – they had never quite found anything to talk about. The gap between them felt awkward and there was the question of Yannis, whom Katerina liked but could never get near because she always felt Antigone needed to put her down in front of him.

'Never mind me. It was Yanni you needed to put down, I didn't figure . . .' said Katerina.

They were lying in bed smoking.

Had she? Antigone couldn't remember. 'Why would I do that?'

'Oh, you had to be the big shot in those days . . .' said Katerina, blurting the words out. '*But*, I like you now much better . . . you've changed a lot, you know . . .'

'So have you,' said Antigone with a laugh; 'maybe you've grown up.'

'Oh, always the same,' said Katerina with a sudden reversion to the tone of a childhood argument, rocking her head softly from side to side. 'You always have to go one better, don't you?'

49

And they laughed at the quotation.

'And how's life at Theia Soula's?'

Katerina was the third of the girls to stay at their aunt's house in Triandria, the suburb of Thessaloniki near the Toumba. Antigone was first, then Fotini, who now shared a flat near the promenade with a crowd from the English department. And now Katerina, who was doing French.

'É, same as ever. Pretty cramped . . .'

'She OK?'

'Just the same. She knows everybody else's business and doesn't have any of her own. She's a cunning old thing . . .'

Theia Soula, their great-aunt on their father's side whose real name was Athanasia, knew everything about what happened in the flats, the street, the *réma*, and half of what happened in Kryoneri as well, the next area which was full of Pontoi, refugee families from Asia Minor. Antigone laughed. The city was just like a village for Theia Soula.

Katerina's hand couldn't help stealing out to the box which lay on the bed and caressing the corner of it. She talked with her head down, the smoke curling into her black hair, her fingers poking compulsively into the gaps in the knitting.

'*Don't* do that,' said Antigone automatically, reaching across.

'Very *Kathosprepei*, *n'est-ce pas*?' said Katerina. 'Hey, tell me about these terrorists. Are they . . . you know . . . good-looking?'

Antigone delivered an evasive account, laced with professional neutrality and descriptions of the extreme romanticism of the boys, pretending that they had dropped down from another planet.

'It's called Utopia,' she finished. 'Ninaki, these people are so idealistic, you wouldn't believe it. They think Greece is being undermined by videos and bottles of foreign milk . . .'

'Anyway, you're going to get them off, aren't you? This is your first case, isn't it? *Ma sœur, vous savez, elle est avocat à Athène . . .*' she said in a swanky French accent. 'That's what I say to my professors . . .'

'How's it all going? said Antigone, partly because she didn't want any more questioning along the terrorist line.

'OK,' said Katerina. 'But I'm only taking sevens and you know that isn't good enough for a scholarship . . .'

'Yes, you need eights,' said Antigone.

'Of course, *you* got nines, you brainy thing!'

It was true. Antigone had just simply been good at maths and any subject that had some kind of technical procedure to master. She saw herself now, at the age of eight, with her little brother, the two dogs and the *kopádi* of goats, looking down from the top of the mountain to where the turquoise waters of the Aliakmon ran in the bottom of the gorge, below the line of the scrub oak, hundreds of feet below them. While he whittled pieces of wood and tried to learn the tin whistle, she counted. She counted goats a thousand times a day. Anything, she counted; she was fascinated by numbers. And pretty soon she wanted to know about negative numbers, and square roots. The world of numbers seemed to her to be frictionless. She could pass through whole realms in a flash; you could travel with numbers. And when she discovered higher maths and calculus life had assumed a new dimension of happiness for her. It was a skill she had started out with, which she thought had nothing to do with anything else. But she gradually discovered that arithmetic was one of the alleyways into the centre of things. She had always been happy to go to the public library at the YMCA building with the other students. But she kept apart, perfectly happy, not groaning in sweaty bunches round the table, or flirting with Costis and getting him to do her maths for her like the others. Antigone was lost in the world of figures she had been taking consolation in since she was a child.

Katerina's breathing had slowed down to a regular heave in the other bed, but Antigone's brain whirled on in this room in which she had spent so much of her childhood.

She was reading about Mexican art and the association between the geometrical cultures of the North, which were all male and had no curves, the sun-worshippers, and the moony, curvaceous, feminine art of the Olmecs in the Vera Cruz area. The person writing the book seemed to think that these associations were inevitable, but she had found, in her own life, just the opposite. Apart from all those years of Latin and ancient Greek which the schools programme had pumped into her, the endless drills and the learning of everything by heart, her mind had been shaped by geometry and mathematics, the two things which she took most pleasure in. Studying for law had been hellish, because it was all rote learning of formulae, but her first experience of Euclid, for example, had been a glimpse of a kind of perfection which had nothing to do with the sort of thing the writer of her book was talking about.

She flipped the page, and dreamed.

Her mind went back to that summer in Chalkidiki, five years earlier, when she and Costis had spent so much time together. She'd been topless at their beaches the whole summer, legs dangling from the back of his snorting *papáki* as they rode to the remote little rocky point they found outside Nikiti, with no road or even a track to it, and whose only drawback was the wasps that constantly came round when the rocks were wet. Costis told her she looked like Nefertiti. Innocent days, before Loukas, before Athens. He dived for sea-urchins and brought her the lovely shells, dark purple, and the wonderful big grey-green one which she still had on her desk in Athens.

Of course then there had been all the panic at the end of the summer. She had thought she was pregnant, missing her period and so on. She had already started working out how to get the money for the abortion. She had been on the point of phoning Sarah in Slough, when she suddenly had a bleeding session like she had never known. And when she had told Sarah, who had been wondering what was going on, she laughed, to Antigone's relief, and said that's nothing, *she'd* had a miscarriage in the lavatory of South Kensington Natural History Museum, amongst the Dinosaurs, so how about that? She'd done her bit for evolution, she said. They had cool, some of these English girls, and she envied them.

And what had happened to Costis, she asked herself, her mind drifting back. Ah yes, Costis had gone as an engineer to Zaire . . .

'Come on,' said Yannis. 'It's become pretty clear what the Government's strategy is . . . to depress the price of labour and institute planned unemployment. You know it's running at ten per cent now. I tell you, they're in the hands of the bankers. It's these EOK people. They're telling them how to run the labour market, putting pressure on them all the time, now the external debt is so high . . . The people are not going to stand for these anti-labour tactics, they're going to come out on the streets. They know PASOK has joined the big capitalist club. Papandreou has turned his back on the people . . . he's just pro big business now, and anti-labour . . . That's what I can't understand about you, Antigone, how you can go on supporting these people . . . you're as stubborn as a donkey!'

Antigone was not a Marxist. There was a tangle of difficulties here for her. Moral, personal difficulties, that made her always think of the individual case. She found Marxism reductive and, besides, she wasn't impressed by the KKE's efforts to deal with the problems of women in Greece, despite the shining example of Maria Damanaki, just appointed Speaker of Parliament, whom she admired personally. She and Yannis had always disagreed about this matter. For him, the thing that mattered was the objective situation of the working class, of which he considered himself a fully paid-up member. Yannis was not interested in subjective opinions. The objective struggle of the producers, as he called the workers, this was what concerned him, first and foremost. As a syndicalist, he was a tactician, interested in infiltration, *blockage*, voting patterns, and at the moment he was doing his damnedest to break up the PASOK faction in the union, split their vote. Recently, Eleni complained, he had been out in his truck more than at home, and talking to all those old New Democracy guys, politicking with the opposition against PASOK's domination of the unions' General Council.

'The public sector's where the big struggle is coming. I tell you. I can tell from what's happening in my union, in DEE, the writing is on the wall. You see, these PASOK union people are in a cleft stick. They are being forced to support the Government's anti-labour policies when the contradiction is clear even to them, and, in private, you can get some of them to admit it . . .'

'Yes, but I'm trying to look at it in a broader framework . . .' Antigone began, her ear half on the struggles of Eleni in the bedroom with little Tassos. 'This Turkish threat is important – look at this last spring, there could be war, you know! And I think if we can get rid of it once and for all with Davos . . .'

Yannis snorted.

'. . . And get rid of the American bases . . .'

'É, Antigone, don't be so *naïve*!' shouted Yannis, pushing his elbows into the lunch plates on the table and getting out his tobacco box. He paused, waving the rizla paper at her: 'Papandreou is the *friend* of the Americans. He's carrying out their policy!'

'But what are *you* people saying about NATO and the EEC? You're not saying anything! We want to get out, to make the southern Mediterranean a nuclear-free zone. PASOK backed up to the Americans over Larisa, at least!'

'It's not important at this time,' said Yannis. 'Whether you like it or not, Greece is carrying out America's spying policy on the East, despite all Papandreou's claims to be a friend of the Gorbachov lot . . . What has Schultz been coming here for so much in the last few years? And America is making the planes for this defence contract which the PASOK government has negotiated for the twenty-first century. This is the reality . . . Oh, no doubt this Hellinikon base will go and there'll be some kind of deal done, but the bases will not go. *É*, he said explicitly in January to the Parliament that he would keep Greece in NATO, what was it?'

' "If the price is right", I know,' said Antigone, as Eleni appeared in the doorway. 'But what did you expect him to say? Greece is a small country. It would be foolish not to face the reality that there will be some cost to us for all this . . .'

She heard them in the other room, Yannis saying 'No, Eleni, no, Eleni, that is not the way!' and Eleni's reply, its qualifications lost in the renewed yelling of Tassos, who did not want to go for his after-lunch nap. Her heart was racing, her blood was up.

Yannis was right, at least to some extent. PASOK had changed. Everyone in the country felt it. After the 1985 elections it was a different PASOK. Antigone had joined the PASOK branch of lawyers in Kipselis in Athens as soon as she had gone down there, and she had been conscientious in attending meetings. There was still quite a lot of enthusiasm amongst the lawyers, because law reform had been one of the great missions of the early PASOK government. But, as Yannis would argue, it doesn't matter how many laws you pass, PASOK's changes were all top-down. There was a gap between what the law said and what people did. Actually, she found she agreed with him but the principle, she felt, served her argument and not his: no matter how many anti-discriminatory laws had been passed in the last six or seven years, the fact was that women had not managed to penetrate the inner sanctum of the male hierarchy.

The stagnation of the economy and the mounting external debt had made PASOK's room to manœuvre in its second term of office much more limited. The tenacity of traditional values, the strength of the old family and the transfer of the rural structure of dowries to the towns were features of Greek social life which were difficult for mere changes in the law to reach, despite the fact that the Greek male was no longer legally the 'head' of the household, and all the other things you could list as gains in a PASOK hand-out or speech. Yannis, who was very conservative about the family – he didn't consider it a political issue at all – was clear about the whole thing. This was a populist, not a socialist, government, which was cultivating a petty bourgeois consciousness in the people, while it manipulated a repressive, bureaucratic caste machine.

'They are Peronising the country,' he had shouted in their last discussion, she remembered.

Now he was trying to persuade Eleni to let Tassos cry, but Antigone knew how hard it was for her. How the child's every dry gasp between tears tore at her and made it impossible not to run to him and pick him up. But Yannis insisted and they came back to the table. While Eleni fidgeted with the sweet and finally pushed it away from her and stared out of the window, he carried on as if nothing was happening:

'The Common Market and the multinationals have penetrated every Greek market – we have to face this – and the Greeks love it. The supermarket chains and the car imports . . .'

'Oh, it's a reality, I know, but it's also a mask,' said Yannis, putting his hand on to Eleni's forearm as she listened, miserably, tensely, to Tassos's long gulps of breathless silence between howls in the next room. He kept his hand on her arm as he spoke. 'It looks as if the consumer boom means that life is getting better for Mr Joe Average, but in fact the value of wages is going down day by day . . .'

'I agree. But you KKE people don't have a policy about the Common Market.'

'Well, it's happened. It's a fact. But the most important thing is to make sure that PASOK doesn't get in at the next election. Coalition, this is what's going to work. There are enough defectors now from Papandreou's repressive machine who are talking about a broad left coalition . . .'

'Now who's being naïve!' she cried. 'You'll just put Mitsotakis back in and turn back the clock thirty years . . . There are so many factions amongst the Left that you'll never be able to hold together! What are you thinking about? This is just Utopian talk!'

'Not from where I'm sitting,' said Yannis, letting go of Eleni's arm. 'I tell you, the writing's on the wall!'

She was convinced he was wrong about this – and there she had no trouble. It just seemed to her a typical piece of romantic syndicalism, even though she knew that the Communist Party did have ten per cent of the vote to dispose and that their refusal to co-operate with PASOK in the last elections had resulted in a big drop in PASOK's share of the vote. She was convinced that PASOK had created a space in Greek politics which it would continue to occupy because nothing else could do it, unless, that is, PASOK broke up in the way Yannis was hinting. Although there had been defections Antigone was sure not only that PASOK was not a spent force, but that also, if Papandreou were not actively supported, the centre ground would be occupied by a re-formed New Democracy party, cloned, by the pressure to compete, from PASOK itself, which could gain a lot of the votes of disillusioned professionals and lower-middle-class small businessmen anxious to protect their interests.

Eleni said she was going to phone her mother.

'*É, paidáki mou,*' shouted Yannis over his shoulder, 'make sure Tombras isn't listening before you say anything!'

They all laughed.

'What a wanker!' said Yannis, shaking his head, 'but they're all in this together . . .'

'Conspiracy theory,' said Antigone. 'Not a good basis for reasoning . . .'

'*É,* what do you want?' Yannis spread his hands. 'This is Greece, *paidí mou! É,* remember Papandreou when he came to power in 1981, what did he do?'

'You mean the Cyprus thing?'

'Of course. He wouldn't open the file.'

'Come on, the two things are not connected . . .'

'Andreas was clearly protecting the American CIA.'

'That is as maybe. There is no proof beyond some flimsy evidence . . . But the fact is, with the Tombras thing, you can't run a democracy, as you well know, without some form of intelligence service . . .'

'Spying on the working class!' shouted Yannis, struggling to light his cigarette. 'It all fits, I tell you. It's a police state!'

Here they were verging on a geniune dilemma for Antigone, and she knew it. 'The police are not the State,' she said.

'You should know, defending these terrorists, trying to assert their rights as citizens . . . against police lying, and fabrication of evidence, and the barbarous execution of that young boy. What's that but the actions of a police state?'

'The Government is ready to denounce the actions of the police, if it can be shown that they acted improperly . . . These are the freedoms, the civil liberties, that PASOK itself fought for and in large measure, as you well know, helped to create. I'm only trying in this case to defend those civil liberties. After all, its PASOK that have neutralised the police and the army, and reduced their arbitrary powers . . .'

'They may say that,' Yannis said, 'but I think they're looking for some exemplary convictions . . . and they're encouraging the police to go on the rampage, so they can be seen to be doing something about the Seventeenth of November, whom they're scared stiff of . . .'

'The police are just defending their own position. It's not the Government . . .'

'I don't know. PASOK are willing to use the law to attack people. They've threatened to use military tribunals and have broken at least four strikes this way in the last couple of years. They even wanted to bring in a *law* to ban strikes last year – or have you conveniently forgotten? – what was the formula they used, strikes "that abuse labour privileges"?'

'That's altogether a different thing,' said Antigone. 'Some of these kids are crazy, and they're dangerous. They're a threat to themselves, and to other people . . .'

'The police didn't need to open fire without warning like that . . .'

'I agree. And I happen to think they're trying to make themselves look good by arresting some of these people without good evidence to suspect them . . . and they're trying to link them with the Seventeenth of November . . . But . . .'

'But?' he said, lifting his chin.

'It's not an expression of the Government's own position.'

'I'll tell you what the Government's own position is,' said Yannis, dropping his voice and listening out for Tassos, but it was Eleni crying '*Ára, manoúla mou* . . .' to her mother on the phone in the hall. 'They're anxious to prove that working-class discontent is part of a plot to de-stabilise democracy and bring back fascism. These poor fools are just part of this process of propaganda . . .'

'God! Yannis, you're as bad as the policemen I have to deal with,' said Antigone with disgust.

'You're not seeing things as they are,' he insisted, 'you're clinging to what you think they used to be!'

And here she did have a difficulty which she couldn't resolve. Perhaps it *was* time for Papandreou to go, and perhaps for George Papandreou to take over, who seemed the most reasonable of the younger people, and highly critical of some of the directions PASOK policy had been taking recently. But would George really command the votes? He was popular, but couldn't be compared with his father, electorally speaking. Antigone found it difficult to admit that there was a policy shift of the type that Yannis was insisting on, because she thought of PASOK not as a governing party, but a state of mind, irrevocably associated with progressive reform. It was not so much what the Party did that worried her, but rather what the Central Committee felt, and surely the Central Committee had always had its divisions – at one hundred and forty strong, what else could it do but reveal its fission?

'Look at that guy Raftopoulos,' said Yannis, moving in with sweet reason in his voice, 'a pretty conservative, middle-of-the-road PASOK chairman of the Greek Confederation of Labour – even he is supporting calls for a general strike!'

Antigone carried the dishes into the kitchen and started to run the water into the sink. Eleni came off the phone, beginning to take the dishes from her and dry them as if by a reflex, and the two of them stood side by side at the sink without speaking, in uneasy silence.

The afternoon was wearing on. Antigone knew that they had wanted her to intercede with Matoula, to take the pressure off them, and she was determined to resist the creeping guilt she felt at not having done so last night. There were, after all, other problems. Nothing, however, would be said about this. She glanced sideways at Elleni, who was simply listening out for Tassos and turning the plates over in her hands, rhythmically, before putting them in the rack.

Antigone walked back into the sitting-room, where Yannis was taking out another cigarette.

'*Yánne mou*,' she said, leaning on the door jamb, 'why can't you just be simple for once and help PASOK out of this crisis?'

'You don't understand politics at all, my little girl, do you?' said Yannis.

She ignored this. 'There is a great danger of a historical step backwards, you know. I am trying to take the broader view . . .'

'You're not living in the real world,' he cried. '*Amán*! What is she saying? This cosy clique of bourgeois lawyers who make money out of these poor devils of muddled anarchists on the streets! And then you come and lecture me about the dirty business of politics as if I had some kind of moral choice in the matter! My God!'

'But we are all on the same side in the end! Do you want those fascists to get in?'

60

'Look, *korítsi mou*,' said Yannis, offering her a cigarette. To her surprise she suddenly took it and sat down again by his side at the table. 'Take this DEE union congress we've just had . . .'

She stared at him while he described the struggle for control of the General Council of Unions in DEE and the tactical withdrawal of the PASOK-controlled union on a technicality connived at by the chairman.

'OK, a technical point,' she smiled.

'All PASOK's points are technical,' said Yannis, 'it shows how bankrupt they are! But do you expect me to just sit there in a spirit of co-operation and take this kind of terrorising legalism?'

'Yannis,' said Antigone, 'I know you Maoists. I know your psychology. You are constantly looking out for the short-term power play. If there are two groups of people, one dominant, you will automatically support the underdog, no matter what class interests they have, because you believe in the dynamics of the dialectical process in the short term!'

'I tell you, these public-sector industries are a contradiction in the classical sense. Half of the PASOK people in the union don't believe in their own Government's austerity programme. Of course they don't!'

'But no one can withstand the outside economic forces which are being brought to bear! It doesn't matter who they are! We know that PASOK's honeymoon period is over, but look what they have done for the general texture of social life . . . Look at what they've tried to do for women . . .'

'We believe that the women's organisations should be free, not tied to the party machinery. Their place in the struggle is autonomous!' Yannis said.

The wailing began again from the bedroom.

'Eleni,' he shouted, without turning round or deviating in his argument.

'On the contrary,' shouted Antigone, banging on the table. 'It is precisely *because* the women's movement in Greece has been tied to the party networks that it has managed to make such a grassroots impact! Autonomy will swallow them all up in the patriarchal process again. We don't have room for the luxury of radical feminism yet in Greece! We haven't enough power! Where are all the women in professions, parliament, doctors, in courts of law? PASOK's reforms have not gone through the system yet . . .'

'It's time for a *change*!' said Yannis, quoting ironically the Papandreou slogan.

'To make that change, we have to support the programmes. We can't just switch away to something else when the going gets tough. There's too much at stake!'

'I tell you, they've blown it. They are going to lose control of GENOP and we shall force industrial action even if we have to make an alliance with New Democracy people! And PASOK will lose the elections . . .'

'Because of people like you! Maoists on the lookout to play the combinations of the voting process, instead of seriously considering what the long-term political goals are for our country!'

'The struggle must go on . . . the people will not rest. Power must be taken away from these bureaucratic capitalists, these PASOKists. My god, they have such arrogance, they think they have this whole country sown up, they think it's their own orchard . . .'

'There are always some corrupt people in politics, but PASOK has many people of good will who have genuinely tried to make progress in this medieval country . . . Look at Tsobolas, look at Melina . . .'

'. . . and look at Koskotas . . . and look at your beloved Prime Minister and his love nest in the seaside boulevard at Sounion. What's he giving Kaloutsis in return for that, do you think?' said Yannis.

'We don't take our standards from the failures, but what we think is right and good,' said Antigone, ignoring her own primness.

Yannis laughed at her. 'Get away,' he jeered. 'You argue like a student who's just read her Plato. D'you think the rank-and-file PASOK member is like that? They are anti-intellectual bureaucrats, I tell you, using their *mesa* like anyone else in this place . . .'

'There's a difference when the ends *justify* the means! If PASOK people use the old means, it is not in the same spirit, there's a goal – a social progressive purpose, as far as I am concerned – in view –'

'Eleni!' said Yannis, '*Ela!*' He looked at his watch. 'You have to go back. *Ela, korítsi mou,*' he said, as Eleni appeared, '*kafedakia?*'

'Done,' said Eleni and disappeared.

'Man!' shouted Antigone, 'you sit there, Yanni *mou*, like a little pasha, shouting "*kafedákia!*" as if Eleni were some kind of slave or servant, while talking to me of the "autonomy," of the women's movement . . .'

But he was laughing at her: '*É*, always the same Antigone *mou*, now you're arguing like a good Maoist!'

'But it's *true!*' said Antigone passionately. 'It's true. It's the whole political process we have to talk about, and that includes every moment of social and cultural life, including life within the family. You union patriarchs are the biggest obstacle to change for women, talking about "the people" and "the struggle" while shouting for your food and your coffee and your bed . . .'

'Eleni!' he shouted, 'come here! I want to ask you a question!'

Eleni came to the table and put her arms round his neck from behind and nuzzled his hair. 'You two!' she said, indulgently, relaxed now little Tassos had finally gone down, 'do you always argue like this?'

Yannis looked across at Antigone, and then looked up at Eleni, caressing her bare forearm with his cheek: 'Don't you agree with me,' he said, 'there's only one political question between a man and a woman?'

'What's that?' said Eleni, bending to kiss him.

'The cucumber. Whether you want it in the front or the back?'

Eleni sprang back. 'Ah, get away with you,' she shouted. 'Don't *talk* like that to me and in front of your sister, too!'

'Sometimes,' said Antigone to Eleni, picking up her bags, 'I wonder why we don't all become nuns and leave them to it.'

They kissed on both cheeks as Antigone said thank you.

'He doesn't mean it,' said Eleni.

'My little brother?' said Antigone, 'Oh yes he does. Every word.'

Their silence in the car did not worry Antigone. Their conversation earlier had been a kind of catharsis, but there had been something troubling her throughout the afternoon and now it surfaced again, as she stared at the peach and apricot orchards flashing by the window of the truck. It was the gossip she sometimes heard from her fellow lawyers, the rumours that circulated about what was going on in government circles. Quite recently, someone had told her something which really perturbed her, and lent, she had to admit to herself, a lot of force to Yannis's arguments, at least to the detail of them, if not the broader assumptions. A rumour that the Bank of Greece had created a change in the banking regulations two years ago whereby it had been possible for all the public institutions − water, the telephones, DEE, the hospitals, even the Church: all of the public sector industries, in fact − to invest public monies in private banks in interest-bearing accounts for periods of seven to ninety days.

This struck Antigone as being either a highly cynical or a highly desperate manœuvre. It meant, as her colleagues − and these were the PASOK faithful − were pointing out, that under the old law, inherited from the Colonels in 1971, there was still in force an act of secrecy which forbade the investigation of private accounts as strict as that of Switzerland or Liechtenstein. Public money was now being diverted into high-interest-bearing accounts, the activities of which couldn't be investigated by public enquiry. If this were true it seemed wrong to Antigone, and surely it was something which PASOK at the highest level had actively created. The cost of the first PASOK government reforms had been huge, she knew, but had things been so bad that they required this kind of remedy? Or were some people just feathering their nests?

Roger was standing looking abstracted on the edge of a company which occupied the middle of the corridor. Evidently the meeting had just broken up. There was an argument going on between Panos and a woman called Thekla about where to have lunch. Panos wanted to go somewhere nearby and Thekla was using all her art to persuade him to go to a quaint place over in Tsingounis, on the way to the airport. The others were standing round smoking in small groups, waiting for a decision to be reached. Panos, whose plans were already made, kept throwing in little objections while Thekla sold him the advantages of her place.

Barbara slipped her way through the group and tugged Roger's sleeve. He looked down, still saying something to the man at his side.

'Barbara, there you are. Meet Stathis. Stathis, my wife . . .'

Apparently, she didn't have a name. She knew that Roger had seen her involuntary wince. She tried to concentrate on Stathis, who was asking all kinds of polite questions about how long she had been here and when she arrived and was she enjoying herself, and so on.

'God, I wish they'd hurry up,' said Roger. 'I'm starving.'

Barbara asked how the meeting had gone.

'Depends on who you are, I suspect,' said Roger, looking at Stathis. Stathis was from the Ministry of Labour.

'It was very interesting, Mrs Wakeham,' he said to Barbara. 'Roger is a very clear speaker and he has a good technical knowledge . . .'

Roger almost blushed, Barbara saw. 'You're very kind,' he said hastily.

'I mean it, Mrs Wakeham,' said Stathis. 'We Greeks need the outside perspective. We are a closed society . . .'

'Yes. It wasn't meant to be an outside perspective,' said Roger, looking piqued.

Barbara deduced from Panos's body language that Thekla was beginning to win. 'I think we're getting somewhere,' she said, remembering to take Roger's arm in good appendage fashion and nodding towards the group which had split down the centre and was beginning to turn away from the conclusion of the argument.

Panos joined them. Thekla had had her way. To such an extent, it seemed, that Panos was now preaching the advantages of her quaint little *mageíriko*.

'I think you'll find it interesting,' he said to Roger. 'It is a neighbourhood, a real old-fashioned Athenian neighbourhood, in which everyone knows everyone else. You would never know it was there. It looks as if it has been totally destroyed by the road from the airport, but the tables are placed on either side of the alleyway and the general impression of the place is of geniune old Athens . . .'

'We saw it last night on the way from the airport,' said Roger to Barbara.

'Couldn't see a thing,' said Barbara, unhelpfully.

'No, I mean *see*,' said Roger, groaning.

'Ah, but you have already been there,' said Panos, about to turn and reopen the argument with Thekla.

'Oh, I don't mean we *saw* it . . .' said Roger, putting his hand on Panos's arm, 'not in that sense!'

'Apparently, we just went past it,' said Barbara to the puzzled Panos.

By the time they had cleared up this misunderstanding they were in Roger's car and heading out towards the airport and Falakras. The others followed behind in convoy. Roger took directions from Panos, who sat in the front while Barbara sat in the back with Stathis, whose gentle face she rather liked, and with Thekla.

Barbara was curious as to how Thekla thought the meeting had gone.

'Don't ask me,' said Thekla under her breath. She laughed and looked out of the window, drumming her fingers on the back of the satchel she had placed flat on her knees.

Panos and Roger were laughing about one of the women in the meeting who had a lisp. Nanopoulou.

'Shame on you to mock her,' said Thekla to the two in the front. 'Anyway, Nanopoulou's a good engineer . . .'

'I don't doubt it,' said Roger over his shoulder.

Barbara had taken Thekla's remark to be a covert invitation: 'Go on. You can tell me . . .'

'You really want to know?' said Thekla through the side of her mouth.

Barbara said she did.

'Shit,' said Thekla.

Barbara laughed uncontrollably.

Thekla laid a hand on her arm. 'Don't quote me,' she said.

'Why?' asked Barbara, still wiping a tear away with a finger.

'Too complicated,' whispered Thekla. 'I'll tell you some other time . . .'

Thekla was a dyed blonde with irregular dental work and a leathery voice, who talked in the same rapid, even tone whatever the subject under discussion. She was from Thessaloniki and had come down with Nanopoulou for this meeting. Her left hand hung at her chest in a small dirty sling bandage.

Barbara was intensely curious about what had gone on at the meeting and managed to get herself seated next to Thekla, not without some artful manœuvering of the type that wives are supposed to do. She was asked to sit next to Roger and Panos, but protested that she wanted to get to know some of the other

67

members of the company and, anyway, couldn't she manage to sit opposite them? They shuffled round and eventually Barbara got her way: they went to another table together.

Thekla explained that Panos was Nea Democratia, not PASOK, and it was not in his interest for the meeting to be a success.

'I don't understand,' said Barbara. 'I'm sorry for being so stupid, but didn't he set up the meeting in the first place?'

Thekla balanced her cigarette packet on her knees and took a cigarette out with one hand, her fingers worming their way without a pause into the matchbox, which she jammed, expertly, into the heel of her hand as she talked. Quite unconscious of her extreme adroitness she struck the match, put it to the end of her cigarette and blew it out through the first clouds of blue smoke she exhaled, all in one continuous movement.

The point was, apparently, that Panos was anxious to get the credit for having set up this meeting, so that when it failed to produce effective security measures he could enhance his position in the company which was PASOK-dominated at the senior management level.

'How did he get his job if he was New Democracy?' asked Barbara.

'Probably already there,' said Thekla. 'Thing is, first factor, he knows perfectly well that everyone is going to go back to their respective departments and they are going to let their notes from this meeting gently slide to the bottom of their trays . . .'

Barbara was intrigued by Thekla. She was wearing a white suit and put her large knees up against the seat in front. She seemed to have far too much lipstick on, Barbara thought, but then she was beginning to get used to this. The cigarette burned down between the blood-red fingernails, which plucked absently at her white tights while she talked.

Stathis was nodding on the other side of her.

'Second factor,' said Thekla, ticking them off, 'Panagopoulos knows we are PASOK and we are from Thessaloniki, so he doesn't invite us to the meeting . . .'

'Then how did you . . . ?'

'I got wind of it. He takes birds from the air, this man . . .' She nodded up the table. 'How do you say it?' she asked Stathis.

But Barbara, more intrigued with the politics than the philology of the situation, was content to let the birds stay in flight and prompted her to continue.

'The installations we are talking about are in Macedonia, you understand,' said Thekla. 'So we have a great interest in the subject. And that is why he doesn't invite us, you see?'

Barbara could just about see. She nodded to keep Thekla going.

'But my boss, she found out what Panagopoulos is up to and she threatened the meeting by going higher up, so Panagopoulos was forced to invite representatives from our office, you see?'

'This is North versus South?'

'North versus South and . . .' Thekla held up her hand with the painted fingernails erect, 'PASOK versus ND at the same time.'

'You mean,' said Barbara, 'that if the Thessaloniki office were not at the meeting, it could hardly be considered a success?'

Thekla nodded.

'It's *Coróna Grámmata*,' she said, 'mmm . . . ?' She snapped her fingers across at him and Stathis said, 'Heads and Tails'.

'Yes,' said Thekla, 'if the Thessaloniki representatives are not at the meeting, then its conclusions cannot be considered to be representative, and if they *are* present, then the meeting will fail anyway, because they will object . . .'

'Ah,' said Barbara, 'heads I win, tails you lose . . . but why?

'Exactly,' said Thekla, laughing. 'Heads I win, tails you . . . very good. Why? Because of the third factor . . .'

'Third factor?' said Barbara.

'Yes. Panagopoulos, he gets a foreigner to do the presentation about the installations in Macedonia, because he knows then that no one will take any notice . . .'

'You mean Roger?'

'Exactly,' said Thekla crisply, in her gravelly voice. 'I'm sorry for saying this but your husband is a *koroído*, *É* . . . ?' She snapped her fingers. 'What do you call it?'

Barbara knew the verb *koroidévo*, it meant 'to mock'.

'A fall-guy?' she said.

'Bravo,' said Thekla.

'Oh my God – politics,' said Barbara.

'We were forced to intervene and make objections, I'm afraid,' said Thekla, 'Nanopoulou and me . . .'

'On what grounds?' said Barbara, looking at the back of Roger's neck at the other table. He was leaning across and saying something, with his hand on Panos's arm.

'Straightforward ones,' said Stathis. 'They asked (and I supported them) why it was necessary for Mr Wakeham's plans to be used, which we know are based on old plans of the original company who built the dams, when the Greek engineers in Macedonia, who had been maintaining the system, have much more up-to-date information on these installations and their present state . . .'

'God,' said Barbara, 'how embarrassing.'

'Not at all,' said Thekla, reassuringly. 'It is true, before all things.' She tapped her satchel.

Stathis laughed. He was enjoying this, the sly smile playing round his mouth. 'So then Panagopoulos and his cohorts . . .'

'Some of the people from OTE were in his camp . . .' said Thekla. She turned to Stathis. 'And that other man, you know, from the Ministry of the Environment. You know, the one from Asia Minor?'

'Ah!' said Stathis, 'Poimenídis.'

The retsina was flowing. Good Athenian retsina. The mussels and the *mezédes* and all the other little bits and pieces were arriving and Barbara felt everyone relaxing all around her. Roger's table, which was a little further up the alley on the other side, was

70

the loudest and Panos was pressing all the buttons by the look of things, because Barbara could see their backs stiffening with laughter in time to his every remark. It seemed he was telling jokes. She heard Roger's bray above the rest. He seemed to be drinking a lot of retsina very quickly. Barbara didn't know anything about the drink-driving laws in Greece, but she was a little alarmed.

Stathis and Thekla were deep into a discussion of the relationship between state-owned industries and monopoly capitalism, when Stathis dropped some oil from the salad on his beautiful, floppy beige suit and had to retire to the toilet for repairs.

Barbara, who was curious about Thekla, took advantage of the opportunity and steered the conversation towards the role of women.

'Feminism is rubbish,' said Thekla roundly, lighting another cigarette.

Barbara was astonished.

'We have other problems, genuine political problems, which take precedence here . . .'

'But you yourself seem to be the best advertisement for feminism there is,' said Barbara. 'A woman engineer, fully qualified, fully in touch with all the broader political developments. How I envy you . . .'

'I'm a PASOK-dog first of all,' said Thekla. 'PASOK is gradually teaching women that they need to vote. Do you know that more women now vote in Greece than men do, one per cent more, at the last count.'

'So?' said Barbara. 'That's a feminist point . . .'

Thekla laughed. 'You don't understand the importance of the family here,' she said. 'Do you think these women would vote for one minute if they thought that by doing so they were leading to the dissolution of family values?'

'What about Margarita Papandreou?'

71

'Look here, her Union of Greek Women is a PASOK organisation first and foremost. That's where she gets her basic support, that's where she gets her network of contacts. It has very little significance in broad political terms, it's just a splinter-group of PASOK women who are her personal friends.'

'And personally?' said Barbara, following the appearance of Stathis down the alleyway between the tables.

'Personally she's no doubt a good woman. But she's got herself into a terrible mess. She likes the power, and the feeling that she's a VIP, otherwise she would have left Andreas years ago. He's had other women, you know. They say Vaso Papandreou was one of them . . .'

She looked interrogatively at Stathis, who nodded: 'It's true, Andreas the ladies' man. And his father was the same . . .'

'But what is she doing, calling herself a feminist and not leaving him, I beg you?' said Thekla, banging the table. 'I don't agree with this behaviour. It's hypocrisy. Preaching to other women that they've got to leave their husbands if there's trouble at home and then unable to do it herself. What sort of a feminist is that, eh?'

'No, it's political. She's not asking for a divorce because she fears that this scandal will damage PASOK. She doesn't want to throw oil on the fire,' said Stathis, trawling amongst the fish with the fork which had been left for him.

The singing had begun. Long, rousing choruses to which even Roger, she noticed, seemed to know the words. Thekla had a powerful voice and, sitting with her back to a large mirror, her head resting against its glass, she and Panos, their enmity apparently dissolved in the emotions of the song, led the chorus. Barbara hummed along while the bouzouki players, who seemed to have emerged from somewhere in the direction of the kitchen, started the gradual increase of pace, leading in the end to Thekla and Panos rising and dancing together while everyone else joined in.

Barbara watched them dancing. Panos was a good dancer,

72

despite his bulk. He moved with ease, a ripple at the hips between each step showing off his grasp of the rhythm. Thekla, despite the sling, was magnificent, Barbara thought, singing as she danced, clockwise and counter-clockwise, her feet, moving and stamping in double time and then single time, dependent on which part of the song was being played. Every time she came near to Panos she looked up, chin lifted, broken wrist wittily drooping, and said a few words to him and he laughed or nodded, a conversation which Barbara would have given her eye-teeth to listen to.

She felt a hand on her arm.

'Let's go,' said Roger.

Barbara shrugged. 'I'm enjoying myself,' she said, looking towards Thekla.

'I'm not. Let's go.' He stepped back and looked at her intensely.

'Isn't it a bit . . . rude?' she asked.

'Nonsense. We've done our bit,' said Roger.

Barbara said her goodbyes and they went out to the car, which was parked some way off down the narrow street.

Barbara was glowing with the pleasure of Stathis' and Thekla's company and her goodbyes had been warm. Perhaps it was the persuasive power of their frankness, but she hadn't asked herself why they were both being so indiscreet with her. Was it because she had revealed enough of herself to let them know that she would be a PASOK person too, if she were a Greek? She realised that this is what, at some almost subliminal level, she had been assuming. But Barbara dismissed this thought from her mind, when she thought again of Thekla's bluntness. The fact was, they didn't care. Or was it that they simply wanted to protect Roger from himself, and this was a simple way to do it. Telling his wife? Or rather, perhaps it was that they assumed that husband and wife were separate people and that it was not automatic that such information would get back to Roger. They were treating her, first and foremost, not as Roger's wife, but as a *person*, in her own right? No doubt it was an illusion, but she thought she marginally preferred this latter version.

'Enjoying yourself?' said Roger absurdly, like a travel agent, as their steps fell in together down the narrow street.

Barbara looked up with her ready smile. 'What do *you* think?' she said absent-mindedly, while she gave herself time to censor properly the mass of information she had just been turning over. She replayed the echo of her tone and heard clearly its unintended coquettishness.

Roger stepped down from the pavement and made a lunge, which she instinctively evaded with a toreador's dip of the shoulder. Left behind her, laughing, he caught her up and put his arm through hers. Uneasily she glanced up at him. The drink had made him rather frisky, she thought, but she didn't want to pull away yet. She let him draw her into his side as they approached the car, swaying together with apparent goodwill, before separating.

She was glad to get round to the passenger side. But then remembered she didn't want him to drive and began to suggest, in what she thought of as her friendly-automatic fashion, that he give her the keys and he navigate. Roger looked at her over the roof.

'This is *Greece*, Barbara!'

'I'm not riding with you when you are not fit to drive!'

'Get in, woman!' said Roger.

Barbara stood silently staring at him. She could feel the slight breeze in her hair, teasing it over to the wrong side, while he struggled to control his temper.

'I tell you, it's OK. They aren't bothered about such things here . . .'

He unlocked his side and jumped into the front seat, reaching over and flipping up the lock for her.

Barbara put up her hand and patted down the lifted strands of hair.

He started the engine.

'Barbara?' she heard him saying from within, leaning across and looking at her through the window.

At last, she opened the door.

'So bloody *awk*ward,' he said, putting the car in gear.

'I told you,' said Barbara, 'I am not riding with you when you've had too much to drink.'

'Then you can damn well walk!' he shouted, moving off, with the door still hanging open.

Barbara stared after him. She wanted to run and jump into the front seat. But she stood and stared, her heart beating.

He stopped the car abruptly and got out.

'So stubborn,' he said.

Barbara held out her hand: 'Gimme,' she said.

He looked at her. She clicked her fingers. He put one hand on the car roof and left it there for a split second while he swung down, apparently to get the keys. But the action was forgotten in a sudden storm of hooting from a car full of young Greeks that had driven up the narrow street behind them and was impatient to pass. Roger waved her in and jumped in on his side.

Barbara bent down and perched primly on the seat with her back to Roger, while she felt the handbrake being released and the vehicle beginning to roll down the slight incline. Obliged to make a choice, she swung her two legs in and pulled the door shut all in one movement.

Roger was laughing as he hunched over the wheel and they tore down the alley.

'You wallies!' he shouted in the mirror.

Barbara was kicking herself. She should have had the wit to hang on and make him capitulate since he had appeared to be ready to do so. She had the battle won, and all she needed to do was dig in and threaten to embarrass him in front of the Greeks in the Renault, who were already throwing their hands in the air and hanging out of the windows, broaching an abusive sequence of Mediterranean dialogue.

They drove over the pavement at the corner and swung out into the four-lane highway which leapt towards the white columns of the temple of Zeus. Above it hovered the thick greyish cloud of pollution.

'It's not the point that nobody cares,' she said.

'What *is* the point?' said Roger reaching over to turn on the radio, his question clearly a rhetorical one. 'I'll tell you what the point is, you just like to be awkward.'

'Killing somebody is the point,' said Barbara.

They sat and listened to the slow clang of the bouzouki number.

'I saw you talking to Thekla,' said Roger. 'What'd you make of her?'

'I liked her,' said Barbara. 'Strong, forthright woman.'

Roger looked across. 'You know nothing. You have a lot to learn. She's a dyed-in-the-wool bitch.'

Barbara stared. Where had he acquired this mixed metaphor? Didn't he mean ewe?

'Tried to screw up my presentation,' he said. 'Deliberately tried to screw it up.'

'Oh?' said Barbara.

'She and that other baggage you were talking to . . .'

'Nanopoulou?'

'That's her. God, these Greek names, how did you remember that?'

'What did they do?' said Barbara.

'Tried to sabotage the whole thing. Asking a lot of irrelevant questions, stalling, all that kind of thing. She's a bureaucrat, not an engineer . . .'

Barbara didn't really want to ask any more questions, feeling herself constrained to play out the role she had been offered. It was more important to see how much Roger apparently understood.

'Slow *down*,' she said, as gently as she could.

Roger took his foot off the accelerator and then said, 'Sorry, I just have to do this . . .'

They screamed round in a U-turn and joined the traffic in the lanes going the other way.

He explained that he wanted to avoid the remains of a demonstration which he could see in the distance, up ahead of them.

'Why do you think they wanted to do that?' she asked.

'How should I know? They just don't like foreigners . . .' he said.

The bouzouki number had gathered speed now and was entering its final phase. This was the moment at which Barbara ought to tell him what Thekla's account of the whole thing was, like a good wife, filling him in on what he didn't know.

But she couldn't. Save it for later. She was afraid he would dismiss her out of hand.

As they went up in the lift, Barbara cast an eye in collusion round Roger's arm at the woman in the mirror. He was holding her against him in an informal *paso doble* and telling her that they had all the time in the world for siestas.

'That's what Greek afternoons are for,' he said, seeking out her face with his eyes, the approving sweep of which she felt suddenly spreading over her like lukewarm water. She felt as if she had perhaps spilt something on herself but didn't want to look in case it wasn't true.

He was burrowing down.

'Mmm? Mmm?' He was insisting into the collar of her costume, while she felt the hand, which had insinuated itself under her armpit, beginning to creep round slowly in a series of spider-like movements of the thumb and fingers at the end of each brief session of stroking, towards its target at the front of her blouse.

The lift stopped, and bounced slightly. She felt his hand under her elbow now as they went out into the marble corridor and stood in front of the door of the apartment. The empty spy-hole stared at them as Roger fished for the keys.

'I want a cup of tea,' she announced, looking down at the front of her blouse where one of the buttons had indeed slipped out of its buttonhole and the white material of her bra was peeping through the butter-yellow poplin.

'In bed?' he asked coyly as he opened the door. The marble stretched away from them in an open expanse of desert all the way, as if on cue, to the closed door of the bedroom.

'If you make it,' said Barbara, letting her eyelids fall on to her cheeks and gathering her strength for what was to come, dimly aware that the gesture would be misinterpreted. For she didn't quite see how she could honestly avoid it any more and didn't feel as if she had the strength to resist. Yet the lack of desire, whose contours pressed back at her like the undulations of a familiar wall, was horribly material and dictated everything. She felt drained all of a sudden, as she took her first steps into the apartment.

Roger tapped her on the arm.

'Off,' he said.

There was nothing for it. Barbara sat upright, crossed her arms as she had done since childhood, and took purchase on the satin on either side. She felt him lift it at the back.

Theatrically, she paused.

'Do you mind?' she said. 'I *can* do this.'

He dropped his hand.

In one movement she raised her crossed arms and up came the nightdress, a tube whose walls were turning inside out, which rose until her arms were high above her head, still crossed, and her face still brushed by the soft, sweet-smelling silver material. She was trying not to disturb her hair too much, bringing it over in front and to one side, and beginning, there, to lift her arms, one by one, out of the straps, when she felt his palm planing its way up and down the curve of her spine, his pudgy fingers rolling on the vertebrae and causing a tiny pattering slap. He came into view in the corner of her eye as she automatically turned the inside-out nightgown back the right way so that she could fold it. His other hand appeared at her front, diving under the material to run back and forth over the slack tyres of her stomach muscles, the fingers dropping each time a little lower, as they passed.

She hopped the material round in her hands and folded it once, turning it briskly and folding it again so that it formed a loose parcel, the straps inside.

'You know my eyes are going,' she said. She was holding the parcel flat on the palms of her two hands, intrigued for a second by the relation between its bulk and its feathery lightness.

He stopped his activity and grunted.

'Don't need *that*!' he said through his teeth as he snatched the parcel and threw it to the bottom of the bed. Her eyes watched it turn over once in the air, keeping its shape, half-unravelling until it hit the corner of the divan, bounce up slightly, the straps shooting out like a couple of arms, and fall like the heroine of a *film noir* over the precipice, the suspended hem just covering the corner of the bed and beginnng slowly to slither towards the edge.

Barbara lay back against the pillows, one leg raised, the foot placed flat on the mattress under the edge of the sheet. She looked up at him, studying ironically his expression as he stared frantically at her stomach. His mouth was open and in the dark skin of his half-shaven neck, amidst the fan of muscles, the column of his carotid artery bulged and slackened with alarming speed. She looked down at her raised leg. The flesh of the thigh was the colour of white Cheddar cheese and two thirds the way up, towards the knee, there was a small, dark-red tangle of broken veins which she particularly disliked looking at and hated anyone to see. She could feel her double chin roll up as she lifted her head and strained to follow the progress of his descending hand. His lips, slackened and elongated, hung down like two flaps of blubber away from his teeth to a point within an inch of her belly, while she felt his hand somewhere further down, invisible now behind his intervening head.

Barbara gave up, closed her eyes and settled back. She felt as if she were in hospital behind a screen. He nudged her thigh and she let it fall slackly over. His hand was worming under her, so she lifted herself to accommodate him.

'Nice,' she heard him say like someone learning English.

The rummaging had begun. She could hear his hands working back and forth, the rustle of hair and skin, more than she could feel them. The sensation was rather like being deaf in one ear. She had a sudden vivid fantasy that both her legs had been amputated and they were testing her for sensations. He was hauling on her other leg, getting her to bend it and push it out wide. This was another vaguely medical exercise, she imagined, to establish feeling. A draft of air blew momentarily, passing like a chill over her various dampnesses, obliterated by the movements of his hands.

'Oh *yes!*' he said.

Barbara opened her eyes and looked at the ceiling. She could hear a distinct rapid slapping sound, but it didn't seem to correspond to any feeling. A finger had tunnelled its way beneath her and she felt it pressing urgently at her, working the partly dry skin back and forth and then trying to push in. She bit her lip. A hair was trapped somewhere. The tears pricked at her eyes with a pain so momentary it had passed by the time her eyelashes pressed wetly together, blurring the image of the ceiling and making its surface appear momentarily convex.

The slapping noise resumed and Barbara felt vibrations in his body at her side. She laid a hand on his shoulder, on the fibres of his muscles, and closed her eyes, moving herself again slightly as much to avoid discomfort as to accommodate. This time the finger pushed in and disappeared entirely from sensation, except for the fact that she could feel herself resting on the palm of his damp hand, so that she knew it was still there. She assumed, rather than felt, that he probably had his other finger inside her too, from all the other evidence and the not always distinct, but apparently continuous, activity that was going on, in the muscle-movements in the shoulder under her hand. But she couldn't tell for sure.

The perspiration had begun to roll out of his hair down the wrinkles in his forehead and gather in his thick eyebrows, which were forming tiny spikes in the wet like the ridges of a helmet. Her eyes roamed over a fold of greyish skin, reddening and thinning towards the corner. At the very point where the black under-eyelash met the end of the eyelid, there was a tiny white patch where all the pigmentation had disappeared. She was reaching up with a finger to wipe the drop of sweat that was dangling from the end of his nose, when he froze, panting heroically.

He turned and stared at her.

'Barbara, you're not breathing properly,' he said, his chest heaving.

Barbara's jaw dropped.

'You're holding your breath,' he said.

The laughter began immediately far down in her belly.

She smiled politely at him, knowing it was down there, lurking independently, ready to start a bubbling throughout her whole frame, but she sought to suppress it, taking advantage of the time-lag.

She swallowed a giggle, her mouth beginning to cave in and feel slightly odd, the saliva rushing, as if she had swallowed a piece of raw lemon.

'What?' she gasped.

Already the rippling and bubbling had begun, however, moving up ruthlessly from the belly to the diaphragm and cutting off her breath. She compressed her lips and heard two quick hoots escape down her nose as she stared up into his earnest face.

'You're holding your breath,' he repeated.

Barbara felt the irresistible pressure building now very quickly. She felt her eyes opening wide, and then slowly her lips began to come apart and a high-pitched falsetto note from the back of her throat came out of them. Immediately it cut off and she was plunged into a tense physiological silence that fled across the gap between them and registered in his surprise, while her body gathered for an irresistible series of shudders that soon set into a spasm. Her mouth opened fully now, giving out a succession of short falsetto cries all abruptly cut off as it sucked at the air with ferocious greed. She began to arch uncontrollably, throwing back her head, eyeballs standing forth.

She raised her head from the pillow and pointed at him.

'You . . .' she gasped, and began the regular slow sequence of two heavy laughs while she kicked her feet in helpless double-time and a whole new set of ripples began to threaten her breath again. Her throat began to ache. She dabbed at her eyes with the back of her hand, seeking to halt the spasms.

'I'm sorry,' she said, and cleared her throat. She took a deep breath. 'I don't think I quite . . .' She tensed again and managed to yodel out the rest of the sentence, '*heard* that right!'

Her body rippled into silent spasm again, tensing all along her limbs as she fought and failed to halt it.

'*I'm* sorry,' she repeated, with a sniff designed to chase away another spasm. But her eyes widened in disbelief at the persistence of the bout of laughter. The tears that started again and blurred her vision of his now expectant, questioning face sent her down into the pillows in an incoherent wailing heap, incapable of covering her mouth with her hand as she rolled from side to side and banged her clenched fist gently against the mattress.

'Not breathe . . . ing . . . prop . . .' she cried, at the top of the spasm, all her pores open and her face hot and red with a mixture of sweat and tears. 'Yoo hooo hoo . . . can't *stand* it . . . Please . . .'

Roger turned away and lay down quietly with his back to her.

The ripples still came, their seismic effects conducted through the mattress, but with greater and greater intervals between them, while she sighed through her dry and aching throat.

Roger lay silent.

Warily, Barbara rose from the pillows and climbed out of bed, trying to disturb her physical environment as little as possible.

'I must just go . . . to the bathroom,' she said solemnly, quite unable, however, to keep the snort out of her voice, which caused another spasm to come on. Bent at the waist, hugging the rigid armour of muscles at her sides, she managed to catch her fingers in her nightdress as she passed the corner of the bed. She padded without a backward look out into the hall, hoisting and settling it over her shoulders and then giving it two or three light plucks to make it drop over her hips and fall in a long, shiny, narrow cylinder to her ankles.

In the bathroom she had tied up her hair and was putting cold cream in broad streaks on to her reddened face, her mouth pursed like a clown's, when his image appeared round the door in his dressing gown. She turned to him and began to say, 'That was the funniest . . .' when she felt something happen to her face just under her eye, while at the same time, somewhere in the room, she heard a crunching sound and her lip twisted outwards numbly as if it had just received a shot of Novocaine. The jar of cold cream flew out of her hand and she staggered, just managing to save herself by grabbing hold of the sink.

He screamed high through his nose like a wild pig, almost dancing up to her on the tips of his toes. This time she put up an arm, but the blow came from above and caught with a dense thud just above the ear which immediately began to sing. She felt her head fly back and strike, sickeningly, on the tiles between the sink and the toilet. Her feet flipped from under her and she almost went down, hanging with one elbow for what seemed for ever on the edge of the sink, remotely aware, while she stared ahead, that this was a silly position to be in, before she slipped again, back and side bouncing off the edge of the toilet seat with a scrape of direct pain.

Now she was lying on her side on the bathroom tiles with her head against the wall and her back against the base of the toilet. 'No more,' she tried to groan, her swelling mouth full of bits, but it came out as 'Bo bore.'

He took hold of her by the ankle and yanked her out, kicking at his face with her other foot, into the middle of the room. He was muttering between pants, 'Fucking teach you to . . .'

She started to scream but the heel of his hand pressed down on her face with such force that she couldn't open her mouth at all. Her nostrils were flattened and blocked. Panic rose in her gullet like a warm syrup pouring away from her racing heart. She snatched at the column of arm that rose above her hand, but it was as rigid as iron. The sound of her suppressed scream backed up into her head like the whine of a dental drill. She began to thrash and kick around on the tiles. He wrenched at the cord of his dressing gown and swept it open with his free hand, while she did her best to bite the hand that was pressing over her mouth. She was already beginning to feel a kind of grey faintness coming over her as she looked up at his face in the shadow above her, remote, unfamiliar, carved like a rock statue, and felt the knee that pressed down succeed momentarily in prying open her legs.

Her head flew back with another dreadful-sounding smack against the tiles that seemed to do something new to her ears: all she could register was the sound of her own high-pitched whining panting as she twisted and tried to close her legs around the knee. He banged her head again, this time barring forearm and elbow across her throat until she gagged, thinking *This is it! This is the end*, and then she felt him slip both knees in between her legs, one pinching her thigh on the tiles as she twisted her head away and started to scream again. But immediately his hand went up round her throat, the stretched web between finger and thumb cutting it across like a blunt guillotine, while the other struck her repeatedly across the cheeks, blows that were so quick, and so sharp, that they brought a fresh set of hot tears springing to her eyes while she saw through her grogginess and her underlay of old, cold tears that he had succeeded in pressing her open with his knees. Her hands, flailing far away at the end of her arms, tried to scrape at his face or catch at some feature, but only banged uselessly against his hair without gripping anything.

Now he was pressing down on her pelvis, working with quick demonic movements that registered themselves in the contemptuous slap of the medallion against her face and the way the edges of the cold tiles beneath her cut repeatedly into her buttocks. She had almost got used to this as the status quo when he made a sudden long push and she felt a dull tear of pain that played above the screech she managed before he cut off her breathing again. He worked in quick, driving thumps that jarred her spine against the tiles, her whole body tensed in anticipation of these dry, smarting blows, each of which when it came caused her to release an involuntary sob.

As quickly as he had started he was off her. She had a glimpse along the floor of his wrist that sank and broadened with his sudden weight. A foot appeared for a moment close to her eyes, and he had left the room, the tasselled cord of his dressing gown trailing behind him round the door.

Barbara lay looking along the reddish tiles, listening for footsteps, her eyes flickering to the gap under the door. Her principal feeling was fear, she didn't want anything else to happen and she was holding herself in, tensely expecting some further . . . In her mind there was a blank at that point, as if she were learning a foreign language and had forgotten the word. Beneath, she felt nothing. A numb lake of shame in the middle of which, as on an island of salt, she had been tied down and abandoned. She was desperate to get up and go to the mirror, to see what he had done to her face, but she waited exactly where she was while she listened, only taking time to press down her nightdress.

Down the hall, through the open door of the bedroom, she heard the creak as he sat on the bed, the rustle of his trousers running up his legs, and then the quick, involuntary stamp he always gave when he had got his shoes on and moved off for the first time. She tensed as the footsteps came quickly out of the bedroom and down the hall. She saw the bottom of the shoes pass and something trail briefly along the floor: a garment, the hem and pocket of his jacket. He paused to unhook an umbrella and then the door slammed and she heard the whine of the elevator. Still afraid, still unable to move for fear, she lay, her eyes running over every little unevenness in the tiles. But he did not return and at last, cold and stiff in every joint, she picked herself up from the floor and stood smoothing the hair back from her face while she stared at last at her image in the mirror.

There was a large, reddish-purple patch on her cheekbone under the eye, which she could probably cover with make-up, but the awful, the pitiful, thing was her upper lip, which seemed to have turned inside out towards the corner and bulged out already in an unmistakable swelling. Barbara gave an inarticulate cry for herself which, however, did not sound, her throat was so dry, but stayed somewhere in her head. No amount of make-up was going to completely get rid of that, because the tissue of the lip had been gashed by a tooth and the split was still leaking thin reddish tears. She took a tissue and dabbed at it, drawing in her breath at the sharp, stinging pain. She could see that her cheek was already out beyond its usual lines.

Without wanting to look at the rest of her body, the waves of shame releasing themselves at the sight of her face, she forced herself to run the shower. Her limbs, particularly her legs, were very stiff and didn't seem to work properly without giving out some kind of pain. Her arms ached as she reached up to take off her nightdress and as she looked down she saw she had reddish patches all across her chest. Her thighs were sore and one of them had a spreading purple mark running down the soft inside, where it had been trapped on the tiles. She turned and looked over her shoulder in the mirror. She had square tile marks here and there over her shoulder-blades, buttocks and the backs of her legs. Her right arm under the armpit, where she had, she remembered, clung to the sink taking her weight for so long, was throbbing.

She trembled all over as she began to soap herself, the trembling getting stronger and stronger until she had to stop because she could no longer manipulate the soap for the vehemence of it. And then, as she stared through the streams of warm water that poured through her hair, rilling down her face and over her stinging lip, she felt the first wave of nausea hit her. She staggered against the wall in her weakness with a groan, the first sound she heard herself make, and then two more quick waves hit like earthquakes, it seemed, and she felt herself going, slipping away, beginning to slide down the wall of the shower. She looked down, watching her bruised limbs buckle, her knee bending into rubber and collapsing before her eyes, until she found herself in a half-kneeling position. Grunting, she supported herself against the corner of the shower-basin, every breath, every in-drawn breath, a shuddering trembling, and she tasted the sourness in her mouth for a moment before there was a further slipping away and nothing seemed to matter now except, before she fell, to get her leaden right arm up against the tiles to support her head, which was already lolling and banging gently against the point where the two walls met.

How long it had been she did not know, but she became aware of the noise of the light pattering of lukewarm water against her skin. The two white tiles in front of her eyes were fitted very close together. She was lying propped against the wall, one knee up, one leg bent backwards, as if she had been frozen in the act of sprinting away, lukewarm water pattering against her head and shoulder-blade.

The cold air of the bathroom was a shock as she pulled back the curtain and stepped over the lip of the shower rim. Shivering all over, she managed to find a towel for her hair. It had gone all flat, as it always did when she washed it under the shower, but she towelled it as vigorously as her aching arms would permit, hoping to restore a little bounce into it by the sheer effort of drying. But it flopped damply, stupidly, over her eye.

As she passed the towel beneath her it stung, and there was a small red stain in the watery patch. Another huge wave of shame immobilised her. She stood looking in disbelief at the blotchy, soggy, alien creature with the swollen face that tried to stare back at her from the mirror, but only succeeded in dropping her eyes back to her damp, greyish limbs which she began to rub automatically, and without much faith, with the towel. Violently, still frames began to click up in her mind: her elbow hanging on the sink, myopic flashes of pain, his first appearance round the door and the dance of the wild pig, the long tear of pain on one side, tiles, tiles, her first sight of herself in the mirror, her collapse in the shower and this desert-like waste of towelling, now – all of them refusing to be memory.

She was holding herself in as she padded down the hall, taking comfort from the three towels that covered her down to the ankles. Thank God she had bought that large bath one in that funny little shop in Tottenham Court Road; the woman had insisted and she thought she had better have one for the trip.

His pyjamas lay neatly folded against the pillow on his side of the bed.

She sat down, plump, on the bed and reached an arm out to open the wardrobe. She had hardly had time to unpack, and now here she was . . . Barbara couldn't face the idea of a suitcase, but she knew she had to pack soon, before he came back. She looked again at the pyjamas folded against the pillow and her mind could make no sense of them at all. She stood, the towels beginning to unwrap in slices of cold from her still damp body and looked out some clean underwear. More splintered images plastered themselves over the inside of the wardrobe, the speed and the ferocity of their appearance, whirling through their sequences without sound-track, making them seem mere abstract flashes of coloured light, weightless volumes of air, that twisted and insisted, as she picked out a black skirt and stepped into it, hooking it round her waist, even noticing now how much weight she had lost since she had last had it on. She blew, and the breath fanned the swelling on her upper lip like a breeze.

The black blouse, she had somewhere. It was a little tight nowadays under the arms, but it would do. And the black tights she had bought. It was all the wrong way round, as the ideas came to her and she stared into the wardrobe, but it didn't matter. She unhooked the skirt again and pushed down the blouse below the line of the waist, doing the skirt up again while the unwanted film show played out some more of its frames, jumping from image to image all over again, but without sequence or meaning.

She took the packet of new tights out of the drawer, split the cellophane with a meaningless finger and watched them spill out in three large folds, the feet settling sideways on the bed below her. She unhooked the skirt again in despair and the blouse sprang away from her waist in large creases. She stood while a fist crashed through the air, overarm, at the top of his stalking pig-dance, which had come to seem absurdly balletic, like Nureyev in something she had seen at Covent Garden.

It had happened to her. It had.

She sat down again and began running her hand down inside one of the tights, staring at the pale mirage of her fingers through the dark material. She pointed her toe and placed it in the pouch provided, her mind suddenly acquiring absurd combinations of words, like instructions. And now the other foot, the fingers spreading like remote daydreams inside the black mesh as she opened the foot-space, holding a black tunnel for the foot to slide into at the end of which she saw, in a series of miniature flashes, his head in shadow above her and heard the high-pitched whining panting with which he accompanied those . . .

Determined, she pushed her pointed toes into the image, which gave way like rotten cheese, little crackling flashes at the margins still seeking to run on, as if in the corner of the eye, but the whole was bisected and disrupted by the advent of her foot, which some other part of her mind pushed into its centre. And she was sitting, trembling again, her hands quivering down to the fingertips as she tried to grip the ruche of the tights with her right thumb and pull it round the heel, working carefully, expanding and contracting over the contour of the foot while she hung again, painfully embarrassed, with her elbow over the basin, staring ahead with stupid goggle-eyes while the pain leapt under her armpit and snatched at her side. Now that the material was over the ankle she could leave it while she went back to the other foot and tried to wrinkle the material together to make the dark pocket for that foot too, but her left thumb felt so weak that she had to stop.

She forced herself to look up at the wall and breathe consciously, deeply, two or three times, so that she could again return to her task. Taking her hand out of the material and looking curiously at her thumb which was vibrating at its base, she could see the muscles in spasm. She turned it over, the soft pad wavering helplessly like laughter, and then back again and then, as in a little screen, she saw it clenched, a kind of large paperclip, round the rest of her fingers as they banged uselessly against the hair on the side of his head. She had broken two nails on this hand and they snagged in the material as she pushed in and formed the pocket again for her foot, just a plain tunnel this time, empty, into the dark of which she pointed her ballerina toe.

She managed to centre her feet in the ruins of the skirt on the floor and draw the tights up one calf, half-way, when again she had to sit up and pause, her breath not coming properly. She detected now for the first time a sour taste of rage come breaking through in her mouth, as she panted with determination and gritted her teeth at the wall. Bending to her task again, she rolled each leg up and over her knees and sat there with the two tight black rolls cutting into the flesh of her thighs. Waveringly, she stood, the backs of her knees against the mattress about to collapse at any minute, and hauled on the one side and then on the other, unravelling the spool of material automatically over her bruised thighs, especially careful on the inside of her right one, which she couldn't help lifting to look at again with fascination, the long purple discoloration running down the flapping edge of the flesh where it had pinched under his knee. Immediately the thigh itself was filled like a screen with wild small images; she felt again the pain and her humiliating weakness underneath him and she felt herself going away again, a strange greyness overtaking her, welling up from somewhere, but she completed the movement. Now the tights were almost up as she stood and hooked both thumbs, swaying with dizziness, under the thinning spools of material and began to run them round, stretching and unravelling them over the clean white underpants she had no memory of putting on with the pink stitching at the hems, like a little girl's, which she had bought for the trip from Arding and Hobbs. Her eyes misted at the thought, but she panted with determination now as she slipped the material over her hips and round her bottom at the back until it was just a tiny thin hem: only a few more turns of the spool and she would have it up under the blouse, its fan of creases round her waist. There was comfort in the black central seam which ran down and under her crotch like the packing of a parcel, an envelope she was going to . . . see herself off in, did she mean that, no, send herself off, she meant to think, to post herself like a package somewhere.

She sat down abruptly, feeling the consolation of the tights pull and crease themselves round her legs, not for once wanting to stand up again and stretch them away from her flesh, but happy to have them encase her tightly in whatever places they wanted to.

Standing again, she pulled the blouse out round her waist. With a gasp at the multiple aches and pains she bent to pull the skirt up over her blouse and finally hooked it at the waist in front, twisting it round to its proper position at the side. It had ridden up and the lining inside was clinging against the tights; she had to twist her thighs together to make a space so she could get her hand underneath it and pull it down against the static electricity. She felt the reminder in the sting of pain under her as she pressed her legs together and the demonic flash arrived, as she somehow expected it to, crackling behind her eyes its replay of those fiercely pressing, merciless knees forcing her apart and the useless flapping of her hands as she tried to grab out at something, anything, to get a purchase on.

The sweat was pouring down her face as she looked down at her open blouse and her feet bare in the black tights with the diamond shape of double material at the toes.

Where were her shoes?

It seemed an impossible question.

Great gusting white-crested rollers of panic swept her away again into her micro-world of buttons and blemishes. Once again, she tried to grip on to herself, make herself not think, force her fingers into the buttonholes of the blouse, obliging them, by a creaking act of will, to fumble hopelessly amongst the tiny black slits. Pushing here and there with movements she remembered as instinctive, but which had suddenly become imperfectly learned, she was distracted by the shape of her broken nails which she paused, senselessly, even while urging herself on, to stare at. But her hands fluttered so much, she found, she had to leave this task too.

She slid out of the bedroom as if in snow-shoes and felt the tights snag on the parquet. Abruptly she stopped and freed her foot, lifting it and pulling it backwards off the splinter of wood. She carried on, sliding the soles of her tights for relief, like a child, on the cool marble and entered the hated bathroom. The woman in black, with her bosom torn open, approached the mirror, her blouse gaping at two creases it had formed to make a big diamond shape around the bra with the little patch of blue ribbon between the cups. She looked in the mirror at the flop of hair, the eyeballs encased by a film of liquid squatting in their vermilion sockets, and wondered where she could begin.

She saw the woman in the mirror throw up her hands a few seconds after she had thought with a strange laugh of doing that herself, almost turn away and then push her face close, tilting it to fetishise the swelling over the cheekbone, to inspect lovingly, mawkishly, the poor torn lip, which now had a dark black strip where it had split in the centre, a chipolata sausage of red shininess. She saw her take the brush in her hand, a little while after she herself had decided that this was where she had to start, and they brushed the hair, together, with single strokes of the brush, finding the parting and then taking it back flatly over each side until she could catch a scrape of it in her left hand, between finger and thumb, and hold it tight, while the other one poked among the things on the shelf beneath the mirror for the hair-grips, crimping the snatch of hair into a roll and popping in the three grips quickly, one below the other, tucking in the stray strands behind the two small, too-small, ears which she had felt from the beginning were so vulnerable and childish that she had said to herself early on in the charade that she hated her ears and didn't ever want to wear her hair back.

Her face was sweating beneath a half-applied layer of cold cream, the sweat drops oozing out through the white cream and gathering on the surface, like brandy butter before it absorbs. She took the tissue and wiped her face completely dry, several times, because each time she thought she had dried it she found new drops gathering at the edge of her scalp or round her ears in the

93

springs of hair that broke free of her tight scrape, wetting and darkening them and causing them to hang down like miniature weeping-willows.

Where had her shoes gone?

It was a worry she was trying to put off as long as possible as she tried to match the bruising on one side with a mixture of blushers. Forgetting, she compressed her lips automatically as she brushed them lightly with pale cream, and the pain shot through the lower half of her face. She opened the mouth and looked inside, inspecting the gums and teeth and taking a bottle of purple mouthwash that he had left on the shelf she sloshed it round, neat, in her mouth until the stinging brought fresh tears to her aching eyes.

Stiffly limping, but trying to keep upright, she walked back into the bedroom in her stockinged feet, vaguely aware that she was looking for something, just grateful to be alone in the place, trying actively to resist the playbacks that kept occurring, brutal flashes of troubled light, while her mind spun on like a shining spool, putting off all the jumble of questions which had begun to press at her. Fear she felt, fear displaced, the fear that he would return, which ran a strange, tautological race with the belief that he would almost certainly want her not to be there when he got back and so would certainly allow her time to go. But the fear was real, the belief hypothetical, and so she began to rummage, panic-stricken again, in her drawer until she found the black silk scarf and the black shawl she took back to the bathroom, where she tied the scarf around her bruised and battered cheeks, trying to avoid getting the powder on it, making herself take her time about tying it properly.

Finally she slung around her shoulders the black knitted shawl, the pain shooting through the arms the woman in the mirror appeared to raise so easily. She let it drop, softly, snugly and for ever, for ever round her shoulders, and now she was collecting the things in the bathroom and tidying up – she wanted to do this but it proved impossible because there was too much attaching to that space in her mind: the tissues with the various smears of blood, even the waste bin, which, when she pressed the pedal, revealed some pink stained horror or other she didn't want to think of, and the least sound, like that of someone walking above across the ceiling, made her wince and recoil. She pulled out the bottom corner of the headscarf from under the shawl because she had put them on the wrong way round – she had put everything on the wrong way round – turning now to look profile at whether she had got the little triangle of black silk free from the swirl of the woollen shawl up her neck, the lovely Scottish lambswool shawl she had bought in that shop in Regent Street. Into the living-room now she went and skirted the table with the maps and papers still on it and went over to the phone in the corner and picked up the curving apparatus which emitted its faithless bleep; she began in her mind to ask for a number she couldn't possibly remember and had to fish for in her bag, unfortunately not a black one but a navy-blue bag, which, as she brought out the address book she had carefully written it in, she had to displace from her shoulder, a thing she was frantic not to do. She sat down to recover herself, hands trembling again violently under the shawl as she fished through the pages of the alphabet for the name, the letters swimming away and the whole point of what she was doing lassoing itself in the wanton loops of the writing until she had forgotten who it was she wanted to phone. The pages flicked by inertly through her trembling fingers while a dreadful pot-pourri of memories possessed her and she wished she could tell what day of the week it was. It seemed a very urgent thing to have to know, what *day* it was, she had no idea and the fear ran through her again, a Gulf Stream of panic-syrup rising up the gullet through the iron bars of stiffness and pain in her chest and rib-cage and she forced herself to breathe again – *you're not breathing properly, Barbara* – her broken mouth twisting into a lunatic smile. What would her children think of her now? She saw their faces and the idea of their ever knowing about this, whatever this was, gripped her with a new shame, flooding into her throat like warm bile; she dropped her hands, possessed of a great weakness, and as the handbag started to tilt and the address book slip from her fingers, she wished she could die now, immediately, without waiting for all her things to pour out of the unclasped lip of navy leather: the deodorant, the papers and bills from the duty-free shop, the London Transport season ticket, the wallet full of drachmas, chequebook, Eurocheques, her plastic credit-card holder falling like a concertina through the air, tissue packs, small white ones, cascading down the shelf of the small Niagara which was her knees, bouncing thence soundlessly on the floor to spill out round her feet.

The telephone. That was it. She was going to make a telephone call. But the effort, as she bent to scoop the objects in all their pathos around her feet back into the bag, was too great and she knew she could not make a telephone call, she just had to go, now, quickly, before it was too late.

She rose, pulled the shawl round her, took the flat keys from the bag and laid them on the kitchen table, turned right into the hall and went to the door. She stared at the horrible grain of the wood. It was easy to reach out her hand for the brass handle, which, as she dragged it back, swung with its own weight quicker and quicker until the door flew against the plaster with a bang, and the cold air of the corridor smacked solid as a wall into her sweating face.

She stepped out, hitched her handbag on to her shoulder, and pulled the door to with a massive click.

In the lift she stared at the woman in black with the pale face and the broken mouth, her eyes slowly moving down the woman's clothes to her skirt, which had some bits of something on it she brushed away with her fingers, and she noted, with abstract disappointment, that she wasn't wearing any shoes.

II

Dancers

AUTUMN 1987 TO SPRING 1988

Autumn

Voula came in about an hour. She took Barbara into the bedroom and examined her, and then she gave her a sedative.

Antigone and Voula discussed the whole thing. Voula thought she had better go back to England when her face had healed. She was in shock. There was no damage to her elsewhere which wouldn't heal soon. She would make out a prescription for some things to help. The main problem was psychic, she thought. She needed to be quiet and comfortable and to rest, preferably away from any associations, any environment associated with this event.

'Would you testify?' Antigone looked at Voula.

'Of course. But you can't bring a case, under Greek law, can you, if they are married?'

Antigone sighed. 'No. It's impossible, of course . . . I was thinking of English law, but I don't know . . .'

'She'll sleep now at least . . .' said Voula, leaving a prescription. '*É, korítsi mou*,' she clapped Antigone on the arm, 'better get some rest yourself . . . ?'

'*Ti prágma?*' said Antigone absently, 'Ah, yes . . .'

Antigone couldn't concentrate on the various bits and pieces of paperwork she had made a mental note to do. She stretched out on the couch, once she had looked in on Barbara and seen that she was asleep and covered her with a duvet, but her mind was ticking on and she lay, alert and tired at once, for hours, listening out on Barbara's behalf for the slightest sound. At one point she got up, irrationally, to see if the front door was locked.

Eventually she rose and sat at her desk, staring at the piles of papers she had to deal with as a result of the tricky process of the preliminary hearing. In fact, this misfortune of Barbara's had taken her mind completely off the various pressures and anxieties that were besetting her. It had been a relief to try and attend to the urgent problems of someone else, even if the suffering that Barbara was going through was disturbing and she feared for her psychologically.

Fortunately they had a mole in the prosecutor's office; Nikos knew someone, a certain Menios, whom they took out regularly and bought dinner for. Menios had been at the grammar school in Constantinos Street, with Nikos, and so they had managed to find out pretty well what was in the prosecution brief, against their three clients, and pretty well what the charges were going to be. She and Nikos had prepared the statement for the press and Spiros had read it out on their behalf, since he was defending the other two. She wrote most of it herself and knew it almost off by heart. She had been looking across at her client, Christos, while Spiros was reading to the journalists:

'The material of the brief does not support the charges and, furthermore, does not support the interpretations which the communiqués of the police are trying to steer the affair towards. A complete picture of the development of this affair cannot be formed without the establishment of a correspondence with the brief concerning the theft of weapons from the Port Authority and the reasons why the enquiry relating to that earlier affair was closed.'

It was perfect. Tactful, low key, but sufficiently aggressive to send out the right signals to the police and prosecutor. What the hell had Christos blurted all those things to the waiting journalists for when he came out of the prosecutor's office, why on earth hadn't he shut up like the others? Because he was young and told

100

the truth? Or because he wanted to make an impression? She had shaken her head at him but he hadn't seen her. The frustration was enormous.

The reporters had surged forward and surrounded him without her being able to get to him. And she had the misery of listening to him, saying that he *agreed*, that in order to have an experience he had stolen the car with Lekas and Thalassinos, without, however, knowing what they were going to use it for.

'Can't you shut him up?' shouted Spiros. She had shrugged behind the ranks of scribbling journalists.

And by the time they got him away he had spilt everything.

'Well, at least it confirms his lack of experience!' said Antigone. 'He's a *paidaréli*, a small-fry, all right; when they print this . . .'

'Won't make any difference to the police!' said Nikos.

'And it's not exactly helpful to us!'

Finally she had managed to get to him, leaning over to advise him not to say anything at all when they got outside and not to say anything more to the police, and that moment was when the photograph was taken, of her leaning over and whispering in his ear, her fingers curled round the back of his neck.

Antigone knew that Loukas, the old goat, would certainly have seen the photo and she was afraid that he would take it the wrong way. He had given her this case, so that she could do a good professional job on it. But if there was any sign of her 'behaving like a woman', he would withdraw his support for her. He had already rung up and hinted that he was watching her behaviour closely. He was jealous, and dangerous. He liked to think he was pulling the strings.

In the meantime Menios had also usefully let drop that the police were now looking for people surrounding the magazine *Dokimé* and that they had been active in Thessaloniki, trying to incriminate the editor of another anarchist magazine, *Mávro-Kókkino*, to such a degree that he had been reduced to giving a hasty press interview saying that, yes, he was an anarchist, but he had never advocated violence and, yes, he had had contact with Preka, but not recently, and so on to cover himself. Now they were watching the anarchist rock group En Route. Antigone knew that Manos was certainly connected with this group which was based in Ambelókypous, an area of the city associated with students and terrorists near his flat.

She wanted to try to find Manos and warn him of the seriousness of this situation, try maybe to get him to put himself in her hands so that she could prepare him for the arrest, or help him to get away. It seemed unlikely that he would be interested in fleeing, that was the problem: these young anarchists seemed to be queuing up to make a point against the police. Christos had flaunted his black eye at the press, and though he had not made any direct accusation, they would all draw their conclusions. Manos would be like a lamb to the slaughter if they found him. She had to get to him first.

Tomorrow morning she would be going with Spiros to start talking to the three in jail, particularly Christos, to try to begin preparing their trial defence. She had been working on the charges. They had fired on the police in the clash at Galatsi, so there was attempted murder, before the incident on the balcony. There was theft, illegal possession of firearms, disturbance of domestic peace, illegal detention, illegal carrying of firearms, and use of firearms. But Christos and the other polytechnic student, Thallasinos, as they had pointed out in another statement to the press, had lain down their weapons and given themselves up as soon as the police asked them to. So Antigone and her colleagues would be working on the relation between these charges and the trial brief some more, and her job would be to go over it all again with Christos. And she had to plan exactly where she wanted her own and Spiros's questioning to lead.

She would not have time to look for Manos until tomorrow evening. Then she would have to chance leaving Barbara and drive over to Ambelókepous, maybe to the Rainbow club where En

102

Route sometimes played gigs and a lot of young anarchists and students gathered. She could almost certainly find someone to talk to her over there. Many of them would have seen her picture in the paper. In any case, a lot of them were quite open about what they believed in.

But she would have to be careful, because the police almost certainly had the place under surveillance, as with all such meeting places and apartments in that area. She simply wanted to advise Manos of his rights on a practical level, she told herself, and of what to do if they did arrest him.

Antigone worked on, prising open the charges. She was particularly interested in the responses of the women, of the Santi family, into whose flat the three young men had entered. Antigone could see all sorts of ways in which some of the charges could be made to come unstuck in a courtroom. Illegal detention of members of the public, for instance. All right, Lekas had asked the father to go downstairs and get his car ready for their getaway, leaving them alone with the mother and two daughters for at least some time in the flat. But they had all testified that they had been treated well, and that they had not objected when they asked if they could go downstairs to Mrs Santi's mother-in-law's flat. The mother was in fact quite sympathetic, and she sent a wreath to Lekas's funeral, Antigone thought she had noticed. This was something to check. Or, at least, she thought there might be a lead there, that the husband had sent it, but Antigone was willing to bet that when they questioned Mrs Santi they would find it was her idea.

The two girls also talked quite well of the way they were treated. Mrs Santi actually said Lekas had said to them,' If all goes well, we'll send you some flowers, we're not bad men, not drug-dealers, but anarchists being hunted by the police!' Antigone could see ways in which this charge and the one of disturbing the peace could be offset, at least for Christos. And then she wanted to interview this other woman, the neighbour, Ellie Papadátou, who wept at the funeral. They would certainly want her as a witness. She had spent some time on the phone talking to the boys, while the police were trying to negotiate with Lekas, this woman, and she was going to be an invaluable witness to their basic characters.

Antigone thought there was a good chance that all these women would testify, and could be interviewed. Which meant that the remaining charges were all to do with weapons, carrying them, possessing them, using them. But Christos and Thalassinos, the other student, had put their guns down and given themselves up immediately. This was going to be useful. Then there was the question of the charge of theft. Again, she had to talk to Christos, but the police were clearly trying to fit them up here. There was no evidence to link him with the theft of these weapons from the Port Authority, but Antigone needed to know why the police had closed the enquiry on this earlier case of theft. Christos needed to help them on this too. It would be invaluable if he had any positive leads, instead of just saying he didn't know anything about it.

Fortunately Spiros was very experienced. The charges against Thalassinos were virtually the same and they would be using the same evidence to get them reduced.

In the morning, after getting the prescription from the chemists, Antigone had to go out and leave Barbara, but she seemed not to want to be disturbed. When Antigone came home for lunch she was still lying on the bed with the duvet over her, slightly sweaty-looking and awake. Probably the medication, thought Antigone.

Spiros phoned in the early evening to say that the police had arrested the whole En Route group and he was trying to get through to Menios to see what the charges were going to be.

Shouting goodbye to Barbara, Antigone dashed out as she was, in her leather jacket and green and white blouse, her jeans, a white silk scarf round her neck. She went straight to Manos's mother's house in Plaka, where it seemed there was no police presence. His brother Alkis, who had obviously been asleep, answered the door, and Antigone asked him if he knew where his brother had got to. Alkis was waiting to join ship and he was a little vague. Might he be at the Rainbow? Alkis thought this unlikely. Why didn't she try the Maimou, round the corner, where he often spent his afternoons.

Antigone parked and went into the bar. There were two or three people sitting around playing backgammon and drinking coffee. Manos had his back to her, sitting astride a bar chair watching a game of cards. He was hooting with delight at something which had just occurred in the game, his strange ovular head rolling back on his shoulders.

She put her hand on his arm.

He turned and the laughter diminished into a smile, the eyes looking away from her as if bouncing off some hard surface.

'Hello, Mano. How's it going?'

'Watch out,' she heard someone down at the card table say, 'it's that lawyer woman, touting for trade . . .'

And someone capped this remark to the general laughter of the company.

Manos did not say, 'What do you want?' as she expected. He asked if he could get her anything.

'Is there anywhere where we can talk?' said Antigone.

There was a certain amount of backchat and sniggering at the table. Manos turned away, ignoring it.

He picked up his jacket. '*Yeia*,' he said over his shoulder and they strolled out of the bar and down the street.

'There's a park,' he said, lighting a cigarette and letting it hang in his mouth. He looked at her reflectively.

'The police have arrested En Route,' said Antigone.

Manos laughed. 'They all knew it was coming,' he said. 'The *Bátsos* have been watching everyone's flats for weeks . . .'

'What about yours?'

'Mine too,' said Manos.

'What are you going to do?'

Manos shrugged. 'What can I do? Tell the truth. I have nothing to fear . . .'

Antigone laughed. 'You should be standing where I am in the courts all day and at the prison with Christos. I'm afraid I don't have much faith in the police at the moment . . . But it's you who should be saying this, not me,' she said as they turned into the park.

Manos was tall, loping along at her side. They went into the deserted playground and sat on the swings.

'I like this park,' he said, gloomily, studying it as if it were his last look, 'but pretty soon it'll be bulldozed like everything else round here . . .' He began to sing:

> 'In the evening
> early evening . . .
> With your mouth full of kisses . . .'

'Why don't you get out for a while?'

'Go where?' said Manos.

'Somewhere up North, or an island? Somewhere out of the way . . .'

He turned to her:

'Why should I?'

'Because,' said Antigone, 'they are going to pull you in very soon along with all your friends . . .'

'So? I'll take my chances . . .'

'Oh, will you? You don't know what it's like, I tell you, to be beaten by them, to have them ask who your girlfriend's fucking with, then, so they can arrest her and all the rest of your friends!'

'I haven't got a girlfriend,' said Manos, 'I'm through with all that . . .'

Antigone laughed.

'I have more important things to think about,' said Manos, 'like what's happening in this video-police-state, this Germanised nightmare. I can't believe it's happening, this.'

She was smiling still.

'What are you being so superior for?' he said. 'You know that's what's happening here in our country . . . you must, you see it every day?'

'See *what*?'

He lifted his legs and swung slowly forward and then back. And stopped.

'The destruction of the values of our Greek community, the creation of a creeping passivity, the tomorrow-worship, the health cards, the boxes of Gala Nou Nou . . .'

Antigone burst out laughing. 'The *what*?'

'Gala Nou Nou,' said Manos, seriously. 'It's a Dutch firm coming in . . . I tell you they are softening up the population ready for a takeover . . .'

He got off the swing and took a few zombie-like steps.

'They're just waiting for the right moment, and then they'll move in and one morning we're all going to wake up and find that this is a West Germany with a seaside . . .'

Antigone shook her head. 'Gala Nou Nou! That's *milk*, Mano!'

'So what? You know, they are making bars of soap out of the Baader-Meinhof people in Spandau!'

He stood to attention and faced the park:

'*Heil*! Klaus Sonnenberg!' he shouted into the wind with great bitterness.

Antigone was taken aback. She realised that life on the streets was pretty paranoid at the moment, but it disappointed her to hear a gentle boy like this mouthing these pathetic, reactionary clichés.

'Look,' she said urgently to him, getting off the swing and catching hold of his arm, 'the police are looking to justify themselves. They are incompetent, and they are flailing about bringing charges against anybody they can find. If you have been spending your time talking like this . . .'

'And writing . . .' he said, proudly.

Antigone groaned. 'Can't you *see*?' she said. 'It's not necessary. It's not going to do any good . . .'

'If it's written, then so be it.'

'You are just a spoilt brat like the rest of them,' she said. 'I'm really disappointed in you. I thought you were different.'

He smiled.

'Think of your mother! What's it going to do to her? She can't afford a lawyer, can she? What on earth good will your martyrdom do for your family? Do you think it will make it any easier for your brothers to get work when you have a police record?'

Antigone was trying everything she knew to break the fixed, glassy, icon-like expression on his face.

'It's all very well for you to walk around pretending you're Jesus Christ,' she said, 'or Saint George. Look at you! You're not *serious*, any of you!'

'On the contrary, I am *deadly* serious. The life of young people is finished. You don't know what it feels like. It's like being caught in a vice and squeezed a little more every day. Every day more pressure, fewer choices . . . Somebody has to talk about this, stand up and be counted. Otherwise no one will survive this kind of passivity!'

'You think I'm passive?'

'You're part of the machine,' he said. 'You think you're not, but you're part of some big law firm. Everything we do makes work for you!'

'You'll think differently when they get you into that cell, and start working on you down at the police station, I can tell you,' she said grimly. 'You will need a lawyer then . . .'

'One lawyer is much like another,' said Manos. 'You're all part of this big state machine that kills the life in people.'

Antigone was suddenly angry. 'I can't waste my time here any more,' she said, turning and walking off.

He sat back on the swing and watched her stalk off into the wind, her scarf flying and flapping round her neck. She turned once as she strode to look back. He was still sitting on the swing with an unlit cigarette in his mouth as she turned the corner and made for her car.

Barbara spent a lot of the time on the sofa, chasing every odd, elusive flicker of feeling and using them as rice-paper playing cards with which to mount a number of draught-defying Chinese structures, visual sequences mainly, whose clarity and definition were high enough to be consolatory. The cold blue current of rage which ran, like a subterranean river, beneath her shame she had not allowed to possess her. But now, at this distance, and with this apparent security (no one in the world knew where she was), falteringly at first, and then with a rush, she let rage have its day.

He came round the bathroom door in the conventional, 'historical' fashion and there were the usual introductory sequences of blows, but then the first thing that happened was that she managed to slip out from under his arm and dodge by him, slithering between him and the wall, blundering into the door.

Here she had the problem of the physical arrangement of the objects in the room. He had half-turned, startled, but now she was faced with the door in front of her, damn it, which she couldn't get round without his catching her. Barbara knew: he took another swing at her, and she ducked like a well-co-ordinated, well-choreographed American girl. She laughed aloud as she heard, with a very satisfying noise, the heel of his hand striking the edge of the door just above her head. Well, that will give him quite a bruise! she thought as she eased herself, tiptoeing with exaggerated music-hall steps across the hall, scoffing to herself and holding her hands like paws, limp at the wrists: a cartoon character, the Pink Panther in silhouette.

No, that was too easy; better go back and flee with a cry across the hall, music sounding in her ears beneath the grunt he gave as his hand crashed with all the venom he could muster into the door-edge.

No, she preferred the cartoon version, in which he reeled back indefinitely, giving her plenty of time to get across the hall. In fact, it was taking him a long time to recover. He was still in the bathroom when he should be on duty chasing her. She looked back. Ah, now here he comes, staggering, his face locked in a frenzy of anger.

She stands watching him at the door of the kitchen, as he runs after her. He has done up the cord of his dressing gown, with a curious modesty, so that she can't see his tackle swinging at the front. Is that right?

No, send him back. He bursts out of the room, cursing, dressing gown flying all around him, two gold cords trailing, one short and one so long that it gets trapped under the bathroom door and begins to extend across the hall behind him, threatening to pluck the dressing gown – medallion swinging up and out, level with his chin – clean from his shoulders, while his purple hairy mess of pottage at the front swings up, too, in a feeble imitation of something free. He half-turns and yanks at the cord from under the door where the tassel has caught, but it won't come.

She is enjoying this, but it's ridiculous. Better speed him up a bit, as he launches himself, closing the gown and huddling the cords round him, across the marble towards her.

She stares at him, as if made of stone, watching his feet rising about three or four inches off the floor as he flies into his arc, teeth clenched, uttering his Japanese battle-cry, and just as he reaches out in his landing sequence, she whips round the door and slams it in his face, listening on the other side for the sweet

110

series of crashes as he lands, the impetus carrying his face inexorably into the door panels with an 'oof!' There are little posterior crashes, as his knees and elbows follow his face into the door, which she hears with bated breath on the other side; breath bated not with fear but pleasurable expectation. Now he is turning the handle and she turns it in the opposite direction with all her might, holding it with two hands while she looks around for . . . the weapon.

Now, let's see what's in the drawer.

She finds that she can hold the door handle with one hand, pushing down on it, with one finger even, while she opens the drawer behind her with the other, and goggles over her shoulder into its depths where there is a magnificent selection of murderous blades. There's a big, almost-triangular Sabatier butcher's knife which she very much likes the look of, there's a meat spike which she hesitates over, but decides against because it's not quite strong enough for what she has in mind, and besides she really needs a blade, and in the end she chooses a brown-handled serrated breadknife, strong but flexible and all-purpose, which is longer than the butcher's knife.

She finds she's even let go of the door handle, but he still isn't able to get into the room. Goodness me, he seems to be taking his time about pressing the handle down and pushing open the door. What is he playing at on the other side of that door? Doesn't he realise she's got an expensive camera crew and lighting team all standing around in the kitchen waiting for him?

At last the door begins to open, and his fingers appear, gripping the edge, and then his shock of greying, curly hair and his head becomes visible. Not very good acting. A touch of the ham, and he makes a great play of first caution and then a smile that breaks over his face showing her his would-be sadistic satisfaction with the situation. She has her back to the sink, scrabbling in the drawer behind her until her hand locates the serrated edge of the blade and her fingers close round the wooden handle. So much better than plastic. As he approaches, slowly, lacing his hands together and cracking the finger-joints ready for what he will do with relish, he is so obsessed with looking at her as a piece of prey that he fails to notice what she's doing with her hand behind her.

Oh come on, hasn't he got to notice? That's the whole point of this scene, isn't it?

No, she decides. Let's run it without his noticing.

Look at his fixed, obsessive stare as he approaches her, his hands reaching out for her throat as she begins to whimper, her fingers closing tightly round the handle of the knife. She is stretching away from him, almost on tiptoe now as his hands make crushing contact with her throat. She can feel the little bones breaking, like chicken wings, in the front of her throat, near her Adam's apple, as he spreads his feet wide apart and assumes a stable position in front of her from which he can do the strangling. But it's quite painless.

Not now. Wait. Wait until you see the whites of his eyes. How on earth do they get the knife out of the drawer and round to the front to strike, these well-built American girls, she wonders, as she stares into his irises, china-blue, flecked with little black anemone-like forms, while the rest of the eyes widen with the physical effort of strangling her.

Now! She whips her hand round and stabs down into his shoulder-blade, just below the neck, with all her strength. But it seems she's using a potato peeler. She's grabbed the wrong thing out of the drawer, but no matter. The potato peeler sinks in about an inch and it's enough to make him loosen his hands from her neck and grunt, reaching round with one hand, to pluck it out.

At this point she has time to scrabble briefly again in the drawer behind her. Better get it right this time. He has fallen away conveniently to the side while he wrestles with this problem of the potato peeler, giving her enough room for a serious strike at the front. She slips away along the sink, holding the breadknife which is glittering, *contre-jour*, her two hands gripping it in the

112

regulation hysterical stabbing position, raises it in a diagonal fashion until it's shoulder height and, aware of his shouting and lunging for it, she jinks it sweetly sideways at the last moment to elude his stretching fingers as it descends, and wallops it down into his rib-cage where it sinks in easily about four inches until it encounters some bony opposition, and stops.

Damn, the blade won't go in past the ribs, it must be jammed between two of them. All the breath has gone out of him as he stares in disbelief at the instrument poking out of his chest, altogether unconscious now, in the moment of his great emergency, of the potato peeler, which is hanging down out of the flesh between his neck and shoulder-blade like something in a bullfight, she thinks.

That's good, that's quite a nice touch. The Hemingway Effect.

Now this is the most difficult moment. Because there are two things that might happen here, which she wants to avoid. One is that, with his behind against the open drawer, he might copy her and reach into it and bring out something like the butcher's knife. He certainly mustn't be allowed to do that. And the other is that he plucks out this one from his rib-cage and brandishes it at her. This also is absolutely out.

Time for some positioning, perhaps, some blocking. She slides away from him down the sink, but when the potato peeler goes in he moves away from the sink, round her, as if to cut her off, into the centre of the room. So that when she puts the breadknife in she's actually moving back towards the drawer, while he is standing in the open space in front of her and she has plenty of time to put her hand inside the drawer and get the Sabatier out.

He's standing there, unable to get a purchase on anything to help him get the breadknife out, tugging vainly at it with one hand across his chest, the other waving vaguely behind him for balance, when she strikes forward with the Sabatier, gripped with two hands in a back-handed hold, so that this time it is travelling upwards as she spins herself slightly, like a discus-thrower, to get a little extra force into her commando launch, pulling the blade round through the air and then following its momentum through as it disappears into the blue tartan dressing gown just below the pocket. Like a woman, a Parisian, say, who leans, one arm extended in resigned indulgence, towards her little dog which is on the end of its expanding leash dragging her towards something it wants, suddenly, very badly.

The Sabatier, which is about seven inches long, whams in easily up under the rib-cage without any vibration coming down its shaft. She feels just the vaguest murmur perhaps of something in the way of its tip, and then a deflection very slightly to the right, and it's in, snugly, right up to its hilt. She lets it go and steps back.

He gives a dreadful passive groan which she doesn't approve of at all because it reminds her for a second of the unutterable pain he must be experiencing, but she sees that he has to have some reaction. She doesn't know whether this is the mortal blow or not, because she can't work out which is left and right. She hasn't time for that. She's far too busy for that. He is spinning slightly on his feet, the dressing gown falling open at the waist, held together only by the bow in the tasselled cord at the front and the knife which pins it to his upper belly on the one side, through a modest blood-stain.

She stares at the greyish purple sacs hanging unequally under the rough crest of dark brown hairs and the other thing lying at the front of them like a curl of pink finger upside down in the act of beckoning, and she reaches into the drawer again. There's still a lot to do, and not much time to do it in, because he looks as if he's starting to go. The arm which has been trying to get at the breadknife in his rib-cage falls away now and he staggers, listing to one side, almost entirely unable to breathe, locked into a paroxysm of pain which achieves fleeting expression on his features before they cloud into some intensely inward, almost introspective sulk – the dropping chin, sagging corners of the lips and roll of the eyes all indicating that he has given up contemplating the outer world, and is now firmly shut in the cell of his own final concerns.

But she means to give him something further to think about before he goes.

Her hand brings out from the drawer a small, horn-handled, narrow-bladed knife which must be for filleting fish. This she holds casually, blade upwards, thumb against the hilt but without any special grip in her right hand while she reaches into the parting dressing gown in front of her with her left. His list is increasing now and it feels as if he is about to go down on one side.

Her fingers cup under the two sacs and for a moment they drop, cold, into the palm of her hand. She is aware vaguely, out of the corner of her eye, of further activity as he vainly tries to take the hilt of the Sabatier in his hand and wrestles with it, gasping, trying with his last ounces of strength to pull it out. This is just a casual comedy, which gives her a few extra seconds, the few precious little beats of the clock that she needs to accomplish the job.

She closes her eyes. The sacred moment, the moment she has been waiting for, has arrived, and now she is balanced exquisitely between impulses, between fear and the driving pleasure of this last payment in full.

She hardly notices the stroke of her right arm as she slides the blade between his two shadowed, olive-coloured thighs. She only feels the two sacs, weighing in the palm of her left hand, as she curls her right arm and strikes back towards her using the circular movement of someone with a sickle, cutting grass. One brief unfortunate sawing through the last strands of hanging flesh, as soft as cheese, and he falls away from her as irrevocably as someone falling backwards from the cabin door of an aeroplane, staring up as he tries to sink on to one knee and fails, his legs buckling instead and his whole body corkscrewing around the thin, rope-like spout of blood she can see between them, which, silhouetted against the curtains, resembles a thin cylindrical strut of metal that appears to support him for a moment like a piece of sculpture, the interruption of one thigh even enhancing this kindly illusion as he rotates and finally goes over, half on his back and half on his side, his head double-cracking, loosely, with a great bounce, she makes sure of this, on the vinyl floor of the kitchen.

He is twitching under the dressing gown, his eyes open in a dull stare, while she is aware of herself standing there holding the knife in the right hand with a single stain on its blade and, still feeling those cool objects under a flap of skin, weighing in the palm of her left. She leans over his faded eyes, and smiles.

'Roger!' she murmurs, 'don't go yet. I've got something to show you. Look here!'

And she dangles them by their greyish-pink flap of blood-stained, goose-pimpled skin in front of his nose, so close that the few hairs sprouting from them like a plucked chicken are almost tickling his nostrils, and swings them from side to side in a mocking, pendulum-motion, watching his eyes follow them involuntarily from right to left and back as he fades. He opens his mouth to say something, which she strains to hear, but which is drowned by the noise of a rasping saw blade which turns out to be a door-buzzer . . .

Barbara looked through the spyhole and saw Robert Graves, in a lemon paisley tie and the palest of mauve suits, staring at her as if he could see her. A beige mac was slung round his shoulders and he was carrying a square box wrapped with a pale-blue ribbon tied in a large bow at the top.

This, she thought, must be an illusion – that was what spyholes were for, wasn't it, to conceal you? – but she recoiled about four feet and stood, looking down at her feet, the toes of her new black shoes placed neatly together.

The telephone she had got used to, but the idea that someone in the body was *there*, at the margins, at the borders, possibly about to step inside and be in the same space as her, was difficult to cope with.

He pressed the buzzer again, this time twice.

Barbara put her hands to her ears at the sound, which was actually, she recalled later, the exact sound of those buzzers they have in American movies of the late Forties that are full of Venetian blinds, something friendly with connotations of material luxury.

The panic swept over her. Her mouth was dry. She worked her hands, kneading them, one into the other, whispering, soundlessly, nonsensical things, fragments of exhortations – *Mustn't* . . . *normally* . . . – as she stared down at the curious way her ankles, very far away, ran into her shoes.

She heard him stirring, his feet on the marble, on the other side of the door.

Barbara took a deep breath and stepped up to the spyhole again.

This time he had his back to her. His white hair settled snowily on a stretch of creased walnut-coloured neck above his pink collar. He was staring – temporarily! – at the ceiling. Barbara dreaded his turning again towards the door. She didn't think she could bear it. She felt a shriek rising within her. She stepped away from the door again like someone on a military parade-ground and stood at attention, perfectly still, her eyes fixed on a blemish in the paintwork just above the lock where perhaps someone had had the locks changed. Yes, yes, it must stem from some time when someone broke in. Or perhaps when Antigone first came, when she didn't have a full set of keys and she had to get the locksmith to come in . . .

Barbara's mind went outside and found the locksmith, a swarthy, chunky type in overalls, benign and charming, who was bending next to her, chipping out the bits of the old aperture,

117

making way for the new one. Kind, patient with her eleven-year-old questions as she stood behind him, quizzing him slowly about procedure; why was he doing this and would he do that next and what came after that? And how did he fix this to that?

Five birds flew across the screen of her mind high up in the sunlight and as they changed course they all caught the light at once and changed colour, from dark grey to blazing yellow, like someone reversing the louvres of a sun-blind. Somewhere she could hear a garden hose, and she was looking out through the french windows into the garden, trying to see if she could see the children who were just round the corner of the house – she could hear their shouts. She had white shoes on and a flowered frock with a gathered skirt, a white matching belt and she was smoking a cigarette. The little girl from Famagusta was shouting '*Ela!*' at Kate.

Barbara stood in the shadows behind the curtains in the corner of the living-room, looking at that blazing path of garden, listening to the scrape of their shoes on the path and their cries and the explosive shouts of their laughter as they splashed each other in the little inflatable pool, made of black rubber – plastics were coming in but they hadn't reached Cyprus yet. Her white handbag lay on the oval coffee table, and she was just about to go out to the officers' club for the evening. Syrmoula would look after them and put them to bed.

The cigarette she was smoking seemed to last a long time . . .

No the cigarette seemed to last for ever as she stood in those cool shadows in their living-room, standing to one side of her life, feeling its volume out there in the heat of the closed space around her shouting, screeching children as something to be observed at a close distance, something from the cool of the curtains tangibly elsewhere in another time and space not very far from her own, but far enough to . . .

The buzzer sounded again and the door shook and rattled in its socket with a rain of knocks.

'Excuse me,' he said, confidentially in Greek, 'but I *know* that you are there . . .'

Barbara sniffed and the sound bit the air inside the hall. She held her breath and a spiral of wind coiled away in her gut with a gurgle that mocked the silence she was trying to keep.

She heard him take a step. The door leapt again and rattled against the jamb, and she gave an involuntary cry, backing away again another step or so, relieved, as she executed them, that these sounds and movements were covered by the noise of the door.

'I know it is you,' he said, laughing briefly. 'Playful, eh?'

Barbara stood to attention, digging her nails into her palms in the centre of the hall in the centre of the silence. She tried to draw in around her, like a comforting veil, all the things she could see out of the corner of her eyes: the pot plants perched just through the window on the balcony and the edges of the plum turkey-carpet running to the corners, the door leading to Antigone's small study she matched against the door on the other side of her leading to the kitchen, centring her perfectly in the space, and behind her, where she couldn't see, she knew there were the two bedroom doors, side by side, dove-grey in colour with yellow facings and knobs. All this wheeled round her slightly, and then stopped, closer, hugging her round.

'You seem to have forgotten, *korítsi mou*, that it is you who let me in.'

Now the silence and the space inside the silence were beginning to crack at the edges, and cold currents were rushing in as if through rents in a physical material all round her. The silence she lived in with bated breath was not holding up, because she felt this intense desire, now, to break it with an action or a sound as if it were beginning to stifle her, silence a kind of oxygen that was beginning to run out.

She was a deep-sea diver in an appalling Eastmancolor adventure movie, in a heavy suit with rubber pipes and ropes and a copper helmet, with a thing like a portcullis in front of her face, her legs weighed down by enormous lead boots and the diver down there with her had just sawn through her pipe with his underwater knife. She could see the eyes behind his portcullis widening with laughter at her plight.

'Come, now, Antigone, enough of this. Let me in!'

Barbara remembered that she had answered the downstairs bell. Before she could think to dredge up her voice to say 'Who is it?' she had, by a stupid reflex, an unthinking movement of the finger she would never ever forgive herself, pressed the release button for the downstairs door which led from the street. She had no idea who it was coming towards her up the two flights of marble stairs, and it was her own fault entirely.

But he, in his turn, had no means of knowing it was anyone other than Antigone, whom this aged dandy clearly knew, and knew intimately. Was this any kind of a comfort? The mutual misunderstanding, which she knew about now, and he clearly didn't?

She was an actress in some long-running stage farce. The door was a flat. The audience was behind her in the bedrooms somewhere. He was out there, absurd Reginald, with his bunch of flowers, not knowing it was she, Daisy . . .

'Antigone's not here!' she said in English, in a hoarse, 1950s elocution-lesson whisper.

'Aha,' he said in perfect English, in his thin nasal whine, 'to whom am I speaking?'

'A friend,' said Barbara.

'I too am a friend of Antigone. I am Loukas. Perhaps I might come in and wait for her?'

'Go away,' said Barbara, coarsely.

Go away, Reginald, said Daisy, shimmying at the door. Gosh, Daisy, it's you, let me in, hooted Reginald.

Now he knew it was her.

'I have an appointment with Antigone,' he said, in a somewhat pained way.

I say, old bean, it's Reggie. Let me in, old girl.

'I don't know who you are. You are not coming in.'

I say, old girl, be reasonable. I've just come down all the way from Charing Cross. You're not going to send me back again, dash it, are you?

'Well then, I have brought something for her. Perhaps you could take this and I will leave a message?'

Barbara stared at the door. She refused to go to the spyhole.

'You can leave it outside and push any messages under the door,' she said.

'Mmm . . . mmm . . . this is absurd,' said Loukas angrily. 'I have come a long way to see her!'

'I'm sure she won't be long, if she knows,' said Barbara.

'It's rather cold out here,' said Loukas. 'May I come in and wait?'

Bit parky out here, old thing. Can't you just let me in?

'No.'

'Ridiculous,' she heard him say to the landing. 'At least you will please tell her to call me as soon as she gets home.'

It was an order, delivered in his huffy, cold, nasal voice.

Barbara jumped up and down. He was going. She compressed her lips with joy and, rising on tiptoe, clapped mental hands together. He was actually *going away*.

Antigone came running up the stairs to find Loukas just beginning to come down. He was furious.

'Who is this mad woman you have in your apartment? She wouldn't let me in!' he called down.

Antigone suppressed the smile behind her hand as she ran round the last bend in the staircase and stopped, staring up at his all-dressed-up-and-no-place-to-go look.

'*É, korítsi mou*, what is this? I thought we were going out tonight?'

'It's Barbara,' said Antigone, wagging her finger at him like Gloria Grahame in *Oklahoma*, 'and you are to be very nice to her, because she's been through some bad things lately and I'm looking after her for a while . . .' And briefly, Antigone explained Barbara's circumstance.

Loukas made a few gestures of impatience:

'All right, all right . . . but where have you been? You're not coming out with me like *that*!'

He pointed at her leather jacket and blue jeans.

She mounted the stairs past him. 'Of course not,' she said, turning from the top to look down at him on the third step, 'I'm going to get changed. I'll just be two minutes . . .'

She ignored the other question, which she hoped to convert into a rhetorical one. 'But,' she bent forward to whisper, even though they were speaking in Greek, 'you can't come in, it would disturb Barbara. Please can you wait out here on the landing. Or perhaps you'd like to go out and find a *kafenéio* and wait for me there. There's one on the corner. It might be more comfortable. It won't take long . . .'

He spread his hands, hunching his shoulders, and looked down at the box.

'This is a joke. You are making a joke out of me!'

Antigone leant forward and took the box out of his hand. She closed her eyes and tendered the cheek.

He bounded up the steps and grasped her by the shoulders, but instead of kissing her cheek he suddenly reached for her hand and took it in his.

'*Magissa*,' he said. You little witch. He bent his white head over her hand and kissed it, pressing his palm upwards into her palm at the same time.

Antigone murmured, withdrew the hand, and turned away with rapid swashbuckling strides – what Yannis used to call the Bouboulina walk – her head tossed up high as he stood sighing against the balustrade. She paused and turned at the door.

'Ten minutes,' she said. 'Where will you be?'

He looked around, throwing up his hands and gathering his

mac around him: 'É, can't I just come in and sit down, korítsi mou?'

'No, I've *told* you!' said Antigone, picking up his childish wail and imitating a mother, chopping the air parodically. 'You'll get the stick!'

He grumbled, turning to go down.

'Ridiculous that people can't behave properly! I shall wait in the car. Don't be long . . . !'

'Shhh!' said Antigone. She turned and placed the key in the lock.

She called to Barbara through the door. There was silence.

When she got the door open, she found Barbara standing in the centre of the hall, her feet together in a prim, old-maidish, slightly military fashion, clasping her hands like a missionary who has just made a conversion.

'He went away!' she said, ecstatically. 'I wouldn't let him in!'

Antigone leant towards her, her finger on her lips, her eyes indicating his presence behind her, and they laughed silently together, their heads touching. Antigone drew back and looked long and hard, the smile still on her lips, at Barbara's bony face and slightly watery blue eyes. The wounds around her cheek and mouth were looking a mite less swollen, and a smile curved its way up through the scab on her broken lip. Antigone grasped her briefly under both black elbows.

'*Endáxi?*' she asked, lightly, but seriously. 'That is Loukas, a friend of mine. I'm going out with him tonight – will you be all right?'

'Fine,' said Barbara nodding. 'I just didn't . . .'

'I know, and why should you,' said Antigone. She turned away, dangling her keys in one hand and beginning to strip off the leather jacket as she walked with the other, lifting her arm high and wriggling her shoulder out, transferring her keys to the other hand while she did it, suddenly aware of herself performing these actions, and taking pleasure in them as she

123

swept into her room, pausing to turn at the door and ask if Barbara would really be all right.

'I'm in a hurry,' she said, holding the image of Barbara, still standing there in the hall, in her mind as she closed the door and completed the action of taking off her jacket. She threw everything on the bed, and put on a bathrobe to go to the bathroom.

Barbara was not there. Antigone peeped and saw her sitting with her shoes off on the long sofa, a book on her lap. She swept into the shower, and then pitter-pattered back to her bedroom in the big bath towel.

Antigone didn't like her hips and the backs of her thighs. When wearing a tight dress, even in company, she had a habit of holding the backs of her legs and smoothing them down as if smoothing down the extra fat. She felt she was short and bottom-heavy compared with some Athenian women she had met, especially her colleagues, women lawyers from good Peloponnesian or Attic families, who tended to be enviably tall and rangy. She turned sideways in the green dress and sighed. She could do with losing a few pounds off her all round, but especially at the back. But with all this work on, she was not going to be stupid and go on a diet. Afterwards, maybe, in the summer, if they were through with the anarchists, she would go to an island and swim and laze around, Samos maybe. She didn't look as good in a dress, especially in these short skirts, as she did in jeans, she thought, but bending to put on her ear-rings, she suddenly felt very much like dancing. She put out her arms, one eye on herself in the mirror, and clicked her fingers in time to some unknown tune. It was ages since she had really had a good dance. Her head went back, and she closed her eyes, lifting her shoulders for a moment two or three times experimentally, trying to remember the last time.

As she picked up her bag, and went out into the hall, the leather jacket slung round her shoulders, car keys dangling, the image flicked into her mind, not of the last time she had danced which she still couldn't remember, but of Thessaloniki days, of herself and Fotini, her sister, singing to each other softly, dancing together very tenderly, very slowly, outside in the garden restaurant somewhere up in Séich-Sou, up above the city, the harbour twinkling below them, doing all the little jinks and half-steps by themselves in the corner of the hedge while the group at the table watched them and clapped in time and the singer at the other end of the garden, an oldish man, with that excessive vibrato of the old-fashioned semi-professional, lifted his hands towards them while he sang the chorus of 'My garifalo'.

She stood in the doorway in the green dress, adjusting an ear-ring.

'Barbara?'

Barbara sat up and smiled.

'You look gorgeous!' she said.

'Thank you. I won't be back until late. Loukas likes to go out on the town and . . .' she twirled, 'I think I might try and persuade him to go dancing.'

'Good for you,' said Barbara. 'I shall go to bed early . . .'

She was doing her best, Antigone saw, to reassure her that she was all right.

Briefly she asked herself whether she should be going out at all, with Barbara in her current state, and then dismissed it from her mind as she thought of the fuming Loukas sitting in his car downstairs.

Barbara came with her to the door. Antigone thought she still looked a little trembly, but stronger.

'I'd like to phone the kids,' she said.

Antigone told her to go ahead and she waved at the black form in the doorway as she launched herself down the stairs in easy, clattering circles, letting herself go limp, her hair bounding, her feet in their flat black shoes fully acquainted with the rhythm of this descent, which she preferred to the lift going down because you usually met no one, and it was a pleasure to feel her fingers still warm from the shower lightly sliding along the cool, polished chrome of the balustrade.

Antigone tapped on the window. Loukas, who was reading, leant over and opened the door for her. He looked up and down, craning his neck to get a good sight of her, while she stood and posed for him, hands on hips on the pavement. Then she bounded into the car, taking the book from his hand. It was a book of poems by Elýtes. She stared at the verses and started to read out loud.

'Ah, but you don't read it right, *korítsi mou*,' said Loukas, and he recited it slowly, rhythmically, by heart.

'Never mind about that, anyway,' said Antigone. 'I want to go dancing tonight . . .' She turned to him, her hand catching his arm as he started the car. 'Can't we?'

'Let's go to Ambélkupo?' he said slyly.

She looked at him. He couldn't possibly know.

'Where did you go this afternoon?' he asked. 'You were so late . . .'

'Oh,' she smiled, 'I had someone to interview in Plaka. Well, someone's mother to be exact. Thought it might be helpful, but it turned out to be a waste of time.'

She sighed as she thought of Manos, sitting on the swings.

'You're very conscientious,' said Loukas. 'They don't deserve you, those people . . .'

'Nikos and Spiros are very good' said Antigone, trying to deflect the direction of this remark. 'We make quite a good team, I think . . .'

'You seem to have let your man talk himself into a lot of unnecessary trouble . . .'

'Well, that was my fault,' said Antigone, ruefully. 'I just couldn't get to him in time when he came out from the prosecutor's office.'

She looked across at Loukas and caught his eye. He was very

well informed, as she expected. She supposed Spiros had told him all about this incident. It wouldn't be Nikos, who didn't know Loukas well.

'Never let them "agree" with journalists about anything,' he said.

'Are you going to give me a hard time tonight?' said Antigone, desperately. She wanted him off this tack.

'Me?' said Loukas innocently.

That was better. What was happening with his yacht?

He began to talk about Skiathos. He had been up to the island in the summer. It was full of PASOK people.

'Halvazoglou was there with that fancy yacht of his, the *Demeter*, with radar he got from EXXON . . .' Loukas sniffed. 'Do you know that yacht isn't even registered? It doesn't have a number?'

'Why not?'

'Because, *korítsi mou*, in our brave republic, there are some people who believe themselves to be above the law . . .'

Antigone was quite used to all the PASOK-baiting which went on with Loukas, whose sympathies were lost somewhere off on the right, but Antigone could never really quite work out where. He was anti-Junta, he was not really a monarchist, but he did not like Mitsotákis. Karamanlís seemed to him the image of a desirable, honourable politician, perhaps. Loukas preferred the older style of patrician conservatism, enlightened, cultured.

'You're jealous because your yacht isn't as big as his!' said Antigone. 'Where are we going?'

'The Dawn Club,' said Loukas.

They embarked on a brief argument about about the wire-tap scandal and Tombras.

'This man is a barbarian,' said Loukas. 'He doesn't know how to behave . . .'

'Well, at least he's fairly open about everything and speaks his mind . . .'

'So much so that he calls his employees at OTE imbeciles! Now

127

they're all out on hunger strike against him. Ridiculous behaviour!'

Antigone was silent, thinking again of Manos in the park and his fanaticism.

'This whole wire-tapping thing's a joke,' said Loukas. 'You know, before they had this digital system the telephones in Athens were so bad that you probably had to listen to about three conversations by other people before you could have the one that you were going to have in the first place . . .'

'Don't tell me you're nostalgic – you're getting old,' said Antigone.

She thought she could risk this kind of banter, but when they reached the Dawn, and they had settled themselves at their table, things became altogether more serious: Loukas spent a lot of the time talking to her about the law firm and what his plans were.

'Have you ever asked yourself how this case came to us in the first place?' he asked.

'I assumed you had a good reputation.'

Loukas smiled. 'For defending terrorists?'

'They aren't terrorists,' said Antigone. 'Let's just get this straight. They're just young men, somewhat confused, who care about the mess this country is in . . .'

'They were carrying arms. Every day the police find more. In my book, they are terrorists bearing arms against the state.'

'But it's not really like that. If you could talk to some of them . . .'

'Your Christos, for example,' said Loukas, 'he has a perfectly respectable widowed mother whom I happen to be acquainted with from my days in New Democracy circles . . . and she wanted me to handle his defence as a favour . . .'

'You mean, that's why you've given it to me, because you felt compromised by it?'

'Not at all. I would do the same job you're apparently doing . . .' said Loukas. 'Any lawyer would be expected to whittle

128

away at these police charges, they're absurd, but don't ask me to believe they are not guilty!'

'He had a gun, true, but he laid it down as soon as they called out to him, and he gave himself up. Is that the action of a hardened terrorist? Can you imagine any of Seventeen N doing that?'

'Well, I can see you're getting all excited about this, but don't get too worked up. They'll all go to Korudallo for a long time before they come to trial. Now they've got them, the police will not be anxious to bring them to court, because they'll get more information if they don't and they'll have a lot more time to pursue all kinds of links . . .'

'That's what bothers me at the moment,' said Antigone. She told him about the inconsistencies and gaps between the prosecutor's brief and the evidence.

But Loukas actually wasn't interested.

'What I am saying, *korítsi mou*, is I don't want you looking for further cases. If you have any ideas about mounting a crusade of a moral kind, forget them. There are going to be a lot more arrests. Don't get involved in taking on any more of these anarchists . . . all right?'

Antigone wanted to shout, 'No! Not all right!' but she was silent, pecking at her souvlakia and watching the band setting themselves up.

The singer, an impressive forty-five-year-old from Asia Minor covered in sequins, was laughing and joking with the bouzouki player, chucking him under the chin in a more than motherly way and mouthing '*Ara brávo!*' as she moved her chair nearer to the front line of the little stage.

'I don't want the office to get that kind of reputation, do you understand?' said Loukas. 'We have a lot of different interests, some of which . . .'

'Are not compatible.'

'. . . positively *conflict* with that kind of activity . . .'

129

'Wouldn't be any of your large, landowning interests in Attica by any chance, some of those that are involved in polluting the coastlines?'

'Ah, yes, typical Romaic style,' said Loukas, changing the subject in a lordly way, as he looked across at the singer.

The band struck up, winding into their introduction. The woman put out her cigarette and wrapped her chewing-gum in a little piece of paper, settling herself on her chair and holding the microphone patiently on her knee, slipping back the coarse, springy curls on either side of her throat in two almost continuous gestures. She swayed very lightly as she listened, looking across to the string player and smiling a very public smile. Suddenly she raised the microphone and her powerful '*Agápi mou*' filled the room, tracked in tight harmonies by the drummer, a young man Antigone couldn't see from where she was sitting.

Antigone was smarting from Loukas's casual prohibitions, his way of laying down the rules with what he thought of as the minutest of shifts in his *bonhomie*. He hardly needed a language to express his ascendancy, it was all so seamless, as he managed the two levels, flipping between them with apparent ease, happy to leave his remarks hanging in the air to do their work all by themselves.

At the same time she felt the urge to dance, the rhythm surging through her as the slow beginning to the song began to beat with the inevitability of a railway train and her arms were beginning, at chest height above the table, to try out a few movements.

'Mmm . . .' She closed her eyes and swayed for a moment, knowing that he was now looking at her again.

Her resentment was still burning, but it was burning cold as she followed his glance back to her own movements.

'How charming,' said Loukas, pushing back his chair. 'Come, *éla*!' and he waved to the waiter to pull back the table.

130

She was already half-up from her chair, looking down at the ruins of their meal, while she felt the rhythm beginning to float into her neck and shoulders.

'*Éla!*' she said to him as she moved along the gap between the table and the wall. 'Come with me!'

'Oh no, my dear,' said Loukas, handing her out, 'I'll watch you . . .'

And she was out into the area between the tables in front of the band. The singer gave her a brief, knowing smile, and glanced at the bouzouki player as Antigone bent from the shoulders and raised her two arms to shoulder height, beginning on a butcher-dance. She was lost in the intensity of the opening slow skips, the long interval in between them serving to concentrate all the bad blood and resentment she felt. She felt with pleasure the artificial emotions of the dance shape her own real feelings, as she bent to concentrate on her feet in the slightly sulky, bluesy fashion the solo dance demanded. Soon she was only intermittently aware of her surroundings as the bouzouki player rose to his feet and moved towards her, emphasising his phrasing slightly more to accommodate her movements. '*Ópa!*' shouted someone across the room as she moved further out into the centre of the space with those tense, understated few steps that act out the dancer's interiorised passion and heroic loss.

Her mouth was open and hanging as she looked down at her feet, her arms raised dramatically high in the slow, deliberate sequence in which there was one exception, when she picked up her leg and swung the calf and foot from the knee in a flash, dropping her leg then, immediately, in the same slow time, as if it had never happened. She adored these flashes of intensity which peeped between the almost funereal steps of the dance, charging its whole sequence with suppressed passion.

But now they had flipped, as the song came to an end, the bouzouki player changing key and stepping up the rhythm into a *zseimbékiko*, and a young man she didn't know appeared from among the tables and put his arm around her waist. She glanced across at Loukas, who was standing and clapping in her direction and issuing some instructions to the waiter.

'*Brávo*!' he was calling, and someone else across the room had responded with an echo, and the whole place had erupted with couples making their way through the tables towards the dance floor.

Antigone felt the rise in her own spirits as they flocked round, and soon the whole room was vibrating to the sound of people singing the chorus, while the loose circle of dancers snaked their way round in the intricate series of little steps. She was laughing in her pleasure at a dance she had been doing since first grade in infants school, far from the contradiction of Loukas's controlling glance, as he sat slightly sideways and smoked, his froth of white hair visible from the furthest reaches of the smoke-filled, red-lit clubroom.

She sang as she danced, hanging on the young man, as the band ran through a series of old favourites, sang at the top of her lungs, as they did '*Leftéri*' and a witty old song about a woman's work is never done which she had forgotten had such good rhymes.

High spirits ruled now. The waiter appeared on the stage behind the band with a stack of a dozen white plates. He came forward, to shouts of '*Brávo*' and '*Ópa, ópa*' and proceeded to smash them very rapidly, almost karate-fashion, indicating at one point Antigone, who laughed and looked across at Loukas.

The white head inclined and he raised a limp hand in the air.

Back at the table, she kissed him on the forehead as she made her way round to her chair. She was panting, laughing, feeling the sweat running on her upper lip, full of the benign spread of good humour throughout all her limbs as she sat plump on the chair and licked her lips hungrily.

'You shouldn't have done that. Now it's time for the sweet . . .'

'You dance like a miracle,' said Loukas, 'a little miracle.'

And she was off to the Ladies while he ordered the sweets and some more retsina and coffee and water, water, water.

The queue was full of Athenian women moaning about the facilities, as they flounced in front of the mirror. Antigone discovered she had to pay a price for her physical exertions. She was surprised her period was so early and had nothing in her handbag. She came out and asked the Athenian women if she could borrow a Tampax and one of them gave her a large sanitary towel.

Loukas was talking to some other people at the table when she got back, two men who were seated, and a large, tall, redheaded woman whose big square freckled shoulders were visible under the straps of her loose one-piece dress and who was standing, being ignored, behind them.

Antigone joined her, standing behind them, looking down at the backs of their heads.

'Hi,' said the woman in English. 'I'm Kelly.'

'Hello,' said Antigone. 'My name's Anti . . .' and she paused to put the stress in the unfamiliar English place, 'Ant*ig*one.'

'That's a beautiful name,' said the woman, routinely.

From one of her unexpectedly, almost absurdly, small ears dangled two discs of silver with a swastika on each side.

'Look at them.' Antigone gestured at the backs of the heads in front of them. 'What children they are!'

Kelly turned. 'Took the words out of my mouth,' she said. 'Smoke?'

'I tell you something,' said Antigone, 'you want to be careful with those ear-rings in Greece.'

Kelly sighed: 'Nobody ever notices. They're not swastikas. They're the wrong way round. Smoke?' she repeated.

Antigone didn't want to smoke, but she stayed politely and exchanged information with the woman since the men were so involved with each other. It seemed she had just arrived in Athens on a visit, staying with her friend. She indicated the curly-headed man on Loukas's left.

'The other guy, the ugly one, he's his friend,' said Kelly, turning to her with enthusiasm. 'How 'bout you?'

Antigone gave an account of herself which was minimal, vague, and serious.

'Well, you sure can dance,' said Kelly, with a broad smile that lit up her brown, freckled face. 'Watched you back there . . . Whoop!'

'Thank you,' said Antigone and bent towards the fiercely animated heads below them.

'Loukas?' she said, hovering over them.

But he was discoursing.

The sweets arrived, including a large *loukoúmi*, wrapped in honey and sprinkled with nuts. Antigone clapped her hands and sat down.

They stood up, nodding over at her, apologising for taking Loukas's time, shaking hands, and insisting on going, understanding perfectly the lack of enthusiasm in the wave with which he apparently invited them all to sit with them.

Antigone was already tucking in to the sweet. She asked who the people were.

'Panagopoulos is a director of DEE,' said Loukas as he watched them go. 'The others I don't know . . . the English is some kind of engineer.'

'And the woman?'

It was clear he had forgotten already about the woman. He waved his hands. 'Some kind of hippie,' he said.

'I suppose it's no use asking you if you saw the ear-rings?'

Loukas smiled; half closed his eyes, and sang in a comically heavy accent:

'And I only 'av eyes forrr youuuu . . .'

'Get off!' said Antigone. 'So what did he want?'

'Panagopoulos?'

The second question meant he didn't want to answer the first. Antigone toyed with her *loukoúmi* and waited.

'Oh, the man seems obsessed with these strikes. Thinks DEE are bound to follow the teachers and the doctors and the bus drivers and all the rest of the revolt of the petty bourgeois against its own kind . . .'

Antigone was thinking of Yannis. How seriously, for all his arguments with her and his tactical voting, he would take a strike and what a struggle it would be if there were one. Whereas Loukas seemed to take it for granted that this was simply the logic of PASOK's dissolution.

'You talk as if this kind of thing is inevitable,' she said hotly, 'whereas people *choose* their actions in a democracy!'

Loukas looked at her under his shock of white hair as large and bushy as a widow's just out from the drier, and his weary grey eyes widened in their pouches:

'Such touching idealism,' he said. 'The sooner you get rid of it, the better. You are going to ruin your career if you carry on talking like that. A girl of your age should be beginning now to learn not to have opinions . . . Opinions are vulgar.' He leaned across and took her hand. 'Use your eyes and ears, of course, but not these twopenny opinions, please. Politics, here or anywhere, don't work like that . . . There's nothing so . . . so petty bourgeois as opinions . . .'

'I believe in PASOK,' said Antigone, simply. 'I believe in what they are trying to do.'

'Please,' said Loukas, 'it distresses me to hear this kind of thing from an intelligent girl like you. Ideas, yes, facts, and technical information, I am open to all of them and will argue with you, but not this evangelical stupidity . . .'

'I'm talking about socialism . . .'

Antigone realised suddenly that she was arguing with a kind of father-figure she had never known. Socrates and she had always agreed on the basic position.

'Socialism!' Loukas sneered. 'Please . . . ' He pointed to the surroundings with his spoon. 'We are out in this pleasant place for a pleasant evening. Please do not spoil all this.

Antigone wanted to shout that she didn't give a damn about

this place they were in. She didn't care about this conspicuous consumption.

'Why should people have to suffer in order that these plutocrats, these shipowners and landowners you are keeping happy, get a little richer than they are already!'

Loukas sailed on: 'I'd rather talk to a Marxist. At least they have a certain logic and are not sentimental!'

'Greece wouldn't be where it is now if PASOK hadn't reformed the country according to socialist principles!' flashed Antigone. 'All right, I know there are problems at the moment, but the basic fact is that they don't want to keep the people *down*! They want to *develop*!'

Loukas laughed mirthlessly, shaking his head. 'Greece wouldn't be where it is now, yes! And where is it? In debt, that's where it is. You see, now even the farmers are revolting . . . and PASOK's great trick was supposed to be the farmers. Let them take a leaf out of Rallis's book when he was Minister of Agriculture! He found out he couldn't give presents to the farmers. This Common Market, it's no good for us! My God, where do I start with you?' He appealed rhetorically to the velvet curtains behind her head. 'Do you think this little company of Romaic gypsies is *progress*? For the nation of Plato and Socrates, of Pericles, of Lysias, of Isocrates and Demosthenes? They are just following passively, aping the style of Western Europe. They have given permission for whole companies of monkeys from the Pontos to stand up and give us their *opinions*, comrades . . .'

'I know all these reactionary arguments, and they just won't wash any more. We need to liberate the workforce. Look at women . . .'

'Women!' he scoffed.

'We've been doing all the work. What happened during the war, when you people went off to fight? My mother, she had to look after the fields. And did women get paid for it? No. And after the war, now that women have made progress with PASOK, it is still difficult for a woman to get a decent wage. These employers are undermining the legislation by just ignoring it. They don't want to pay fair wages. How can you justify such things?'

Loukas turned. 'Ah, the band!' he said. 'They're back . . .'

The bouzouki player began at once to wind into a heavier music than before, its Turkish rhythms wheedling and insinuating their way into the atmosphere, and the singer began to strike the tambourine she carried in her hand against her bare thigh, having pulled back her sequined skirt, with slow inviting strokes. She sang through her nose, her phrasing crammed with atonal grace notes which sounded so good to Antigone that she pulled back her lips in a snarl of pleasure.

Loukas was nodding.

'Yes!' he breathed, 'A *tsifteteli*! Ah, *yes*!' His hand came across the table in invitation. 'Come!'

'I don't want to,' she said, and she meant it. The argument had been infuriating because he hadn't taken her seriously at all. *This* was what he wanted. To watch her, as she danced, to show her off to the other members of the club, the other diners.

'No!'

And yet the music was irresistible. Her mother, Matoula, had shown her how to do this dance from a little girl. She could remember standing in the garden, practising throwing up her right arm and locking her tiny pelvis into a forward slope and then bringing up her left arm level in front of her face, and beginning to twirl the hands round one another, only restricted movements of the fingers to begin with, as she learnt to bend her knees, and plant her thighs apart.

Loukas led her without a word to the corner of the table, and throwing up her chin she launched herself slowly into the dancing space. Each braced leg carried forward her jabbing pelvis in time to the music, while she began to ripple the rest of her, from the bottom of her stomach to her breastbone, the little movements of her shoulders and arms beginning to shake her breasts under the green dress.

The delight she felt in being able to co-ordinate all these different, quite separate movements outweighed the knowledge she had of Loukas's watchful eyes and puppeteer's hand. Antigone was already dancing for herself, she was dancing for her own past, for all the pleasures of the family and of her childhood and girlhood. She was doing this not because he asked her to, blackmailed or pressured her into doing it – she knew perfectly well this was what he wanted, to be able to display his manhood by proxy – but because she herself, first and foremost, took pleasure in the rhythm and the elasticity of her limbs, and this dance, these movements, belonged inalienably to her.

She was vaguely aware of people rising and clapping at the back and along the sides of the room as she edged forward in the posture that emphasised, with mad eloquence, the lower half of her body. Inching each leg forward to begin with, but then suddenly doubling her step and relaxing at intervals the tense lock of her knees, she twirled, once, twice, three times, to their shouts of 'όpa, όpa, όpa!' and found herself moving forward with steps so tiny and rapid, so melded with the rhythm of the players, that they were almost imperceptible to her.

The bouzouki player now produced a little reedy pipe and to his furious scales she lifted and moved her buttocks in tiny circles. Finally, as she brought her arms inwards towards her throat, the whole column of her neck slid easily back and forwards.

She set her jaw with the intensity of her pleasure, signalling her intention to increase the pace, to bring even more parts of her body into movement, and she paused on her back foot to begin the lateral sway of her hips that added to all the others until she swung and twirled and rippled all at once, the movements perfectly independent, and even sometimes contradictory, but all part of her living, moving self. Each time she threw back her head to begin another sequence and glided towards the crowded tables where people were now standing and applauding, she felt herself dive under the movements, pushing them from below and then, effortlessly, like a lifted prow over water, riding above the turbulence of her limbs, actions which she had neither time nor need to intend, because the wanting was, for once, all part of the doing.

She was hardly aware of the waiter. He might just as well have been an architectural support in the middle of the room, as she danced round and round him, using the displacement of the space, the rearrangement of physical reality which his presence created, to perform new variations, new disappearances and reappearances for her audience. They were whooping with joy now as she started to spin and reverse-spin in a cunning sequence, not ceasing the rippling of belly and behind under the green dress for a moment, supported perfectly, as if floating in a heavy medium, by her arms and elbows held at shoulder height which controlled the spins, initiating them and slowing them down with sweeps of the shoulder that gave orders to her feet to displace and replace themselves in a lightning chain of substitutions, which begged in the end for her shoes to be kicked off so that she could get more purchase on the arches of her bare feet. Whenever she looked down, theatrically, at intervals and directed attention to the various independently rippling parts of herself the crowd could restrain itself no longer, stamping, howling, and crying: 'Brávo! Brávo, korítsi mou!'

The music finished, she stood, breathing heavily through her nose, suddenly aware that she was in the middle of all these people and that the waiter had been waiting all along, probably, to give her what he was giving her now, a gardenia. She smiled shyly as she took it and looked towards Loukas, many of the heads, she noticed out of the corner of her eye, turning with her, to acknowledge him as he sat, one hand raised to her like a circus performer – 'I give you . . . Antigone!' said his gesture.

She bent to look for her shoes. Someone came running up and clapped her on the bare shoulder, crying 'Brávo, korítsi mou, you're marvellous! Trelathékane! They're going mad . . .'

139

Antigone felt confused, suddenly aware of the gap between what she had done for herself alone, and the reactions of everyone else, especially of Loukas, who sat, old, dangerous, and snowy, amidst his admirers who had been applauding spontaneously, she knew, she felt it, and who looked back at her now with different eyes.

Antigone had been interviewing clients all morning and taking their statements at her office, along with Nikos, but she managed to get to a shoe shop before they closed at two, fighting her way with raw lungs through the streets, and bought Barbara a new pair of size thirty-eight sensible flat black shoes, and went home to make her a nice lunch of village salad and various salamis and cooked meats.

Antigone was pleased that Barbara ate heartily and even drank a glass of retsina and soda water. She gave her a lively account of the morning at the office and the various statements and Barbara seemed interested in the whole thing. But all the time Antigone was wondering how she could approach the question of what they were going to do with her.

At last Barbara raised the matter herself, as if reading her mind, thanking her profusely for her hospitality and saying that she couldn't be a trouble to her any longer.

'Nonsense,' said Antigone, 'you must stay until you are completely well . . .'

There was then a question in the air.

Antigone saw Barbara look down at her plate and swallow.

'I've been thinking . . .' she began.

'If you need money for your flight back to England . . .' said Antigone, 'there's no problem . . .'

'I don't want to go back,' said Barbara.

She reminded Antigone of a stubborn little girl when she said this, and she laughed and reached over for her hand. 'Why not? What about your children?'

'That's just it. I don't want them to know about . . . this.'

'But won't they call the apartment?'

'Not for a week or so. I've already talked to them and I wouldn't have called them for a week or so. I don't want them worrying and trying to come out here. There'll be all sorts of fuss . . .'

Antigone was silent, taken aback. She had been assuming that Barbara would want to fly back to London as soon as she could.

'I'll tell them in due course,' said Barbara, 'but in the meantime I don't want this to spoil my trip to Greece. Why should it?'

Antigone lit a cigarette and nodded. She didn't think this was at all realistic.

But Barbara had obviously been thinking it all out. She had her savings. She would stay at the YMCA or somewhere, get a room, and look for a job. She felt she had given everything up in England and she just didn't like the idea of being there. She smiled her lopsided smile. 'D'you see? It would be a defeat. 'Whereas . . .'

Antigone stared back at her battered face. The bruises were coming out now, particularly the one under her eye on the cheek-bone, which was yellow and embossed with an umbra of purplish black. She looked slightly crazy to Antigone as she lifted her chin stubbornly for a moment and stared back at her.

Antigone nodded, her mind beginning to skip over the possibilities for Barbara. She waved her hand sympathetically as she looked into a future of streets and jobs and people, trying to fit Barbara in, trying to give her a context. 'What about him?' she asked.

Barbara's eyes narrowed above her wounds.

'What *about* him? He's nothing to me. I don't need him to get along. I've been independent from him for years . . .'

She glared across at Antigone and she felt the waves of intensity radiating from Barbara's hesitation, as she went on: 'That's not to say I wouldn't like to . . . punish him for this . . . Good God!'

She buried her face suddenly in her hands in a sudden cry of anguish and then, to Antigone's surprise, her face emerged again just as abruptly, and she said with a kind of dead calmness, her light-blue eyes looking at nothing, unseeing: 'I think now I'd like him hanged, and then taken down at the last minute so that I could address him just before he left this world.'

Her hands were clenched into fists on the table.

'And what would you say to him?' asked Antigone.

'I would tell him that every hour of every day since he did this thing to me I had been praying that he burn in hell for ever, but that now the moment had come . . .' Barbara paused and unclenched her fists, '. . . now the sweet moment had come, such a prayer was no longer necessary, it no longer served to express my feelings for him . . .'

'You mean you would forgive him?' said Antigone, who felt her own anger rising and was about to protest.

Barbara laughed shortly.

'Those feelings could only be relieved by one thing, I would tell him, and I'd had him brought back to life for a moment to understand this, the true and certain knowledge that he was going to . . .' Antigone saw her pick up thumb and forefinger and throw a silent, delicate, invisible dart, accompanying the launch with a puff of the lips, '. . . cease to be.'

'*Brávo*!' breathed Antigone.

And it was at that moment, as they burst into laughter, their heads nodding together like two old ladies out on the balcony, that she first had the idea of sending her to Theia Soula.

Spring

Kelly sat in the *kafenéio* nursing a *frappé*, trying to get it all in proportion, The Relationship. The big R with Rog, big R of the big R. These new things about his wife that this Greek girl had told her when she came to get the suitcase had rocked her, unexpectedly, partly because she secretly felt the whole thing was kind of getting out of control anyway.

Jesus, they hadn't been *doing* anything much, since she arrived – i.e. all winter – except screw. And hell it was *boring*, that is if you wanted to travel, especially with that ape Panos around all the time. Roger had to show off to him. All that competitive stuff which she somehow got infected with. Couldn't resist it, and she found herself trailing behind the two of them as they laughed and drank and dirtyjoked their way through two or three strip clubs a week. All boys together.

Much better when Panos wasn't there, she thought. Roger could be very sweet. She'd never met anybody so obsessive about her body. It was kind of flattering, but a bit . . . well, you had to get used to it.

Their first time she hadn't told him about her little weakness. She never told anybody about it. She called it her little weakness because she didn't know what else to do with it. She told them part of it, if she had to: she had to be on top to take her pleasure. But there was more. Fact was, the only way she could do it was to pretend to herself she was strangling whoever was underneath.

She had practised it until she'd got it down to a T and a lot of the time they never knew – all she had to do was reach out with her hands, just start to reach, and then everything just . . . clicked into place. There it was. She thought of it as her little weakness because it didn't fit with any of the rest of her, which was healthy and good-humoured. Real normal. Kelly couldn't think of anyone more normal than herself. Didn't have a drink problem. Didn't have a shrink. Never *had* had one. Health foods, good exercise. Liked being in her skin . . .

She took a deep breath and stared at the man behind the bar, washing the glasses.

They were comfortable with each other because Rog liked her on top. He didn't know about the other at first but she'd gradually given it away. Her little secret.

Turned out he loved it. Used to smile, ask her with his eyes, stretch out his neck for her. She was scared to start with. Thought she might throttle him for real. But he had a tough neck, Rog. She soon learned she could really get a grip on him and it didn't matter a damn. Then she could really . . . ride up there in peace. After that, it was like the song: *Relax, don't do it, when you wanna go to it*. She didn't know where the hell he had his fingers or his cock sometimes. Didn't give a damn, either, because she found that once she'd got over that tense first one it was all plain sailing, just on and on into it. First time she'd ever known *that*. It really made a difference. Sex was a whole different ball game. At last she'd found somebody who understood her. Somebody who liked it *her* way as much as she did.

The man was looking over at her.

'No, no thanks. Nothing.' She must have been smiling out loud.

She'd always be grateful to him for that. The apartment was neutral space. They didn't need to do anything. So they ate and slept when they needed to, sometimes eating ravenously and smoking Js in the middle of the night. It was great to start with.

Then Roger had started 'developing' it. It began with her playfully saying she needed a pee and starting to get off him. He got hold of her round the waist and held her there – all dreamy like – and said:

'Let *me* have it?'

She got up off him, didn't know what to make of this. Yuck, did he really mean what she thought he meant? Then he was somehow manœuvring her over his face and his mouth and she could hear his muffled voice begging for it.

So she bared her teeth and let him have it.

Good God, there was no end to it then! She had to wash those sheets, all of them, and the mattress. No end to it. He was following her to the toilet, kneeling down by the side of her putting his hand down between her legs underneath while she took a pee. Kissing her thighs and sniffing her like a dog. Said he liked to feel it running over his hands, hot, straight from her like milk from a cow. Drink it by the pint.

In the end she managed the mechanics of it quite well. Never soaked the bed like that again. Found she could control the outflow. Dribble it out. Draw it out, tease him. Gweedy boy mustn't have everything at once, eh? Wait till gweedy boy *deserved* a drop or two. Yee . . . es.

Where had they found that bit of suede lace, the one she had tied a knot in? Couldn't remember now, but that was when things really began to get interesting for her. Started out tying it round his neck, but then they got into some new things. They pushed up the bed right into the corner of the room. Had to knock that cupboard down to do it, take it off the wall. The neighbours complained at the noise. Anyway, she liked the feeling at the beginning of pushing him, getting him up in that corner. It was beautiful! Lining up his white back between those two walls. Him whimpering, and her kneeling there behind him, breathing softly. Both of them laughing like a pair of drains, while she made the first few flicks over his white back, waist and shoulders. It was sweet. Just a few little tramlines. That was all. Couldn't describe it, it was so sweet and sharp! He insisted on doing it back to her. That was OK but, well, it just didn't compare with the other way round. That was something else. That was the best thing. Ever.

But then he wanted to bring Panos in to watch. That was where she drew the line. Hell, have that bloated reptile googling at them? No, sir! That was when it all got really boring. She really needed some fresh air.

But what were they going to do now?

She thought about all the investment she'd made for this trip after Roger had left England. She'd spent the next few months thinking about Greece. She'd begun to take out books on Greece from Richmond library and read a whole history of Macedonia. Yeah, really got into the whole thing, especially that story of Queen Olympia and the murder of King Philip II. What a woman! There was a miniature bust of her somewhere with a twisted, downturned mouth.

The part she'd been drawn to was the funny business about the spells, the Mystery cult of Samothrace. Olympia was from there, apparently, and she and Philip had spent their honeymoon on the island. How Olympia had consulted the priests on the island about the assassination and taken part in one of their ceremonies (what did they *do*?) before getting the all-clear from the auguries to kill him, at the triumphal games at Vergina, and put her son, Alexander the Great, on the throne.

Kelly had started poking around in Greek art and religion after that, all last summer till she came out in the fall, really getting into the cult of Dionysus and these weird *Kaboiroi* of Samothrace. After spending weeks staring at colour photos of the Krater of Derveni, which she pinned up all round her studio, she started making pencil sketches of the gold reliefs on the vessel, celebrations of the marriage of Dionysus and Ariadne, erotic figurines of long-bodied Maenads and Satyrs and the strange Dionysiac figure of a bearded man dancing with one sandal on.

146

What had finally really obsessed her, however, was the magnificent frieze of the Rape of Persephone in the tomb at Vergina and, in particular, the figure of Demeter mourning for her daughter.

She just *had* to make the trip. She had to go to Vergina. She just had to go to Samothrace. It was karma.

But she couldn't see Rog coming along. No way she'd drag him off to some cold island! She really needed a girlfriend she could talk to. She wished Sal was there. She liked the look of this little Greek lawyer. She reckoned they'd be about the same age. College girl, but looked OK. She really needed to spill the beans. See what she had inside her head.

She felt in her jeans pocket for the card she'd wormed out of the girl. Antigone Kara something, what's that, Karagouni, it said.

She thought she might just call her up at that. Do her good to get some of this stuff off her chest.

Kelly breathed in, and thought.

Antigone was waiting in her car at Averof.

Kelly had let drop to Antigone in the course of her monologue some titbits of information and Antigone was turning over in her mind what, if anything, she should do with them. The main one was that Panagopoulos was in frequent contact with a German who, as far as Kelly could tell, was the proprietor of a massage parlour in Paradise Street. Perhaps he wasn't the proprietor, thought Kelly. Antigone knew better; she knew from Loukas that he was the bully-boy of the establishment. He was the one they took the girls to, and he showed them his collection of pistols and instruments of torture in order to persuade them to work for the appalling rates they paid them. And secondly, that Panos and this Englishman had been hanging around quite a lot with people from DEE. Antigone thought about Yannis, but he probably wouldn't be interested in such manoeuvrings.

Now that Kelly had told her everything, much of which she'd rather not have heard, Antigone's main problem was what and how much to tell Barbara when she went up to Thessaloniki. All the signs were that Barbara had made it through the crisis and was making a new life for herself up there. Katerina liked her, and so did Theia Soula, and they were quite happy for her to stay as long as she wanted.

She drummed her fingers on the wheel: she had driven there to pick up Manos, who had told her that he wanted her to come with him 'to a ceremony'. He wouldn't say anything else. She had assumed that it was the funeral of his three-legged cat.

At last he appeared, ducking under one of the trees in the square, and jumped into the car.

'Where to?' she asked.

He was carrying a wreath of spring wild flowers mounted on a frame made from a coat hanger. Antigone noticed tall red poppies, interspersed with Roman camomile, the golden variety, bedded down on Queen Anne's lace, and studded every now and then with little blue flowers she didn't know the names of, and bound with white and yellow marguerites.

He laid it with infinite care on the back seat.

'Straight ahead, Leofóro Metaxá,' he said, chopping at the windscreen with his hand.

'Did you make it?' she asked.

He nodded. 'Picked them at dawn this morning and had them in water . . .'

'What are we celebrating?'

'A death.'

'Stop being so mysterious,' said Antigone.

'We have somebody to pick up,' he said, so solemnly that she laughed through her irritation.

At Calabria Street in Ambelókypous, where it met Evrytanias, a young man and a girl were standing. They had a similar wreath. Sophia and Apostolis.

They all drove down to a spot on the seaside road coming from the airport, one of the busiest boulevards, and parked the car up on the pavement. All the way down Antigone just listened to the way the others were discussing the police, comparing notes on surveillance and the near squeaks they had had on the night of the student elections.

Apostolis was bearded and had long, greying-black hair tied in a ribbon at the back of his head. Sophia was close-cropped and blonde, wearing jeans with holes in the knees.

They were laughing at the thought of Michael Dukakis winning the American elections and becoming President.

'Greeks really believe it,' said Apostolis. 'Do you know what the cleaning woman at Zamano said to me the other day, that in revolutionary times the Americans almost adopted the Greek language for their parliament? The motion was defeated by one vote. What a joke!'

'Really believe what?' said Antigone.

'That they're going to have an empire again,' said Apostolis.

'Dukakis is from Lesbos,' said Sophia, 'I used to know someone who knew his niece . . . rich family.'

Antigone got out of the car with them and followed to a spot on the pavement where Manos halted.

'Here,' he said.

There was nothing that Antigone could see which marked the spot as any different from any other of the intersections of pavement tiles that stretched out as far as the eye could see. She stared at the cars careening by in both directions, the noise so great they had to shout to each other.

Apostolis knelt on the pavement and Sophia handed him their dripping wreath. He laid it carefully on a tile and then stood back up again and they stared down at it, fitting perfectly like an emblem, a wet circle inside a square of dry paving-stone.

Manos was already in the centre of the boulevard when they looked up again. He halted at the first of the blaring horns and knelt on the pock-marked beige asphalt as the cars began to brake and lurch, their drivers shouting and throwing their hands in the air.

A taxi screamed to a halt behind him and the driver, leaning far out of the window and making a kind of underhand shovelling motion with his open hand, as if scooping Manos up and bulldozing him out of the way, shouted, 'Where are you going, you imbecile!'

Behind him, a queue of drivers began lurching and weaving to a halt, desperate to get by if they could see a way, all leaning out of the windows to see what was going on, banging the heels of their hands on their horns.

Manos knelt, oblivious, on the boulevard and contemplated the wreath lying in its small spreading pool of water. He stood back, as if he were in the middle of a rural cemetery, and bowed his head. On the other side of the boulevard the traffic going in the opposite direction slowed as the drivers hung out of their windows to try and see what was happening. Horns were beginning to be deafening as the cars backed up for a hundred yards now.

Antigone walked out into the road and took him by the elbow. 'Please,' she said, 'Mano, you must . . .'

It was the first time she had used his first name. She was not thinking, just acting instinctively. She looked around at the chaos of throbbing engines and irate drivers behind them and made a gesture of reconciliation. Manos did not move.

Antigone looked back at the other two who were contemplating their own wreath, equally oblivious, on the pavement. She tugged at Manos's sleeve, but he ignored her.

Doors slammed and people began marching up the boulevard on the outside lane. A bus disgorged several passengers who began gesticulating and hastening towards the scene.

'Please,' said Antigone, 'someone will call the police!'

As she looked at the wild motorists she thought it more likely that some kind of physical battle would break out before anyone said anything to anyone.

Manos stood with bowed head. She tugged again at his sleeve, but he stayed where he was. She felt most peculiar, torn between real anger at this latest prank, wanting to leave immediately and get back in her car, and drawn to stay with him in his exposed situation to see that he came to no harm and to help him get away if the police should be called. She stood, like Buridan's Ass, slightly behind him, frozen to the spot.

His body flew forward from the first push, his arm detaching itself from her gripping fingers, as he flung it in front of his face to protect himself. They were round him in a flash, shouting, kicking, and one of them bending to punch him in the face. Antigone glimpsed the expression of ferocious impatience as he waited, this man, to find a gap in Manos's flailing arms through which he could punch him. He was about sixty years of age, she estimated, collar and tie, silver hair neatly combed back. She looked down. He was standing on the wreath of flowers, his feet grinding them into the asphalt as he hopped to deliver his punches. A little stream of green from the crushed leaves began to ooze down the camber towards the gutter.

Antigone stepped forward with restraining arms.

'That's *enough*!' she shouted at them. 'I'm his lawyer, and you will be prosecuted for assault if you carry on with this . . .'

She hauled at the silver-haired man, whose locks had fallen over his panting face, and repeated herself.

The motorists had stood back for a moment, shouting what was he doing, the imbecile, disrupting the traffic in this way? Was he crazy? She got them to get him to his feet and he put one arm round her shoulders as they frog-marched him to the pavement and hurled him down against the litter bin. Apostolis and Sophia stood by their wreath looking stoically on.

The motorists stood briefly in the centre of the road, dusting off their hands and explaining to the other motorists who came

151

running up what they had done. One of them, a young man, came jumping on long legs to where Manos lay wiping his bleeding mouth against the litter bin, and cursed him in a stream, delivering an extra kick from his large, crêpe-soled, beige suede shoes.

Manos got to his feet as they marched away and started up their engines and Antigone stood by his side to watch the traffic begin to flow again, staring at the wheels passing over the wreath and breaking it up into large shapeless fragments of green, flecked with occasional red, and scattering the soggy bits of leaves across the carriageway. One section was tossed in the air over the massed bonnets so that two yellow camomile flowers, still twined, climbed briefly on an air-draught before plunging back into the roadway, to be run flat, sticking in the treads of a removal truck, Antigone saw, and carried away in the roaring mêlée as if they had never been.

Antigone and Manos watched until they could see that the road was completely empty of all trace of the wreath, and then they turned away to the car.

'OK,' said Antigone, handing Manos her handkerchief, 'would you now like to tell me what that little protest was all about?'

Apostolis and Sophia came up.

'Oh, didn't you know?' said Sophia. 'It is the place where Panagóulis at the beginning of the Junta tried to put a bomb under Papadópoulos.'

Antigone stared at Manos. She frowned.

'Wasn't that in December?'

Manos grinned. 'We haven't time to wait for the anniversary . . .'

She glared at him. 'You didn't tell me?'

He shrugged. 'You came?'

She unlocked the car and they climbed in.

'Let's get out of here,' she said.

They dropped Apostolis and Sophia off at Psychico and went

back to his flat. As they came through the door, the three-legged cat came running, tail up, and rubbed against his trouser leg.

It had survived an amputation, an infection, and a series of injections of antibiotics by Manos and his friend.

'Not only that,' said Manos, bending to pick her up and rub his unshaven chin against her nose, 'but she's hungry, aren't you, eh? Time you went on the streets again . . .'

'Aren't you going to keep her?' asked Antigone. She took off her leather jacket and tossed it on the sofa. Then she dropped down with a great heavy sigh.

'What would I do with a cat?' said Manos. 'This isn't the type you give all these fancy tins of foreign stuff to, you know.'

'What's the point of saving her if . . . ?'

'She's an alley cat, aren't you? You'll have to get back down there in the dustbins scavenging, that's what you like, isn't it?'

The cat sat back on its haunches and howled in miniature – comic, wretched, lopsided, but vociferous and strong.

'You're a survivor,' he said.

'Not without you,' said Antigone.

She didn't understand anything, she thought, as she lit a cigarette in the sunlight. Everything about Manos seemed to be a contradiction. Nothing made very much sense. He seemed to have such a strange combination of strength and vulnerability. She didn't understand what she was doing there, was she waiting for something? Some clue that would allow her to understand him? Or was it that she understood him already, but wouldn't admit it to herself? She saw again the good citizens kicking and punching him down on the road and she wondered for a moment if perhaps he had invited her in order to make a point. But he wouldn't do a thing like that – he had done this from passionate desire, not calculation.

She put in another strip of Stimorol and blew out a spume of smoke over the yellow cushions towards the dirty, sunlit window.

153

She could hear him singing in the little pantry just off the corner of the room as he boiled the coffee on the two-ring electric stove he had there. It was a Byzantine Church hymn. On the wall, there was an Ioanou cartoon of Andreas Papandreou, standing by a wall, on which he had just painted a whole barrage of slogans – such things, she saw, bitterly, as 'Americans Out' – and he is turning to his cabinet who are lined up on the pavement behind him, saying: 'A word of advice – it doesn't matter what the slogans are, it's *who wrote them* that counts!'

The squeeze box lay in the corner of the sofa, half under an Indian print cover. A guitar was propped up on the arm, over which lay a sheet of paper with some staves and notes scribbled on it. The bookshelves were full of technical books on veterinary surgery, textbooks on anatomy and physiology, Kropotkin's work and Marx's *Theses on Feuerbach*, and Manos's copy of the *Little Red Book*.

She suddenly found herself envying him the little space he had, the freedom from the clutter and the compromise of her own life. The family pressure on her. He had no phone. She thought of the phone calls she had made and answered in any one week, last week, say. Her mother alone had rung every day with some new problem or facet of the old one, with some new request that she bring this or fix that. She was tired, sometimes, of just being there. Then Loukas had rung three times. He wanted to know what she was doing in the Christos case. He wanted her to take up some other thing. He would explain the whole thing to her.

Antigone was tired of just sitting somehow in the middle, while the Government's situation seemed to get worse every day. Now there were no buses, trolleys, no trains – or unpredictable trains – Athens lay stifling and immobilised under the cloud. There was no oxygen even. Hospitals were very erratic indeed. Meanwhile the politicians shoved the issue of whether the shops would open in the afternoon back and forth. They debated the prohibition of odd and even numbers of cars from the centre of

Athens on certain days. PASOK was running into the sand, wasn't it? She felt it acutely, *É*, all right, outbreaks occurred in Greece, but it all seemed as if it was slipping away before their very eyes and she felt the frustration herself, in her own life, in the squeezes, the pressures, the constant feeling of running to keep up with the shadow of her own overstretched commitments . . . Here, in this little place, you could sit and play a chord and jot down a few notes for a song, study, go down and see your friends and listen to some rock music, and argue about politics as if you weren't on board this sinking PASOK ship . . .

He came in with the brass *kafenéio* tray and set it down on the floor where he squatted cross-legged. There was a slight ooze and a caked streak of red from the corner of his lips.

'Why did you do that?' she asked.

He shrugged. 'There are sacrifices that have to be made. Things that have to be done . . .'

'But Nikos and Spiros and I have been breaking our necks all winter putting together the defence case for these people . . .'

She was trying to justify herself. Why? For this young man? With his desultory studies, his cats, and his easy life?

But she knew it wasn't a question of that. It was something else she saw in his face. He was like those Buddhists who sat cross-legged in some square, carefully shaking over themselves the last few drops from the petrol can and, after dropping a match into the flow, placed the can calmly to one side and never moved again.

She saw there was absolutely no practical way to get on terms with his attitude to life, but she couldn't resist saying, 'If you leave your studies, you'll have to go to the army. Then you will do something for Greece!'

He handed her the little cup, stolen from the *kafenéio*, no doubt.

It was all so stupid, her being here. What did he want with her, or any woman? She stared down at the thick coffee and felt the grains on her lips as she swallowed it down. He reached over and took the squeeze box from under the cover of the sofa.

Antigone rose, bending to put the coffee cup back on the tray in front of them, when he began the introduction to some song, pulling the sides of the pentagonal instrument with his fingers carelessly half-slipped under the straps, and holding it on his lap while he stared up at her, glassy and tender over his chords.

She reached for her leather jacket. 'I have to go,' she said.

He stared up at her, his whole face appearing to open with the light of his expression, and sang:

> 'Black eyes, black eyebrows, curly black hair,
> White face like a lily and a mole on the cheek.'

'I have to go, I said.'

'Wait a moment,' he whispered passionately, looking at her all the time as he screwed the slow, minor chords out of the little instrument.

> 'Such beauty, ah my sweet flirt,
> We never met in all the world.
> My black-eyed one, because of you I've gone crazy,
> I'll die, I can't stand it, I'm half the man I was.'

Antigone turned away from him to the window, in a storm of helplessness, throwing up her hands a little way, her breath filling her throat in troubled clouds.

She was conscious of the jacket hanging over her arm; not able to move, yet wanting to do something, perform some action, anything, even to shift and clear her throat, which she thought of doing but couldn't. Instead she looked down at the creases in her jeans while he finished the song, his perfect nasal whine flying a fifth above the single top note of the squeeze box in a metal-bright harmony:

'I have hidden pain in the depths of my heart
When you look at me, my light, with your bewitching eyes.'

He had stopped. He was standing near her shoulder, his olive-coloured oval face completely open, the skin as soft as a ripe apricot's. My God, she thought, how innocently beautiful he is, even with his dirty, unshaven chin and hands hanging round the squeeze box.

Antigone did nothing to arrest the movement of the jacket as it began to slip from her arm.

The wind was driving the rain across the deserted quay. No one was in the white kiosk that said 'Tickets' and it didn't look as if anyone ever would be again. Kelly laughed. In fact, it looked as if it might lose its moorings and blow round the harbour in a minute. Where the hell was the ticket man? Who cared? She was excited, getting ready for the trip.

Well, this had to happen. She couldn't spend any more time cooped up in that God . . . *damned* apartment with him. He was a great guy and she'd miss him. They'd had a lot of laughs. Make no mistake. But it felt right.

The ride up to Thessaloniki in the Toyota had been something else. He was real mad. She told him she was going on to Samothrace without him, and it was best they split. She had to get some air. He said – well, he didn't say anything for an *hour*, for Chrissakes! – came over all heavy, y'know. Jeez, just like a kid. Started driving real fast, all the old stuff, trying to get between buses and trucks, heel of his hand on the horn, trying to get past everything on the road. She knew what was going down. So she just put her hand on his arm, just leaned over and looked him in the eye and said, 'Let me out now. Right now.' He pulled over by the side of the road. Bluff, she said. He reached over and opened the door, and gave it a push. She sat there for a moment collecting herself, put on her shades and stepped out. Goddamn bags were in the trunk. She didn't know whether he had the key or not. She stepped round the back and tugged at it, but he'd locked it all right. Damn!

She went back in the car. He was grinning, a kind of a sneery kind of a leery smile, as much as to say, 'You can't do without me you know!' Shit!

Thing was, she *did* need him. He had the Greek to help her get around easily. She was seriously interested in some of these places and he could have acted as guide for her. Like the first time she went to the Benaki Museum in Athens, he talked to that guy and they'd opened up all this fabulous stuff for her, because old Rog said she was a jewellery maker, professional thing. It was terrific – all this Islamic stuff they had in the basement, in the stores. She could go in, said the nice lady, any time she liked and they'd get it out for her to copy the designs. She filled her sketchbook with this most terrific stuff. And she wouldn't have been able to, you know, get that on her own. But . . . so what! Time comes when a gal just has to split.

Good talking to that Greek kid, Antigone; I ask you, what great names they had. Antigone. She had her head screwed on right. I mean, that asshole Panos, what a jerk, what did a guy like Roger want with him?

He's sitting there in the front seat when she gets round the side, singing that calypso: 'The more you stroke 'em, the more they like your technique!'

Well, she could do all the intro stuff for herself. It was just she didn't have the Greek like he did. Couldn't get into conversation with people like him. And that Panos. He could open doors. Some of them had – no, most of them had – some pretty unsavoury stuff behind them. Like that German guy, Pieter Paul Somebody, they brought back, and that little dark Greek girl he had in tow, and all the guys are there drinking beer. And old Rog tells her I'm a masseuse. Jeez. Then it all comes out about the massage parlour.

Oh-oh, I say, shaking my finger, I'm a *real* masseuse. Little bitch, trying to persuade me to go down to this Paradise Street and help them out. Help them out!

I mean, what is a person like Roger doing with people like that? Scummy types. Even this girl, OK she turned a trick or two when she had to and she, Kelly, could understand a thing like that once in a while. But you see it all the time, this German guy has some kind of a hold over her, a threat. She's not Rog's type at all, though he pretends they're great people and he wants to go out clubbing with them for Panos's sake.

A bad trip. Just went wrong somehow. Started off so well, until Antigone had told her about that thing with Barbara way back. If she'd known about that, that would have been that in the first place! Would it? Or was she willing to say OK, let's draw the line now, because they'd run out of gas? What's the difference? People are people, they just do things. Bad karma, though, is bad karma, and this was – man, was this – bad karma.

Kelly laughed at the rain, drew on her cigarette, barrelling away in her head to her friend Sal.

So he's sitting there like a jerk at the wheel, saying he's not going to open the trunk. Rocking back and forth and banging his hands on the wheel.

'Great,' I say, 'what am I supposed to do now?'

'Get in. You're not going anywhere,' he says in that uptight-Brit-officer kind of a way he has sometimes. When he's mad.

'Dead right,' I say. 'I'm not going without my things. I'm no Barbara, buddy boy . . .'

He doesn't like that so he takes off again. Same routine. He's aiming the Toyota like a bullet at one hundred and eighty kilometres an hour down the centre of this Greek three-laner. I shut up this time. No point if he has the cards. My time will come.

After a bit, I look at him. His face is all wet.

'What am I going to do without you?' he says.

'Aw c'mon, Rog, you're a big boy now,' I say. 'Whole big wide world out there!'

'A desert!' he says. I ask you, Sal! I hoot with laughter, looking out at all them rocks in the rain. It looks true. But I ask you – what a bullshit line. He purses up his mouth. *A desert!* Joseph Cotton stuff. Thing is, he is so fucking *weak*, just like all those characters Cotton plays.

'Look, Rog, why don't you get yourself down to Paradise Street with old Panos and get yourself a nice blowjob off that little Greek black bird, what's her name?'

'Kelly, you're so *hard*,' he says. I kind of never quite know what he means when he gets that tone. He kind of drawls and sneers.

'Look. I've told you, I'm splitting, and nothing's gonna change my mind. Understand? It don't matter whether it's here by the side of the road or when we get somewhere. I'd actually prefer Salonika to the side of the road, but if I have to . . .'

'But why?' he says for the thousand and oneth time, 'for God's sake.'

I'm rolling up a numbrero now, with my feet on the dashboard. 'Hey, Rog, knock it off. Let's get with some good sounds!'

He looks across at me. 'If that's the way you wan' it,' I say, the roach squeezed between my teeth, 'let's roll . . .'

'There are police on this stretch past Larisa,' he says. 'Put it away!'

'OK,' I say, 'but for Chrissakes, cheer up a bit,' I add, in my best British. All in the front of the mouth. Chirr-up-a-bit. Like that.

Then he's laughing. I see it. Shaking his head.

'Hey,' I shout, 'hey, that's it, man! Whoopee, my man, somethings's gonna come and say hallo to Valerie, give her all my salary! Whoo-*eee*.'

I'm relieved.

'What a girl you are,' he says, and I know I've got him. Phew!

160

So we get another couple of hundred kilometres on this. Then he makes the mistake, come to think of it maybe it wasn't a mistake at all, of putting the Stones on – 'You can't always get what you want' – and we get another outbreak of the heavies. Oh God! Another period when I can feel him all tense and backed-up in his seat. I can feel it coming through the upholstery like soundwaves. I reach over to massage his neck and he shakes me off.

Here we go again.

'You bastard!' he shouts, kind of bracing his arms to hold the wheel. 'You're just doing this to fucking torment me!'

I am not saying anything. This is truly dangerous. I am looking at the road.

Then thank God there's this road block and a lot of cops are checking people's licences and so forth. He gets out of the car and he asks somebody what it's all about. The football fans have set Larisa on fire; whole town's blazing with police and riot squads and barricades, the lot. Some doping scandal. Larisa had won the league cup for the first time in Christ knows how many years and then they go and dock four points off them because of this one player. Fans go completely wild and attack the city. Police are advising people not to go there. Airport down, everything.

'See,' he says, 'I told you not to do that thing.'

'Yeah, that was two hundred miles back . . .'

'What did I tell you?' says he.

'Hey, horseshit, Rog,' I say, but he's so pleased with himself he just goes on crowing.

Well, this gets us to Salonika. Well, not far away, to that castle up the hill, where you turn down in that dip and then up again sharp right by the sea. Then he has another attack of the mumpsies. Jeez. And so on, till we make it into the streets of Salonika. Good town by the look of it.

'Pity you won't be seeing any of it,' he says.

I agree. It's a pity. But who knows. Maybe I'll be calling in on my way back.

'When are you meeting Panos?' I ask.

'Oh, a couple of hours,' he moons. 'Stay with me till then?'

Low down. He'll try anything.

But I stay. And at least he gets me to the Kavalla station. Jeez, I'd never have made it if it hadn't been for that. They have all these different bus stations hidden away in the back streets. Different for every goddamn town, I ask you. Weird kind of a Greyhound system, I don't understand it.

Anyhow, there we are. The couple of hours pass in a café, with him trying to persuade me to go back with him and Panos and stay in Thessaloniki and me just shaking my head. Amateur dramatics again and threats and the whole boring routine. Phew, am I glad to get to this Langada Street place and on the bus and get the old Walkman on and get dear old Bonnie Raitt doing some, 'Nobody's Girl,' she says and that's about it. A whole damn winter . . .

Oh-oh, Kelly thought. What's he staring at?

She was tracing out a pattern on the tablecloth of the fish restaurant she had drifted into, lost in thought. The guy in the office had said there was a boat at five, so she had four hours to kill, while outside the rain and wind lashed the quays and bounced along the road in little needle points, whipped up into mock hurricanes of dirty white spray. She was trying to contain her excitement. There was only one boat, and she'd got it – purely by chance – she'd asked Rog to call the Port Authority for her, but there was too much shenanigans for that. She'd shimmied into the agent's office, to the amusement of the guy behind the desk who thought she was some kind of mad German. He said it was going to be real rough, but what the hell! She was going!

What was it going to be like? She hadn't a clue. She had a mental picture of a hulking mass drifting in the dark sea. And then

162

these weird *Kaboiroi* people, spirits. She just couldn't wait. She felt like a kid on Christmas morning: most important thing, what was inside the sack they brought into the dormitory in the morning at the home, whichever one it happened to be.

Oh-oh. He was coming over. Oh, *no*. She just did not need another pick-up situation, with a well-spent night at the end of it.

But at least he was young.

Kelly watched as he threaded his way between the tables and came towards hers at the entrance.

'See down there?' said Antigone, bending over the rail.

She waited for Barbara to come and look down. They could see into the lighted basement window: a bed, two very plump undressed legs and a pair of bare shoulders. A cigarette in a hand appeared in the top corner of the lighted square.

'What did I tell you? Did you see?' said Antigone, pushing on up the yard and round the corner in front of Barbara, feeling apprehensive, all bustle and *bouboulina* walk. She turned, waving her hands. 'It's a brothel,' she said. 'It's famous.'

'I'm impressed,' said Barbara as they sat down inside the taverna. 'It's the first time I've ever been in a restaurant in a brothel.'

'Well, it's not exactly "in", more "next to".'

Antigone frowned at the next table. There was a noisy group of people talking a mixture of Greek and English. Professors from Thessaloniki University, by the look of them.

'Well? Tell me your news!'

Antigone stared at Barbara while she responded. Out of her black for the first time, Barbara looked remarkably at ease with herself. No ornaments whatsoever, no rings, no bracelets. The hands folded in front of her looked red and slightly raw. Antigone took one of them casually in hers and turned it over, while Barbara talked. It was cold and damp.

163

'Just gardening,' laughed Barbara to her question, and pulled a stray flop of grey hair away from her eyes. She became serious, the smile fading as she added, 'Thank you for bringing my things. I naturally never thought I'd see them again . . .'

'Oh, it's nothing . . .' said Antigone, scanning the menu to change the subject. 'Would you like to have a look at this before we start? And then we'll see what he's got when he comes . . .'

It was a difficult problem to know how much to tell her. She had decided to wait and see what condition Barbara was in before venturing on any plan. She had been delighted when she arrived at the *réma* at Sandy Island Street after the long drive from Athens and found her in such good shape. She had taken the suitcase out of the trunk with some confidence and Barbara's reaction had been fine. She didn't need her things, she thought. She'd been living without them all this time. But it was nice to have them . . . et cetera. Naturally, there was the unspoken question about whether she had seen Roger and what reaction he had had and so on. But Barbara had not ventured anything and they had left it in the air, while Antigone talked to Theia Soula and Katerina.

She stared at the swirl of stiff, greying hair on the crown of her head as Barbara bent forward to read the Greek, knowing exactly what was at issue. Barbara would be using every scrap of information she was given as evidence.

'Thessaloniki suits you,' murmured Antigone, still trying to think how to broach this subject and how far to go into it. Her instinct was to tell her all, because she felt – she knew – Barbara trusted her implicitly.

'You went there. You saw him?' said Barbara at last, sitting back after they had ordered.

'Yes. There was someone there . . . an American woman. Did you know about her?'

Barbara looked away.

Antigone let it rest for a moment. 'This retsina's not bad,' she said.

164

Barbara nodded absently. 'Young?'

'About my age.'

Barbara smiled, worn but steady. 'It's all right,' she said, her finger playing absently over the fork in front of her, 'I knew there had to be someone. Where? When?'

'Easy, easy,' said Antigone. 'Let me tell you what I know – from the American, by the way – yes, she came to see me and talked and I told her what had happened . . .'

'I suppose she's attractive?' said Barbara, and then, with a rush, her hand straying across the table to Antigone's arm, 'I'm sorry, I . . .'

Antigone laughed softly. 'All right, I suppose. A hippie who makes jewellery . . .'

'The medallion, *of course*. I knew he had to have someone. The way he was behaving . . .'

'Anyhow, I made sure she knew everything! You know, he hadn't told her about you?'

'I can believe it!' said Barbara bitterly.

'She knows now.'

Barbara put her hands up to her face. 'Am I red?'

She wasn't red, just a bit pink and moist around the eyes.

'You know, I really have stopped thinking about all this while I've been here. There've been so many other things going on. It's strange to go back to it all now. It's like a dream. Are they . . . ?'

'Still together? I don't know. The last thing I heard she was going back to discuss the whole thing with him. But I can't think they will be together for long, judging by what she told me she had already said to him.'

'She told you quite a lot then?' said Barbara, suddenly curious.

'Volunteered it.'

'Poor you,' said Barbara leaning across again and squeezing her upper arm, 'you must be sick of this business. I'm sorry . . .'

'It's nothing. My own life's not exactly been quiet . . .'

Barbara didn't respond. She was too busy thinking of something else.

'He did it deliberately,' she said, 'to get me out. But where . . .'

'She was in England. He met her there . . .'

'Must have been when . . . I had my operation.'

'I think so.'

'*Ma, ti eídos anthrópou!*' said Barbara suddenly. What kind of a person!

'*Brávo!*' said Antigone, '*Etsi . . .*'

'Do you realise he let me think . . . ah, so that's why he was so reluctant in the autumn. I couldn't understand it,' she said to herself, 'why he was so lukewarm all of a sudden about my coming out. And then, when I saw the medallion, I knew something was going on . . . or *had* gone on, rather, because I didn't think he was still . . . it could still be going on.' She smiled to herself bitterly. 'He must have got into a panic . . . is that it?'

'Yes. She was almost on her way when you arrived.'

'On her way from? Oh, I see, England. Of course . . .'

Barbara had begun again, mining back through all the narrow tunnels of the past, looking for the tiniest nuggets of understanding. She went on doing this while Antigone sat back, answering the odd question, wondering why she didn't feel that whatever responsibilities she had in delivering this news were now absolved. It was quite the opposite, she discovered, as she watched Barbara piecing together the whys and the wherefores.

The food arrived, and they tucked in. Barbara ate heartily and talked about being able to walk along through Séich-Sou. Antigone was horrified, as Barbara described her ordeal. How she had forced herself to go through the gate.

'I . . . I couldn't do it again,' said Barbara.

'*Ah, éxeis kouráyio, korítsi mou,*' said Antigone. 'But you're foolish . . . I would never dream of doing such a thing.'

The professors were going, smiling and laughing as they went.

A slim dark lady with black eyes clapped her hand on the bespectacled Germanic-looking man strolling in front of her and said, as they passed, in a deep smoker's voice, '*Ah, Viktoráko mou . . .*'

Barbara looked at Antigone. 'You said your life had been turbulent recently?'

Antigone laughed. She thought her little remark had escaped Barbara.

'Did I?' she said.

Barbara put a forkful of *tsoutsoukáki* in her mouth and lifted her eyebrows, waiting.

Antigone felt her clarity of vision clouding as she turned her thoughts inwards. How easy it was when it was other people's lives. Somehow you could see the issues so clearly, but . . .

Barbara took a mouthful of retsina. 'Manos?'

Antigone nodded.

Barbara was silent. Antigone was aware of her, calm, expectant, full of gentleness. Then she said, 'Was this wise?'

Antigone shook her head.

They laughed.

He stood in front of her table. Very quick, buzzy, decisive, and said something in German.

Kelly shook her head, and looked out at the harbour.

Again she had the impression, from the quick lift of the hands as he talked, that he was speedy.

'I saw you on the bus,' he said, 'you know you were not sitting in the best position . . .'

What an opener.

But he turned out all right, Nikos.

'Let me explain it,' he said.

'Look,' said Kelly, looking into his wide dark eyes and pale skin, his humorously pointed nose, 'I don't need someone to

167

explain to me that I was sitting on the wrong side of the bus. Do you get that?'

But she was already smiling. He was so eager, so sincere.

He turned out OK. He was a soldier, finishing his national service, very excited, because he had twelve days to go. He was in the Intelligence Office in Thrace, based in a place she would never have heard of.

'Try me,' said Kelly.

'Soufli?'

'You're right,' she said with a grimace, 'where the hell is it?'

Then he explained to her about the river Evros, and the garrison towns there, and the way the river formed the border with Turkey. It was very tense, he said, not this nice world of archaeology. All soldiers.

'You are an archaeologist?' he asked.

Kelly smiled and preened. She was flattered.

'What makes you think that?'

'You're going to Samothraki. No one goes there at this time, unless they are an archaeologist. But, I do not know where you are from. You are not a German, I believe you now, you are not an English . . .'

Kelly was brimful of questions already. She couldn't get a word in edgeways with this guy. How did he know she was going to Samothrace?

'I watched you.' He smiled. 'I saw you go to the ticket agency.'

'You've been *following* me!'

'No, no. I too have time to kill . . .' He looked at her and smiled shyly. 'Twelve days.' And then he leaned over and said with passion, 'Twelve more days before I come out. I count the hours . . . the minutes, the seconds!' He tapped the face of his watch.

'So what are you doing here?' said Kelly, still checking this strange, appealing boy.

He recovered himself. 'I will tell you. If you will tell me,' he said.

168

'It's a deal,' said Kelly. 'You like to sit down?'

He sat. How wide apart his eyes were, she thought. Trying to get used to his face. Now he looked different from when he was standing over her. Younger.

He was from Thessaloniki but his wife was from Evvia. And guess what, he had a son of eleven days. He had been delivering a letter for an officer, in Drama.

'So important, you see, it must go by hand.'

'What's it all about?'

'I know nothing about what is in the letter.' He did a Pontius Pilate: dramatic wiping of the hands. 'All I do is give it to the man personally at the officers' club.'

'And now?'

He smiled and shrugged.

'I have a pass for a few days. They don't mind where I am because I have worked so hard . . .'

Well, well, well, thought Kelly. Imagine that.

'And you are from where? American?'

Yes, she was a kind of American, she explained. A native American.

He whistled.

'You are not an ordinary American. I have never met an Indian before.' He pointed at her wrist. 'Is this yours?'

Kelly turned her wrist over to show him the bracelet with the two triangles, one above the other. 'Yes. This top one with the point upwards is the Mountain . . .'

'And this smaller one . . . how do you say it . . . the wrong way round?'

'Upside-down,' she corrected, smiling. 'That's the Heart. D'you know the tarot?'

'The?'

He looked so completely blank that she laughed.

'*Tarrow?*' he repeated.

'Cards?'

169

His eager boy's face lit up.

'Ah, yes, I *know*.'

'Well, the Heart's the cup in the tarot pack. It's an ancient symbol . . .'

He shook his head. 'I studied tourism.'

He brightened up, holding a finger vertical. 'But I know much history. We had to study Thukidides and many others . . .'

Kelly was very amused by the way he checked his files. If he knew something, he was cock-a-hoop. If he didn't know it, he wanted to find out everything about it, his eyes grew blank, and he radiated helplessness. But when he knew something, he was very confidential, nose tapping and all that. He talked a blue streak when he got going, passing from one thing to another. She was puzzled, trying to think what it was, that expression, when he didn't know things. It was as if he were disappointed because he was almost at the point of knowing *everything*, and here was this little something else, but never mind, we'll just quickly absorb that and then . . .

Kelly asked him what he was going to do when he got out.

'I have a scheme. I want to know your opinion.'

She offered him a cigarette, and they set off round his scheme: To make his own boat, a traditional boat, a *kaike* – he knew someone who makes them – and then to make trips to the coast of Chalkidiké——

'Where?' said Kelly.

'The three *pódia*? That stick into the Aegean . . .' He waved his arm, back towards Thessaloniki.

Kelly had a sudden flash of Roger, mocking the English tourists who called it 'Halkee-deekeee'.

'To just have cushions, crates of beer, and dive over the side to swim. Small parties. Good business. Weekends. Germans.'

'Do you know Germans?'

He smiled. 'Sure I know Germans. I was there.'

'How long?'

'Seven years. In hotels, in the tourist business . . .'

'Do you like them?'

He smiled and put his head on one side.

'É, there are good and bad ones. But I don't like their way of life. They are crazy with stress. Me, I do not want this. So, I find a business to make money which does not have the stress.'

'What happens if they get drunk and fall over the side?'

He laughed. 'No, but what do you think?' he asked eagerly. 'It is a good scheme?'

Kelly opened her mouth.

'No,' he interrupted, 'they are all crazy. They work, work, work and then they get drunk to make themselves ill and guilty to work another week. It's *nevrotiká*. They are robots. Greeks are not like this . . .'

Kelly couldn't say. She didn't know many Germans. But talking of nationalities, why did Greeks hate Turks? What did he think of Turks?

He stopped. He backed off, and did some of his nose-tapping stuff. 'You haven't told me. You haven't filled up your part of the . . .'

'Bargain?'

'Yes. Now. You tell me.'

He offered her the floor. Or rather the table.

She told him she was going to Samothrace because she wanted to find out about the Mystery Cult. That she was looking for designs for her jewellery, when she got back to England. Put it down to research.

'Bravo!'

He was thoughtful. *Bravo*, he repeated under his breath with a gently absent current of self-questioning in it.

'You are . . . alone?'

'Yes.'

He smiled his eager smile. 'Bravo! I too want to go to Agion Oros . . . alone . . . to find a certain Father Barios. He is the one who has the answers to certain questions, theological things . . . I want to ask him . . .'

'What sort of questions?'

'These men are very pure. They are alone.'

'Is this the place where no women are allowed?'

'Yes.'

'I can't accept that.'

'Listen, if a man goes there he must live a simple life, getting his own food. There are two orders, the communistical order, and one which is based on solitude. These men know things, because of the way they live. They do not join the stress and the work . . .'

'The rat race?'

'Excuse me?'

How beautifully blank he was. She laughed easily, almost put her hand on his arm. 'It's an expression.'

'I want to make money for my family,' he said. 'But I have seen how they live, these Germans, and I don't want to work for anyone else. I want to do something where, É, I work in the morning and I take a siesta in the afternoon, I see my boy growing, I teach him things. I have time for this . . .'

It wasn't a neurotic energy, she thought. It was kind of good vibes she had off of him. But boy did he give out some wattage!

'I have *enthusiasmós* . . .' he said, as if trying to find out what his own character was like. 'How do you . . . ?'

'Enthusiasm,' she said.

'Of course. A Greek word.'

'Why, so it is,' said Kelly.

They laughed.

'Do you know this word, *philótimos*?'

Kelly did not.

'It means someone who wants to work, who wants to get things right? One who loves honour.'

'We don't have it,' said Kelly. The idea seemed a bit quaint to her.

'I have many questions about religion,' he said thoughtfully.

There was an easy silence.

'You like something?'

He motioned at the waiter, who went into the kitchen. A small boy appeared and came to their table.

'You like *ouzáki*?' he said to Kelly.

'Why not?' said Kelly, offering him a cigarette. He didn't smoke, but he would try one. He tapped it on the table, eyeing the boy who stood, impassive, his stomach touching the chequered tablecloth.

'*Férte más káti mezédes. Ti éxei?*'

The boy recited them with indifference.

Click, click, click. Nikos picked three.

'*Mia poikilia, kai ouzo. Ti ekei?*'

Again the indifferent catalogue of ouzos. In the end they had to have Tzsandali.

Kelly was doubtful about who was paying, and tried to share it.

'Please? I have twelve days. I insist you help me celebrate . . .'

She gave in. If that was what he wanted. But did he know it was more democratic to share?

'I invite you,' he said.

The boy came back with a slender blue bottle of ouzo and glasses, water and an oval silver tray with the *mezédes* on it. Nikos stared at the tray and there was an altercation. The boy closed his eyes, scarcely raised his eyebrows, and scarcely raised his wrists, to indicate that they hadn't got it, whatever it was. Kelly didn't even know. They watched the boy's back.

He had won.

'He's good,' said Nikos, arranging the two forks on each side of the tray and pouring out two tumblers of ouzo and a splash of water.

'*Stin yeiá mas!*'

They clinked and knocked it back. He spread his hands. 'Eat!'

'I'm kind of not . .' said Kelly.

173

'No. It is important to have food with the ouzo. It is the way we take it . . .' He had already turned and he was summoning the boy again for another bottle.

'Believe me, it is my first time to do this for a long time . . .'

What did he mean the boy was 'good'? Kelly thought he was an arrogant little s.o.b.

'No, no, he doesn't take orders. He has learnt to work his own way. Even though he doesn't bring what I want. It's good . . .'

They laughed. Kelly looked more closely at the boy when he brought the second bottle. Nikos engaged him in conversation a little, but he remained firmly within his role as the indifferent waiter.

The bottles were two and then three, slender empties, left in a row on the table.

'Eat, eat!' said Nikos, reaching over and picking up her fork. He dug in the tray and found her some paste, strongly flavoured with garlic. 'It's good.'

They laughed at her helplessness, because now they were both slightly drunk.

'Didn't answer my question about Turks,' said Kelly. Why was she asking this?

He pulled back, trying to think.

'You see, they are different from us. They are not a developed people . . . The Greek . . .' He tapped his temple repeatedly. 'He was thinking always ahead, looking up into the skies to find, *É*, the stars, always looking to develop. If the Greek conquered a territory, then it was because he wished to *develop* it . . . but the Turk, when he was over the Greek, what did he do? How did he do? He let everything be as it was, he did *nothing* . . . It was four hundred years of darkness . . .'

'C'mon,' said Kelly, 'the Greeks had slaves, they had an empire based on military conquest . . .'

But they lost it, laughing at each other.

He raised his hands. '*É*, I tried,' he said.

They were silent. Kelly wanted to laugh at nothing.

'I think we are drunk,' he said, breathing, blowing out his cheeks.

Kelly nodded. 'You just could be right.'

He looked at his watch. 'One hour to go. Listen, what you say I come with you?'

Vague alarm bells. Vague disappointment. Here we go.

'What about the army?'

'I told you . . . I have made myself so useful. They won't say anything. I have worked their computer. Put the office on-line. This officer, my boss, he is high up. The others will do as he says. If I deliver the letter, I can have a few days off, that's the monkey . . .'

What the hell was he talking about monkeys for?

He was roller-coastering, calling for the boy, making the sign of writing on a pad.

'But you haven't got a ticket?' said Kelly feebly.

Jesus, why did this always have to happen?

'No problem. I have time. I will get one now. I just pay the bill, and then you stay here while I get a ticket, and we go. Yes? What do you say?'

She looked at him.

'Twelve days!' he shouted and clapped his hands together.

'But supposing you screw it up?' said Kelly. 'It won't be twelve days, it'll be gaol . . .'

'I am not counting gaol. There will still only be twelve days!'

'But you don't know when the next boat comes back?'

'The ticket man, he will tell me. There are more boats to Alexandroúpoli than here, and it will be on my way to Evros . . .' He pulled out a wallet and carefully counted out the bill, not offering the boy a tip.

'You stay here,' he said, 'while I get a ticket. Yes?'

Kelly sat back, drunkenly, in her uncomfortable chair, the crude basketwork seat of which was cutting into her thighs through her skirt, and reached for her cigarette packet. *Go with the flow, girl*, she said as she watched his disappearing enthusiastic back, clad in its light-tan leather jacket. He felt so young. And he *would* be useful with her Greek, good for arranging things, smooth the way. And he was kind of fun . . . But damn it, this was *her* trip! Why did it always have to happen? There always seemed to be some guy there, trying to tell her what was good for her.

Where the hell was he?

She hadn't noticed her own change of mood, but he seemed to be away a long time. The boy and a fat girl of about seventeen stood in the doorway of the kitchen staring at her relentlessly, without dropping their glances or exchanging a word. At last they moved away and started pulling one another about, and laughing ritually.

Kelly was edging into moroseness by the time Nikos appeared again, bouncing between the tables.

'It's OK,' he said, holding up the ticket. 'Boat to Alexandroúpoli, Friday, so that will give me four days . . .'

He put his hands on his hips and whistled.

'I was so drunk,' he said. 'I'm not used to this!'

The restaurant looked OK again, thought Kelly, and the cloud lifted. Yeah, what the hell!

She rose, to the question in his eyes, standing over her.

They hit the squally rain and he took her arm.

'Your bag?'

Kelly groaned.

They ran back into the restaurant. There it sat on the table. Classic stuff. She felt completely light-headed. A bus went by with a single blast of the horn. They all do only one, she thought.

He took her arm again.

'All do only one,' she said aloud.

'*Whaaat?*' he shouted against the rain.

'Greek buses . . .'

He shrugged. 'We must wait till . . .' he said.

Kelly was nodding. 'I know. Till we get there,' she said.

They huddled together, penetrating beyond the customs house barrier and the deserted, official-looking white offices of the harbour authorities and followed a length of chain along the floor of the harbour, to where three people stood by motorbikes and a taxi was circling at the edge of the quay. A man in uniform stood and waved, unnecessarily, to the taxi-driver who spun his car with one idle hand on the wheel.

The black steamer, its rear end already agape, was slowly approaching. Two men stood, staring towards them, on the rear lip.

Nikos put something in her hand. 'See this,' he said.

Kelly looked down. It was his army card. It had a photo of him, passport style, and various details of a biographical nature. She noticed he was twenty-six. Younger than her, by quite a bit.

She blew the rain from under her nose. It was driving down on them, into her hair. They watched the man up on the top deck giving his instructions to the engine-room as the boat came to the slipway and ground slowly up it.

Kelly stared at the metal ramps which were dropping from the stern of the ship. There was a revving of engines and a truck bearing a load of sheep rolled off and bounced up the slipway to the harbour, accelerating away round the quayside.

The man standing at the stern beckoned and the motorcyclists kicked up. Kelly and Nikos made their way up the ramps and presented their tickets which the man tore enthusiastically in half. Kelly followed Nikos up the steep green-painted metal staircase.

'Up again,' he shouted.

They stood on the top under an orange awning, the rain and wind whipping in and lashing the deck.

Kelly was still holding on to something. She looked down. She was clutching her half-ticket and the army card, which was beginning to curl in the wet, and the ink to run. She nudged him.

'Thank you,' he said, taking the card and kissing it theatrically.

He drew back and hurled it into the air as far as it would go. It flipped upwards before dropping like a stone, as if it had mass, driven fiercely down on a squall of wind. Kelly watched it float briefly, a green patch in a grey harbour wave.

'Twelve days!' he said.

'You're crazy,' said Kelly, shaking her head, feeling her cheeks fill with a smile.

After the taverna they walked down, arm in arm, to the harbour and strolled along the esplanade towards the White Tower. Barbara held the umbrella, which squalls of wind threatened to turn inside out, and sometimes Antigone held her hand, to help steady it. They had fallen into silence, Barbara didn't know why. She was trying to think about Roger and this young American hippie. That explained a lot, but by no means all.

It felt far away, thank God, now, a kind of abstract problem of the past which could only have an abstract solution. Barbara had given up thinking about justice or redress, only too happy to sink into anonymity here in the *réma*.

The legacy, she thought, was a new world of fear which she had never experienced before. She was afraid of many things now and sometimes had to force herself out of the house in the morning. Night-time was the worst, despite the hospitality of the Greek night. She could get on the 13, or the 17 or the 37, from Triandria and go into town on her own to the movies (if Katerina didn't want to go), but it was an effort. In the cinema itself the pleasure was always tempered by the feeling there might be someone behind her. Sitting on her own, as the titles went up, she felt the nameless fever of expectation she had done when a child. What could it possibly be like? In a moment it would have begun. What would *that* be like, and so on. Intense childish excitements still belonged to her, she had discovered, but at the same time, as she bowed her head, listening idly to the conversations behind her, the back of her neck began to prickle and she hoped the light of the screen was not picking her out in any way. She couldn't bear to be in the middle of a row, and always went early so that she would get the end seat.

Even in the daylight she had noticed a different pattern to her moods. When the postman came, or Theia Soula came down with the letters, as she sometimes did, Barbara felt a nameless dread as the letter came into her hands. It was addressed to *her*! This was not just the rational fear that something had happened to Lewis or Kate, or Rachel, which she carried with her all the time, quite lightly, and accepted as part of being a mother. This was quite different, a different level of insecurity, something which flickered in broad daylight, in any situation, like a physical palpitation of the heart, sliding into her moods unbidden and corrupting any happiness she might feel, any simple spontaneity. It was like the knowledge that she was condemned, a feeling that *something was going to happen to her*, and she felt it at the oddest time, even in the middle of a laugh. One night they had all gone out to a taverna, and Apostolis had told a stupid joke he had heard that day. Barbara laughed before everyone else, because of the way he was telling it. And immediately it flickered like a tongue whispering in her mind; so that when they all erupted she found herself bewildered, dislocated.

She told herself it was natural, because she no longer lived with the presence of Roger in the back of her mind; she no longer consulted his image, even half-consciously. Now there was no one's image to consult. Only herself.

But she wasn't convinced.

The sun had set behind Mount Olympus, but there was still a huge vague blaze in the Western sky. The shuttle, OA262, the aeroplane on which she and Antigone had first met, blinked in along the shoreline, banking out into the middle of the harbour to begin its descent to the airport. Towards them along the esplanade strolled straggles of families, bearing coats and umbrellas against the rain. Two urchins were trying to heave an old anchor into the harbour, against the remonstrations of an old lady.

Barbara bent to look under Antigone's curls. She wanted to see the expression on her face. She couldn't gauge her mood, she seemed to have withdrawn into some private preoccupation all of a sudden. She could see the light falling on the set of her lips, and the firm silhouette of her pointed jaw stood out against the blaze of pinks and blues on the water.

They looked down at their feet, long ago fallen into step.

'We're a long way past the White Tower,' said Barbara.

'Never mind,' said Antigone, 'let's just . . .'

The wind snatched the rest of her phrase.

Barbara thought of the scene at the *réma* when Antigone had arrived with the suitcase. She had insisted on Barbara forsaking her black, for tonight, because tonight was special. She wouldn't take no for an answer and had bundled Barbara off into the bedroom where they went through her things in the case.

How genuinely surprised she had appeared at the beautiful clothes Barbara had, holding up the tops and skirts and dresses against her with a sigh. In the end they had chosen a turquoise and orange dress and a necklace of red wooden beads and some red court shoes. Antigone had sat on her bed, smoking impatiently while she waited for Barbara to come out of the bathroom. She had whooped and clapped when Barbara had appeared in the doorway, shy, not knowing where to put her hands, not able to stop touching her hair.

'Don't move!' she shouted, and fetched Katerina, who looked, Barbara saw for the first time, more beautiful than Antigone, in a slinky red number. Katerina and Antigone applauded, fussing her, asking her to turn round, and Barbara, who had felt positively sticky with embarrassment at the thought of shoulder-pads and the image of confidence they were supposed to project, had been

180

filled with a simple pleasure at their enthusiasm. She wobbled round on the unfamiliar heels and hiked up her skirt, for a joke, leaning in the posture of a model against the door jamb, hands wide on hips.

'*É*, you're beautiful, *korítsi mou*,' said Antigone, coming over and kissing her with a laugh on the cheek. 'It's true, Ninaki, isn't it?' she turned back and asked.

Katerina, from the bed, gravely assured her it was so.

Barbara remembered how the illusion had swept back for a moment with that sweet '*korítsi mou*', that she was not an old, chalky-boned, menopausal English thing at all, but a part of them, setting out for a bop with them on a Saturday night.

'What beautiful long legs she's got!' said Antigone with a sigh to her sister. 'I'd give *anything* for legs like that!'

And she held the backs of her own perfectly ironed jeans in mock agony as they swopped another cigarette; Katerina doing her best to convince Antigone that she was OK compared with *herself* . . .

Barbara smiled now in the dusk and squeezed Antigone's arm.

'You know what I was thinking. . . ?' said Antigone. 'How great it was to be in my home town again . . . People are different up here, you know.' She sighed. 'You know, sometimes you're set on a track in your own mind and it turns out to be quite different in reality . . .'

'Loukas?' said Barbara, guessing.

'Yes, partly, all that,' said Antigone. 'I've been talking to the women lawyers federation of Greece, recently, and those women, they're really quite something . . .'

She explained they were going to mount a campaign after Easter to try to get Sefertzis and her son out of Korudallos. The women she had been talking to made her think again about her career.

'What d'you mean?'

'Well, it doesn't have to be like it is. Some of these women had children . . . they worked part-time.'

Barbara looked at her sharply. 'This is not like you . . .'

Antigone looked away at the polluted wavelets of the gulf and took a deep breath, as if she were about to say something. Then she let it out slowly, blinking, Barbara saw, in silhouette against the lights in the water.

'Let's get a taxi,' she said.

Across the stage hung a huge red banner: EXW OLES OI VASEIS APO TEN ELLADA! All bases out of Greece!

The atmosphere was reminiscent to Barbara of an old Labour Party do in England. There were children everywhere and one hundred and fifty people sat in groups at different tables with their friends. The dancing took place on the stage, under the banner, where girls of all ages, dressed in party frocks of the most extravagant kind, twirled with each other, locked in hit-parade-dominated, mutual trances, while their parents looked on indulgently.

Antigone had found a table with some people she knew – Thessaloniki lawyers, she whispered – and plunged immediately into all kinds of discussions. It looked as if they had missed the speeches, but Barbara was just sitting there trying to read the signs, grateful for the space to get her bearings. Flanking the stage there were two more banners which read: GREECE A NUCLEAR-FREE ZONE.

She waved. Katerina was up on stage in her red dress, dancing with a small girl of about eight or nine who had white socks on and shiny black ankle-strap shoes, a heliotrope satin dress ruched at the waist with a large yellow bow at the back, and a matching yellow bow which bobbed on top of her perfect, shiny blonde hair. Katerina winked roguishly and after a minute or two, when the number was over and she and the girl had solemnly curtsied to each other, she came over and sat with Barbara.

'She tell you she was pregnant?' she said.

Barbara shook her head. 'I knew there was something,' she said.

'She's chatting up these guys to see if there might be an opening here,' said Katerina.

'Is she going to keep it?'

Katerina shrugged. 'Who knows? It's going to be a great Easter, this year. PASOK in trouble . . .'

She was just starting to reel them off, the catastrophes, when Antigone leaned over:

'Who says PASOK's in trouble? Look at all these people here, they're all PASOK people. Get up and dance, both of you!'

Katerina and Barbara drank another glass of retsina and then made their way to the stage. They turned easily together, Barbara taking the man's part.

'Is it true?' she asked. 'I mean, confirmed?'

Katerina nodded. 'God, I'd be scared.'

Barbara moved her round so that she could see over her shoulder. Antigone was tremendously animated, waving her hand at the man opposite her, who nodded continuously as she advanced some proposition, thrusting forward that pointed chin under her curls, her green PASOK scarf still tied at the throat in a loose knot, and passionately chewing her Stimorol, the cigarette between her fingers constantly knocking against the lip of the central ashtray.

Barbara turned Katerina again, first half, so that she faced the back of the stage, while Katerina waved over her shoulder to someone down at another table, and then a full turn. She saw that a man across the table from Antigone was staring at them intently. He seemed to be doodling on a piece of paper, his ear cocked at the animated conversation going on on his left, between Antigone and the man with a small goatee beard, and staring at the stage where Barbara turned Katerina easily from the waist, pump-handling her arm absent-mindedly, as she tried to think what this news could mean.

'No one else knows?'

'No.'

'She must be feeling . . . bad.'

'Terrible.'

'Is it that crazy boy?'

'Yeah.'

'But he's so young!' said Barbara with a groan. 'What is she thinking of?'

Katerina clung to her. 'I *love* this bit,' she cried, looking down at their shoes and doo-dooing to herself.

'She was trying to tell me something down at the harbour,' said Barbara.

'No sweat,' breathed Katerina. Barbara assumed she didn't mean it. But it did matter. Obviously it mattered a lot. Barbara tried to imagine what Antigone was thinking. Of course she was old enough to know how to handle this, but it was a potential disaster for her.

They threaded their way back. Katerina darted off to see her friend. Antigone gave Barbara a grimace and a smile from across the room when she sat down, assuming, Barbara saw, that Katerina had told her. The noise was now tremendous. Antigone pointed at the toilets in the corner of the room.

'Why didn't you tell me you were such a wonderful dancer?' she said, Barbara noticed, still trying to make her feel good.

'Nonsense,' said Barbara. 'I just . . . followed Katerina. I don't even know the steps.'

'Wait till afterwards,' said Antigone, 'when things really get going . . .'

Inside the toilets, they joined a small queue.

Antigone looked up at her. 'She tell you?'

Barbara nodded. 'Manos?'

'I'm trying not to think about it,' said Antigone. 'I'm much more worried about whether he's OK or not. Did you hear? The anarchists bombed the centre of Athens last night . . . It's this guy

184

Melistas' trial, a cop, who shot a fifteen-year-old boy two years ago. The anarchists have been threatening to do something for weeks. Huge demonstration, in which they bombed the OTE building in Solonos.'

The toilet door opened and out came Thekla, adjusting the waistband of her white slacks, the sling not in evidence. She looked over and came to kiss Barbara.

Introductions all round. Thekla had a woman in tow called Elsa, another unionist in a *diamanté* black evening dress and bouffant hair.

'All these beautiful women,' said Barbara, 'they turn out to be traffic engineers or something!'

'Don't you believe it,' said Antigone.

She didn't know how many had been arrested. She thought three or four. She was waiting for a call from Spiros from the office any time now, to find out whether Manos was among them.

On their way back to the table she seized Barbara's arm.

'See the guy next to the guy with the goatee beard? He keeps asking after you . . .' She went up on tiptoe and whispered, 'I think you've made a hit.'

'Who is he?' said Barbara, looking over to where he was still doing something with a pencil.

'Stathakopoulos,' she said, 'architect, I think . . .' She ground her teeth. 'My God, I wish I were in Athens right now, so I'd *know*.'

When they sat down again Antigone introduced her to Mr Stathakopoulos, who solemnly handed her a small envelope, addressed to himself. Barbara thought he was just helping her pronounce his name, but he was smiling and shaking his head through the racket all round them. He made a gesture with his fingers for her to turn it over. On the back was a sketch of herself, sideways on, obviously done at the table. It traced her bone structure in a single line of the pencil, the hair looped up slightly higher than it was in reality.

Antigone leant forward. 'Cartoonist,' she said, 'for the Thessaloniki papers . . .'

They were three hours hammering their way past Thassos in the March winds. Sitting down in the empty, elliptical bar Kelly and Nikos talked and argued the toss. They had the boat to themselves, drinking coffee and testing each other out about Samothrace. Nikos had also not been. They both knew about Mystery Cults from Elevsina. Kelly had read a bit of Eliade during her Richmond library period.

'OK,' she said, fingering her spinach pie from the little bar, 'so, what's the mystery?'

'What?' He was wide-eyed.

'As in Mystery Cult, dope,' said Kelly. 'What's the mystery of the Mystery? What do these guys *do*?'

'Sacrifices to the ethnic deities . . . ?'

'What's that mean?'

'The old religion, the fertility of the earth, so we're coming at the right time. There would be bound to be spring rites . . .'

'What *kind* of rites?'

He was puzzled. He didn't quite get her drift. She laughed.

'Well, they said the god had frozen their tongues. Once you had been initiated, you couldn't speak of what had happened . . .'

'So – what did happen?'

'Well, the usual sorts of things, I suppose: sexual initiations of various kinds, sacrifice of animals, eating of raw flesh, special prayers to Demeter, and the gods of the Underworld, Kore, Hecate, the celebration of the holy marriage between Pluto and Persephone and the union of Persephone and Demeter, the fire ritual—'

'What's that?' Kelly interrupted.

Nikos laughed. 'Hey, what is this?'

'You're Greek,' Kelly accused him through the spinach pie.

186

'I know only the story that Demeter tried to create an immortal – she put the son of one of the people at Elevsina in the fire, but she was discovered in the act and it didn't work, the boy remained a mortal . . . so there's a ritual with fire in the mysteries. They probably incinerated people . . .'

'What about the Kaboiroi?'

'They're twin ithyphallic demons . . .'

'Ithyphallic?'

'They have erect phalluses.'

'Any more? What do they *do*?'

'*É*, what d'you think?'

Kelly looked at him. He would do fine, she thought. He could get on terms with the locals, get her off to a good start, then he would be leaving. Perfect.

'Why do you really want so much to go?' he asked.

Kelly reflected, but then decided to keep her thoughts to herself. 'I told you,' she said, 'I'm looking for designs for jewellery.'

They were up on deck, staring at the grey hulk of Thassos finally receding on their right as they shifted course out into the open Aegean.

'Look!' he cried, pointing. 'Dolphins!'

Kelly rushed to the rail and hung over it, watching them roll and slide. She counted five or six blackish-silver backs.

'A good omen,' said Nikos.

They went down to the bar again and got talking to the barman about Samothrace. He told them the inhabitants spoke a dialect that no one could understand.

Kelly asked about the Kaboiroi.

'Ah,' said the man and looked at Nikos.

'Who are they?' Kelly persisted.

'The Greeks call them *Dioskouri*,' said the barman.

'You know,' said Nikos to Kelly, 'Castor and Pollux, the twins . . .'

'Hey, the Dolphin and the Octopus,' said Kelly, happily.

'They protect people at sea,' said the barman.

Nikos and Kelly sat down again with some more rum and cola.

'Now I know where I am with these Kaboiroi,' she said. 'You remember these two triangles I showed you . . . ?' She held up her wrist.

'Your bracelet,' he said.

'Well, the Mountain and the Cavern—'

'I thought you said the smaller triangle was the Heart?'

'Well, it is. But it is also the Cavern, as opposed to the Mountain. You see, when you know about how to cut stones, you know the old tradition of Solomon's seal. These twins are triangles, the one never apart from the other – by its form – but also one goes inside the other, like the Cavern goes inside the Mountain . . . and the ancient way of cutting a stone was to give it the form of Solomon's seal, one small inverted triangle inside another larger one, which then gives you four facets, each one triangular.'

Kelly took a pen out of her bag and looked round on the table. In the end she found a guide to bar snacks which had a blank space on the back in which she drew the figure. 'The small triangle stands for all forms of "littleness" and the big one for "bigness" and what the Cabbala calls the Microprosope and the Macroprosope . . .'

'Ah, Greek words.'

'Are they?' said Kelly. 'I wouldn't know . . .'

'They are,' said Nikos. 'The Little Face and the Big Face.'

'Well, stones are cut with these faces sometimes,' said Kelly. 'I've done it myself.'

'I'm lost,' said Nikos. 'I don't see what they have to do with the Kaboiroi . . .'

'Well, the twins in Hindu mythology are sometimes called "The Two Birds in the One Tree", or "The Two Who Have

Entered into the Cavern", but they are in fact not one, but two, from the point of view of eternity . . .'

Nikos threw up his hands.

Kelly laughed at herself. 'Yeah, I know. Everybody says I'm crazy when I get going . . .' she said.

'Samothraki,' said the barman, pointing through the window.

They went together and stared through the bucking porthole at the rugged saw-toothed peaks that looked as if they had newly sprung out of the heaving sea.

'My God, we have to get up on deck for this . . .' said Nikos.

They made their way past the foul-smelling old blue smokestack along a narrow passage to the prow. Kelly took the joint out of her bag and lit it in the wind.

'Moon Mountain,' she said. 'That's it. You know, if you asked me again why I wanted to come here, know what I'd say?'

Kelly took in a couple of substantial mouthfuls of smoke, whipping them back between nose and mouth and holding them down. She stared for a moment at the beige rocks in the distance. Then she let it all out in a gush of blue smoke and laughter.

'Know what I'd say?'

Nikos was giggling already. 'My God,' he said, holding up the J, 'this stuff is so . . .'

'I *know*,' said Kelly, with a big smile, so big her mouth ached. She nudged him. 'Wanna know what I'd say?'

They burst in a rain of giggles.

It was absurd. She sounded like Lauren Bacall.

'What would you say?' said Nikos and burst out laughing again.

Kelly howled. 'This could go on for . . . it could become a major occup—'

She put her hand on his arm and their heads clacked together in the wind. The joint was now a tiny shrivelled brown end. Solemnly, he extracted the last ounces and hurled it into the sea, holding his breath. He stood there looking down at her, his lungs full of the last smoke. She cocked him a wild eye that made him

189

start to laugh and forced him to breathe it all down or lose it on the wind.

They swayed, hanging on to the rail.

'Wanna?' she said again.

He nodded.

'Sure?'

He nodded.

'I wanna find the centre of the world,' said Kelly.

There was a silence, while they both became aware of the roll of the ship's deck, as if it were a telepathic secret.

Nikos cupped his lips to her ear. 'What are you going to do when you get there?'

Kelly stared at the escarpments of the island. Now she could see a tiny scatter of white buildings along the flat shoreline beneath the precipitous vertical faces of the mountains, folded one behind the other in deep rifts.

'I'll know,' she said, 'I'll know.'

The second session was a bouzouki band.

Antigone glanced across at Barbara who was talking to the man who had drawn her cartoon. She looked so much more full of confidence, as she inclined her head to take in what the man was saying, already, Antigone could see, formulating some objection, some disagreement. She could tell from her rhythm, which was familiar to her now. She glanced with satisfaction at the orange and turquoise dress with the square shoulder-pads, remembering the struggle she and Katerina had had to get her to wear anything other than her black. Dignity, she had.

She bobbed her head, looking for Katerina. She was easily visible in the red dress. At the table, she bent to whisper in her sister's ear, asking her to keep an eye on Barbara while she went out to get her phone call from Spiros.

Katerina glanced back lewdly. 'She looks as if she doesn't need an eye keeping out for her!'

190

'Oh, you know what I mean,' said Antigone. Her hand squeezed in a slight rebuke as it passed over her sister's bare shoulder.

One of the lawyers had said she could use his phone. He was one of the organisers and his office was upstairs in the same building. She sat at the large desk and sank back in the spring-backed angled office chair, waiting for Spiros to answer, an unlit cigarette between her fingers and a fresh strip of cinammon Stimorol between her lips, which she folded back slowly into her mouth with her tongue while she waited.

At last it went.

'Spiros?'

'Antigone, where are you?'

'Thessaloniki.'

'Ah-ha, bad news here, I'm afraid. Our friend Menios just rang through from the prosecutor's office—'

'And?'

'There were three arrests after the bombing . . . and your friend was one of them . . . I have the list here. Manos, Manos . . . just a minute . . .'

'Alexiou . . .' said Antigone in despair.

'Yes, that's right.'

'Charges?'

'Not known yet. You know the form . .'

'Yes. What happened?'

'Well, they were all out – about three hundred of them at the Propylaia at about six this evening, all shouting 'If Melistas gets off, the centre of Athens will burn!', and then they got down to Odos Solonos by about nine p.m. and somebody threw a Molotov cocktail into the OTE building there . . .'

'I don't understand it,' said Antigone. 'Didn't they *read* the charges against Melistas?'

'Hmm, "murder with intent, while the balance of the mind was disturbed, surpassing the bounds of self-defence . . ." '

191

'Well? Aren't those pretty good?'

'It's all pressure, though, isn't it? They're still afraid he'll get off, so they want to put as much pressure on the jury as possible. I'm sorry,' said Spiros.

Antigone sat back in the chair and looked at the framed cartoons on the wall. One of them showed Andreas Papandreou as a puppeteer tied up in his own strings, vainly trying to reach from below for the wooden cross-piece to work his own hopelessly tangled, limp, puppet-limbs.

She lit the cigarette and stared at the image, not really taking in its significance, thinking only of Manos.

It was not a surprise, of course. She had expected it all along. But now that it had come, it was a shock. Now that it had assumed depth and consequence, and she knew the kind of pain and discomfort gaol was going to be for him. She badly wanted to go back to Athens immediately that night, but decided against it, because nothing would be known for several days, and she had to make up her mind about a lot of things in between.

She didn't know whether it was Spiros or Nikos who was systematically informing on her; she suspected Nikos. Someone was keeping Loukas informed and if it was Spiros he would already know about this phone call. If it was Nikos, then perhaps she had better let him reveal himself before she played into either of their hands – and indeed those of Loukas – by trying to visit him. The police would immediately want to see her and goodness knows what Loukas would want to say to her. But she had a good idea, she thought grimly as she pulled the door of the office to, and put the key in her bag.

Actually, she was almost certain he had been wrongfully arrested if they were going to scapegoat him with having actually thrown the petrol bomb. She didn't believe Manos would have done it. It would be ironic if it was wrongful arrest, because it had got him what he wanted – martyrdom for the cause.

She walked slowly back to the hall, vaguely aware of the

rhythmical clapping and the twang of the *bouzoúki* that was getting louder with every step. What was she doing mixed up with such a crazy boy? She was relieved he hadn't got himself killed, that was at least something – he would be safe in gaol, whereas on the streets she had her doubts about him.

But there were other things to decide. What was she going to do about the baby? She had already decided that whatever decision she took about that, it would be independent of him. He could hardly look after himself, let alone her and an infant.

For now, she decided, as she pushed open the door into the crowded hall and caught a glimpse of Barbara's dress near the stage, turning and turning in time to a *zeybékiko*, her face and head momentarily shielded by the cartoonist's back, that she would follow the original plan. Tomorrow, a quick visit to the village, and hopefully to see Yannis and Elleni, and then back down to Athens the following day. She needed some time to think; even though the village, in her present state, would be an ordeal, it would at least give the enforced space to contemplate what to do.

She sat down at Barbara's table, watching the dancing, trying to take in the blow she had just received. How good-humoured the atmosphere was, she thought. Didn't everyone know that the third round of talks about the bases had been fruitless and had ended in disagreement? Why were they all so gay, and friendly with each other, when it seemed less and less likely that Andreas would be able to carry off his promise made at the elections? You only had to go outside this hall into the driving rain and you could feel the tension and despair, physically, in peoples' lives! And yet here they were, saying *mía chará*, what a long time it had been and so on . . . PASOK had drifted a long way since the autumn. Something was going wrong with the party's machinery. Even respected people like Vaso Papandreou were openly criticising the leadership, the way decisions were being made without consultation, and Yorgos, too, had even got it together to criticise his father by implication in the newspapers. Antigone knew what people were saying about Andreas, of course – that he thought like an American; they didn't forget he had been head of the American Economic Institute at Berkeley, and the prospect of his ditching the Americans was simply improbable, and yet within the ranks of the party faithful, at gatherings like this, there was a real belief that such things would happen.

She grimaced. How Yannis would crow. Here they were dancing for the removal of the bases, and there were nearly two million people out on the streets. Even the street cleaners had joined the professors at the universities and the teachers in secondary schools and the pupils. The doctors were out, the public servants, the private schools were out, even. There were no taxis, in Athens at least, and no petrol to run them anyway. There were no buses, no trolleys. The bus strike was still going on in Thessaloniki and the army trucks had been working for nearly three weeks now. Price rises went on being relentlessly announced. The external debt was ballooning. She'd even read an interview with the Englishman Tony Benn, she meant to tell Barbara about, in which Benn, who presented himself as a friend and admirer of Andreas, commented on how he was in the hands of foreign bankers. Ironically, Yannis's industry was one of the few which *wasn't* on strike!

The song came to an end and they came threading their way back to the empty table. Barbara's face was radiant, she thought, as she went in front of the cartoonist and turned back once or twice to share some remark with him or to listen to something he was saying. Once they paused in the aisle, entirely unawares, and held everyone else up behind them.

Barbara flopped down next to her with a sigh of pleasure.

'My feet!' she said in English.

They called for more retsina. Barbara was already bent forward towards the cartoonist, trying to decipher what he was saying above the racket, when the band struck into 'Synnéphiasmene Kyriaké' and everyone all round the table began to sing, leaning back into the song; Barbara looked at their lips, Antigone saw, and tried to follow the Greek lyrics, mouthing them stumblingly after the event. Antigone looked across at the cartoonist to see if he was helping her and saw that he was already scribbling on his sheet of paper and pushing it in front of Barbara, who looked across and gave her, Antigone, a quick glance and a shy smile as she began to sing from the paper:

'Cloudy Sunday, you're like my heart
That's always cloudy, Christ, and the Holy Virgin

You're a day like the one I lost my joy;
Cloudy Sunday, you make my heart bleed.'

Antigone looked around. Everyone was singing, conducted by the bouzouki player from the stage. The room was like a ship reeling blindly through the seas, the passengers in the state rooms seemingly unaware of disaster, and yet the song itself said it all.

'What an incredibly sad song!' said Barbara to Antigone's proffered ear.

Antigone smiled. 'But look around you. Look at the passion,' she said. 'Greeks love pathos.'

'When I see you rainy and I can't get a moment's peace,
You make my life black and I sigh heavily.'

It was true. She watched them, all round at different tables, lingering lovingly over this last line.

'It's just like the Welsh valleys,' said Barbara.

Antigone nodded, though she knew nothing about the Welsh valleys, wondering how much more appropriate for the Macedonian mountains the words of this song could ever get.

*

195

Things were going pretty well with the preparations. They had almost everything they needed.

Kelly was poking around in the rocks on the north shore, not far from Paliopolis. She'd been doing this for several hours. She had one half of the equation, a long thinnish cylindrical black stone, and now she was looking for the other: a large black stone which had been worn away, in the manner of a flint, until there was a circular hole in the middle of it, through which at least the nose of her cylinder would pass. Both stones had to be black, but fortunately – or maybe, she began to think, it wasn't just luck – all the stones on the beaches of Samothrace were a mottled greenish black.

They had spent the first day up at the site, getting to know the buildings and fitting them to the plans in the guidebook which was in Greek. Good job she had Nikos with her, to translate. It was hard work. They went up there on the motorbike they'd hired for the day from Kamariótissa, the harbour where the boat had landed. It had all turned out like a dream. Kelly just couldn't believe it. She had a lot of *déjà vu* fizzing around in her brain.

The site wasn't really open at this time of year, but there was a little community of people who lived around the area near the perimeter fence, including Ritsa, who occupied the workshop at the front of the building in the basement, and put potsherds together. She lived opposite, in a tent in the white cottage garden, when the weather permitted. The boys who were actually digging the site were friendly and they let them in for nothing, and Nikos had managed to get one of them, Takis, to open the museum for them, so Kelly could have a preliminary shufti at the objects. There was some pretty amazing stuff there, she thought.

The weirdest thing had been the bezel of the Kaboiroi. The most impressive bit of surviving proof that the Kaboiroi were part of the rites was the inner stone of a ring found in the later 1930s, which was circular and showed the emblem of the Kaboiroi: two snakes attached at the tails, in a reversed 'S' shape, and two stars.

When she read about this Kelly nearly went berserk. My God, how luscious! She could make a copy in clay and then work it in silver when she got back.

Takis had let them into the little museum at night and they spent several hours in there examining the cases of objects. When she came to the place where the bezel should have been, Kelly couldn't believe her eyes. There was nothing but a small round black-and-white photograph of it. Goddamn it! It turned out to have been stolen during the Second World War when the island had been occupied by Bulgarian soldiers. Kelly made a sketch all the same, issuing a formal curse against all Bulgars.

She looked up and shaded her eyes against the light with her hand, cocking an ear for the sound of the engine. Nikos had gone along the northern shore to Loutra, looking for flowers. Takis had managed to get the keys of the little tourist hotel and now they were able to bed down in a couple of rooms there. Perfect, no hanky-panky, just peace and quiet. No hot water and no kitchen facilities beyond a fridge and sink, but it was all they needed.

She thought they had almost everything, except the stones.

She had the two baskets, the one large and the one small; bread; she'd found two purple silk headscarves covered in glitter and gathering dust in the back of a little supermarket in the village at Kamariótissa. She had a piece of white muslin in her backpack for a veil. She had an egg painted one half white and one black. Nikos was supposed to pick up several ears of corn and the flowers on the bike.

She rummaged some more in the gusting wind, liking her reflection in the rock pools, humming to herself. To start with, she had felt weak from their fasting. The only thing they were allowed was a joint at night, last thing. But she seemed to gather energy rather than lose it and she hadn't been hungry once since they arrived.

The other great thing in the museum had been the frieze of the dancing girls some Frenchman had found in the 1860s. Oh boy,

197

was that weirdly beautiful! She just couldn't get it out of her head. There were two big stone tablets with eight dancing girls on each one. Their faces were in bad condition because somebody had taken it away from the site in the Byzantine period and stuck it in the wall of one of the watch-towers near the shore and all that weather had worn away a lot of the relief. The faces of most of them were gone, or looked like hags or death's-heads, but there were two girls' faces, one on each tablet, whose features were still perfect.

Kelly had stared at them in astonishment: to imagine the whole thing, each individual girl holding the next by the wrist, judging by the evidence of these two, was to know you were in the presence of a great, ruined piece of art.

The girls wore loose decorative garments that left them entirely naked behind. At the front a gathered, fringed sash hem passed between the breasts at an angle of thirty-five degrees and covered the left breast, leaving the right one entirely exposed. From this sash, at a point roughly under each breast, hung two fillets of material, loosely dangling, and in between these fillets, covering the front of the torso, hung a broad piece of material, a stomacher, which terminated in a frilled semicircle between the top of the thighs. Attached to this, on the inside, ran down another loosely-gathered piece of material, widening towards the bottom, which hung free at the front between the ankles parted in the step of the dance.

Each girl stared alternately in the opposite direction to the next whose wrist she was holding, though from the waist down their bodies all faced the same way. The guidebook said this was an archaic mode of dancing which was well-known in the early period before Christ. On their heads they wore a little frilled circle of material, gathered and tied, like the top of a jam jar, and in front of each ear dangled two more fillets of material, like pigtails.

Amongst them, one played a stringed instrument and one a

flute, and one was beating a tympanum. These last two had gone, but they had been witnessed by the Master of Ancona in Italy, in the fifteenth century.

They probably culminated in a group displaying the Holy Wedding of Kadmilos and Armonia, the Pluto and Persephone of Samothrace.

Kelly spent hours sketching these girls and she knew every detail of their posture and dress.

It looked as if they were keeping the centre of the building on their left, with a suggestion of a turn in the opposite direction. This would make their ritual polar rather than solar, unfolding anti-clockwise from the south to the east and the east to the north, moving from the Cavern to the Mountain, from the gate of the humans to the gate of the gods, like a polar masonic ritual in which the throne of Solomon is placed in the east instead of the west ... maybe because in these rites the gate of the gods is placed in the north, but faces the east, the side of light and life, and the gate of the humans is situated in the south and turned towards the west, as the side of shadow and death.

The girls that turned to the right, then, Kelly thought, were recalling the kingdom of the shades.

Kelly shifted and listened. All that was for the end of the thing anyway. She and Nikos would be going the other way. They had spent a whole day planning how it would work. The correspond-ences between the year and the day. They would go from midnight to midday, and then midday to midnight. Midnight was the winter solstice and midday the summer. Midnight was the gate of the gods, which they would return to via the gate of the humans. Every two hours was a month. The first two thirds of the year, Axiersa, the Samothracian Persephone, was above ground, and you ran through the whole cycle of spring and summer. But after the harvest, July, at four p.m. exactly, she disappeared below ground to Pluto, Axiersos, and they entered the kingdom of the shades to emerge transformed in the holy marriage of Kadmilos and Armonia at midnight again. But this time they were emerging in the blinding light of non-manifestation. And they were going to be guided by the demons, the twin earth spirits, the Kaboiroi, who governed the two gates, Capricorn and Cancer.

They were going right through death and out the other side.

Kelly stared at the stone her fingers had clasped around, and smiled at her hoisted-up skirts and bending face in the water, hair wild in the wind. She stood up, her skirts billowing wetly, the stone lying wet and very black in the palm of her hand. They might well do. She scrambled to the bank and made her way across the pebbles to where her bag was. The tip of the cylinder passed into the aperture for about three-quarters of an inch. That would do nicely. She stood and listened to the scrape of the stones.

The Yamaha was invisible, but she could hear Nikos change up and open the throttle along the coast road towards her. Good.

Kelly shaded her hand against the light and started down the road. She had scrambled up the bank from the beach and was waiting for him. There was something odd about the dot in the distance as it flashed in and out of the clumps of half-leaved trees. He seemed to be holding on to a greyish parcel while he rode – very erratically, she now saw – with one hand, the bike weaving about the road from one side to the other. Damn good there was no traffic, she thought, as she watched him swerve about and nearly fall off, wrestling to keep the parcel in position.

As he approached down the last open stretch towards her she saw what it was. Nikos was holding a bad-tempered sucking-pig, its back legs tied with string, slung across the petrol tank, while trying to keep the bike, which also seemed festooned with plants poking out of plastic bags at the back, on an even keel.

He lurched to a halt on the loose stones by the side of the road in front of her, his smile infectious.

'Jeez, I wondered what the hell . . . Where d'you get *that*?'

'Get on,' said Nikos.

As they rolled up the track to the Tourist Hotel, he told her, over his shoulder, how he had found it loose in the ravine at Loutra, just up from the baths. Two children, a German girl of about twelve and her little brother, had obligingly trapped it and were poking at it with a stick when Nikos had rolled up on the bike. It seemed to take no notice of anybody, just rooted about in the weeds by the side of the stream in the *réma*.

As it wriggled and gave a great scream Kelly smelt it and almost retched. 'Brilliant,' she said bitterly to Nikos. 'What the hell are we going to do now?'

'Help me tie the front legs up,' said Nikos, and they all rolled off the bike together, the little hog bouncing in the dust and giving off blunt squeals in threes while it thrashed about in a circle on the floor, dragging the tied back legs as it dug in at the front and tried to rise to its feet.

'Run,' said Nikos, trying to prop up the bike. 'In the kitchen drawer there's some twine . . .'

Kelly couldn't get the key in the door, but in the end she threw down her bags and forced it, ran in and snatched up the twine, still in its cellophane packet.

Kelly stared down at the animal, vaguely aware of the bike wheels spinning while Nikos was ripping open the cellophane packet. It was pale and grey, surprisingly bristly. Was it wild? Hardly pink at all.

She shook her head. 'No, no, no,' she said. 'This is wrong. Take it back!'

'Take the *laimó*,' he shouted, 'the neck! Lift it!'

Kelly's hands closed round the grey, bristly column of the neck. It felt like a leather bag fully of jelly, tough and roly-poly at once.

'Don't let it go!' shouted Nikos.

But it was desperately trying to get its snout round to where she was holding it, a snarl drawing back its lip at the side.

201

Alarmed, Kelly dropped it, and stood back, pulling her hair back out of her eyes.

'*Don't* let go!' said Nikos as it tried to fasten on his bare arm. Now he had the green twine loosely round the legs and rapidly he wound it round and crossed it over, trapping them provisionally while he let more of it out. The rate of squealing had almost doubled now, Kelly saw, and she knelt in the dust and tried to talk to it.

'. . . It's OK,' she said ridiculously.

They stood up and back, and let it thrash its way round and round on its back, continuously working its legs and biting at the string, between high squeals.

'I *said* a chicken!' said Kelly, passing her hand through her hair again in despair. 'This is too much!'

'No. It's right. Don't you know you sacrifice a pig always to Demeter?'

She looked at him. 'You trying to make a fucking monkey out of me?'

Nikos smiled a charming smile and raised his hands. 'You want it right?'

Kelly was in despair. She went into the hotel and left him there in the yard with the creature on the ground wriggling in front of him. To hell with him! What the hell is it with this Greek idiot! she was thinking. He is going to screw up the whole thing.

She had been thinking a chicken. There wouldn't be so much blood. The corpse is manageable. And you could see them poking around in those cottage gardens near the perimeter fence. You could easily buy one, or steal one without too much fuss. Easy to keep. No fuss, no bother. But a goddamn hog!

She sat at the kitchen table. Why was it always the same? She should never have teamed up with this Greek goon, he was just the same as all the rest. He wanted to take over the whole show, that's what he was doing. He kept telling her how to run her own rituals, when *she* was the one who had the idea and it was her trip,

202

not his! He had just tagged along for the fun, probably thinking he could get in her pants. Well, Mister Smarty Alecho, she had news for *him*!

Was he really trying to sabotage her ideal? Kelly got up and looked through the window. Nikos was dragging the creature off, fully trussed, towards the corner of the garden. Its squeals were audible above the crash of the sea.

After an hour he came in, panting and weary. He said he had rigged up something in the corner against the old fence. He said it had calmed down.

'Come and look.' He was proud.

She went and stood in front of it. It was lying on its side, breathing very quickly and didn't look at all happy or well.

'For God's sake, let it go!'

'No. You must do this thing right!'

'*I* said let it go. A chicken will do!'

'Look,' he said seriously, 'you can't just sacrifice a chicken because it's *convenient*. É, the gods will not be pleased!'

He was trying to make a fool out of her. She was sure of it. She stumped back into the hotel. Damn it, how had she been fool enough to land herself with this jerk! They would hear that thing squealing a mile off! The villagers.

He came in and started to wash himself in the sink. He stank of hog, his casual shoes covered in yellowish-grey excrement.

'Chicken is voodoo,' he said, running the tap. 'You can't have that.'

'But it's . . . cool,' said Kelly.

'A pig is *choiros*. Do you know what that is? It's the female sexual organ! Archaic soldiers' Greek!'

'How do you know?'

'I'm Greek. I tell you, if you sacrifice that . . .' he jerked his thumb towards the garden, 'it's equivalent to sacrificing a young girl . . .'

'But, I don't *want* to sacrifice a young girl!'

203

'Exactly. *É*, so this is a good ritual substitute . . .'

Aggressive, competitive. They were all the same. You could trust them to mess everything up.

Barbara took home the cartoon on the back of the envelope and put it on the sideboard. She propped it up against her studio-photo of her three children, which they hated, arranged in a pyramid all with their adolescent mirror-faces on, Lewis with his arms wide round his two sisters' shoulders, drawing them in so that their heads lay inclined towards his chin – the photographer had insisted – on either side. She knew Mr Stathakopoulos was keen, but she refused to give him Theia Soula's telephone number.

'*Archóntissa*,' he breathed as he left, raising the back of first one and then the other of Barbara's hands, both of which he was holding, interlaced, and kissing them lightly through his moustache.

They teased her briefly in the taxi on the way back to the Toumba, but Antigone quickly fell silent, the smile visibly wiping itself in the glow from the lights outside, as Barbara looked across at her from under her delayed-action halo of warmth. Katerina, paying no attention for a moment to her sister, flung a bare elbow over the front seat and tried to keep up the worn-out old line, but Barbara felt acutely the anguish on Antigone's profiled face. She put out a hand, raised a finger to her lips for Katerina's benefit, who immediately turned her attentions to the driver, and then dropped the hand gently, palm up, into Antigone's lap. She jerked out of her reverie of misery and Barbara felt her open palm fill with the back of Antigone's own hand: small, sinewy, dexterous, responding with a tender but absent stroking motion. Barbara felt her distress as if in physical waves.

'What is it?'

Antigone shook her head and looked out of the window.

At home, over endless cups of coffee, they got it out of her and sat around on Barbara's bed speculating about what was going to happen in a way that was, as Antigone said, futile, but which helped to share her dilemmas.

Katerina was shocked she wasn't going immediately to Athens, but Barbara could understand her caution. There were all kinds of decisions she was going to have to make, and she needed some space and time to think about them.

She shook her head. 'How could I do something like this? How *could* I!'

'Are you sure?' asked Barbara.

'Yes. Voula – you remember Voula – ' she flashed a smile, 'examined me. Five weeks.'

'You've got eight weeks to make up your mind,' said Katerina, rolling over on the bed and lighting a cigarette.

'It's not that. It's *him*. What's he going to do now?'

'Well, as you say,' said Barbara, taking the practical line, 'at least he's safe . . .'

'I mean,' said Antigone, 'what am *I* going to do with *him* if he's convicted? He'll go down for a long time . . .'

'Does it hurt?' said Katerina. 'To . . .'

They both looked at her while Barbara grimaced.

'It's excruciating,' she said, 'the most awful pain you can imagine.'

'Oh great,' said Antigone. 'Just my luck.'

Barbara was immediately ashamed that she had burst out in this way by reflex; she tried to explain that she had done so because there was so much propaganda around that made it sound as blissful as an image from an insurance company advertisment that she wanted to tell the truth. But she couldn't really find a way of digging herself out of the pit she had made and had thrown Antigone into. They all went to bed in gloom and concern for Antigone's impasse.

Antigone lingered at the door, eyes moist, tongue bitter.

'It's not easy, you know, to make a mess of your career and

your life in a single afternoon. You must give me credit for that!'

Barbara murmured she was sorry, hardly knowing what to say. She did not want to counsel her to abort. It was Antigone's decision. But it came, the question she had been dreading:

'What would *you* do?'

Barbara laughed incredulously, desperately trying to fend off a straight answer. 'Me?' She gestured to her rumpled flannel nightdress, the red knees just showing under the hem.

But Antigone insisted. 'I want to know.'

Oh well, thought Barbara, what are friends for but to ignore.

'I'd ditch him – he's not your type at all and it would be a disaster to prolong your relationship – this *thing* with him – and I would have an abortion as soon as possible on the grounds that your career comes first! But, I mean, it's not my business to . . .'

Antigone smiled, the lipstick cracking on her full bottom lip. 'It's logical,' she said, 'but somehow not very Greek.'

Kelly had explained everything as best she could to Nikos. The little mysteries started at twelve midnight and went on until midday the following day. They were divided into what you say, what you do, and what you show. This period is known as the ascendant period and even kids can take part. It's a general introduction and dedication to the great gods.

'Kind of getting acquainted,' said Kelly brightly.

'So long?' said Nikos.

'Well, we'll be following the sun round through the six months of the year from the winter solstice, Capricorn, to the summer solstice, Cancer, which is June, the centre of the year. It's two hours for every month; so six o'clock in the morning will be the spring equinox . . .'

'And what happens after twelve noon?'

'Well, that's when the fun really starts – the great Mysteries, which are completely secret . . .'

'Why not just skip these little ones. It's so long!' complained Nikos, 'and it will be cold up there!'

'Because you can't do the big stuff until you're initiated . . . there's some Greek words here . . . help me out will you?' They spelt out together: '*teleté*' and '*epopteía*'.

'So what happens?'

Kelly swallowed in excitement. 'Well, for the first period, Kore is still on earth. I mean, that's all the way from midnight to four in the afternoon, because this represents the two thirds of the year when she's up above. The crops are sown by the spring equinox, that's six tomorrow morning, when we'll have a ritual representation of that, and harvested by the end of July, or beginning of August, that's four o'clock tomorrow afternoon—'

'Wait a minute,' Nikos went to the window, 'I think I hear our friend . . .'

He went outside and listened.

'I'm just nervous,' he said. 'You know you have to be careful! Have to look after him . . .' He sat down. 'Carry on.'

'Well, then we have the descent into the underworld. Because this represents the rape of Persephone. She has to go down and be with Pluto until midnight when she comes up again at the winter solstice in a blaze of glory. This is called the descending phase.'

'How are we going to do that?'

Kelly held up her little Russian doll, the smallest of her set.

'This is Grade A White Lightning. Made by a friend of mine in California, so I know it's good stuff. I am going to drop this at exactly four . . .'

'You?'

'Yeah, only me, I'm afraid. We have to have somebody straight on that site. It's too dangerous. You'll have to be my priest and helper for this journey. Now, it says on this pillar thing – column, whatever – they found outside that you can't go in unless you're initiated. Neither you nor I are initiated?'

'Is?'

'What?'

'*Is* initiated. It's grammar . . .'

'No. no. We don't say that in English.'

'It's ungrammatical . . .'

'I don't know anything about that. I'm trying to tell you about this difficulty we have to overcome, Nikos . . .'

'So we must get someone else, mmm, how you say it, third person?'

'Third party?'

'That's it!'

'That's not it.'

'Or, *É*, what? We go home . . .'

'No. We initiate each other. I'll be priest to you, and you to me. Get it?'

'But who can be first?'

'What?'

'Who will be the first priest?'

'Whoever wants. Personally I thought I——'

'No. I mean how can . . . *É*, how can either of us?' He threw up his hands and scratched his head.

'What are you talking about? The priest just listens while the other one does the responses, right?'

'The priest isn't initiated?'

Kelly looked away. He was just making *trouble* here. That kind of sarcastic tone of voice.

'You are trying to make trouble?' she said suspiciously.

Nikos was looking sceptical. Kelly thought maybe he wanted to back out.

'Oh please, Nick,' she gushed at him as best she could, kissing him on the cheek. 'It's my big chance to get straight with the great gods . . . Look, if you feel excluded, we'll do the whole thing over the following night for you, I promise!'

Nikos sighed. 'It's not that. I have to get the boat back to Alexandroupoli and rejoin my unit. I can't stay that long . . .'

'We only have time for one shot?'

'We only have time for one shot.'

'Too bad,' breathed Kelly.

She looked at him. Jeez, he couldn't be trying to back out, could he? Was it the mention of acid?

'Niko,' she put her hand on his arm, 'I've come a long way for this, believe me; help me, please?'

He looked at the sea, a bleak grey-green, raging now in a heavy swell beyond the kitchen window. 'You know, there are soldiers on this island. We're not far from Turkey. The army's here. There's a garrison somewhere up beyond Chora. If anything goes wrong . . .'

'Nick, it won't go wrong. You can always run for it and leave me to take my chances, anyway.'

'What, completely stoned . . . ?'

'I'm a nut,' she shrugged, 'American nut who doesn't speak properly.'

He was hesitating.

'What about our friend?'

'What about him?'

'What if he squeals?'

'We'll put some nice sleeping pills in his mash, so he's real groggy when the time comes?'

Nikos laughed. 'He will be stoned too.'

Kelly smiled. 'That's right. We'll all be stoned, except you. You can have a ritual J, but nothing more. Otherwise, I'll never come up at the end of the day, but I'll be stuck in Hades . . .'

'Isn't that a risk anyway?'

'Maybe. But much smaller with you there to guide me. And do the final honours . . .' She smiled meaningfully. 'Know what I mean? Nikos, I *have* to do this. I have to dedicate my jewellery to the great gods. Krishna has to give way to Arjuna, has to enter the dark, so that it can become light again.' She grabbed his arm. 'Think of what it must be like to live without fear of death, Nick!

That's what this means for me. If I can go through this I'll never be afraid of dying . . .'

'But what for?'

'Nikos, don't you wanna be *fearless*?'

Nikos shook his head. 'No,' he said. 'Someone who is really without fear is . . . stupid.'

'Well, I don't agree and I wanna make my peace with the great gods right away. Oh, Nick, please, you must do this for me!'

Nikos looked at her and she wondered for a moment. They seemed to be standing on the brink. She was striding up and down, waving her cigarette.

'I want this,' said Kelly in a tense, tear-filled voice that thrilled up from her belly, 'more than I have ever wanted anything.'

She thought of Ruth Windcloud, arms pumping, running towards her, with that last frown on her face.

'OK, OK,' said Nikos, 'calm yourself. Have some coffee, water, orange juice. Something.'

Kelly took a deep breath and bowed her head. 'Thank you, Niko. I owe you. OK?'

'Sure,' said Nikos. He didn't really understand. But what the hell?

They sat down at the Formica table to plan the rest of the ceremony.

Nikos was puzzled. 'It's the drugs,' he said. 'Why do you need them? Me – I want to go to Agion Oros. There is a particular Father I want to see there. I shall ask him about certain theological matters. I shall live simply there with the Fathers for a few days. I shall ingest nothing but simply food. And I shall come away refreshed and informed about what I must do in life. I don't need drugs.'

'Can *I* go to Agion Oros?' she asked sarcastically.

'No, of course not. But that doesn't mean—'

'I'm a woman!' she said. 'Cybele, Hecate, Demeter, Axiersa, Persephone. These are my people!'

Nikos smiled sweetly all of a sudden and broke into song in Greek:

> 'The Mother of Alexander
> Went looking for witches under the moon . . .'

Kelly didn't follow and had to have it translated. 'Hey, so you're into that too!'

'Sure,' said Nikos, 'you've heard of our Olympia?'

'Quite a mother,' said Kelly, not listening, getting out her notebooks and spreading out her ringback binder, leafing through the pages of sketches and diagrams of the site, of the solstices and equinoxes and the phases of the moon, the signs of the zodiac, and the emblems of the Kaboiroi.

'Hmm . . . now look.' She traced her way through the labyrinth of biro scribble, black underscored with red, until she found what she was looking for. He had better have this now. 'You have to remember these. These are the ritual sayings that occur at the various states while we're up there. We'll drink and pour libations, while we recite these . . .'

They worked at remembering them, practising together, solemnly intoning in the kitchen of the Tourist Hotel:

'Earth shows burning desire for lofty Sky
Passionate desire to be one
When the celestial spouse lets fall his rain
Earth grows big and gets green shoots
For the animals, and the fruits of Demeter for the humans,
The apple ripens on the bough through this marriage with moistness
So, it too, is caused by me,
Zurinthia Aphrodite!'

211

This was the hymn that kicked it all off at midnight, the first of the *legómena*, the things that are said.

'*Zurinthia*?' said Nikos. 'That's not Greek. What is it?'

'I got it out of some book or other. Couldn't tell you.'

'Is this correct? What happens if you offend these queens of the dead?'

Kelly looked at him and slowly bared her white strong teeth. 'They tear you to bits,' she said.

They stared at each other for a moment across the table and then Nikos crossed himself.

Kelly laughed. 'I'm kidding. I think you have to stay in Hades.'

'Where's Hades?'

'Nowhere. It's a series of rooms you're not allowed in. You have to stay for eternity in the hallway.'

Barbara crossed the road under the electricity cable and went up in the lift to call on Theia Soula. The old lady had said she wanted to get some *chorta*, some greenery, and she had brought two plastic bags with her from the drawer in which she kept, tightly crammed, more flattened plastic bags than Barbara had ever seen, carefully smoothed into layers of her recent life.

Theia Soula, the spirit of the *réma*, planted her bow legs wide and talked in a high shout, hoicking up one wool-covered knee under her black dress to counterbalance the slope of Sandy Island Street, and dug herself in for some gossip. Individuals approached her like ships, manœuvring inevitably alongside and docking in whatever space the street allowed. They bumped into the postman on the grass by the side of the *réma*, who, backside in the air, postbag abandoned for the present, was clutching his own plastic bag, on the same search for greenery. They discussed the price of things as they poked in the bank, Barbara not quite sure what she was looking for, but too self-conscious to say, like a child: 'Is that it?'

Theia Soula asked about the postman's cousin, the one who had the Swedish wife and had gone to live in America. Was he doing all right abroad? His mother seemed to have plenty of money, if he didn't mind her saying so? When were the children coming back to learn their Greek? Two other people, temporarily aground outside the *kaféneio*, had cruised into stationary positions on the opposite side of the road and were shouting contributions to the conversation, together with someone sitting on a chair outside the electrical shop. A peacock screeched regularly from behind the fan of trees, and the clouds bowled in the wind over the top of the Toumba above them.

As she did her share of poking, Barbara stood back from the scene, so strange, and so familiar at once. She asked herself, as she took her trial leaves over to Theia Soula and had them brusquely identified, which ingredients of the scene made for familiarity and which for alienness, and she couldn't really find a way of separating them. She looked at the spaces between them all – there was something unfamiliar about this. They were very large, and no one seemed to worry about shouting above the noise of the traffic that poured into town down Konitsis Street and rumbled immediately round them, descending from Triandria. A man stared from the doorway by the wood depot on the corner of Sandy Island Street. A woman beating a carpet she had hung over the railings of her balcony shared the disposition of people dotted about the street – their curiously halted, becalmed attitudes. Even the action of carpet-beating, despite the woman's energy, was performed with quick glances back inside her opened balcony door at something, her strokes no more than a contemplative thrash.

Barbara was standing in the middle of the marshy grass listening to the steady interrogations of Theia Soula, when she became aware of the car turning in from the street with a lurch, and then slowing down to walking pace, as if the driver were looking for an address. She couldn't see the person at the wheel because of the reflections of the trees and sky scrolling up the

213

windscreen and side window. Everyone broke off and simply stared at it: the three people across the road, the two women on the balcony – the one even stopping beating her carpet altogether – and even Theia Soula herself broke off a question that was an answer, and stared in a mixture of alertness and curiosity.

Barbara was still mentally pulled back from the scene, her plastic bag at her side, forgotten. There was complete silence by the time the car actually stopped and the driver opened the door and stepped out. He stood staring for a moment over the roof of the car, all around, and then he waved.

Everyone turned and stared at her.

Barbara heard Theia Soula say, 'É, *korítsi mou*, he's looking for *you* . . .' and tried to recall her floating faculties from the clouds and the wind and the figures placed at intervals in the street, as in a painting, to the sudden force-lines of purpose that had entered the scene.

It was Mr Stathakopoulos, she saw.

Barbara felt like a teenager, standing in the grass with the half-filled plastic bag, painfully aware that everyone was guardedly resuming the conversation, now that this new subject had entered their ambience. She put her hand to her forehead and frowned against the light, launched, abruptly, into the centre of this event, her mind empty of all resource.

They were twisting and turning in a clash of wills. If only she could get *out* there in free fall.

She managed to get him to stop looking out of the window at that fucking animal every five minutes and sit down at the kitchen table. To concentrate on the itinerary and help her work it out. She'd written it all down – all the stages, and all the things they needed at each stage – and she wanted to go over it with him and make sure he knew what to do and what to expect. But also she needed to check the guidebook and only he knew what was in there because it was in Greek. Goddamn place, dug out by the

214

Americans, and the guidebook written by the University of New York archaeological department, and there was no copy in any language but Greek! So she needed him to check the buildings with her.

'Now look, here's how we go. At midnight, we start at the whatdyacallit—'

'The *Anáktoron*. The – how do you say?'

'The Palace. OK, now here's the building. Here. Number twenty-three, OK?'

Nikos was murmuring. He half got out of his chair.

'Niko, I need you here! We can't do this if you are going to be worrying about that goddamn hog all the time!'

She wondered what was the matter with him. Maybe he was a frustrated hog-farmer or something.

She put her hand on his arm. 'Niko,' she snapped her fingers, 'wooee, Niko? You missed your vocation, buddy boy!'

She passed him a cigarette. He waved it aside and pulled out some Stimorol from his pocket.

'OK, now, Niko, pay attention. There used to be a great torch outside the main door of the building. Snake's head in bronze with the fire in the open mouth and the body twisted round the stem.'

'A caduceus?'

'What?' Always interrupting.

'The wand of Hermes? With two snakes?'

'Hey, that's real neat. Yeah, Kadmilos, he's Hermes up here. Anyhow, it's the Kaboiroi . . .'

'Why only one?'

'Niko, we are never going to get through this. Because one snake is always two! Remember the emblem: two joined at the tail with two stars, right?'

'Worms . . .' he said with a laugh.

'Anyhow, we are then going, having drunk the sick—'

'The what? Oh, the *cyceon*. OK, that's a mixture of barley water and wine, isn't it?'

'Let me take care of that. Then we say the poem outside the main door. The hymn of Aphrodite Zurinthia. Then we go in and sit in the main hall. Now look, there is a little room here at the end of the palace and a door. See that, remember what it is for?'

Nikos stared at the diagram, helpfully provided by the archaeological department of New York in 1978. Kelly waved her finger, trying to attract his attention.

'Remember, it said there were . . . Oh, Niko' – she whistled satirically – '. . . two big bronze statues of the Kaboiroi – here – guarding the entrance to this little room with their hands and their . . . things *raised* . . . First thing is we have to get ourselves initiated, both of us, outside, then we go into the main hall and you are going to pour a libation to the Great Mother and we'll offer a three-breasted effigy to her which I have made . . . and we'll pour libations to Kadmilos. There was another big whatdyacallit—'

'Ithyphallic?'

'One of those statues of him in the main hall. There is a pit in the corner of the main hall: see this little circle on the diagram?'

Nikos was nodding, but she could see his mind wasn't on it.

'It's just like going to church,' he said absently.

'These are only the little Mysteries . . .'

'How long does all this take?'

'These stages will each be performed every two hours when the month changes.'

'You mean we have to wait *two hours* outside the door of this place? Can I take a book?'

'Yes. No. Then when we have sacrificed to the great gods at the pit, we get to go into the hall at the end of the room, the inner sanctum of the Kaboiroi. There we will pour a libation to Dardanus and Aetiom.'

'These guys are not Greek. Who are they?'

'Search me,' said Kelly, 'I'm just going by the book.'

'They are from Asia Minor.'

'OK. Then we're going to do the . . .'

'Sacrifice?'

'Yeah, the chicken.'

'How do we do that?'

'You cut its head off and pour the juices over me in the pit, OK?'

'But we haven't got a chicken.'

'We get one from up the track, right?'

'We are going to be very popular if we steal—'

'We'll *buy* one, OK? Anyway, what about that thing outside? Whatever . . . Then we'll roast it, and eat it, OK? It's only you who thinks of stealing . . .'

'That's a found object. *You* said steal one, I remember . . .'

'Just a manner of speaking. It has to be alive when we do this, that's all. I don't care how you get it, but you're in charge of the chicken, right?'

'This is like being in the army.'

'Niko, we have to have some order in all this. Otherwise we'll both be so drunk and stoned, we'll just flop on the ground and go into a coma, for Chrissakes. It's all in the interests of managing intoxication . . . so we don't make any mistakes.'

'Buy a chicken off them?'

'I will do it if you—'

'If I'm chicken! Hah ha ha . . . Hey, that's good, don't you think?'

'Greek humour being English? Very funny. Ah, what we also need are the magnetic rings we wear for the strength of the Mother of the Rocks . . . Oh *God*.' Kelly wailed and put her head in her hands. 'I forgot them! And they had the magnets in that village shop . . .'

Nikos smiled and put his hand on her arm. 'It's OK,' he said, 'it's not a German coach party. Relax.'

'But we have to have everything *right*.'

'Hey. Have some coffee. I'll make it . . .'

He got up. His eyes, she saw, on the window. Damn that hog.

How were they doing? She looked at her watch. It was six o'clock already. They only had a few hours and they would be 'on'. She felt as if she were doing a show.

Kelly thought she would go into the bedroom and meditate for twenty minutes. She really needed to relax. This was nerveracking.

'I have to go out and look at him,' said Nikos.

Fine, fine, let him go.

'Don't forget the chicken,' she heard herself call, like a suburban housewife, as he went out of the door.

Kelly squatted on the end of her bed. She tried to get into her meditation but she couldn't get beyond first base. What happened after the chicken? Then she went and sat on the altar thing in the middle of the room while all the initiates stared at her, and the priest asked her if she had done anything. Then she declared the things she had done with the two baskets. And then what? She was asked if she wanted to show something. Then they went out of the building and round the paths with the lantern, to impersonate the Great Mother looking for her lost daughter, Persephone, and they wound all round the building of Arsinoë and the Sacred Temple, because Arsinoë had a daughter whom she lost, and that's why she built that round thing there, to the Great Mother. And then they came back into the *Anáktoron* and the priest asked her if she had anything to show. Then she had to show an ear of corn, and she could take her place amongst the initiated. By then it would be twelve noon.

It was all so goddamn complicated. Had she got it right? And that was only the little Mysteries, the first bit.

What was she getting herself so all fired up about?

He came striding across the grass from the car towards her like someone in a movie towards the camera.

'I didn't recognise you,' he said.

218

Barbara's heart was thumping unpleasantly. She raised the plastic bag and let it drop. Her hair. God, how awful.

She looked across at Theia Soula, who was making that circular movement of the hand which seemed to mean 'Nothing human alienates me', and heaving on each leg to get her feet out of the grass.

'Hallo,' he said with a smile. His hand extended, coming towards her. She raised her hand into his, and slipped into some kind of social gear at last, relieved to find the mechanism working.

'*Yeia sas*,' said Barbara automatically. His eyes came at her like a sheet of blue, a very nice shade of blue she had to admit, like an almost sapphire patch of sky glimpsed through the walnut furniture of his domed forehead and healthy cheeks. His hand was warm and soft.

He rattled off something interrogative in Greek that she didn't understand.

'I'm sorry,' said Barbara in English, feeling foolish.

'I said, are you enjoying this kind weather at last?'

'Yes.'

'You are working, I see. I shall not steal your time . . .'

'Come and be introduced,' said Barbara. She turned and clutched at his arm, finding contact somewhere just above the elbow, dragging him over to where Theia Soula was bent over fishing in the grass.

'Theia Soula, may I introduce Mr Stathakopoulos . . .'

He was excellent with the old lady, meeting unflinching and unfazed the frank appreciation of her gaze. She spoke little, and stood off from him, assessing every detail of his clothes and attitude. It was impossible for Barbara to tell what she thought of him.

'I've come to ask you something. Would you perhaps like a coffee or something? Or is there somewhere, even, we could walk?'

Barbara glanced up at the Toumba.

'Yes, let's,' she said, giving the bag to Theia Soula to empty into hers and explaining that she was just going to take a walk with Mr Stathakopoulos.

'*Aide, korítsi mou, yeiá sas*,' said Theia Soula and made a small ushering motion.

They climbed the steep bank between the small home-made shacks built like irregular post-war English prefabs into the side of the Toumba, their breath beginning to blow alternately in the silence.

'You know why I didn't recognise you?'

Barbara was blank. She couldn't think why he should or shouldn't.

'For a moment, I thought you were a Greek woman.'

'Ah, my clothes, yes. I'm sorry, I'm not . . .'

Barbara looked down at her rumpled black skirt and the black tights that ran down into her black shoes.

'Don't apologise! Why do you say you are sorry?'

'It's a habit. I'm sorry.' She laughed. 'There I go again . . .'

They paused while he looked around.

'Interesting. I am here all my life and I don't know this area at all. Here is a stranger leading me through the back streets of my own town . . .'

'We mustn't go too far,' said Barbara to herself.

They stared down at Sandy Island Street below them. Theia Soula and all the rest of the people had disappeared. The chair outside the electrical shop was empty.

'Can we get up?' he asked, turning towards the mound. 'There must be a wonderful view . . .'

'Yes. It's not easy, but there's a path towards the end of the street on the right that will take us up.'

He too looked different from the night at the bases' dance. He looked older in casual clothes. His mustard-coloured sports shirt beneath his jacket, his grey terylene trousers and his Italian slip-ons should have made him younger, but curiously they had the opposite effect. He was tanned and healthy-looking, but not young. Barbara was relieved.

They turned up into the track and scrambled, laughing about old bones and pulling one another up, to the top, where they stood in the wind looking at the view: at the back, the Fortress, Séich-Sou and the Seven Towers, and in the front the bay strewn with cargo ships, and to the side of them, the White Tower and a section of the empty promenade.

'Ah, o . . . o . . . 0!

'*Ómorphi Thessaloníke* . . .' he sang, into the wind, sweet and easy. '*Ta mayiká sou vráthia nostalyó.*'

'I am nostalgic for your magic nights,' said Barbara. 'What is it?'

'An old song, I don't remember,' he said. He glanced around and they sat down for a little on the coarse grass that blew in the wind, apparently just beneath the scudding white clouds.

He pulled out a stalk and chewed on it, talking about the excavations that had started in a half-hearted kind of way on top of the mound.

'There are objects in the museum, you know, from this place. I believe they have been inside from below, from the street . . . You know, by the bus stop, where there's a kind of depression in the side of the bank?'

'Why don't they dig it properly?' asked Barbara.

'Usual thing. No money.'

Barbara sat up, her legs under her, skirt pulled over them. She tore at the grass while she talked, and thought.

Mr Stathakopoulos had done his Ph.D. in Paris. He loved France and spoke fluent French. His two children had been to Paris many times and he wanted to make sure that they were Francophone. Delphini was eleven and her brother, Agamemnon – Menios for short – was nine. They called him 'Poulpe' – octopus – because he was so much arms and legs.

Barbara laughed.

'You will like them,' he said, his gaze catching her in mid-laugh, her mouth soft and open.

Barbara drew breath and snatched at another piece of grass, looking down at the mess of stalks in her hand.

'And your wife?'

He sighed.

'She died. Two years I nursed her. We all loved her very much.'

'What was it?' Barbara asked. He was not bitter, she thought.

'Cancer, of course.'

'I'm sorry,' she said, and then felt a fool as he gazed at her again.

'Don't be. She knew everything. She was beautiful and brave, a real fighter.'

Barbara was silent.

'I feel she's with me. We all do. Even poor Poulpe. We discussed it. Life must go on, do you understand?'

Barbara never quite knew what people were asking her in Greek when they asked if she understood. It really meant 'I hope you see what I mean'. She looked at the wind sweeping across the top of the Toumba flattening the grass, lifting the hem of her skirt, insistently.

'And you?' he said, putting his head back to look at her.

The wind was also lifting the hair round the small bald patch in the middle of his head. His voice was a rich tenor, full of inflections and shades. His walnut colours made him seem strong and healthy and alive. Barbara had never really put into words what had happened to her in the last six months and now she found it surprisingly easy, when the time came, to deposit these secrets in exchange for his own story. He exclaimed at a certain point: '*Ma, Panagiá mou!*' What distress!' She stared at him while she talked about her life here, the language school, the Toumba, Antigone and Theia Soula, her Greek lessons and what it all meant to her.

222

Forgotten until then, the thin vein of fear pulsed in, as he sighed, lying back on one elbow, and took her hand in his.

'It seems we both know misfortune.'

She got up, shaking the straws from her black skirts and pulling that awful flopping lock of greying hair of hers against the wind as she stared meaninglessly at the dusk that was settling over the bay, waiting for him to rise.

'Do we go on?' he said.

'Yes, let's.'

Why did she say that? Why not go back when he had given her the opportunity? Barbara didn't know anything. She was all right with him, she told herself, she just didn't want him to touch her.

They scrambled down again towards the lane that ran by the side of the Toumba. Gallantly, but humorously, he held her under the elbow, at arm's length, a conscious parody, she thought, as she said primly, 'I can manage, thanks!' and then regretted it, as she slid on some loose stones and cried 'Whoops!' between her teeth.

Up the steep street towards Krioneri they walked, their talk varying back to the bases' dance and the state of Greek politics. Vangelis – he insisted on her calling him that, but privately she always thought of him as Mr Stathakopoulos – discoursed on the bloated construction industry and the failure of PASOK to invest.

'They throw money at things,' he said, 'and, of course, they get it wrong . . .' He sighed. 'You know, they haven't really managed to create an industrial class beyond the old power blocks between the big fish – the shipping millionaires, they easily avoid PASOK's restrictions by flying under another flag – and the petty bourgeois self-employed small businessmen in goods and services . . .' He gestured round him at the basements. The one opposite, labelled PETALOUDES, seemed to fit the bill.

They went over and stood looking down into the basement where two men sat at a table, one sewing on a machine and the other doing the accounts. In the window stood four cages full of various linnets and canaries trilling in the dusk.

'Brothers probably,' he said. He walked on. 'Ah, traditional Greece! Will it ever change?'

'Do you want it to?' she asked.

'Of course. Somehow there has to be a bridge between big business and these people . . .'

'The young haven't come through yet,' said Barbara. 'Have patience. PASOK's educational reforms haven't had time to work. But look at my friend Antigone, for example, she's a PASOK person . . .'

'A PASOKzou?'

'Yes, and she's the very product of their policies. I'd trust her and her like with the future any day . . .'

'But it's a mess! My kids have done nothing this year, they've hardly been to school at all. Now we don't even know whether Delphine' – he used the French intonation – 'will do exams or not. She doesn't read. She's involved with all the strikes and union activity at her school . . . but . . . what about her education?'

'It's good for her. It's all part of her education!'

Barbara stopped, passionately, in the middle of the street. She told him then about her own children who had been to a small comprehensive school and all the rows that were under way in England about whether the Sixties' philosophies were of any good at all. It was *true*, they couldn't spell, she argued with a laugh, but they knew their politics. They had a sense of the social world.

'I believe in the old methods,' he said firmly. 'I agree with whoever thinks you have to be rigid to begin with. I ask you, how can you learn a language in the beginning without such rigidity? *É*, it's built in to the whole process . . .'

'I know you all believe that here. My teachers keep shouting at me not to *think*! It's incredible how antiquated the methods are here.'

'Yes, everything by heart. But it's *good* . . .'

'Not *necessarily* . . .'

Off they went in the dusk, leaning together and bumping shoulders and then walking apart, as they constructed argument and counter-argument, fishing for examples, running their hands over the railings between the buildings, stepping off the pavement and pulling each other back as a big green tricycle carrying window frames almost sliced them in half.

As they turned and came down the hill again towards the Toumba, a gloom settled over them. Michael Dukakis had just lost the Democratic Primaries in Michigan.

'Greeks are always optimistic, you know. Everybody here really thought maybe they would get a foot in the White House.'

He turned to her, his face glowing in the lights from the shops.

'Barbara, I came to ask you something,' he said, as they came within sight of Sandy Island Street and Barbara smelt the familiar smell of drains. They paused on the corner and stared down into the *réma*, at the roof of the shack, the tiles weighted down with stones and Katerina's bike propped against the wall underneath the stovepipe chimney that poked out above its saddle. They were playing backgammon and watching TV in the dusty *kafenéio* across the road.

'I want to invite you to my house, to meet Delphine and Poulpe. Will you come? We can have a meal?'

Barbara stepped back. 'I . . .' she said.

He waited. Eager, but patient.

You can't. You can't.

'I'd love to,' she said, smiling across at him in the dark, the dread tight round her heart.

*

She had her feet in the cold water and her head felt really spaced out. They couldn't sleep, either of them.

'Do you think the tide's going in or out?'

'In,' said Nikos, his voice muffled under the elbows that supported his head.

'Yeah, I think it's coming in too. Be up over your shoes if you go to sleep . . .'

'No, *in*.' He sat up. 'In . . .' and shooed it out to the horizon.

Kelly looked at him, bleary. 'Oh – get it. Well, that's *out* where I'm coming from.'

'Well, we say, goes *in* . . .'

'Yeah, but you were speaking English, for Chrissakes, Niko . . . How d'you expect me to know?'

'It's more logical. Think about it. The sea goes in, meaning into *itself* . . .'

'Jesus,' said Kelly, 'that's real twisted, man. The sea goes *out* from the land, from where we are – see? Look at the thing!'

'See the sea? Hah ha!'

'Oh, my God . . .'

'There you go again, you Westerners. It's your ego interfering. You can only measure it from where you are. Whereas we scientific Greeks, we measure it objectively. We let it have its own life . . .'

'That is really, really weird,' said Kelly turning herself over, away from him. 'You mean it's going out when it's coming up the beach over my . . . ? Wow, that is so . . . fucking—'

'We have it in our language,' said Nikos, as if it were a kind of bag that Greeks carry around with them, into which they put meanings.

'For Chrissakes,' said Kelly, 'so do we . . .'

'Ours is older. It's more scientific. Yours is primitive . . . anthropomorphic . . .'

'Anyhow, it's tideless.'

'No.'

'Yah,' she jeered, 'almost.'

But she was pleased about how it had gone last night. First half. They were both initiates now. Second session, the big stuff, could begin tomorrow noon.

Her head kept going on and going on. Couldn't stop it. She heard the plop of the waves on the big stones as if they were made of treacle, or some heavy viscous material.

'*Teleté* and that pop-thing . . .'

'You wh—?' said Nikos.

'Oh sorry, just thinking aloud. What's the name of that final ritual again?'

'*Epopteía.*'

'Why the hell is it I can remember the one and not the other?'

He was silent.

'You cold?'

It was cold up there on the site. Real cold. She wondered what they did in the old days. Lit plenty of fires, she guessed. They must have needed a lot of extras to do whole companies of people. Whole buildings full of sacrificial animals, stinking and lowing, rows of feasting tables. She started to laugh. She imagined them all stretched in the *stóa* like a dorm one hundred yards long. Jeez, must have been like a Jehovah's Witness conference to organise all that. Little men with togas and name-tabs on their chests. Stand, sit, go here, use the path there, kneel. Toilet and drains must have been something else. Big forty-hole stone privies with a run-off into the *réma* to take it all down to the sea. The harbour. Or maybe connected up with the town sewer somehow. Armies of women, you can bet, baking and roasting stuff round the clock. And people selling trinkets, ritual statues all over the place, racketeers. Place must have been like Disneyland. Huge. Teeming with people. Boats coming in every day. Docking right up near the temples. Nice and convenient. Silted up now.

Most of it was OK. Nikos muffed his lines a couple of times and she'd had to put him right. But most of it was OK. The bit where

227

they went looking for Kore was great, she thought. And that first dedication of her jewellery and the dedication to the Kaboiroi. Getting into that inner room. She could just *see* those two huge bronze statues with the erect phalluses and the hands in that strange position. The only bit she didn't like was getting down in that pit and waiting for him to do the chicken. It took him for ever to get through the neck and it was real smelly crouching down there. She listened out for the knife-scrape on the stones. Good she'd taken the top off her dress because there was a lot more blood coming down out of that flapping thing than she'd thought. Plastered in her hair. And when they changed round he was covered in it too. The thing was still running when she got up and did Nikos. Christ, she thought she'd never be warm again. Ice-cold body and all those little quick hot drops like candle wax all over her shoulders.

Didn't feel like eating it somehow, but once he'd plucked it she supposed it would be just like any other chicken. In the old days they'd have roasted it right there and then. If that. Maybe torn it apart raw.

But the wine they poured eased it all a bit. She never felt drunk in the ordinary sense of the word, though they must have got through some booze during the course of the twelve hours.

She felt like she once had after a French country wedding. You didn't know whether to go to the toilet, close your eyes, stay awake, walk, lie down. You just didn't know what to do with yourself.

She looked up behind them to the coast road to check the bike was still there.

Nikos's leg jumped in relaxation like a dog's.

It had been fun at the *tavernoúla* in the garden and now they were twisting and turning their way through the narrow streets down to Mr Stathakopoulos's – Vangelis's – house.

Barbara thought his kids had the perfect mixture of boldness and shyness. Delphine was held in a perfect crystal – she was adolescent, she had entered the tunnel yet she refused to let it disturb her.

Barbara glanced sidelong at her. She was talking easily about what the Union was trying to achieve, the problem of grading in schools and the new grading system which Tritsis, the Education Minister, was trying to force on them. Barbara could see the presence of the mother in her, calm and strong in her manner. She was going to need it, Barbara thought. She looked at her perfect skin and thought of the sweating ravages of self-doubt and hormonal imbalance that were soon to beset her. But for the moment she had the easy fluency of a child and the dignity of an adult, all in one beautiful, contradictory form. Barbara thought she couldn't have learnt that from her father, Vangelis, whose basic trick was to tease about everything, and then get serious. Over dinner they had talked about horoscopes and characters and names, and he had teased Delphine about being a female monster in ancient Greece, the dolphin. Delphine was a Capricorn. Her horoscope told her not to get angry in her efforts to persuade people of her own positon, because this was a time when she had to learn to approach others with delicacy.

'*Anoisia*!' she shouted at her father. 'Rubbish, Dad!'

There was a pause, as she remembered.

'Sorry, Dad. I have to learn to approach with discretion your sensitive points. It says so in my horoscope.'

Poulpe was a complete gaggle of arms and legs. He was dreadfully clumsy and managed to knock a glass of water over Barbara's cream trousers which she had just had dry-cleaned. He flushed and stood by the corner of the table staring at her flouncing efforts with the *pezéta* to dry herself. She put out a hand, and he looked away, his flush deepening. 'It's only water. It's nothing,' she said.

Vangelis was severe and silent.

'Dad . . . I . . . I—'

'Just look out next time, OK?'

'*Nai*,' said Poulpe, adjusting his spectacles and running round the table like an aeroplane.

Barbara discovered during this conversation that she herself was a medieval Italian saint.

'Oh, I always thought I was a bearded lady.'

Delphine laughed. Vangelis looked puzzled.

'Bárbaros, Dad.'

'Oh.'

'Don't you think of me as a barbarian?'

Delphine looked keenly from one to the other as Vangelis leaned forward over the little silver trays and said softly: 'You are very at home with us.'

And when they were leaving the taverna, Poulpe came unexpectedly of his own free will to help her down the steps before running off into the darkness, arms extended. A sudden moment of shy grace, in which he formally held her hand sideways, in gallant style, and pointed out to her the unevenness of the white steps down from the garden.

'Amazing!' said Vangelis as they set off down the steep slope away from the lights into a well of darkness. He held his arm crooked for Barbara to put her hand through. 'Careful here,' he explained, 'there are no pavements and the road is rather uneven . . .'

'It's his horoscope,' said Delphine in the dark on the other side. 'He's a Leo and it says he mustn't show to people that he underestimates them but that he simply wishes to express himself . . .'

There was a crash from the bottom of the street. Somewhere in the darkness.

'Look what you're doing, Poulpe!' said Vangelis and detached himself to go on ahead.

Delphine put up her hand and whispered in Barbara's ear.

'Watch this!'

Vangelis ran off into the dark.

A moment later there was a peal of laughter from Poulpe.

When Barbara and Delphine caught them up they were still laughing. Poulpe had an infectious laugh, completely uninhibited. In his mirth he had dropped his hands, Barbara could see. In profile against the lamp at the crossroads his mouth hung open in helpless glee.

'Lies!' he shouted, pointing at his father who shrugged ruefully. Poulpe started to honk infectiously, laughing as if he had a klaxon in his throat, in long single bursts, like a chesty cough. In the gaps they all laughed at him, standing round on the corner of the street under the light. And of course he tried to keep it going and went right over the top and lay down on the ground and had to be picked up and shushed.

Then he ran on again.

But suddenly, after a street or two, he appeared again and asked his father for the keys. He wanted to run on and open the apartment for them.

Vangelis gave them to him and he disappeared.

'He's a character,' said Barbara. 'I like him.'

'Yes, he has a sense of humour.'

'Sometimes I wish he didn't,' said Delphine. 'Especially in the mornings . . .'

And they went on to explain the morning practical jokes which Poulpe just couldn't resist trying to play, even though they both knew exactly what he was going to do. Barbara explained about the English institution of Ellisdons and the 'black-face soap' that used to be advertised in the paper and they laughed, and said that was just him.

When they drew near the apartment, they put their hands on Barbara's arm to restrain her.

'Now you're going to get the chance to find out what his jokes are like,' said Delphine.

They counselled her that she must go on into the flat through the open door, nonchalantly, as if nothing was happening, and she must say, 'I don't know where Poulpe's gone. I can't see him at all.' This was the standard procedure. Then she would hear a giggle.

'I understand,' said Barbara, and stepped out of the lift first.

The hallway of the apartment really was pitch-dark and she paused, suddenly unsure, putting out her hand but feeling nothing.

She felt her feet on the marble floor land with surprise, as if at any moment she would step out on to nothing. She could hear the boy's breathing now, but not where he was. She opened her mouth to speak and nothing came. It was a dry void. Where were the others? She couldn't hear them. Behind her somewhere, quietly waiting. She was rooted to the spot, unable to proceed further and incapable of turning back to them for support. She heard the boy breathing through his nose, and a draught raise the curtains somewhere. Otherwise nothing. She tried again to speak, but was too preoccupied with what had happened to her feet. She pushed one forward again and stood. And then one more and it stepped right on to something large and soft and jelly-like.

Barbara screamed, and staggered, as a pair of hands closed round her ankle.

The light snapped on.

'Ah, you spoiled the joke!' said Poulpe from the floor. He was lying in the middle of the expanse of marble.

The others came up from behind.

'You didn't *do* it properly!' he said to Barbara and walked off to his room.

'I'm sorry,' she said to Vangelis. 'I'm such a goose these days!'

'I get scared too sometimes,' said Delphine. 'It's better if you keep talking and pretending aloud you can't see him, and then he laughs and you can figure out where he is . . .'

They sat her down and gave her a drink of whisky. Delphine

said she was going to bed and kissed her. Barbara hugged her close and said thank you.

Vangelis poured himself a drink and sat comfortably in the armchair opposite. He said he would drive her home in a few minutes.

They were silent.

She looked around, to distract herself from the pumping of her heart. A photo of them all, variously entwined around a seated dark-haired figure, sat on the bookshelves in the corner of the room, together with two separate photos of the children, arms at their sides, staring direct into the camera, details from some group pictures which had been enlarged and cut off. Pouple's ears were enormous and he looked tiny.

The apartment was full of very old-fashioned things. Lace everywhere. Old dark furniture.

'Not Rania's or my taste. It's my mother's apartment,' said Vangelis.

'Is she . . . ?' said Barbara.

'Oh, very much alive,' said Vangelis. 'I couldn't manage these two on my own!'

He explained it was a temporary arrangement. He was having a house built in town which he had designed himself.

'We won't have to be camping with my mother much longer,' he said.

Now Barbara noticed a lot of other framed photographs at the other end of the room, on the wall.

'Barbara,' said Vangelis, leaning forward to place the empty glass on the shiny coffee table, 'I want to ask you something.'

'Yes?' she said, finding it suddenly very interesting to tilt and slosh the centimetres of whisky round in her glass.

'We have a house in Chalkidiké. The children and I would love you to come and spend Easter there with us. Will you come?'

Mentally, Barbara's cheeks blew out. She looked up, euphoric with relief.

'I . . . I can't think of anything nicer,' she said.

'But you have plans?' said Vangelis. 'I quite understand.' He waited, generously, she thought, to let his escape clause sink in.

'It is, of course, very short notice,' she heard him say, with a sigh, as he got up.

'It's not that,' she heard herself say as if she were sitting by her own side on the sofa, 'I'm . . . I don't know if I'm ready for . . .'

She stammered out the clichés about needing her own space and placed them carefully, her cards, on the table between her anxious face, which had begun to twitch somewhere round the mouth, and his grave, concerned, watchful stare.

His hands asked her to stand. Barbara felt as if she were being crushed in a vice padded with velvet. He touched her lightly on the elbow, helping to draw her to her feet as she started to rise from the sofa.

His eyes flickered once, almost-sapphires in their walnut case of forehead and temples, and his lips unpicked themselves in a gentle smile. He was shorter than her, she realised, by about an inch.

'My mother will be there. She will cook for us. She is an excellent cook, if you like traditional Greek food . . .' He bent and picked up his car keys. 'Just give it some thought,' he said.

Barbara said she would give it some thought.

All the way to the Toumba, they drove in silence. He pulled in off Konitsis Street and they rolled, the tyres crackling on the gravel of Sandy Island Street, up to the grass verge above the shack. Barbara thanked him and opened the door.

He smiled across at her.

'Well,' he said, 'did you give it some thought?'

They stood and stared at one another amongst all the mothers with their sons, and the husbands and wives making their friendly racket of embraces and happy talk. She had brought him some *tsouréki*, and a magazine about drugs and pharmacology. The guy at the desk took the *tsouréki*, absurdly, and examined it. Unwrapped, he handed it back to her.

'How have you been?'

He looked thinner than usual and there were great dark shadows under his eyes. He didn't answer beyond just nodding.

'I was up in Thessaloniki. I heard about it from someone.'

'Two of the kids in here have killed themselves quite recently . . .' He said this without any intonation.

'Why?'

He threw up his hands. 'What can you do?' he said. 'There's quite a lot of people in here without trial, waiting . . .'

'I know.'

'Gets on peoples' nerves . . .'

'Manos, tell me what happened. I've been worrying about you . . .'

'I didn't throw the Molotov . . .'

Antigone sighed. His face looked pinched and unshaven, grey prison shade. She tried not to be angry, but she felt a brief rise in her internal temperature.

'Of course not . . .' She half turned away from him, watching the other people holding hands and leaning forward to each other eagerly.

'I told you this would happen. I warned you . . .'

'And what will happen now, tell me that, *mágissa*?'

'We shall have to wait and see. They'll hold you and gather information . . .' She ignored the irony and reached out for his hand. 'Listen, I've got something to tell you . . .'

But he was already into one of his rants about the state machine, raising his hand in the peoples' salute and shouting:

> '*Ótan oi mbátsoi skotósoun ta paidiá sas*
> *Tóte tha byéite ap' ta kloubiá sas!*'

235

(When the cops have killed your children
Then you'll come out of your cage!)

It's you who's in the cage, she thought, but knew it wouldn't
do any good at all to say it aloud. It would only provoke him. He
had the aspect of someone who had been recently brainwashed. If
so, he had brainwashed himself.

'Listen to me,' she said again.

'What did you come for? Shouldn't you be seeing your client?'

'Don't, Manos. Please, I want to . . .'

She stood back and looked at him, not knowing how to
interrupt his bluster, but feeling that he must know, and she must
know his reaction.

'I'm pregnant,' she said quietly.

He smiled broadly, and put his hand out to her.

She waited.

'That's good,' he said.

'Good for whom?' said Antigone.

'Just good. A little *moraki*.'

He smiled all around. She saw that he would announce to his
fellow prisoners when he went back into the cells that he was a
father.

They were standing there, on either side of the barrier, their
hands clasped. He asked her several questions about when and
how had she found out and so on, which she answered in a daze, a
daze caused by the detachment from him that she was beginning
to feel. She had always said, from the beginning, that she would
have the baby independently of him. His capacity to imagine her
situation was willing, she saw, but limited. He had no idea what
this meant for her.

He put his hand through the bars.

'Let me feel you,' he said.

Antigone placed her stomach against his hand, laughing.

'There's nothing to feel. Yet.'

236

'I want to feel him,' said Manos.

Antigone laughed again.

'How d'you know it's a son?'

'It is. I know it is.'

'How can you know?'

'Sometimes you just do . . . You wait till he starts kicking. You'll see I'm right.'

Her face must have clouded. She was looking for something else.

'I'm not sure when you—'

'Oh, don't worry about me. They'll have to let me go. I haven't done anything . . .'

'Manos, the fact is . . . I . . . don't think I can—'

'Yes, you can wait.' He caressed her hand with his dirty nails, sure, telepathically, of the end of her sentence.

'Go through with it,' she said.

'You can, you can.' He patted her without change of tone, not taking in, she could see, what had been said.

'You understand?' she said. 'There are many pressures. My career. My family. It's wrong timing for me . . .'

He stared at her, following her expressions through the bars, attentive now.

'You mean, you don't *want* him?'

She saw that he had no idea of the kind of compromises she was used to making every day of her life. He was indignant.

'Our son?'

'I don't want to talk about this now. I just want you to trust me to understand the position I'm in. I have people dependent on me, Manos. My sisters, my job is paying for their education. You know it is. If I were to have this baby I would have to give up everything to do it . . . It isn't rational. I'm going to let everyone down. I can't do that.'

'And what about us? Me?'

'Don't do that!'

237

'Well?'

'Don't, I say!'

He turned away in exasperation. 'You come here,' he said, 'you threaten me with killing my son while I'm in here! Don't you have any courage, or respect for me?'

He raised his voice. She saw the guard, behind the pillar at his desk, look round the concrete support to see what was going on.

'Please don't, Manos . . .'

He was silent, kicking the base of the bars over and over again.

She folded her arms, ready for a tirade.

'Don't you realise how cruel this is?' he said suddenly. 'Why didn't you just get rid of him? No need to tell me. Why come here and torment me like this? It's crazy . . .'

She found herself unprepared for this.

'I know what it is,' he looked at her with scorn, 'you've already decided to do this and you just want me to help you feel better about it! So everything's nice, just like it was!'

'No, that's not it.' She unfolded her arms and let them hang at her sides, like an actress stuck for a gesture, as his words struck home. *It is partly true*, she said to herself.

'Bourgeois cowardice!'

'I've tried to explain, Mano . . .'

'Look at Sefertzis, she's got a child and she's in here . . .'

'She's hardly a role model. We're all trying to get her out. She should never have been imprisoned, but . . . no, it's just that I felt you should know about this before things went any further.'

'Don't give me all that democracy stuff!'

She had recovered herself now.

'It's a simple moral right,' she said. 'You should know.'

'Perhaps it would have been easier not to tell me. Now what am I supposed to think? Am I supposed to go way into my stinking cell and think: I'm glad I helped her to decide to kill my son? It was a sound moral procedure!'

'If you can't be realistic then think of me for once! Why should

238

my career be ruined, just because we both did something? The reason I've come to tell you is you're involved as well, not just me!'

'But you have all the power. You can do what you want. I'm stuck here. I don't know what you expect me to say, but I tell you, I'm not having it. I want my son. D'you hear me, I want my son!'

The guard was looking at them again. The woman next door turned to them and said through her teeth: 'Shut it. You'll get us all thrown out!'

'Mano, listen to me . . .'

'You've got my son! I want him!'

'Listen, the fact that you're in here is irrelevant. It has no bearing on what we did. You weren't in gaol then . . .'

'You'd let him live if I wasn't in here?'

'Mano, don't play the lawyer with me!'

'Well, don't play the lawyer with *me*!'

'I *am* a lawyer, remember?'

'You're just defending your property rights!'

'What nonsense!' said Antigone. 'This is a moral argument, not a political one! And I insist that you understand my position as a woman with a career. Can't you think beyond your own slogans, your own little world, to the situation of someone else?'

'You talk about what I believe as if it were just inside my own head, but you know what this world is like. You just haven't the courage to face the position you've put yourself in. You've crossed the line, *korítsi mou*, whether you like it or not. If I weren't in here, I'd be saying exactly the same things to you. I wouldn't be any different. So why do you say my being here's a separate thing? I'm in here because of what I believe!'

'I'm vulnerable, I tell you. It's my right to let you know this. You should have already thought about it. Why do you assume I'll want to have it?

'Because you've created it!'

239

'Aren't you responsible?'

'Of course!' He squared up and took a deep breath. 'I'm willing to——'

'Responsible to *me*?'

'No more than you are to yourself!'

'I don't understand that!' She was shaking her head.

'You've done something. You must acknowledge that.'

'I do acknowledge it. But I haven't done it alone. You are also involved.'

'It's *me* that *wants* him!'

'No. Listen. Because you are involved you have a responsibility to me . . .'

'But what about your responsibility to *me*? You seem to forget that——'

'I am the person who would be having this child. I'm the one who would have to give everything up. You can't support me! And why *should* you? You're not ready to be a father. I accept that. I wouldn't dream of asking you, Mano, to change your life . . .'

He flashed with pride: 'I can work!'

She shook her head again: 'No. It's ridiculous. Then you would learn the bitter way what compromise is . . . I don't want you on those terms!'

'You come here to dictate terms to me!'

'I can't do it, Mano. I appreciate your pride and your honour are involved, but that's no basis for me to——'

'You are making a laughing-stock out of me,' he said bitterly, and walked away.

The guards at the door in the back of the room came forward and took him, unnecessarily, by the arms. Without turning his head he disappeared through a door set into the back wall.

At about eleven she heard the noise of a car through the window. A blue Ford pick-up swung with violence into the compound of the Tourist Hotel and a guy came over to the back door. Kelly couldn't make head nor tail of what he was saying, but he kept gesturing towards the pig which was digging around fairly peacefully behind the piece of galvanised iron in the corner of the yard.

The man had a couple of teeth missing. He was grizzled and stocky. She heard 'Loutra' and '*Astynomía*' which made all too much sense: Loutra was where Nikos had found it and the other word meant police. He wore a stained blue shirt and his bandy legs had irrevocably shaped the ancient pair of filthy Levi's which hung on them.

He advanced on to the threshold, reaching out for her and beckoning towards the truck.

Kelly shrunk back. Where the hell was Niko? This pig business was going to fuck up everything. They were in deep shit with that animal from the first, she knew it.

Kelly waved her arms at the man and pointed at the inside of the hotel. In reply, he crossed his two forearms at the elbow like a pair of shears and made a sudden gesture that strongly conveyed the impression of decapitation.

They heard the noise of the bike coming up the track and they were obliged to stand there, the man's body still facing her but his head turned towards the sound, waiting impatiently while it buzzed and faded behind the trees, then emerged into hearing again. It bounced and turned into the short drive, faded completely round the side of the building and finally appeared, swinging into the yard, Nikos loaded up with candles and wine and flowers in the basket they had strapped for him on the back. He hauled it up on its spike with one expert heave backwards as the engine died.

Kelly explained that their friend had come for his pig, and he seemed to want to transport them both with it off to the police station. He was emitting rhetorical questions like threats as he and Nikos approached each other, Nikos beginning to do the same. Kelly went over to the bike and freed the basket from its rubber octopus bands. Firmly ignoring the yelling, she carried the basket into the kitchen.

She had checked all the items, candles, oil for the paraffin lamp they had found in the cupboard in the Tourist Hotel and the wine she was decanting from its plastic container, when Nikos appeared.

'Well?'

'It's all fixed . . .' He held up his hands, palms towards her.

'*What's* all fixed?'

'The pig. We can have it. I've done a deal with him, Mr Tsakalis. He says he won't go to the police . . .'

Kelly laughed. 'You Greeks! How d'you manage that?'

Nikos was rubbing his hands. 'Just a little – er—'

'Hey, I smell a rat . . .'

'There is a little something we have to do for him in return . . .'

'Come on, Niko,' said Kelly, 'spit it out!'

'Well, the idea is he lets us have the pig and we pay for it by working just a week in his restaurant in Loutra . . .'

'What?'

'Yes, it's pre-season, so the work shouldn't be too heavy . . .'

'What's this "we", Niko? I thought you said you were going back to join your unit?'

'I am.'

'So it's not "we" who'll be doing all this not very heavy work, it's *me*!'

'Well, yes, but it's not heavy . . .'

'What kind of work, Niko?'

'Oh, waitressing, bit of dishwashing maybe . . .'

Kelly sat down with a thump. 'Jeez, that is just wonderful!'

'We have no choice. He's mad. He'll take us both to the police and then we'll be in bad trouble. It was the only thing I could think of at the time . . .'

242

'Tell me something: does he think we're *both* coming to work for him?'

'He does . . .'

'So I'm going to have to turn up and absorb this guy's wrath?'

'You could blame it on me. You could say I've run out on you . . .'

'I never wanted that damn pig in on this. Now I've got to go and labour in some shit kitchen and wait table for a *week* to pay for it?'

'Ah, yes, unfortunately it may not just be a week, if I'm not there . . .'

'You mean he'll double my time?' Kelly ran a hand through her hair and lit a cigarette. 'Jesus Christ, I cannot believe this!'

Nikos looked at his watch. 'It's a quarter to twelve . . .'

'Oh my God,' said Kelly in a monotone, 'we're late. We must leave *now*. Oh no . . . I'm not dressed . . .'

'I'll get his tether on,' said Nikos, smiling at her like an imbecile. 'We'll have to talk about this later . . .'

'You bet your sweet life!' said Kelly, ripping the stems of the daisies apart and pinching them at double quick speed with her thumbnail. 'We surely will, Mister Nicholas!'

Kelly was dressed in white, the chicken stains washed out with partial success, her tiny pancake of white gauze threatening to blow right away from the crown of her head in the wind, her fillets gusting about wildly. She had the various vessels and the books in her deep shoulder bag, the candles and the paraffin lamp, the stones and the ears of corn. In her hand she carried a plastic container, like a petrol can, full of wine. Dragging the pig by the rope and resisting its every attempt to pry in the verges of the track, Nikos told her to go ahead and start without him. She looked at her Mickey Mouse watch and saw that it was noon

243

already, the sun high behind a fuzz of clouds. She was furious.

This time she could simply come over the bridge and in through the gate and down the little path past the kiosk. The lads were on a dig up in the Byzantine section up to the north-west. Thank the Lord they didn't have to get the hog over the fence like they had the chicken! Kelly hurried to the starting point which was the Holy Rock.

Nikos arrived and hastily moved himself into position. He had tethered the pig somewhere up on the north-eastern side, where there was some vegetation for it to snout around in. They had filled it full of beer before they left, out of the Tourist Hotel freezer, which it lapped up by the canful.

'Show me the things you have done?' said Nikos.

Kelly took the two baskets and placed them out on the parapet rim of the Tholos. She placed the stones in the small basket and then took out the long stone and passed it carefully into the ring three times. Then she took out the long stone and held it between her breasts for a moment. She replaced the stones in the large basket.

'I have fasted,' she replied. 'I have drunk the *cycaeion*; I have taken the things that are in the large basket and, having manipulated them, I have placed them in the small basket. Taking them from the small basket I have placed them again in the large one.'

She took the two vases, and when the priest asked her, 'What have you done?' she filled one half-full and left the other half of the water in the other, then stood them side by side on the parapet. Silently, she turned them round, exchanging them one for the other.

They collected the pig and processed down to the Rocky Altar. Taking off everything except her underpants, Kelly knelt, head bowed, in the pale March shadow of the rock, her neck just beneath its ragged lip. She wasn't looking at what Nikos was doing, but she could hear a lot of struggling and the rasping of the pig's coat on the surface of the rock before at first the drops, then the flow, began. She felt it spatter in her hair and on to her shoulders. He had made a small hole in the jugular and trussed the thing's back legs. He then held the front legs to prevent any thrashing around.

And a sequence of piercing squeals, the substance poured over her, hot as wax, in a stream that rose and subsided with each pump of the heart. It snorted and kept flicking up its head as if it had just been stung by a wasp.

Kelly looked up at the thin drift of cloud. 'Sky, rain!' she shouted, raising her arms.

The blood was coating the back of her neck and running in streams that coagulated rapidly in the wind down her arms and between her breasts, forming a pool in the hollow of her belly and spreading in an extending stain into the waistband of her white underpants.

She stared down at the rocky dust, and spread her arms towards it: 'Conceive, Earth!'

It was gathering at the end of one of her nipples and dripping on to her thigh with a rapid plopping sound.

Above her, hanging over the edge of the rock, the pig's head lifted rhythmically and jerked, and with each jerk the spout renewed from the hole in the neck, subsiding to a drip almost immediately afterwards. She heard it swish and spatter on to the caked deposit on her neck and shoulders. It ran down in her hair and was dripping from its ends in dull globules that seemed almost gold against the light. Every now and again the animal gave out a small grunting squeal.

Kelly turned to the south and repeated her formula, receiving the hot spoutful at the base of the throat as she implored the sky to rain. The substance spread, with a dreadful sweet stench, in a fan over her chest until she was heaving and retching violently, the tears pouring from her eyes with the effort.

She turned again towards the west as planned and the spout

245

poured directly into her ear, matting the hair over it in strings and running down the outside of her bicep and dripping off at the elbow. She turned again after a moment to the north, facing the sea, and repeated the formula, receiving another thick sheet over the back and shoulders, wet and bright, over the dried caking mass that was sticking now absolutely everywhere she looked; in her hair it matted, under armpits it squelched, sticking one strand, one surface, to another.

The leg she could see under Nick's hand was twitching continuously. The snout hung open over the rock, giving out small grunting squeals now without stopping, the saliva pouring out of the corner of the mouth in a thick mounting foam that mingled with the other streams down her shoulders. There were little red pools around her now in the dust, two on one side and one at the front, and no doubt they were behind her too. It was just as if someone were squeezing a sponge which kept filling up again and needed squeezing out again. With every squeeze of the sponge – the pumping stream – came a train of noises from the twitching, jerking, saliva-covered snout, accompanied by a fresh wave of stench. All around her sore knees, in the rocky dust, the pools were spreading and threatening to join up. She watched the spreading edges move towards each other, diverted sometimes in little streams amongst the pebbles like the deltas of meandering rivers, and Kelly felt herself going, very comfortably, falling sideways into the side of the rock, down into the stench and the stickiness and the greyness that rushed up to engulf her eyes.

Nikos's hands raised her, in a daze, to her feet. She caught a last glimpse as she stumbled away of the snout, flies beginning to gather on its pink wet surface, silent now, hanging open, a trail of silver liquid swinging from the jaw in the wind.

The sea was icy, and the shock made her start to scrub at herself, at the caked dark patches all over her shoulders and breasts. Nikos stood waiting for her, holding a large towel from the Tourist Hotel bathroom, which was soon to be soaked in red stains.

Nikos looked down at her. 'It is certain you cannot go on,' he said.

She was shivering violently. She had not really succeeded in getting the stuff off her, and her hair was now matted with salt and blood in thick strings. It flapped in the wind against her shoulders and face like leather strips.

He started to scrub her sides and back.

'I must. My robe. The scissors! Where's . . .' She looked around wildly.

He pointed to the bag and heap of clothes on the pebbles.

Sick and cold, she waited a few moments more until he had scratched his way down her freezing thighs with the sodden, blood-stained towel before staggering over the stones and picking up the clean pair of white underpants that lay ready on top of the robe.

There were red drops here and there in the soil of the track as they went back up past the museum and under the trees back to the site. Each time they came to a new one, Nikos rubbed at it vainly with his shoe.

Kelly could see the redheaded girl with the ragged, chopped-off hair was hesitating, but she knew she had to run when Nikos dropped her hand. A quantity of thorn bushes loomed over the winding track. For some reason there was a fierce-looking owl perched on every one which came and went with a popping sound and a flash of gold-dust. Behind her eyes Kelly could hear a loud crackling noise which seemed to correspond to a series of shifts in the light, rippling between flaming pink and lemon green. Kelly saw the girl in grubby white start to run between these grainy clouds of colour into the shadow of the track, ducking under the overhanging branches and dodging round the rocks and the marble pillars that had fallen in her way.

Kelly saw the girl in the remote distance above the site, a tiny, berserk figure on the sheer escarpment of the mountain, swarming from one position to the next, fragments of a wreath of battered poppies and daisies clinging to her copper-coloured head.

Kelly even had the illusion – at such a distance it had to be an illusion – that she could hear the sharp intake of her breath. She could imagine well, as she shaded her hand against her eyes, the girl's saliva-less throat behind her foam-flecked lips.

Now she was coming down the track on the eastern side, past the Byzantine towers and the southern necropolis. There was a brief moment when Kelly could have sworn she was watching an old movie in crackling flames – a panting messenger was approaching. Then the figure disappeared, plunging into the shadow of the track.

But Kelly thought she could still hear her, gulping to catch her breath behind the trees and she ran – irregularly, from the sound of her feet – with cries each time she bumped carelessly into an overhanging branch.

Then she was round the corner into view again, swinging in a loping run, her knees and shins barked, towards the Propylon of Ptolemy.

Nikos was shouting: 'Down!'

Slithering down the loose pebbles by the side of the building, the girl entered the tunnel and was lost to view. She stopped dead. The tunnel was full of rocks. They could hear her steps pick themselves uncertainly for a yard or two and then stop.

'Don't stop!' shouted Nikos, running towards the building through the site.

She was there before him and saw the girl's terror.

There was something already in the tunnel which lifted its head at the shadow she made.

The girl was paralysed by the bell that sounded through the fizzing darkness, coming and going in a continuous ribbon of hooked faces. It approached through the smoking dust, a hideous, pale-blue bearded face, a bell ringing. Its eyes gleamed yellow in the darkness, fierce diamonds. She sank whimpering on to the rocks as it towered over her, bearded rubber lips champing. At the other end of the tunnel Nikos appeared.

'Get up! You mustn't stop!'

The overpowering stench of excrement and a tattoo of panic-stricken hooves filled the tunnel as Kelly helplessly watched Nikos drag the girl past the creature and out the other side into the air, sudden and sweet, where they ran together now, the girl unable to keep up, her head rolling on her shoulders.

They ran to the theatre where Nikos let her go and she stood heaving deeply. Someone was banging a drum now, slowly, and, filing into the amphitheatre, round the girl, Kelly saw the chain of white dancing figures, each holding one in front by the wrist, fillets and stomachers swinging, as each alternate girl turned in the opposite direction. One of them was playing a square harp, holding its frame high in front of her as she performed the graceful, rising steps. The air was full of the bang and shuffle of these white figures, all round the stationary form of the girl in the centre of the round, stepped space.

Lights began to spring into being. Kelly could see Nikos dimly running from one candle-holder to the next. He waited until there was a gap in the dancers and then came forward and put one in the girl's hand. The dancers seemed to have brought their own.

The wind blew a wall of thyme and camomile hitting her nostrils in one impossible blow of fragrance whose elements took hours, it seemed, to separate themselves. They seemed to have got this into the film. Quite an improvement in technology, Kelly thought.

Darkness had really fallen now and Kelly found it more difficult to see the girl. She found she had to move nearer to her.

After a number of scatterings, which Nikos virtually had to do for her, the procession swept round to the foot of the Temple. Kelly saw that she was standing in the midst of the dancers as the

249

drum slowed to a single expectant beat. Nikos the priest began descending the steps between the pillars, several things in his hands. She clutched her cellophane lantern which flickered in the wind.

Nikos asked her to put out her forearms and these he touched with a stick. To turn them over; he touched her palms, and then, rapidly, the top of the breast, the collar-bones and lastly the soles of the feet. He touched all the places with the things he had in his basket, the bread and the stones, and he rubbed each place with meal.

The beat became more insistent and he invited her, hand extended, to mount the first step. She raised a leg with difficulty and planted it on to the next block.

She held up her arms towards the pillars that towered above them. 'Brimos!' she cried.

She mounted the next step. Kelly saw she was trembling in every limb now.

'Brimos!' she cried again.

The dancers were all left at the bottom staring up as she climbed away from them.

Nikos came to the edge of the top step and stood above her in the flickering light, hands outstretched, as she moved falteringly upwards towards him.

She reached the edge of the top step and stepped out blindly between the great pillars. She was not standing on the edge of the temple at all, she discovered, but at the edge of a great plain full of waving grasses.

Kelly turned to say something to Nikos and felt only the embrace of the other woman.

Mother and daughter, together at last.

'Brimos!' they cried in unison, raising their arms with a new strength, their voices clear. 'Sacred Brimo has conceived a sacred infant, Brimos!'

Nikos turned and stepped towards her, putting forward his

closed fist. Kelly strained forward to look, her outline blurred by the second form that bent forward with her. He turned it over.

On the palm lay four green ears of corn.

III

Witnesses

MAY, 1988

'É,' said Yannis, sitting on Antigone's sofa and sipping at the glass of beer she had put in front of him, 'you should have seen them. They were all there . . .'

'Koutsoyiorgas?'

'All the PASOK high and mighty . . . and all the party officials, nodding away . . .'

'Raftopoulos?'

'Exactly. He has a few opening remarks and then he turns on the communists, KKE in particular. All these PASOK ministers start nodding when he says he has a lot of respect for the history of their struggle, and so on and so on, and you know he's going to turn it all round . . .'

'And did he?'

'Of course. Enormous respect for them et cetera, et cetera, but the present set of choices they were making were bringing in enormous dangers for the unity, the orderly continuation, and the bargaining effectiveness of the union movement . . .'

'Well, it's true!' said Antigone.

Yannis, for once, ignored her.

'This guy used to be a liberal, middle-of-the-road character. Now he's doing their dirty work for them . . .'

Yannis lit a cigarette and offered her one. She stretched and patted her stomach.

'I forgot,' he said with a grin.

'PASOK has always had difficulties with May Day,' said Antigone. 'Remember when they changed it to a peace march? Now everyone behaves as if it's an occasion for reminding people of government policy . . . but that's no bad thing in itself.'

'Wait,' said Yannis, holding up his hand. 'Here, in Constitution Square, under the blue flags of the proponents of "Remission" and the red flags of those whose slogan is "real change", *laissez-faire* economics and state intervention have formed an unnatural but stable association which has culminated in their campaign against the government . . .'

Antigone started to laugh. Yannis stood up and waved his arm over the crowd.

'Comrades, you are making a mistake. You are going down the slippery slope! "Real change" is not carried out by joining with the forces of reaction. In the arena of social, political and class struggles, it is not possible to identify the aims of ESAK-E with its allies who are openly undermining the process of democracy and the elections of the people!'

'*Brávo!*' said Antigone.

'What do you mean?'

'He's right!'

'It's just PASOK union talking. But there's no way they'll be able to keep that position!'

'Why not?'

'Because the right and left in the unions will form a coalition and outvote them . . .'

'Is that what's happening to you?'

'Exactly. The PASOK lot are constantly campaigning against industrial action. But they'll have to support it in the end, because they will be outvoted . . . I hear this kind of speech all the time from Gikas and his PASOK cohorts in the General Council . . .'

'D'you think DEE will go on strike?'

'For sure. The union has drawn up an agreement for the industry . . .'

'What are you asking for?' Antigone looked at her brother. He was passionate, totally involved, serious now, as he explained their demands: index-linking, increases in benefits – eighteen per cent for dangerous work, family benefits increase, better working conditions – prevention of accidents and no to price rises in electricity.

'It's a whole package we want them to sign. PASOK are wriggling and attempting to get out of it, but they can't. But the directorate of DEE, still trying to carry out government policy – because, as you know, the PASOK bureaucrats have a majority on the Committee – insists on this link between salary increases and increased productivity. It's a head-on collision . . . the strike is planned . . .'

'D'you think you can win?'

'Of course,' said Yannis.

He was bullish. She didn't want to argue with him. Normally she would be trying to pick away at him; perhaps it was the baby, she didn't know, but she could see the point about the thin end of the wedge. She could see that they would have to make a move now.

'But what else can the government do?' she asked, benignly.

'Well, they can do something more than these endless "dialogues" they keep offering with the Left. They are just hollow, they're an election ploy. They don't mean to talk about anything in particular. Just vague words. No content . . . Why don't they protect their workers?'

He had predicted the situation last October during their last real argument, and when she looked back he had been, on the whole, correct. On the other hand, she persisted in her general belief that the Movement was a good thing – realistically, what was there to replace it?

But now, to her dismay, as she stared at the way Yannis's red check shirt opened in a vee round his deep-brown throat, she realised her whole attitude had shifted over into a negative and pragmatic justification rather than a positive political faith.

257

*

Barbara's stay at the Stathakopoulos's house on Sithonia had been potentially delightful, but actually something other. The weather had been good. She was already used to all their company and Poulpe and Delphine welcomed her as warmly as children who are distracted by their drive to possess friends can. Vangelis was attentive and his mother cooked heavy meals which they ate slowly at three in the afternoon and eleven at night. In the afternoons Barbara slept unashamedly, and dreamlessly on the whole, reading a little from her Greek primers and trying to do the exercises. They took tea at six after which she and Vangelis, with or without the children, went down for an evening stroll along the harbour walk.

The family fitted easily round all her quirks of temperament and mood, she found. She had only to say she felt like going to her room and a smiling Vangelis was standing with the kitchen door open, ushering her out.

'Please, please, Barbara. Do you have a headache? Is there anything you need?'

She talked about cooking with his mother, who spoke no English. Barbara managed, limpingly, to give an account of her views on home economy, her children, her attitude to shopping, clothes and the things she liked and didn't like – one had to be careful here: not exactly didn't like, so much as found strange – and many other topics of this kind, like so many encyclopaedia articles with headings. SWIMMING. Only like it when it's warm, blood temperature. Disapprove of topless bathing. Barbara found that her Greek was only up to clichés, and rather than be silent or gaping like an ignorant foreigner, she invented clichés for herself. She attributed opinions to herself of the most sublime banality. RAIN. It is always raining in England. That's why it's so green. FUNERALS. Important to get them over with at once.

258

The old lady couldn't help really testing her, she saw, and she seemed by this method to pass her ordeals with minimum upset.

But Barbara hated herself for it. The more she told herself it was only for this week, the more she wanted freely to express herself and the more she despised herself for having started such a thing.

It was a joke she had trapped herself in. All the more when Vangelis saw that his mother approved of her and that the two women got on so well. He made no secret of how delighted he was by this and left them alone in the kitchen to talk their 'women's talk' while he went off upstairs to his room to work. In the evening, on their walks, he usually asked at some point what his mother and she had been talking about that morning and Barbara, to her own self-disgust, compounded what after all, she told herself, was a set of white lies brought about by linguistic necessity, by repeating a glowingly edited version of the *Home Encyclopaedia*. SMOKING. Don't like it. Not only bad for the lungs, but bad for children. Sets a bad example.

The truth was that Barbara had never cared one way or another about the topic. But when she remembered her reaction to Roger, she became confused. The fact was she didn't like smoking particularly, but she had only found it alarming because it had signified a change in him she couldn't relate to. It made her feel insecure at a time when she required support, she told herself. No, it wasn't the content of the *Home Encyclopaedia*, that was always untrue. This wasn't the source of the discomfort she felt. She could usually rationalise it both ways – she could find both rule and, obligingly, the exception that proved it, no, it was the tone of it all that made her feel so unfree. And when she multiplied the old lady by the inevitable cousins and aunties and their mothers who, she feared, would be coming in from the Peloponnese to inspect her pretty soon, she despaired of ever emerging from beneath her own joke. She was trapped for ever in the *Home Encyclopaedia*. It wasn't really her inability to manage nuance, though that was certainly the case and did affect her relations with people, it was her way of handling the expectations which were being thrown over her like so many blankets, so many pieces of material, just like those sold by the man with the truck who came round in the mornings shouting 'Couvertes' and from whom, she confessed it, Vangelis's mother couldn't help buying too many.

This feeling of self-disgust and basic dishonesty had been growing throughout the week. These were good people. Vangelis, she saw, was a good man who wanted a new wife as soon as possible to repair the breach left by his old one. Barbara seemed to him perfect, and he made no secret of the fact. The children took her by the hand and they strolled on the beach as soon as she arrived. Poulpe came into her room to show her his new Focke-Wulfe plastic dive-bomber. Delphine did her horoscope, asking her minute questions about when and where she was born and then drawing the lines on the ready-made chart, while they digressed into Barbara's past and discussed some titbit of information she would reveal without thinking about her childhood in the North-East.

Vangelis showed her the plans of the new house in Forty Churches. He discussed in detail the internal arrangements of the house, showing her all the rooms and who would have which. Certain rooms were blank, unassigned. Her study, for example, he hinted. The master bedroom. Where exactly should it go, did she think?

Barbara didn't think. She stared at the folds in the plan and the fine lines of Vangelis's drawing and wanted to be away.

When the children had gone out of the room, he came and sat next to her, the plans in front of them on the table. He took her by the hand. Barbara's smile, as he did this, became fixed and inane with tension; she felt it wreathing about her mouth like a rubber inner tube filled with air. She spoke through it when he asked her how the week had been, how she had felt, did Chalkidiké please

260

her, was her room comfortable, the food had not disagreed with her, had it?

To each question, fired off in soft Greek, she gave an answer turning towards him the trembling inner tube of her lips – she was still conscious of the scar at the most inconvenient moments – in a manner that she imagined must resemble the mouth of Coco-the-Clown. But each question seemed to give way to another whose grammar became just that little bit more obscure, and whose articulation just that little bit more rapid and blurred, until he was raising her hand to his lips, kissing it and glancing at her over it with his almost-sapphires, while she picked imaginary bits off her apple-patterned skirt and smiled until she was aching with tension and rigidity. Then he repeated: '*S'agapáo*, Barbara, *s'agapáo* . . .' with a sigh, and asked her with his firm dry lips, puckering them towards her, for a kiss, which she smiled at absurdly when he bent forward and took it in the lightest of manners, not moving her head while the smile still spread at the corners of her mouth so as not to acknowledge, quite, that it had happened.

'Is there some way . . . ?' he began.

Barbara looked down, her hands plucking blindly, and shook her head. 'Please, I . . . can't. You've all been so kind . . .'

He got up off his chair, still holding her hand, and stood over her.

'You must understand. I love you, Barbara,' he said in English. 'I am asking you to be my wife!'

'It's too soon,' said Barbara, immediately regretting it.

Why on earth had she said such a thing?

'I can't think of such things,' she said vaguely, trying to add the impression of finality she had failed to give before.

'I understand,' said Vangelis, bending and raising her hand against his slightly unshaven cheek, 'I am waiting for you.'

He stared down at her, an expression of undisguised yearning drawing down his normally optimistic features into a mournful

261

scowl, persisting with a gesture of the head that burrowed ostentatiously beneath her dropped glance and raised it up to his own.

He caressed her shoulder kindly, with a sigh.

'I know what you have suffered,' he said.

Barbara looked up at him, sitting intimately in the shadow he cast.

'Thank you . . .' she managed to get out, but couldn't say his name as she felt she ought to have done. Without the requisite confidence the reply was meaningless and bordered on, she felt, an insult.

And indeed he seemed almost to take it that way: 'Thank you,' he repeated, as he gathered up the plans. 'How strange you English are!'

She came back from Chalkidiké to find the Toumba anticipating a state of siege. The cuts in electricity began about a week later. At first, no one paid any attention – it was only for a few hours and what if the lift did go off? The government announced price rises in electricity and telephones, of between nine and fifteen per cent, Barbara noticed from the paper. Back at the language school it didn't make much difference to her personally at first, because most of her teaching was in the morning. In the afternoon, in her language classes, the classrooms in the basement of the old school building were dark and it was difficult to see their books or what was written on the blackboard.

Theia Soula was effectively imprisoned some mornings in the apartment block because these days she depended on the lift. At the beginning the cuts were of two hours' duration, but since the lift had to be reactivated from the button on the roof there was no one there to go up and switch it on until the end of the day. Progressively, they moved to longer and longer periods, until they stood at twenty-four hours and then forty-eight hours.

All day long the fire brigade received phone calls from people trapped in lifts in different parts of the city. The hospitals were in chaos since the doctors and the cleaners had already come out. DEE declared that they were making rigorously sure that power was supplied to essential units, but nevertheless the whole city was in complete chaos and any business that depended on refrigeration was in serious trouble. All over the city the cake shops and the delicatessens had stopped functioning for fear of mountains of melting sweets and gâteaus and the same went for any business that depended on refrigerated meat.

It was strangely beautiful, Barbara thought, like a medieval city. There were no lights in the streets, but you could see candles everywhere in the house windows, while people sat in the dark on the balconies and gossiped as usual.

Spirits amongst the population were good, but there was a run on candles and all forms of lighting. One night Theia Soula had said that they needed some more lamps. She gave Barbara strict instructions about how to find the shop on Papafi Street where they sold lamps and Barbara set out through the darkened streets listening to the susurrus of conversation on the crowded balconies which were full of people she couldn't see. The electric and neon signs were all gone, the advertisements had ceased to exist and in the back streets, if you saw a glow, it meant that someone was keeping their shop open with an oil lamp. Traffic was severely reduced in the city because of the petrol shortage caused by a strike of the distributors, so the usual roar whose reverberations she'd become so used to had almost ceased. Early in the evening, it felt like the middle of the night.

It took her some time to find the shop. She had lost her way several times and once, near an old broken-down orange neoclassical building in Homer Street, she had jumped out of her skin when a toothless old creature had suddenly put her arms through the gate begging for money. She lived there with her dogs which were leaping all round her. She gestured to some steps behind her which, Barbara could just make out in the dark, led up to a door on the first floor lit dimly by a candle. Barbara offered her some of Theia Soula's lamp money and had to wait to be blessed and stroked by the gnarled old hands, the colour, in the dark, of copper, and webbed with flaps of skin.

The shop was milling with people when she arrived. They were out on the street trying to shove their way into the crowded interior. A woman with a purple bandanna wrapped round her head, carrying one child and grasping another by the hand, was appealing to people inside to let her pass. To Barbara's surprise the wave parted and in she pushed, people grasping her by the shoulder and helping her through into the suffocating interior.

Barbara was standing outside watching and wondering how on earth she was going to get in and get a lamp after all this lot had gone, when a hand touched her on the arm.

Vangelis stood before her, offering to kiss her on the mouth.

Surprised, she tendered her left cheek and then her right, forcing him into politeness.

'I rang and rang,' he said accusingly. 'Where have you been hiding?'

She mentioned the language school, her classes. She pleaded her marking with the one and her homework with the other, but the truth was she had been contriving to be busier than she really was in order to put herself out of his way. Once he had appeared in person at the *réma* and offered to take her out to dinner, but she had pleaded pressure of work and he had understood, he said, which meant that he would allow her to escape this once.

Now he stared at her, keenly, as she gestured at the crowd in the shop. He took her by the arm. 'Come! This is impossible. I know another place across town where we can find a light . . .'

They set out.

'I mustn't be long. Theia Soula's waiting for me . . .'

'You'll be quicker this way than if you tried in that chaos. Anyway,' he laughed, 'by the time you get to the counter, they won't have any lamps left!'

This seemed reasonable.

264

They turned left and went down to the harbour past Radio City cinema in the narrow streets that led to the sea. The ships' lights were unaffected and seemed much more dominant out in the bay than usual. The esplanade was crowded and yet the great highway between the shore and town, Vassilis Olgas, had been empty when they crossed it. Everyone had walked, for once.

'Ah bliss!' said Barbara, 'no cars!'

He was talking about the terrible loss to business of the whole thing.

Barbara thought of Antigone and Yannis and what she had told her on the telephone about how hard the struggle was going to be. She talked about the strikers' demands and the attitude of the government.

'Most people seem philosophical about it. In England they would be outraged. There would be a massive hue and cry . . .'

'You seem well informed,' he told her.' How do you come to know all these things about DEE and GENOP and so on . . .?'

She explained about Antigone's brother.

'Every day you learn something . . .' he said, not without, she thought, a shade of irony.

They fell silent, looking out at the coasters planted closely about the bay, the lights in their bridges corresponding with the candlelight of the apartment blocks behind them so that the whole environment appeared continuous, land and sea a deep dark, pricked by galaxies of lights.

Dramatically he stopped amid the bustle of families that backed up and began to flow round him like water.

'Barbara?'

Drifting and dreaming along, looking at the lights, her reverie was broken. She stopped and slowly walked back towards him, ten yards or so, in the flow of the people.

'You can't keep me waiting for ever, you know?'

She stared at his open-necked shirt, and almost-sapphires, so familiar now in their walnut cases, and she thought with a shudder of the years of the *Home Encyclopaedia*.

She shook her head.

'I've decided,' she said, suddenly.

Three policemen, laughing, out for a stroll, collided with them and issued some charming ritual apology.

'Well?'

'I can't marry you. It isn't right . . .'

He stared out at the ships and swallowed. Barbara felt a sudden wall of sewage-stench hit her nostrils.

'Do you mind telling me why?' he said.

They were standing a foot apart.

A ball rolled between them and came to rest at his feet. He kicked it savagely away without looking down.

'Of course, you are a very good friend to me, and your children are wonderful, but I can't think of you as anything more than that. I'm sorry.'

He clenched his fists.

'I'm offering you a whole future. You need someone. We both do. It's ideal, it will *work*. I know it will!'

'No.'

'You don't love me now, perhaps. But . . .'

'I love it here, but the time will come when I shall want to go back to England . . .'

'You'll find work here easily. We'll be happy. My mother – she already adores you. She's always asking when you are coming . . .'

'That's the prob––' said Barbara and bit back the words.

'You don't like my mother? You didn't say anything when we came back from Chalkidiké. You said you liked her! You told me – I remember – how nice you thought she was!'

Barbara swallowed.

'It's not her personally, Vangelis, it's the whole context. I don't think I can fit in. I've been on my own too long. I can't play the role of housewife and mother any more. My life's changed while

266

I've been here in Greece in all sorts of ways I hadn't anticipated. I've only just realised it myself . . .'

'But . . .' He put his hand on her arm, about to launch into a fierce piece of rhetoric, but she stepped back and held up her hand:

'Please! Let me finish . . .'

'Yes, but—'

'Please!'

He was silent, looking away, his mouth muttering. She caught '*Panagiá mou*' and he went on in a stream. He had switched over, irrevocably perhaps, into Greek now.

She plunged on. 'There are many things I suddenly have the strength to think about now, for the first time. My friends have seen me through a period when I didn't know whether I would survive or not. You don't know. I thought I was going mad, I . . .' The memories bubbled to the surface of her mind and gave off their poisonous gases of recollection. 'I was on the sofa at Antigone's for weeks . . . immobile . . . I thought I would never be able to live in the world again—'

'I am not the world!' he said.

'That's exactly it! I really do mean the world, not the family!'

'I don't understand. I don't understand at all. What have you been telling me with your every glance for the last weeks?'

'I'm sorry if I appear to have misled you . . . but I have been very confused myself, things have not been at all clear. It's only recently I could be touched by anyone without my skin crawling . . . and these dreadful fears I still have . . . I still don't think I could ever . . . be a wife to anyone ever again . . .'

'Is there not some way we can—'

Barbara shook her head. 'No. I've given it a lot of thought, Vangelis, it's quite impossible . . . I'm sorry. I feel absolutely awful saying it like this, but . . . there it is.'

They turned as if by mutual consent and began to stroll through the advancing families, wave upon wave of grandmothers and children and parents of all ages walking apart, walking with linked arms, hand in hand, looking up, looking down, looking away from each other. Everywhere the sound of children crying out '*Mamá! Éla liyáki! Mpampá . . . a . . . a!*' punctured the velvet darkness.

For a moment, she thought the crisis was over. But Vangelis came at her again and again with the persistence of despair and she was obliged to explain herself so many times that in the end she began to stress quite different things and it was easy for him, speaking rapidly in Greek, to pick out the inconsistencies in her account of her feelings.

By the time she reached the Toumba everyone had gone to bed. She had, of course, forgotten all about the lamps; she undressed in the dark and fell, ashamed and exhausted, across her bed, face down, her eyes open against the sheets, her mind flickering on in an unstoppable, unsynchronised series of released memories.

Antigone sat across the table at the fish taverna which Loukas had insisted on taking her to, waiting for him to finish the small talk and get on to what she knew he really wanted to say to her. They had already traversed the usual PASOK-baiting repartee, and he had told her about the latest developments in the Cretan Bank scandal. Rumour had it, Loukas said, brushing the crumbs from his pearl-grey double-breasted jacket, that Papandreou had had a meeting with Koskotas in which he had been set up to be PASOK's press baron, in exchange for a change in the law on investments. Loukas was in his element, she thought, feeding his romantic young provincial protégée with seedy titbits of Athenian gossip, and then watching the milk of her complexion curdle, the copper currency of her smile corrode, in this laboratory sink of leaks.

'So how's the Christos defence?'

He raised a bushy white eyebrow.

'You know about the film?' she asked.

He inclined his white head, as much as to say, *Yes, but tell me about it . . .*

'Well,' said Antigone, complying with the ritual because she couldn't think of anything else to do, 'some neighbour turned out to be an amateur photographer, and took a film of Christos giving himself up and laying down his weapon . . .'

'And?'

'The police dismissed it as irrelevant . . .'

'Well, it is—'

'No, we think it's useful, Spiros and Nikos and I . . .'

He picked at a nail.

'So you're just waiting for the Attorney's office?'

'Otherwise, yes. Although all this stuff about the guy from the Port Authority is a useful development because it shows Lekas to have been the main perpetrator . . .'

'Hmmm . . .' He was bored with this. 'And this . . . other *paidarélli* you've been associating with, how does he fit in?'

'Manos Alexiou? He's been arrested . . .'

'Quite,' said Loukas, searching her face. 'So why go to see him?'

'He's full of useful background evidence. He's been very helpful to our case . . .'

'I'm sure he has,' said Loukas dryly.

Antigone put her chin out. 'What do you imply?'

'He's your lover, isn't he?'

He toyed fastidiously with some fish bones and then leaned back with a sigh.

'Don't bother to answer. Just listen. I know everything. I know what you've been doing with this young *gávros* . . . I am surprised and disappointed in you, *korítsi mou* . . .'

'How do you know? You've been having me watched, you—'

He held up a hand.

'Before you say something you might regret, I have a proposition for you. I want you to stop seeing him . . .'

'But I am not seeking to defend him, on your instructions! I haven't done anything wrong!'

'You are becoming a liability. You are hanging around with too many of these women lawyers who have . . .' he sighed again, '*causes* . . .'

'That's my business! It has nothing to do with—'

'Your business is my business. You seem to forget that up till now you have been working for me . . .'

'Up till now?'

He leaned back, and put a knuckle on the red and white check tablecloth.

'Spiros will handle the Christos defence from now on . . .'

So Spiros had been the spy. She might have known.

'What else have you got for me?' she laughed bitterly. 'Land disputes in eastern Thrace?'

'Not a bad idea,' he laughed pleasantly. 'No, the proposition concerns property in Attica. Some villas near Sounion, not far from where your great leader used to have his love-nest, as a matter of fact . . . I want you to represent some clients in a muddle they've got into with the government. Advise them, sort out their rights, win their confidence, generally mediate, and handle any litigation which may arise . . . But, there is a condition—'

Antigone had begun to say something indignant.

'You are not working for me at this moment in time. Beforehand, I want your assurance that you will not see this hunger-striker any more. I can't have someone from my firm hanging around with riff-raff like that!'

'Hunger-striker?'

'Ah, of course you were away at Easter in your village, weren't you? He and a number of other prisoners have been foolish enough to go on hunger strike against the conditions in Koridallo . . .'

270

He snorted with amusement at the idea.

Antigone ignored the fact that he was scrutinising her face. She was genuinely shocked. She had to take it in. Ah, Manos! It was typical of him. She felt a flood of guilt. Did their last meeting have anything to do with it?

She shot to her feet and he rose slowly with her.

'Wait,' he said, 'I . . . want you to think . . .'

She slung her bag over her shoulder, and turned on her heel.

'Take some time to think,' she heard him say behind her as she ran out into the sunlight and down the paved pedestrian walk to look for a cab.

In the waiting-room the man on the desk, whom she knew slightly, tried to tell her she couldn't see Manos, because he was on hunger strike, and she was forced to produce her lawyer card and threaten him. Eventually after a lot of shuffling they brought him in behind the bars on a stretcher, which they placed on the ground, and retreated to stand at the wall.

Antigone knelt by the bars. 'Mano,' she whispered.

His face was turned away and when he turned to her she was shocked by the thinness of it. He was haggard. It was almost as if she were talking to someone else. His eyes were glittering above his grey cheeks, the arches of the eyebrows even more prominent than usual. He smiled wearily and she put her hand into his through the bars.

'*Agápi mou*,' he said. 'What are you doing in this horrible place . . . ?'

His voice sounded tired, the word tapering off without any energy of expression. He almost sounded too bored to speak.

'What's happening?' she asked.

'I decided to do this . . .' he gave another of his weary smiles, 'to get them to improve the conditions. They're terrible. There are kids ready to kill themselves in here . . .'

271

'How long have you . . . ?'

'I don't remember. Is it . . . ?'

'Two weeks,' said Antigone, 'since you were first here.'

'They don't like it. They are trying to isolate me as much as possible to reduce the amount I talk to other people . . .'

'I brought you . . .' she said, 'but they confiscated them, some magazines and some books . . .'

'This guy here?' he asked, jerking his head round on the stretcher towards the man at the desk.

She nodded.

'That's all right. He's all right, that one. I'll get them later,' he said. 'So what's new?'

She laughed.

'Mano, please forgive me . . . I was wrong. I've talked to my family and they're behind me . . . I've decided to have it.'

Easter had been difficult for Antigone. She had meant to conceal her pregnancy from the family, but as soon as she had found herself facing Socrates it had all come tumbling out and her greatest dread – her guilt over the economic situation, and the contributions she would be unable to make in the future – was allayed by the way they all took the news.

Matoula was delighted for her, instinctively, that is, but as soon as she began to explain about Manos, then she became disappointed and got rather awkward. Antigone had stressed that she intended, and had intended all along, to bring up the child independently of Manos.

At that time she had reasoned that she would not have to lose her position, though obviously she would give up her present job. If she moved back to Thessaloniki from Athens she and Katerina could find a flat together and share some of the baby-watching during Katerina's final year.

She thought perhaps there would be some more interesting things to do in Thessaloniki. She badly wanted to set up a shelter for women, a rape-crisis centre, and see if she couldn't get her friend Voula to come in with her. Perhaps even Barbara, as a trained nurse, could be persuaded to help.

The crucial thing had been Matoula. The mention of coming back to Thessaloniki outweighed her distaste for the idea of Manos, and this had been decisive.

Manos laughed, and sighed to himself:

'I could see it in your face . . .' he said, 'I knew you would.'

She looked at him closely, squeezing his hand as she told him about how all the sickness had gone and how her indigestion had started, how she felt as if her stomach was being pushed up under her chin.

His eyes had huge hollow shadows under them, and he was unshaven, the beard about one inch long now.

She started to tell him about the meeting she was just about to go to about the campaign for the release of Evangelia Sefertzis.

It was a group of women lawyers. They had approached various bodies for their support because Sefertzis had her child with her in gaol and it was clear that there was room for a claim that the child was being deprived of a suitable environment and was experiencing psychological damage. Christianopoúlou, who was a member of the Greek Council of Lawyers, was guaranteeing the support of the Movement for the Defence of Citizens and their Social Rights and Váso Karaháliou was there as well, a lawyer from the Co-operative Council of Women. They were planning to come to Korudallos and make a series of public announcements to the press, displaying her behind bars with her child.

There were no colours, they said, in the cell, no materials for the child to play with and the little boy was more than one year old now. They wanted the educational psychiatrists to go in and examine the child's development and announce the process of his retardation to the press.

'That's good. She should come out then, soon?'

'We'll see. We're just waiting for the psychiatrists, but the lawyers are behind it . . .'

273

'She's a real fighter, *lebéntissa einai* . . .'

'She's the *polytechneío* generation,' said Antigone, nodding.

'Yes, she attacks them whenever she can. She's not frightened of really letting them have it . . .'

'Manos, I'm going up to the village again. I'll be away sometime during the next week or so, for a day or so . . .'

'Why?'

'DEE is going on strike and Yannis is involved. I may be able to help . . .'

'When exactly are you going?'

'I don't know. Soon.'

'Don't make it too long,' he said, looking down at his body on the stretcher and wriggling to ease the leather straps round his chest and legs.

'Are you going to be all right?'

'Of course. Don't worry about me. With your news I've got everything to look forward to now . . .'

He lifted up a thin, yellowish arm to wipe the sweat from his brow and she realised suddenly how wasted he was. The hand she was holding was in a cold sweat. She looked down at the huge half-moons of white at the base of the nails.

'They think they're going to break me . . .' He smiled. 'They think I'm going to give up . . .'

Antigone was on the verge of sharply reminding him that she was having his baby, but she bit back the words and nodded.

'The mice are interesting . . .' he said vaguely.

'How can you stand it?'

'They have long bodies. Anatomically interesting . . .'

'Manos . . .'

'Yes?'

'Make sure you . . . don't go too far. I don't want to lose you, you know, just when I've found you . . .' She put on a brave face.

'Worst thing is the stench,' he said, 'but I'll be getting out of the cell soon . . .'

'Why?'

'They'll be transferring me to the medical block.'

'What for?'

'So they can pretend I'm ill . . . it'll be easier to force-feed me there.'

'What?'

'Well, I'm banking on the fact that they won't want the publicity if—'

'If what?'

'If anything should happen to me.'

'But . . .' she said, leaning down and kissing his hand and holding it against her cheek, 'nothing's going to happen to you. I want you to promise me something?'

'What?'

'That you won't let this go too far, please?'

He smiled his faded smile that made her bowels turn.

'Of course not, now I'm a father . . .'

'Promise?'

'What?'

'You'll stop before—?'

'Have a little patience,' he said.

'Promise, Mano, promise? I need you . . .'

'Have a little patience,' he said again with a crooked sort of smile, and again she felt the churning deep inside her as he began to sing in a querulous, old man's voice:

'Don't despair, he won't be long;
he'll come to you one dawn
asking for new love
have a little patience

Chase the clouds from your heart
and don't lie awake crying;

So what if he's not in your arms!
he'll come back one day, don't forget it.

Some sweet dawn he'll wake you
and desire will be reborn;
new love will live again;
have a little patience.'

When he had finished he smiled again that crooked smile, and as she watched him being carried away towards the door in the wall Antigone felt the idea which had been sidling up throughout the last few minutes step boldly into her mind with one stride, and become the conviction, that she was never going to see him again.

She clutched the bars. She rattled them.

'Mano! I'm coming Sunday!'

The yellowish hand raised itself in acknowledgement, but then, as they passed through the door, she glimpsed the way it opened after this salute and fell back, dangling over the edge of the stretcher, impeding their progress; the second man, nearest her, was obliged to reach down and tuck it in, like a piece of cloth, before they could proceed.

Barbara sat in the back of the orange DEE pick-up as they drove out from Veria. There was plenty of moonlight and it picked out the faces of the two men opposite her, Kostas and Michaelis, the bear-like one of two Michaelises she had been introduced to. If she twisted round she could see the mass of Antigone's black curls brushing the glass behind her in the cab, as she turned her head to talk to Yannis who was driving.

They took the road to Vergina out of Veria and climbed away from the plain up on the southern side of the Aliakmon gorge, the mountains great looming masses all around them which Barbara felt rather than saw because only occasionally, whenever the little convoy – the pick-up and the Opel in front and the VW van behind – twisted and turned round a hairpin bend, did they distinguish themselves from the paler dark of the sky.

The two Michaelises were telling jokes which came and went as they rolled together round the bends. One of them seemed to be about some scientists from Venus who had met an expedition of earthlings and had asked them about their reproductive methods, requiring them, in the spirit of science, to demonstrate the method. There happened to be a woman on board, and she agreed to participate in the demonstration which was highly successful from a scientific point of view. The Venusian leader commented that his team had found it all quite fascinating, and it had shown them the method quite clearly. But there was something that puzzled them. Was the infant produced immediately after coupling? The earthling scientist leader replied that, no, the incubation period was nine months. Then why, asked the Venusian with genuine perplexity, were they *hurrying* towards the end?

Barbara looked at her watch. It had taken ten minutes to tell the joke and three for the laughter to subside. Now it was 2.30 a.m. and she still had no clear idea what was going to happen. She had been up to the village before, taking the old road from Veria over the top of the mountains, but this road, which was new and had been built by DEE, hugged the side of the gorge, as far as she could see, about a third of the way up its sheer side.

They passed the first dam at Asómata without stopping, just able, once they had climbed away from it, to look down at the reservoir below them. Then the tunnel intervened and when they came out the other side they could get no clear picture of the river in the bottom of the gorge.

Twenty minutes and two jokes later the convoy drew up at a bend in the road, and everybody started getting down. Antigone came back for her. The pick-up and the rest drew over at the side of the gorge, where there were notices everywhere saying that it was forbidden to go down to the reservoir. They stood and watched as the men dragged the dinghy over and four of them, including Yannis, disappeared over the edge.

'What's going on?' said Barbara.

'They're going upstream to the dam,' said Antigone. 'Let's go and look . . .'

They walked further to the corner of the road, hugging the side of the drop to the river, and there, lying below them, lighted up and looking to Barbara's eyes like a space station, stood the dam. The road gave up at a huge security gate and a blockhouse just up ahead of them, and then behind the fence it ran down steeply to the hydroelectric station buildings and the enormous wall of the dam, built on a sharp corner in the river so that it actually faced directly the southern bank.

They peered over the edge of the gorge down into the bottom, but couldn't make out anything.

'We won't see the boat until it gets round the corner and picks up the light . . .' said Antigone.

'What are they going to do?' said Barbara.

'They're going to shut it down,' said Antigone. 'The one higher up is already not working and if they can shut this one off the other below can't work either, because they're in a chain . . .'

Yannis appeared back over the edge of the gorge by the road a little further down, picking his way between the weeds. Barbara could smell thyme strongly, crushed by the boots of the men.

Yannis waved them back into the cars.

'Wait,' was the word.

One of the men from the pick-up's cab was in the boat, so that left a space for Barbara and she climbed in on the outside next to Antigone.

'Don't want to spoil the surprise,' Yannis grinned.

They stayed out of sight of the gates and the blockhouse for a while until Yannis judged it to be time and the convoy headed out towards the gates, the DEE pick-up leading the way.

278

They stopped at the gates and a figure came out of the blockhouse and waved to them. Yannis waved back, and shouted:

'Ol' endáxei?'

'Kala!' said the guard and went back into the blockhouse. The gates in front of them gave a click and started to swing open slowly.

As they nosed through and down the steep approach road to the power station they could see the shadow of the dinghy, with the three men in it, out on the lake heading for the wall opposite the turbines. By the time they had reached the bottom and turned into the car-park, directly under the mass of the dam wall, Barbara could see the little boat rocking violently in the swell from the three great turbines as it crossed the lake and approached the concrete wall opposite them.There were two figures in the lights out on the bridge under the heads of the turbines, cupping their hands and shouting across to the men in the boat.

Everyone got down from the cars and went through the control building whose door had been left open down onto the bridge. On the stairs they met a number of men coming up. Barbara heard a brief exchange as they brushed past.

'The engineers,' said Antigone. 'They're coming out in sympathy . . .'

By the time they got down on the bridge above the lake, the swell had subsided and the men in the boat were able to keep in near the concrete wall on the far side quite easily with the oars.

Barbara looked up. In the huge lighted windows of the control room there were a number of gesticulating figures.

'It's off,' said Antigone to Yannis, who nodded. 'They've switched it off! She turned to Barbara, eyes shining. 'They've switched Greece off!'

'It's deep there,' said Yannis, 'forty metres. They can't do anything else. If that boat were to capsize in the turbulence from the turbines, the lads would be drowned. They'd never come up in that amount of drag . . . They're afraid. They've got no choice but to switch off . . .' He laughed. 'I bet the phone's busy up there!'

Barbara looked up at the sky above the gorge. The grey-pink of the dawn was just beginning to flush, and to change the colour of the water below them from black to navy blue. The Michaelises in the boat opposite kept it stable with paddles while Kostas hung on to a ledge to hold it in position as the last of the giant bubbles from the turbines broke white on the surface and lifted them vertically, rocking, about three feet up the rough shuttering of the concrete.

Kelly was leaning idly on the rail of the boat looking at them all along the promenade under the awnings lashing into their fried octopus amid bursts of Greek rock. She was glad she was leaving. She was exhausted. She had never worked so hard in all her life as she had at Mr Tsakalis's restaurant.

It was all very authentic, the taverna. The big fat Germans were themselves and Mr Tsakalis's wife was herself, that is, she suspected Kelly of trying to turn her husband on with her Indian print wrap-arounds that kept coming slightly undone in the breeze, and Mr Tsakalis had been very firmly himself, lecturing her on hygiene with his eyes on her cleavage.

She drew up an orange chair and put her feet up on the rail, watching them waving a truck full of sheep up the ramp. She had just had to brace herself and serve out her time. Nikos had disappeared back to his base, saying he would meet her up on the Evros at Didymótoicho on the twentieth, which was tomorrow.

Poor old Niko. He'd been kind of subdued when he left. She was a bit worried about all those marks on his neck. She sniffed and scratched her nose. She hadn't remembered anything about it. Just woke up in the same narrow bed. He was black-and-blue. How was he going to explain that when he got back? No doubt he'd think of something. He was pretty fly, she decided. The card he'd chucked away had only been his pass card for the barracks at Soufli and since he was only in a kind of small billet, just three or four of them together, everyone knew who he was and he wouldn't have to produce it.

The chain dropped and was reeled in as the boat scraped off the ramp and they slid away from the promenade, leaving Kamariotissa to stew in its own octopus juice. The docks were full of waving families. A German teacher was reading, feet on the side rail, pen poised over the text. Preparing for the summer semester? Her friend had two kids. One in a pushchair and the other, her boy, sitting on her chest as she lay full-length on one of the benches and tried to rest. A young man with a bottle of water was sitting on the red life-jacket box, his knees drawn up under his chin, staring persistently at a pale girl who stood at the white railing, her gaze fixed towards the shore as they began to cruise past Paliopolis.

Kelly could see the site beginning to emerge round the rocky bluff above the skirt of fields on the coast road, the pillars of the Temple, the Tourist Hotel down nearly at shore-level like an architect's model, and she even made out a gleam of white from the museum and the cottages higher up the track amongst the trees.

She turned sideways along the rail and saw the pale girl was weeping calmly. Kelly sat down to write her diary as they pounded slowly along the length of the northern shore, the jetty below Loutra coming into view now, the road up to the baths, the *réma*, and the hated restaurant which was somewhere up in the square out of sight.

She looked up. The young man was offering the girl his water bottle and standing by her side.

A little later, as they were leaving the north-eastern tip of the island ready for the crossing to Alexandroúpoli, Kelly moved over to the bench under the awning and fell asleep to the sound on her Walkman of Jerry Garcia singing 'Ripple':

'There is a road
(no simple highway)
Between the dawn
And the dark of night

And if you go
No one may follow
That path is for
Your steps alone'

She woke as he sat on the end of the bench, her mouth dry and full of sleep. He was smiling and offering her his water bottle.

She sat up and took the bottle. She held it up:

'Cheers, mate,' she said in Eel-Pie.

'Your health.'

'What happened to her?' Kelly nodded at the girl who had now occupied the life-jacket box and was leafing through a magazine.

'Her grandfather just died . . .'

It turned out he was just about to go into the army. He asked if she was a writer. He had seen her scribbling. He had thought of being a writer, poetry, or very short texts, but it was hard. He was in limbo, he said. He was glad he was going into the army. He didn't want to go to college. He was unteachable, he said, with a smile.

As the low straggle of palms and harbour buildings came into view at Alexandroúpoli, Kelly declined his offer to accompany her to Didymótoicho, feeling very practical and purposeful as she confined him to the bus station.

Everybody was crouched on the little low parapet above the water, talking. Yannis was carrying the loud-hailer and calling to the people in the boat. In between these bursts of encouragement he and Antigone talked to some members of the garment-workers' union who had arrived in solidarity. Even some pensioners from the bakers' confederation had come, Antigone discovered.

Every now and again someone would sing and they would raise a fist.

They heard the helicopter beating up the gorge long before they saw it. Eventually it rounded the bend in the river and dipped thunderously towards them across the artificial lake. It was fully light now, and she could see one of the riot police who looked like a Japanese warrior sitting next to the pilot.

'Here comes trouble,' she said to Barbara.

Barbara grinned. She didn't seem at all afraid.

The helicopter swung round behind the installation and settled in the car-park, disgorging a crowd of riot police who ran through the control block and down on to the parapets.

The word came along for them to link arms, and they all rose to their feet and stood, impassively, facing the police. Antigone heard the boy next to her say that they had frogmen.

The leading policeman waved his club and clutched his riot shield. He ordered them in the name of the Greek Government to come off the parapet in an orderly fashion, and he turned to the water without pausing and waved his arm at the men in the boat who were still clinging to the wet concrete retaining-wall of the bank.

'Out!'

Antigone stared at the dark uniforms standing astride, clubs at the ready. There were about eight of them. On the narrow parapet of the dam, just above the sluice-gates, stood about thirty strikers and supporters.

The leader of the riot police, accompanied by the manager of the station, repeated his request and the negotiations began. Various strikers spoke, justifying the action as a majority decision of the general council and pointing out that it was highly dangerous and irresponsible to run the plant without a full and proper engineering staff. The plant should not be in action when all they had to run it were a few scabs, shouted Yannis through the loud-hailer.

The police leader shouted that they were endangering Government property and their presence on the site was illegal. He and his men would be forced to take steps to remove them unless they ceased this occupation immediately.

A ripple ran through the people standing on the dam and they tightened their arms. Antigone glanced at Barbara. She was clinging tightly to the two people next to her, an eighteen-year-old boy and an older man with grey hair dressed in an orange DEE overall.

The police chief stepped back to confer with the manager, the two men standing back from the line and waving their arms at one another.

'They're waiting for reinforcements,' said someone.

The word was passed along the line that national production of electricity was down by fifty per cent now, and a cheer went up from the union ranks. Yannis reported this through the loud-hailer to the men in the boat and one of them waved his cap.

Antigone found she had very little grasp of the passing of time. The riot squad from the helicopter had stood down for the moment and everyone on the parapet relaxed. Some people began to sit down, cross-legged, and wait for the next set of developments.

It was a beautiful spring day, the sun climbing high over the gorge, the green beginning to shoot everywhere along the banks. The strikers had undone parcels and they were passing cheese and spinach pies and cans of Fanta along their ranks, sharing them out as best they could.

Antigone could see through the big window of the control room at the dam crowds of people milling around. Every now and then someone came to the window and pointed down at them, discussing some tactical manoeuvre. There was almost a festive air, she thought, as she looked along the line and watched them talking happily and joking with one another. Barbara was discussing something with the grey-haired man on the other side of her. The boy on Antigone's left said that the Communist MP for Thessaloniki was with them in solidarity. He pointed him out to her, standing in his suit on the parapet, chatting to someone from the leather-workers'.

Antigone was just thinking they must have had instructions to be extra careful about using violence because the Government couldn't afford for anything to go wrong, when everyone stiffened and heads turned towards the lake again. They could plainly hear an engine of some kind.

Round the corner of the lake appeared a large inflatable dinghy with an outboard motor. Inside it sat about ten men, a mixture, Antigone thought from their uniforms, of police and army personnel. They were heading at speed for the three men in the small boat at the side of the dam.

'Look!' shouted Barbara to Antigone, pointing up at the bank.

A single file of infantry was beginning to wind its way down through the security gates and past the blockhouse on the approach road.

Kelly was walking along the road out of town towards Turkey.

She came to the Holy Rock with the shrine on her left and then the small tannery came up on her right, the chimney belching out foul clouds across the road. Just before that there was a small café with a terrace under an arbour by the side of the road and she flopped into a chair. Everywhere seemed deserted because it was silent, but if you looked closely there was a figure standing or moving in the fields at almost every section of the road.

Nikos was supposed to meet her at the French Bridge which was a railway bridge over the Evros.

Kelly thought Didymótoicho was a pretty weird place. The bus arrived in the dark. As they came over the Evros the fairy-tale castle, with its illuminated crinkle of Byzantine walls, dominated the town like any other tourist attraction. But the place itself was strange and frenetic: full of discos and young soldiers trying to pick up girls, and the arrival of the bus seemed like an aircraft landing at a remote bush settlement; people swarmed around it delivering parcels and messages, taxis purred on every side. But in an unbelievably short space of time, the time it took Kelly to climb down and get her bag out of the yawning hold of the bus, they had all vanished and the square was empty under the moonlight.

Kelly had walked off up a side street, thinking she would soon come to a hotel but after a few streets she began to feel this was not the case. She came across two girls sitting on a step and asked them where there was a hotel and they said it was five kilometres, waving their arms. They understood 'rooms' OK, but they waved their arms again, as much as to say there weren't any.

Kelly was lucky: she retraced her steps to the square and found a stray taxi there who had not picked up his fare. She'd managed to ask him to take her to a hotel in town which was not expensive, and he nodded. He took her two blocks, almost to the place where the girls had been on the step.

The hotel was right by the spot.

At the café the man squinted at her. She asked for an orange and he brought her a glass and a bottle and a straw, moving slowly and never ceasing to squint in her direction. In the end, wiping the table, he asked her if she was German. 'Americanída,' she replied and he repeated it, going into the little café and staring at her openly through the window as she raised the glass to her lips.

He came back out across the terrace to her table.

He pointed at the small white building on the hill opposite about half a mile away:

'Barracks!' he said. 'Nix go!'

He levelled an imaginary weapon at her.

She nodded. 'Yes, I know. Only me to bridge!' she managed.

He went in again, but continued to stare at her through the café window.

When she got up, he came shooting out again. '*Verboten!*'

'How much?'

'*Hundert. Verboten!*'

'Yeah. *Only bridge*,' she repeated as she picked up her bag and set off quickly under the clouds of rank brown smoke that drifted across the road from the tannery.

Kelly heard him continuing to talk behind her, but she didn't look back.

Behind the white slaughterhouse the bridge came into view as she rounded the bend in the road. Painted a pale green, it was a simple one-span, round-topped steel affair. Behind it, up on the hill, overlooking everything, stood the barracks. She could see the Greek flag now, hoisted outside it.

Up ahead, the road crossed the railway line which ran over the bridge. Kelly paused when she reached this road. On the other side of the track, where the road continued along the side of some fields planted with sweetcorn, there was a battered, rusty metal notice: FORBIDDEN ZONE.

Kelly decided to walk along to the bridge itself on the other side of the railway line, where a footpath, or at least a space between the line and the fields, ran, technically not crossing into the forbidden zone, but skirting it. She thought that would be OK. It all looked peaceful, but no doubt they were watching from the barracks.

There was a rumbling along the track and a goods train arrived and banged its way interminably over the bridge. On its way to Istanbul, she guessed from the notices on it.

On the other side of the track she could see a Muslim woman working with a hoe in the field. Kelly wandered to the bridge and stared into the sluggish Evros. She must be looking at Turkey on the other side, but because of the way the river wound round through the fields it was not clear how the border worked. Perhaps it was still Greece, because the barracks was on the other side of the bridge, she now saw, set up on a little rise that overlooked the flat, wooded river valley.

She sat down on a rock under the dank shadow of the bridge. According to her Mickey Mouse watch it was eleven o'clock, and Nikos had said he would meet her there under the bridge at mid-morning. She took out pencil and pad and started scribbling her diary entry, breaking into diagrams every now and again, when the idea for a setting took her. Since the island she'd been feeling really good and she felt ready for a creative winter working up some new designs for her stuff back in England. The only immediate question was a little bitty bread to get her back without having to wait table again and Nikos had promised her some after he had done this deal, whatever it was.

Kelly put her hand up to her hair. It was growing fast, she thought, but she'd hardly looked in the mirror recently to see. No waves yet, to speak of, but they'd come back. She laughed. She'd had a terrible shock the first time she'd caught a glimpse of herself. She was a pale, long-faced, slightly mad-looking stranger with this slashed and tufted haystack of red on her poll.

She sighed and crossed her legs as she scribbled the events of her recent trip for her record. She was at peace with herself now. She had decided she was going to take her mother's name when she got back to England. Her Sioux name, Kelly Windcloud. She thought fondly of herself before. She always had this itch whenever she got near water to whip up her skirts and plunge her tush into it. Perhaps she would never feel that again. Whatever, the muddy Evros didn't give her a single vibe in that direction.

The voices she heard from some way off and she packed up her flowered notebook, wrapping the elastic band around it with a frown. There wasn't supposed to be anyone else, as she'd understood it.

Two shadows fell across the arch and she heard the slip and crunch of boots and an exclamation in Greek on the steep earth by the side of the bridge.

'Hey, Kelly!' said Nikos, standing and holding out his arms.

The other young man stood behind him, grinning and nodding.

As she kissed him Nikos was already drawing away and turning to him, saying that this was Kelly and this was Melik.

'We waited for you at the bar,' said Nikos.

'What bar?'

'You know. You must have seen it. The Turkish bar.'

'Did you say that?'

'I mentioned it. Just in case. You pass it on your way out of town . . .'

Kelly raised her hands and dropped them, looked towards Melik. 'You just said the bridge to me . . .' she said, shaking hands with Melik. 'I don't understand. What's a Turkish bar doing in Greece?'

'There are many Muslims here. It's a typical border town. There's even a mosque in town which they use. Melik here is Greek . . .'

He spoke to Melik in rapid Turkish and nodded. 'But come . . .'

They shepherded her out into the sunlight and they walked back along the side of the bridge.

When they came to the notice Nikos turned unhesitatingly right into the Forbidden Zone.

Kelly stopped. 'Didn't you see that?'

'It's OK . . .'

Melik nodded.

'Niko, I'm not stupid. It says it's forbidden. Even the guy at the café told me. He *saw* me, you know . . .'

Nikos gave her his sweetest smile.

289

'It's OK. Trust me . . . They don't really police down here any more. Besides, it's the spirit of Davos at the moment!'

He turned to Melik and they laughed.

As if to prove his point, three boys on bicycles rounded the bend and tore past them over the railway line, laughing and jostling each other as they peddled for all they were worth under the line of poplars deep into the Forbidden Zone. Kelly could hear their shouts echoing under the trees, growing fainter.

'OK,' she said as they set off again in the wake of the bicycles, 'you convince me. So where are we going?'

'Just down to the river . . .'

'But we're already *at* the river!'

'A little public this spot . . . I'll show you . . . it's much prettier further on. Melik's people own some land down here; they work the fields, don't they, Melik?'

Kelly glanced up at the barracks sitting, apparently deserted, up on the hill.

'Don't *worry*,' said Nikos, trying and just failing to put a comforting arm round her shoulder because of her height. 'We're just out for a stroll with our friend . . .'

The path wound on as they talked, catching up with all their news. Kelly showed him she was furious with him about the restaurant deal on Samothrace, but he replied that he had warned her in advance, which was technically true.

'You didn't tell me I'd have to endure the attentions of Mr Tsakalis,' she said wryly.

'*É*, I'm not a prophet . . .'

'But you are a civilian . . .' Kelly decided to make peace. 'And you don't look any different to me . . .'

Nikos clapped Melik on the shoulder. 'Inside, I am a totally different man! Free! Not theirs any more!' And he shook the grinning Melik in time to his words to give them emphasis as if he were totally inanimate.

Every now and again he turned to him and they exchanged

rapid question-and-answer sequences in a quite different, rather urgent tone. They had come to a crossroads and Melik stood scratching his head.

'He doesn't know the way,' said Kelly. 'I thought you said he had property down here?'

'His family did, in his childhood. But it's ten or fifteen years since he came down here and—'

'He can't remember the way?' Kelly was incredulous.

She turned behind them and saw that they had not yet gone out of sight of the sleepy-looking barracks.

After more hesitation they took the right-hand path which crossed a tributary stream and were lost to view amongst the foliage. But it still felt to Kelly as if there were people about and sure enough, at the next bend, they came across a small pony waiting patiently under a birch tree. A man called to them from the other side of the stream. He was digging at the bend, making a trench in the bank. He stood up and leaned on his spade.

Nikos engaged him, asking the way and explaining, apparently, who they were.

'You're Dutch,' he said to Kelly as they moved away, 'a friend of Melik's family from Holland . . .'

'Why lie?'

Nikos repeated her question to Melik in Greek and they laughed.

'There's *kósmos* and there's *kosmáki*. Melik knows the guy, but he's not a friend. There are friends and there are . . .'

'Acquaintances?'

'Exactly.'

The sun was up and the muddy path was actually getting dusty. Everything around them was bursting into foliage. But Kelly couldn't get rid of the feeling that they were out in the middle of a plain walking on eggshells. As they walked together, Melik and Nikos unconsciously lowered their voices.

Again they stopped and had a conference together, during

which she wandered off to the side of the track and stared stupidly into the birch trees.

They had rounded a corner and the track had petered out. It was a question of whether to go on, or go back to the crossroads and take the other fork. In front of them lay an expanse of scrub which stretched for several hundred yards until it terminated in a fan of high trees.

Kelly was impatient. She wanted to get somewhere.

'Come on, you guys. Make up your minds . . .'

'Yes. On,' said Nikos.

'What are you looking for?'

'The river.'

'But we crossed it, didn't we?'

'No, no. It winds round in front of us somewhere in these fields . . .'

They sauntered on in silence while Melik kept up a steady stream of conversation in a Greek that was laced with Turkish expressions.

'Ah,' said Nikos, quickening his pace, 'I think . . . something here ahead . . .'

They came to an open, sandy space in front of the fan of high trees. The three of them pressed forward now with sudden energy. Sand dunes of a miniature kind sprang up around them and they crested one of them ahead and stopped.

Nikos took her arm.

'That's it,' he breathed, 'Turkey.'

The Evros wound past about ten feet beneath them, flowing faster here through the meadows. The fan of trees was actually, Kelly saw, on the other bank, set back and separated from the stream by about thirty yards of thick undergrowth and bushes. On the other side the pale sandy bank made a cliff about eight feet high.

'Behind those trees there are villages,' said Nikos, dropping his voice to a whisper. 'At night you can see the lights . . .'

'What are you whispering for?' said Kelly, in a whisper, as they stood back and searched the undergrowth on the other side with their eyes.

It was quite hot on the parapet now. People were shielding their eyes from the bright sunlight as they squatted down and talked in low voices. Barbara looked around. The dam looked like a fortress under attack: there were troops and riot police everywhere, walkie-talkies buzzed in the hands of a dozen people as they walked about and a handful of journalists had arrived on the scene.

The process of change was almost as imperceptible as the growth of the day's heat: the car-park behind the control block was now full and people must be leaving their vehicles up on the road and walking down to the site, she imagined.

There was a ripple of tension amongst the people on the parapet. Something was happening down on the lake between the people in the inflatable and the three in the dinghy. One of them turned towards Yannis standing with the loud-hailer on the parapet and gave a wave. It was as much as to say: 'We're coming off now. Can't stay here any more . . .'

Yannis shouted down to check, and the reply confirmed it. They were coming off the water. Two men, leaning over the side of the inflatable, were still conducting intense negotiations with the three inside the dinghy. One man behind them actually had his hand on the rim of the larger vessel, Barbara saw, and was in the process of trying to board the smaller one, but he was restrained by one of the others. Chins were thrust forward, arms waved, but they couldn't hear what the terms were. It seemed, from what Barbara could glean from the shouting, they had a warrant signed by the director-general of DEE for the personal restraint of one of the men in the boat and he had decided to give up.

Now the party on the parapet were suddenly in a vulnerable position. They had no protection. As long as their colleagues had been in the boat they had felt reasonably secure, but as the three in the dinghy made their way to the bank Barbara felt a rush of mingled energy and fear go through the human chain.

Antigone gripped her hand.

It looked as if defeat was staring them all in the face. They had no leverage now, and there was nothing to stop the other side from starting up the turbines again.

Barbara looked across to the point where the police were standing in groups. One man in particular seemed active, talking with someone in the inflatable on a phone and nodding vigorously as he looked over towards them.

'*En'taxi, en'taxi*,' Barbara could see his lips cutting into the silence in between bursts of sound from the instrument he was holding to his ear. The army chief stood by his side, arms calmly folded across his green fatigues, scanning intently the people on the parapet.

With a roar, the inflatable opened up its outboard and moved off downstream. The dinghy had already reached a point where the three men could scramble out and Barbara could see they were just about to do so.

Antigone clutched Barbara's arm. Something was happening with Yannis. He was actively involved in some kind of bustle occurring over in the middle of the parapet. He was holding a rope and talking quickly.

He took up the loud-hailer and said quickly along the line: 'OK. Link arms. The lads are going down!'

Barbara saw them go over backwards, three of them, two of them abseiling down the ropes to hang, braced, over the sluices and one just over the parapet, hanging about a foot down.

Antigone was jumping up and down. 'They've done it!' she turned to Barbara, 'd'you see? They can't switch on now!'

The human chain tightened as everyone looked towards the

control-room window, where there were a number of people looking down.

Barbara could see a triad of people in earnest conference outside. The police chief, the army man who still looked cool, and another man whom Barbara thought must be the director of the dam, crossing his two arms and giving the sign for 'It's all over!'

Barbara could see his gestures quite clearly, and the corresponding intensity of the conference of the other two as they looked towards the crowd on the parapet – defiantly linking and singing something that she joined in with, though she didn't know the words – suggested an imminent assault.

She looked back at the strikers patiently hanging over the sluices, talking up to their colleagues on the parapet. Yannis was kneeling and giving something to the highest one. He looked round and snatched up the loud-hailer: 'Brace yourselves, comrades!'

The control-room area was swarming with people now and files of troops were clattering down the walkways towards the parapet.

'I think they don't yet have the authority,' said Antigone, 'otherwise, why don't they charge us?'

It seemed there was a stand-off.

This happened three or four times over the next hour or so. Then there was a sudden 'crump!' and a cloud of acrid silver-grey smoke drifted into them.

'Tear-gas!'

They braced again, handkerchiefs and whatever they could find tied over their noses and mouths, as the boots rumbled on the gangway steps to the parapet and the police chief appeared in front of them at the head of a column of armed police. He was visibly raging:

'You people!' he shouted. 'Come off, now, or I'll drown the lot of you!'

He took out his pistol and waved it above his head, shouting hoarsely: 'Come off, now, or you'll all go in the water!'

To Barbara's surprise the human chain began to murmur and show signs of anger, shouting that this was a legitimate protest and that the Government was not going to intimidate them like this.

Suddenly Barbara felt that Antigone had let go of her arm and she saw her go towards him, beginning to upbraid him: 'That's no way to talk to us. There are women here!'

'I'll shoot you!' shouted the police chief, holding the pistol high. 'I'll shoot the lot of you!'

He looked behind and waved. There were two more crumps and clouds of tear-gas drifted in towards the strikers from beneath which appeared a crowd of special forces in dark-blue uniforms, armed with clubs. Some of them had spray cans which they were directing at the strikers while others began to tug at the chain, prising their arms apart from one another.

Antigone was still standing forward from the rest of them.

'Why do you want to arrest me?' she shouted. 'What have I done? I haven't committed any crime!'

She stepped nearer to the police chief who was waving his men on, turned away for a moment.

'I'm a woman!' Barbara heard her shout, almost into the police chief's face as he turned towards her. 'What are you going to do with that pistol?'

'Here!' He directed them with an encircling arm. 'Over here! This one!'

Antigone was shouting with an intense anger so close to him that Barbara thought she was going to grab the gun out of his hand.

'Are you going to do something against women and children with that pistol?' she shouted. 'Shoot women and children!'

They were all round the back of her, all of a sudden, the blue uniforms. Barbara counted seven of them and she could still hear Antigone crying out in the middle of them with passionate sarcasm.

'Shoot women and children! Go on! Shoot women and children!'

Barbara saw the knee of one of them raised as they pulled back Antigone's arms and she heard the deep thud as it ground into the small of her back. Then they hauled her away and through the gap she left came more of them, hacking down on their arms to work the chain loose.

One man close by went down, slumping suddenly as they led him away, the blood pouring from a wound on the temple.

There was total chaos now on the parapet. Three men came to the spot where Barbara was standing, still linked to the young boy and the older DEE worker on the other side of her, and shouted at them. One of them raised his club and threatened to chop down on to their arms if they didn't release each other, while two others took them roughly by the shoulders and tried to drag them along the narrow parapet.

Barbara was terrified of falling into the water and dragging the young boy with her. She felt suddenly dizzy and sick in the clouds of smoky tear-gas as she stumbled away down the parapet towards the steps.

She looked around. Everywhere the chain was breaking and individual groups of protesting strikers were being led away surrounded by policemen.

As she neared the steps, Barbara glanced up at the control-room window and thought she was hallucinating when she saw Roger, with Panos by his side, pointing down into the mêlée.

The two policemen dragged her, amongst a group of other people, underneath the window and they began to mount the steps with her, thrusting her from below almost as if she were a parcel. As she came to the top of the steps she was almost level with the control room and she could look across again through the corner frame of the big picture window and see him against the light in the control room, quite clearly, bending forward, staring down intently at the mass of struggling figures on the parapet and turning to Panos to point out some overlooked point of detail, some nicety of the pattern.

Before Barbara went limp, letting herself be borne away towards the car-park and the waiting police vans, there was a split second when a ghostly protest reared up from deep inside into the back of her throat, a cry she didn't have to suppress because she couldn't have uttered it, but which, she knew, as she nursed its almost unintelligibly close blend of utter helplessness and raw power, would have bitten the air like the first cry of a baby.

They were all three staring at the shore when a figure sprang out of the undergrowth and stood motionless, staring back at them. Kelly saw that he had something in his hand.

Melik nodded, and clapped Nikos on the shoulder, as if to demonstrate that he was a friend. There was a brief exchange between them in low Turkish which carried perfectly across the sluggish expanse of brown water. He nodded towards Kelly, and she too was explained, she saw.

The man was dressed in a ragged, collarless shirt and shapeless trousers held up by string. He came to the edge of the sandcliff above the water and asked a question. Melik shook his head. Kelly saw the hand draw back and something small and dark flew like a skimming bird about a foot above the surface and smacked into the bank.

Melik waved. The man turned without a word and vanished into the bushes.

They scrambled down the crumbling bank and ran to the spot where it was half-embedded in the clayey soil.

Melik prised it out and held it in his hand. It was a black, oilskin parcel, with a roll of string round it. Deftly, he undid the knot and rolled it along the palm of his hand and up his extended wrist.

Nikos reached forward and lifted up, delicately, by the corner, the chunky cellophane, bulging with white powder.

'Oh my God!' said Kelly and covered her mouth.

Melik laughed at her and crisped a dirty finger and thumb.

'Hundred per cent pure,' said Nikos.

He put his arm round her.

'It's OK, we're only the postmen . . .'

What was he playing at? She only wanted her air fare.

'My *train* fare would have done!'

But Melik could hear something as they came back to the end of the scrubland where the track began in the corner. He bent low and scuttled up to the corner where the silver-birch copse began.

They were all three crouching, peering at the track, trying to make out through the trees where it began and ended.

'Hsst,' said Melik, and ducked.

Nikos pushed Kelly down.

But she had seen. Two of the birch trunks were not trees. They were soldiers standing staring towards them.

Melik, who was kneeling and burying the parcel in the undergrowth, indicated that he would try to go round through the wood on the other side and motioned them to take the cornfield on the left-hand side of the road where the cover was best.

'Slowly,' said Nikos as he and Kelly crawled on their bellies down to the field and slid over the margin into the young corn spikes.

'You bastard,' said Kelly softly to his back, 'you absolute fucking schmuck! What have you got me into now?'

He turned round, maddeningly, and held his finger to his lips.

Barbara was sitting down in the *réma* on one of Theia Soula's six plastic chairs, the other five around her in an empty circle on the grass. Katerina lay on her stomach with a neglected book on the grass nearby, legs up, ankles crossed behind her, monitoring the finer points of Antigone's character with the pedantic intensity that only a younger sister's envy can manage.

Barbara glanced around this slightly insanitary bowl of green. Up above them, on two sides, zoomed the evening traffic, largely unseen now the trees were coming into leaf. It was good to be there and to have gone to work that day, like any other Monday.

The events of the weekend seemed to have reached some sort of conclusion. Antigone was already in Athens, visiting Manos, who, to her delight, had given up his hunger strike. Yannis had been arrested along with eleven other people and was being held in Veria while the police got the charges together. She and Antigone had stayed to join the street protests against the arrests in Veria, then driven back down to Thessaloniki on Sunday. For some reason she'd been unable to tell Antigone about seeing Roger and Panos in the control room at the dam. Like a secret, festering sore she'd been keeping the knowledge to herself, squeezing painfully and futilely at it from time to time, telling herself madly it was not public and treatable, it was hers, and she had to bear it.

That morning, Yennimatas, the Minister of Labour, had signed the union agreement with the Electricity Company.

There was a shout from across Sandy Island Street. Barbara craned while Katerina scrambled to her feet. The squat figure of Theia Soula was waving from the balcony of the block of flats.

'Telephone,' said Katerina.

It was Antigone. She talked to them all in turn. 'Did you catch the news? Isn't it marvellous?' she said. 'We *won* . . .'

'Yes,' said Barbara. '*Who* won exactly? Sorry, I . . .'

She felt a heel immediately, because she was thinking of Roger's face against the light in the control-room window. But Antigone was at her best, ignoring her, toughing it out:

'Come on, Barbara, the workers, Yannis, everybody together, they risked their lives . . . lots of them were PASKE–PASOK

300

people you know – who were very strong and solid when it came down to it . . .'

'How's Manos?' asked Barbara, who could hear shouts and clinking behind Antigone.

'Not good,' said Antigone. 'I . . . I've just come from the . . . He's still in a hospital. Very weak. They're afraid he might have gone too far . . .'

Barbara was wretchedly silent. 'Is that a party?' she managed in the end.

'Yes, some DEE people,' said Antigone vaguely, her voice leaving the receiver for a moment as she looked around. 'Listen . . .'

It came back now, strong, definite, close to Barbara's ear.

'On the news. After the pictures of them signing the agreement. There's an item about heroin smuggling up on the Evros . . . I want you to look at it on the six o'clock news and call me back . . .'

'Why?'

'It's *her*. The hippie. I'm ninety-five per cent convinced of it. She looks completely different. Hair's all cut off, but I *know* it's her . . .'

The camera was somewhere above. The girl sat, eyes on the floor, under the ragged hail of flashes from newspaper cameras during the three-minute transmission. On a table by her side, mounted on a dark square of oilskin, lay a long, sausage-shaped cellophane packet of white powder. For the purposes of demonstration it had been broken open and scattered across some brown paper in little heaps. On the other side of the table stood the other two, an unshaven young Muslim with a gap in his teeth and a young, sharp-faced Greek.

A soldier's boot was a constant presence in the corner of the screen. At one point the camera panned round a number of feet under the table. The young Greek, smoking a cigarette, stared at the camera, talking constantly. The Muslim Greek was hangdog by his side, sniffing once without looking up.

They had been all caught *in flagrante*, apparently. Charges were being prepared at the prosecutor's office. It was thought the case would be treated with particular severity as an example to all young people, but also because of the presence of the Muslim.

Barbara stared at the girl's thick, pale lips. The face was pale, too, and she seemed to have a variety of red spots on her forehead under the punkish copper-coloured spikes of hair which started, like an Indian brave's, along the ridge of her skull. To Barbara's surprise, when she opened her eyes briefly to look at the floor the girl looked faintly oriental. Barbara saw now that she had high cheek-bones that sat beneath flat, almond-shaped eyes. From her tiny ears dangled two swastika ear-rings made of the same sort of metal as Roger's medallion. Under a crêpe flowered skirt that came down to her ankles her high black boots were splayed out hopelessly in front of her. Her arms lay in her lap.

She looked like a Mongol.

Barbara stumbled out of the house and went down into the streets. There had been a shower while they were indoors and a fresh warm wind was blowing the grass along the top of the embankment. She had no coat. Down in the *réma* garden she could see big drops of rain on the plastic chairs.

So that was it. *That* was the creature.

It scarcely seemed possible. Could Antigone be right?

When she got to the top of Sandy Island Street, still in the grip of the television images, she climbed the steep, wet streets against their coursing, arbitrary rivulets, towards Kryoneri.

It had released something in her, she knew. She didn't want to ask herself why. She simply wanted to enjoy the almost laughable change of scale. Those images she had of the past which she thought of as 'demonic', unintelligible, a film she was frightened of seeing again, had suddenly become Grand Guignol.

What she privately called The Street of Caged Birds was strangely silent after the rain. Barbara fished around briefly for the hidden entrance to the path down into the other branch of the *réma*, trying different streets until she found it, a narrow alley of home-made concreting between shacks, deeply funnelled for the water run-off.

The steps were too long so she was obliged to shuffle to deal with their length, the awkwardness, she suddenly felt, part of a particularly strong *déjà vu*, something to do with these long, sloping steps that frustrated the rhythm of her descent, the wet vegetation brushing under her skirt and the dank trickle in the bottom of the creek, the improvised foot-bridge, the rail made out of old piping. She stopped for a moment and sniffed the same insanitary air. Something in the past.

'*Kosteeeeeees!*' screeched a woman's voice from one of the apartment blocks that towered above her, and broke the spell.

Barbara went on her way, climbing up the other side of the *réma* now, gingerly putting aside the wet sprays of elderberry leaves.

Their awful smell.

She remembered an old pram.

She stopped and turned round, clinging to the rail and looking down at the bridge in the bottom of the creek she had just crossed.

No pram.

Voices above her and the sound of steps made her move again. Two people came into view, the woman first. He was behind her saying, 'About eight thousand . . .'

They stopped and she climbed up beyond them in silence, pressing against the rickety railing as she passed, the thick, dank stink of elderberry invading her nostrils — so mysteriously familiar, yet the overlap had still not taken place, and the memory, whatever it was, refused to come, like a stammer in her brain — as she climbed on and up the winding concrete steps with

303

their shallow risers and long, downward-tilting slabs marked by tiny, regular, star-like indentations that were so tantalisingly familiar they were like a name on the tip of her tongue.

She shook her head, pursing her lips with the effort of recall, aware of, even trying to explore, the gap she was living through. She had always wondered, when she was in the casualty ward, what it was like to have concussion. Perhaps this was it. A strange gap, like this, that refused to fill.

At the top of the steps, she thought it would come, but it refused again like a perverse spirit and she drifted on past the cemetery and the two marble workshops.

Another street and she reached the green gate into the pine wood, her wet feet sinking with relief into the carpet of dry needles.

With a kind of silent click and a flooding of images it came to her at last. It was the little creek by the housing estate at South Shields. From some buried layer of her mind rose, like a fume, the condensed essence of dull afternoons and soft summer evenings as she and her friends rambled back from the rec, over the brook and the rickety, makeshift bridge; that same combination of dank smells and the pram that lay sunk and rusting for years, half in the trickle of water, one piece of dirty, pale-blue upholstery still clinging to the back of it. That was it.

It came to Barbara then, with a sudden sweetness of confident perception, that *this* was her life, this moment now, because it had all, always, been her life, even the blind horrors and astonishments of her recent past; the present was not, as she had been thinking of it, some abstracted piece, some interlude of recuperation, suspended in brackets waiting for a future that joined up again with the past.

It was one elderberry smell, not several. She laughed aloud at the thought.

*

Antigone gripped the scrap of paper in the trembling leather of her black gloves and scanned the sea of faces over its edge. She hitched up the collar of her leather jacket and adjusted the red scarf at her neck. She cleared her throat.

'Shhhhh . . .' said several people.

'I just want to say to you all,' she began, and waited for one of the staff of *Dokimé* magazine to stop talking, 'that I'm proud to be Manos's widow, and I'm proud – and my family and Manos's family are proud, I know——' here, she couldn't quite see where Manos's mother was, but she knew where she ought to be and smiled in that direction, 'that I'm bearing his child. Whether it's a boy or girl, this child will be a freedom fighter like its father. Of course, I have my own personal memories of Manos and his . . . beauty,' she swallowed and looked down, catching a glimpse of Barbara and Yannis starting forward in front of her, and shook her head at them, 'and they, of course, will live for ever with me. But I'm not going to speak of them because Chatzidákes has put it so much better than I can and, in a minute, Manos's brother, Alkis, will read his beautiful translation of Shakespeare's sonnet one hundred and six, which expresses everything so perfectly, I think, about my personal sense of Manos's loss . . .'

She saw them all round her now, quite clearly – Socrates and Matoula, Yannis and Katerina and Fotini, Eleni and Tassos, Barbara, holding tightly on to Theia Soula's arm, and Manos's family standing with folded hands – and she crumpled the paper in her fist as her eyes rose to fix on the tiny, silver dot at the head of a vapour trail, the glittering point slightly detached from the body behind it, that steadily made its way, a needle pushed by calm old fingers, through the fabric of the cloudless blue above them, the words coming louder and more confidently now.

'No, it's just that having known Manos, especially watching him in these last days, I've learnt something important which

305

has changed me. I've learnt that we belong in the future, and the future belongs in the present. For anybody who knew him, Manos, of course, lived in Utopia . . .'

There was a murmur and someone laughed.

'He did, that's right, and we argued a lot about this. But in Manos's Utopia there's no harmony, no respite from a perpetual difference. Manos's Utopia isn't a place to escape to – where everything's fine and dandy, Elysian fields and all that where everything's *stopped*! – it's a place of conflict. In fact . . .' She laughed, her chin lifted, her eyes on the steadiness of the glittering point, darning with its silver thread the blue above her. '. . . It's a place very like this society we're in now . . .'

Someone began to cry. She couldn't look down to see who.

'But with one crucial difference. In Manos's Utopia there are no outsiders. Every one of our voices, man or woman, rich or poor, black or white, counts and will count, and count absolutely . . .'

The needle had reached the hem of this particular patch of sky. Busily, it made its way in, and was lost to view, drawing after it a progressively fraying thread. Antigone dropped her eyes to the group packed unevenly around in B *nekrotafeio*:

'Because it's a state of mind, you see, the future's a state of mind, and it's only then, when we have that state of mind, that we shall *truly* come to appreciate the significance of Manos's life and of what he stood for. That's all I have to say. Thank you. Alkis? Where are you? Alkis?'

From within the ranks of Manos's brothers, Alkis stepped forward and began, stumblingly, to read.